THE MAN WHO LOST HIS SHADOW

The Man
Who Lost His Shadow

A NOVEL IN FOUR BOOKS

by Fathy Ghanem

Translated from the Arabic
by DESMOND STEWART

HEINEMANN
LONDON

THREE CONTINENTS PRESS
WASHINGTON D.C.

Heinemann Educational Books Ltd
22 Bedford Square, London WC1B 3HH
P.M.B. 5205, Ibadan · P.O. Box 45314, Nairobi

EDINBURGH MELBOURNE AUCKLAND
HONG KONG SINGAPORE KUALA LUMPUR
KINGSTON PORT OF SPAIN NEW DELHI

ISBN 0 435 90223 7 (AWS)
ISBN 0 435 99414 X (AA)

First published in Great Britain
by Chapman & Hall Ltd 1966
First paperback edition published by
Heinemann Educational Books 1980

Published in the United States of America 1980
by Three Continents Press
4201 Cathedral Avenue, N.W.
Washington, D.C.

ISBN 0–89410–207–9

Set in Monotype Garamond
Reproduced, printed and bound in Great Britain by
Fakenham Press Limited, Fakenham, Norfolk

BOOK ONE

Mabruka

I

MY NAME IS MABRUKA ABDUL TAWAB. MY LATE HUS-
band, Abdul Hamid Effendi, was a primary school teacher. I am
still young and pretty. My figure is graceful: my hips are on the
plump side, which pleases me, but my breasts, being small,
annoy me. Men still stare at me and I like this. I'm vital, restless.
I can't sit still even when I'm at home. I must cook, wash or
sweep. In the evenings I go out to look for my son, Ibrahim. If
I find him playing football, I drag him home by his *gallabya*, to
see that he does his homework. After that I bath, and comb out
my hair. And then come the long hours in which I lose myself
in the hatred devouring my heart.

My only emotion now is hatred – hatred for one man whose
death I dream of – a slow lingering death with plenty of pain. I
would like to knife open his belly, pull out his liver and grind it
with my teeth. I would gouge out his eyes, or drink his blood.

The man is Yusif Abdul Hamid, my husband's son by his first
wife.

Sometimes I wonder why I have come to hate him so much,
and what will be the end of it. He obsesses me day and night.
Sometimes when I look at Ibrahim, his face blurs and becomes
Yusif's. I feel an urge to smash his ribs, but then a faint voice
whispers: Control!

It is a long time since I first saw Yusif. I was a little child. I
knew nothing of the world. I was hardly ten and worked as a
servant in a big house in Giza. I didn't know what being a
servant meant. All I knew was that one day my mother had
taken me from the village by train, with Sheikh Dessouki who
chattered with her all the way. I paid no attention because of the
strange things happening. This was my first train; the world
which ran to meet the train was vast; at stations where we
stopped people climbed up while others clambered down. And
a rough man in blue serge approached us; my mother pulled

me close to her. The man examined me with cruel eyes which made me frightened. He asked Sheikh Dessouki how old I was and examined our tickets. Then he went away, still staring at me for no reason I understood.

I stayed frightened as I climbed down from the train into the big city. The wide road with the speeding cars frightened me – they looked like the dwellings of ogres. And the people frightened me. They reminded me of the man on the train. Any moment they might seize me and ask my age – for no reason I could understand.

We boarded a train. I thought it was another train. My eyes could not focus on what was happening near me. I squatted on the floor near my mother's feet, holding the skirt of her dress. I would not lift my head whatever happened. I even stopped myself from crying. I was afraid that if I cried people would notice me.

We left the train and walked down a wide road lined on both sides by houses and gardens. The sight of greenery once more helped to calm me. Mother said not a word to me but went on talking to Sheikh Dessouki. They walked fast while I ran behind, clinging to my mother's dress, frightened she might forget me, and I'd be lost.

We reached a house with a garden. A black man in a big turban sat at the gate and Sheikh Dessouki asked him:

'Is Rateb Bey at home, Uncle Osman?'

The man's eyes moved between me and my mother:

'The Bey's gone out and not come back.'

'And the old lady?'

'At home.'

'I'll call on her, then.'

Sheikh Dessouki left us to enter the garden. But he did not use the white staircase I had expected. Instead he disappeared round the back of the house while my mother and I sat down near the man called Uncle Osman.

He stared at us a moment, then said:

'Don't sit in front of the gate. Go and sit inside.'

'Inside where?'

He pointed to where Sheikh Dessouki had vanished.

Mother seemed at a loss, so the man got up slowly.

'Follow me.'

Half-way up the garden he pointed to a passage along one side of the house. He told us to go and sit at the end of it. We did as we were told, sitting down near a chicken-coop. A man in a white cap came out of a narrow door and stood in front of a pot cooking on the fire. From the pot came the smell of food and my mouth watered and my stomach rumbled.

Time passed while I looked at the chickens and smelt the food and stared at the man's strange cap. Every now and then he looked in our direction but said nothing. Then Sheikh Dessouki came out of the little door, beaming.

'The old lady agrees, Layla. If she proves good, she'll get sixteen shillings.'

The sum astonished me. Sixteen shillings – a fortune! But who would the old lady be giving it to?

Mother got up and took my hand. We followed Sheikh Dessouki indoors and my fear came back. I didn't take in what I saw; it was like entering a magic world. We climbed up a long staircase till we reached an open door. Sheikh Dessouki coughed, knocked and told us to go in.

I saw an old lady whose face was as shining as the full moon, wrapped round as it was with a white shawl. My mother covered her hand with her black head-cover, before stooping to kiss the lady's hand, praying God to grant her long years and lasting bounty. Turning, she prodded my shoulder:

'Kiss your mistress's hand, child.'

The old lady withdrew her hand before my lips touched it.

'What's your name, girl?' Her voice was feeble.

My mother quickly nudged me:

'Tell the lady your name.'

I lowered my head.

'My name's Mabruka.'

Mother, nudging me once more as if I had done something really bad, corrected me

'Your *servant* Mabruka. We are all your servants, Madame.

We live thanks to your breath and the breath of the great Bey.'

Mother then began praying for the old lady, who said to Sheikh Dessouki in her faint voice:

'Enough – we have agreed.'

The lady put her hand to something by her side, I did not know what. She looked at it, then said:

'It is not yet noon.'

We then went down the stairs again and sat by the chicken-coop. Sheikh Dessouki left us to sit with Uncle Osman, waiting for Rateb Bey.

Sheikh Dessouki was gone a long time and the smell of food came to my nostrils. I was hungry but dared not ask my mother when we should eat. If I asked her, she'd be bound to slap me. That was her way with me and my brothers and sisters. So we never asked when we should eat or complained if we were hungry. We would wait till she brought us food. If she didn't bring it, we went to bed hungry and practised patience.

A second man joined the man with the cap and both got busy. The new man put a red sash round his waist and began carrying out plates piled high with food, meat, water-melons and rice.

I watched him, astonished. My eyes were glued to him till he vanished behind the door. Hunger gripped me so that I almost munched a handful of mud.

But my pains did not last long. The man came out again, carrying a tray loaded with plates and loaves of bread. He put the tray before us and left, saying nothing.

The sight of so much food – lumps of meat, rice and *melukhia* – dazzled me. My mother seized a loaf and bit into it hungrily, then told me:

'Eat, child.'

I ate and ate till my plate was empty and my stomach ached: but I was happy. When would I taste such food again?

'Mabruka,' my mother said suddenly, 'you're going to stay here.'

I didn't understand what she meant and so kept silent as she continued:

'You'll stay with the old lady and serve her, you understand.'

I said in terror:

'But mother, you'll stay with me?'

'Stay with you?' she snapped back. 'What for? I go home to your brothers.'

I was on the edge of tears. She looked at me harshly:

'You'll eat meat every day and wear clean clothes.'

I knew she would hit me if I went on talking. I was afraid of her, but even more afraid of this large house. My pleasure in the food had vanished. It could not replace my mother or my brothers or my village and it could not remove my fear.

I said trembling:

'Mother, I'm scared.'

She cursed me, saying how I was to be envied. If it had not been for my brothers and sisters she would herself have left the poverty and hunger of our village for this house of plenty.

Sheikh Dessouki came back smiling: it was time for him and my mother to leave. Tears came to my eyes and I clung to her, circling her tightly with my arms. She pushed me away and slapped me; then pounced to hug and kiss me. She was as upset as I was. She called to the man who had brought us the food (he was watching us from the window) and implored him to take care of me, making him swear to this in the name of God and the Prophet.

The man led me inside the house. At the same time my mother walked away with Sheikh Dessouki, muttering prayers on my behalf.

2

DAYS PASSED, AND MONTHS, AND THE WORLD CHANGED round me. I didn't realize that I was changing too. The enchanted world, as I had imagined it, turned by stages to three storeys with bedrooms, dining-rooms and sitting-rooms. The man who wore the cap was the cook. The man who wore the red sash around his waist was a servant like me. 'Uncle' Osman kept the gate. The object by the old lady's side was an alarm-clock which she always carried so as not to miss the times for prayer. The old lady was not the only woman in the house. She was the mother of Rateb Bey and we called her 'my old mistress' for there was also 'my young mistress', Rateb Bey's wife, to say nothing of 'my mistress', Suad, Rateb Bey's daughter, a little older than myself. There was also my young master, Midhat. He was my age and he went every morning to school with Suad. When they came back in the afternoon they would first go upstairs to sit with their grandmother. She would give them each a piastre and then they would come out on the roof and bat a small, white ball across a green table. Long months passed before I learnt the game's name: ping-pong.

In the evening their tutor came. He was a fat, red-faced man with a grey moustache. He and Midhat used a room at the top of the house for lessons.

Sometimes the teacher's son came too. Yusif was the same age as Midhat and both would study together. Sometimes the teacher's son came early to play ping-pong with Midhat, while they waited for his father.

I would stand watching. If the ball went over the roofs, Midhat asked me to fetch it. I would hurry to my old mistress and get permission to run down into the garden to fetch the ball.

Years went by and I continued to serve my old mistress: carrying her alarm-clock for her, massaging her feet after evening prayers, washing her clothes, sweeping and cleaning the upper storey and the roof. When I had time to spare, which was not often, I would watch my young mistress mending Midhat's pyjamas or Suad's petticoats. Thanks to her encouragement I learnt sewing and needlework.

As I grew up I became aware of my real position in the house, a servant who had forgotten her past and whose other brothers and whose village were a fading dream.

My whole life, its joys and griefs, was linked with what went on in the house. I was happy whenever I inherited one of Suad's dresses. I was sad when my old mistress was ill. I thought of this house as if it were the world. I had no connection with the other world outside.

With the passing of time, Midhat no longer needed lessons from his tutor, though the latter still visited the house occasionally. He was, I knew, a relative of Rateb Bey's. Yusif would also visit us but always went to the top of the house to be with Suad. The two of them looked out at the street, exchanged whispers or were quiet together. If they sensed I was near, they would look embarrassed and Suad would ask me to bring her a glass of water or buy a packet of melon seeds.

Sometimes I saw them lurking behind the door or sitting together in the gloaming. Once I saw Yusif sit so close to Suad that their cheeks touched. He planted a quick kiss on her forehead while Suad sat motionless. He pulled back and they stood in silence, for Midhat could be heard coming upstairs.

I knew Suad and Yusif were in love, and I was jealous of Suad, comparing her situation to mine. She'd marry Yusif, she'd have a house like this one, with servants to wait on her. But who loved me? Whom could I marry?

One day Midhat came home and went into his bedroom. I heard him shouting for Ismail, the servant. No one answered, so I went and knocked at his door. I opened to find him in his underwear, holding his suit in his hands. He was so embarrassed he looked down at the floor, shyly asking:

'Where's Ismail?'

'I don't know.'

Cursing the fellow, he handed me the suit and asked me to take it quickly to the cleaner and get the ink spots removed.

I looked at the suit and cried:

'What ever's happened to your suit, master Midhat? It's ruined!'

I pretended to scold him while he still looked at the floor. I knew I was being bold, lingering in his bedroom while he was almost naked. My heart beat fast and I ran out of the room.

It was then a crazy notion occurred to me. Midhat was a boy, I was a girl. Why shouldn't he love me and ask me to marry him, just as Yusif would Suad? Midhat would defy his family, and insist on marrying me. I'd leave the house for another, similar to it, where I would be mistress, waited on by servants. Why shouldn't this happen? Was it too much for me to achieve?

From that moment I made constant advances to him. I took new care of my appearance and my clothes. I borrowed the scented soap from the bathroom and cleaned myself with it. I learnt how to comb my hair in front of a mirror. I rushed to Midhat whenever he shouted. I took care to be in his way and to speak to him in soft and tender tones.

But my dreams were punctured by the very different tones in which the cleaner flirted. Awad noticed me when I used to bring clothes for ironing. He was a slim, dark-skinned young man with black woolly hair. He had a beautiful voice in which he liked to accompany the radio, singing the songs of Abdul Wahab and other popular singers. Awad would receive each servant with a different song. For one he would reserve: 'The world, my love, my tears, my smiles'; for another: 'Love, who knows what love is?' But for me, he sang Farid al-Atrash's song, 'I am hopelessly in love, but my heart is happy.'

I used to ignore him. Instead I would speak to the other cleaner, Hassanein; he was more mature, being a married man with four children. But Awad never gave up. During those days I heard people talk of 'war' but didn't understand what they meant. I wondered at the anxiety of people's faces and, when our street was darkened and young men in khaki shouted outside the houses, 'Lights out! Lights out!' I thought that war must be, like jinns and goblins, a thing associated with the dark. I noted that my young mistress stored up sugar and paraffin. She came into the kitchen once or twice and got angry with the cook. Sometimes we went without meat for several days.

Our life was changing. We would hear Midhat shouting out news he had heard on the wireless. He would rush up and down stairs telling everybody that the Germans had beaten the French, then that the Germans were on Egyptian territory. People's faces were solemn, their voices had an edge I was not used to. As for my old mistress, she raised her hands to heaven.

War was one reason why Abdul Hamid, the teacher, no longer visited us often. Every now and then, though, Yusif would call in on his way back from university with Midhat. Yusif studied law, Midhat engineering, but Suad had not gone to college, having twice failed her school certificate.

Yusif was still obsessed with Suad – I knew this from the way he watched for her to appear. Suad was fidgety and restless whenever she knew that Yusif was in the house. She would go from her mother to her grandmother, then shout for me at the top of her voice; then go to wherever Yusif was sitting, greet him, and return to her room, shutting the door – only to reopen it and buzz about like a bee, all over the house.

Sometimes, book in hand, she would go in and tell Yusif what she was reading. Or, Yusif would bring her a book. I wondered what prevented him proposing.

Then one day Rateb Bey came to the old lady's quarters (something he did rarely).

'Congratulate me, Suad is engaged to a doctor from the Sarwat family, a surgeon with a future: he works in Kasr al-Eini Hospital but also has a private clinic.'

'A thousand congratulations, son. The Sarwats are good people, neighbours, for their land joins ours. Now it is Midhat's turn.'

And she sighed, adding:

'I hope to see him married before I die.'

A malicious pleasure filled me, not for Suad, but for her misfortune – since she would not be marrying Yusif, but a man she did not love.

Suad made no resistance to the marriage. She seemed dumbfounded, witless. Her eyes were sad; I was the only person in the house who knew why.

Then one morning Yusif came at an unusual hour. I was up on the roof having hung out some washing. I rushed downstairs to greet him.

'Master Midhat's not back yet.'

'I want your mistress, Suad. Go and tell her I'm here.'

Suad hardly believed me.

'He's where? In this house? He said he wanted me?'

He was waiting for her in the hall. His voice sounded sad.

'I'm sorry . . . but the library wants me to return the book.'
He told her its title.

'All right – but won't you sit down?'

'No, thanks – I'm in a hurry.'

She was disappointed, I could see. Then he tried to put
humour into his words:

'Congratulations, Suad.'

She gave, in a faint voice, the conventional answer.

His laugh was strange, choking.

'You're really marrying?'

'Yes, I am.'

'You're happy?'

'About what?'

'You're marrying – why?'

'What else should I be doing?'

Silence, then Suad said she would go and get his book.

'If you've not finished, don't bother.'

'Thank you – I don't need it.'

She went to her room. I was in the dining-room. I heard her
call: 'Mabruka! Mabruka! – What are you doing down there?'

I had my answer ready.

'I was seeing about my mistress's yoghourt.'

She stared at me for a long moment, clutching the book, then
snapped:

'Go upstairs, look sharp about it.'

She took him the book, did not delay, returned to her room,
locked the door, and stayed there the rest of the day. Only
bombs got her out.

For that night the siren sounded and for the first time bombs
dropped. I went down with my old mistress, carrying her alarm-
clock and prayer-mat. We were all gathered in the basement.
The old lady repeated the *Verse of the Throne** without stopping.

* Koran, ii, 225.

Midhat tried to laugh. Rateb Bey scolded him, smoking cigarette after cigarette. He sent Ismail into the garden to see if the cigarette showed outside. He kept telling me to pull the curtains tighter. He sat under a pillar which he had chosen so that even if the house was bombed he would be safe from rubble.

We were all frightened, but not Suad. She sat indifferent, leaning on her hand. When the All Clear sounded, everyone went upstairs very relieved and happy. Except Suad who said: 'If it goes again, I'll not come down.'

Her mother laughed.

'So you'll get yourself killed and have your bridegroom's family on our necks? No, you must come down.'

The old lady looked at her clock, sat down on the sofa and stretched out her legs, asking me to rub them. She began talking about the time of Arabi's rumpus against the English. She had been a little girl then and gone into the streets shouting 'Down with the English!'

I listened eagerly, glad that Midhat, too, was listening to these stories and sitting near me.

'What was the rumpus, my lady?'

They all laughed, including Rateb Bey.

'It means revolution,' Midhat answered.

I was filled with conceit because he had thought me worth answering. Thanks to a murderous air raid, I thought, I am sitting talking to Rateb Bey and Midhat as if I was one of them. When my old mistress talked about her father, the officer who had been with Arabi, I imagined that my own father had been this same officer.

Air raids frightened me. At the same time I waited for them, since they gave me the chance to sit with the family and be one of them. Then one day a surprise attack found me in the cleaner's shop. I was waiting for Midhat's shirts, as he was going on a trip early next morning. The warning went at nine-thirty in the evening. I was terrified for my old mistress. I wanted to rush back across the street to join them in the basement. But anti-aircraft guns started before the sirens stopped. Awad seized me and dragged me into the shop, locking down the shutter. I was frightened by the noise the shutter made as it clattered to the ground – more than by the guns. I was alone in the shop with Awad. No one would hear my shouts or help me.

I tried to get out. I battered at the door. Awad thought it was the air raid that frightened me. He tried to calm me but I did not understand what he said. My eyes watched his hands. My heart quaked at any movement he made. I expected him to close with me any moment, to seize me.

But Awad did not approach me. Little by little I took in what he was saying. His voice was harsh, sad, tinged with bitter laughter. He imagined I looked down on him, although he had plenty of money and his intentions were honourable. He loved me, he wanted to marry me.

My head whirled; Awad observed my silence. Emboldened, he took a step near me.

'Please listen, Mabruka. I'll treasure you as my two eyes.'

I screamed in terror:

'Get away from me – don't touch me!'

He stood where he was and said mockingly:

'Why so frightened? Do you think I'm going to eat you?'

The All Clear went and saved me before his mockery turned to anger, when God knows what he might have done.

Awad ran up the shutter. Saying good-bye politely, he handed me Midhat's shirts and I ran back along the road.

But the idea of marriage held my thoughts. As the days passed I realized he was serious. He no longer greeted the other servants with songs. He did not sing to me, either; he treated me as soberly as his friend Hassanein. I began to pity him. Then to think again.

Why had I rejected the thought of marrying him? Would I find a better husband, or would I wait and wait till I became an old maid, when I'd have to accept one of the boys from my village and return to the same life of poverty lived by my mother?

These new ideas dragged me from my silly dreams of Midhat. I compared myself to Suad. She loved Yusif and was marrying the doctor. I had dreamed of marrying Midhat, but would marry Awad.

This comparison comforted me.

Suad was getting ready for her wedding. Every day she and her mother went out to buy things. One day she came back with a lot of cloth. She was very happy as she opened her parcels and inspected the dress lengths, hanging them against her body and looking in the mirror. I was consumed by jealousy. That moment I decided to marry Awad. I went and sat down by my old mistress, to massage her legs. I told her of my decision.

She listened gravely, did not interrupt me. She seemed more interested than when Rabet Bey had told her of Suad's engagement.

'How old is he, Mabruka?'

'About twenty.'

'He's got enough money to set up house?'

'He says so.'

'Let him come here so I can see him.'

I was alarmed. How could Awad come into this house in my master's presence, in front of Midhat and the others? If Rateb Bey saw him, he would turn him out. I didn't want Midhat to laugh at him. I didn't want Suad to take pleasure in the difference between him and her rich doctor husband. I preferred them to have a vague picture of Awad: only a name, a bridegroom. I didn't want them to see him as he really was, in his cheap *gallabya*. I could see my engagement was landing me in trouble. My old mistress broke into my thoughts:

'But take care he doesn't lay a finger on you! Don't let him get you alone or he'll say you're his wife already and seduce you.'

'I'll not see him at all,' I said in terror. 'I'll not set foot outside the house.'

She smiled as though pleased by what I said.

Nevertheless, I did go out, and she knew but did not object.

I told Awad – now I had accepted his proposal – that my mistress wanted to see him. His face flushed with pleasure. 'She'll have to give me something to get married on.'

We chose a moment in the morning when none of the family was at home. We reached her room unnoticed.

He was in complete command of himself, turning his head to take in all the furniture and hangings of the house.

'Where can I take you, after this paradise? This, Mabruka, is a palace, not a house.'

It turned out that my mistress had known Awad for years.

'You want to marry Mabruka, young man?'

He swore he loved me as his two eyes – all he wanted was her approval. He would defend me against all harm, and treasure me as his life.

I was terrified she might not give her consent. Awad's words fizzled out in silence.

Then she spoke quietly:

'Good–you go now, my son, and may God effect what is good.'

Awad hesitated, then asked:

'Does that mean you approve, my lady?'

She simply repeated what she had said before:

'May God effect what is good.'

Awad looked at me, puzzled: had I understood what she meant? I went with him to the door. As he went out he whispered:

'I don't understand a word she says!'

He was angry. He prodded my shoulder.

'You tell her to give us some money.'

My mistress was praying. When she had finished, she smoothed her face with her hands and said tenderly:

'So you'll marry, Mabruka, and leave me?'

'No need,' I blurted, 'for me to marry.'

She smiled a little.

'May God effect what is good.'

Although I hoped she'd say something about Awad, she was sunk in silence.

When I told Awad that he should expect no help from my mistress, he began to shout curses and insults at the rich.

'If I was you, Mabruka, I'd handle people like that in another way. Find some way – a bracelet – a gold watch.'

'For shame! You want me to steal?'

He laughed in my face.

22

'I want to be rid of such people – once you've had your rights.'

Although I put Awad's words down to anger, I did begin pondering my rights. I had saved £34 with my mistress over the years. I now asked her for £10 so that I could buy things for the new house. From the way she answered, she might never have heard about my marriage.

She gave me the money, reluctantly I thought. When I went shopping I found prices terribly high and the money was not enough. When I got back I felt wretched, and compared the things I had bought with Suad's.

The old lady had meanwhile told Suad and her mother of my plans and of the £10 I had taken. They pestered me with questions about Awad. They opened the few parcels I had brought. They fingered the cloth. They asked me, how much?

Suad said enviously:

'You certainly know how to shop, Mabruka!'

Then she laughed and said to her mother:

'Look at these night-dresses, mother!'

To me she said sarcastically:

'You really wear a night-dress, Mabruka?'

Hiding my anger with a smile, I left them laughing at my expense. Carrying my clothes I sat down on the roof, longing for the day when Awad would take me to his room, safe from this house.

While I was sitting, I noticed two large sheets hanging on the clothes' line. Automatically, without thinking, I touched one of them, to feel its texture. I thought of the bed on which I would sleep, its mattress, its sheet. Why shouldn't the sheet for my bed be one of these? This house was full of sheets. On a sudden impulse I snatched one of them, rolled it up and hid it in the little room where Midhat used to study and which was now used as a store-room.

I had no idea of the fuss my young mistress would make over this sheet. She asked Ismail who asked me, and would not credit what everyone suggested – that the wind had blown the sheet into the road. I myself went and hunted for it in the garden and the street, asking at neighbours' houses, too, if they had seen it. When the uproar died down and I knew I was not suspected of the theft, I took the sheet, wrapped round my stomach under my dress, to Awad's shop. He gave me a cunning look.

'Where did you get this sheet, my girl?'

'I bought it.'

He laughed back at me. 'Can't you find something better? I can bring you a thousand sheets any day.'

He knew everything, and I did not know what to say. Perhaps I could take Suad's dresses, or her jewellery. Once I had crept into her room and opened her wardrobe, and gazed at her frocks. But I felt terrified and quickly ran out. My mistress was sitting asleep, clutching her clock. In my fear I felt she clutched it to keep it safe from me. I sat and stared at her, terrified. I sat for hours. Darkness came. I tiptoed to the door but suddenly she spoke:

'Where are you going, Mabruka?'

'Are you awake, my lady?'

'Listen to me, Mabruka. This boy Awad – my mind's not at rest about him. I'm afraid for you, my daughter.'

My heart dropped to my feet. She knew! But how? Did she have some special link to God?

Four days later Suad and Midhat called for me.

'Mabruka, the police have arrested Awad.'

His home had been found full of stolen goods.

I was in terror and despair, shut in the house. One moment I decided to go on as a thief. The next I repented for the sheet I had stolen. My old mistress seemed to have the miraculous power of Sayida Zainab.

I would never leave her! Perhaps my loyalty would gain me God's pardon. He had lately increased her penance, for her stomach was in continual pain. More than one doctor came first to examine her, then to make light of what was wrong.

But on going out they would whisper with Rateb Bey. There was a dismal atmosphere in the house. It astonished me how Rateb Bey was now visiting her morning and night, spending long hours with her. My young mistress and her two children did likewise. If there was a raid, they refused to go down into the basement. They stayed in her room. In the middle of their gloom I realised that her end was near. I sat alone and wept. I pondered on what my future would be after her death.

3

RATEB BEY FRETTED ABOUT SUAD'S MARRIAGE. IF HIS mother died first, there would be long delays for mourning. Better have the wedding soon, in the old lady's lifetime.

The night of the wedding the house was packed with guests. Among these were Abdul Hamid al-Sutfi and his son, Yusif. Yusif sat alone, gloomy. When the press of guests increased he stood hesitantly in the hall, then walked through the door towards the garden. But it was cold and he came back into the hall, looking about him as though undecided. I saw Ismail give him a glass of sherbet. He took it but did not touch a drop of it.

What he did after that I did not see, for I went upstairs and sat with my old mistress. Suad and her groom had visited her at sunset after they had signed the marriage bond. I was by the sickroom door when I heard Midhat's steps. When he saw me, he whispered:

'Is your mistress awake or asleep, Mabruka?'

'I'll just see . . .'

She was asleep. I felt his breath on my neck as he gazed at his grandmother.

'Better shut the door,' he said, 'or she'll wake.'

I did so and turned to find him smiling at me:

'She's still asleep. Why not go downstairs for a bit?'

'I'd better stay by her. She may wake up.'

'No, no – you go down — Why should you be the only person not to enjoy the wedding?'

He suddenly seized me in a manner unexpected and unusual. I found myself in his grip, staring into his eyes. I felt his lips on my cheeks as I surrendered to his arms. But when he put his lips on my lips, I resisted, whispering in panic:

'No, no, Sir – please, stop!'

He paid no attention, but put his hand on my breasts, seizing me and kneading me to his will, pushing me against the wall where I could not resist him.

'Master Midhat, Sir, stop . . . please.'

Still holding me, he whispered hotly:

'I love you, Mabruka. Believe me, I love you.'

Then my mistress woke.

Midhat ran downstairs leaving me alone, my breast pounding in a way I had never known before.

From that night Midhat pursued me. My old dream of marrying him returned, of having a house like this one. Happy one minute, downcast the next, I decided to bring things to a head. The next time he approached me, I would say that what he wanted was the right of my husband only.

One evening when the household was sleeping he forced my body against the wall. He grabbed my thighs and almost threw me to the floor. We were both crouching. I was fumbling for the words I had prepared when suddenly my old mistress's door opened and I heard Midhat's mother come out screaming.

'Midhat – what are you doing?'

She stood there shaking. Midhat withdrew from me. 'Go to your room!' she shouted at him. Lowering his head he went downstairs. She slapped my face, pulled me by my hair, threw me on the ground, much of my hair still in her grip and began to kick me in the breast, on the legs and head, while I cowered in terror. But again she grabbed my hair.

'Get up, you slut, get up!' She pulled me to my feet, pushed me into her room and locked the door.

I was sure she meant to kill me.

'For God's sake,' I implored her through my tears, 'it was Master Midhat, he did it against my will.'

She cut me short with a blow.

'Shut up,' she screamed in fury, 'shut up.'

I could not prevent my screams getting louder. She shouted in a voice trembling with anger:

'Lower your voice, girl. Do you want to disgrace us?'

Instead I screamed louder. I saw my screams frightened her. She was suddenly quiet.

'Be quiet, girl, be quiet.' Then, 'What did he do?'

'How do I know? Didn't you see what happened?'

She tried to control her anger.

'How long has this been going on?'

'Ask him.'

'I want you to tell me. What did he do?'

'When he saw me alone – he took me – I said, Stop, Master Midhat, for shame.'

She seemed frightened.

'Did anything . . . happen?'

I answered with pride:

'Nothing, my lady.'

'You slut. You can't stay in this house a moment longer. I'll send for your mother to fetch you.'

She ordered me to go and shut myself in the basement and stay there.

I didn't move, I wouldn't eat, but finally fell asleep exhausted. I woke in the morning black and blue with bruises. Perhaps I should get up and leave the house. But to go where? Hour after hour passed. Then Ismail came down to me.

'Go upstairs. The Bey wants you.'

'No, I'm not going.'

'Do as I tell you. The Bey's dressed and wants to go out.'

'I'm not working for them,' I insisted, 'any longer. I'm going.'

'Going where?'

'Going – that's all.'

He hesitated, puzzled.

'You want me to go, and tell the Bey that?'

I nodded, without speaking, then felt frightened and submitted. 'Wait – I'll go.'

I found Rateb Bey and his wife standing in the hall. He gave me a long look, then said very quietly:

'Listen, girl. If what happened yesterday happens again, I'll kill you, I'll skin you alive. Understand?'

I was on the verge of tears.

'I want to go to my mother.'

'If your mother knew, she'd kill you for very shame. Now go upstairs to your mistress and don't let me see your face downstairs again. Understand? And I don't want you to say anything to your mistress. She thinks you've been ill.' And he added: 'She's dying. If it wasn't for this, I'd have shown you . . .'

'It wasn't my fault, Sir,' I said, with a return of spirit.

'Shut up, you bitch. You do as I tell you. If I see you talking to anyone but your mistress, I'll kill you.'

I hated Rateb Bey and I hated his wife.

But I went back to my mistress. She was lying stretched on her back, breathing with difficulty. When she heard me, she whispered:

'What's wrong, Mabruka?'

'Nothing, my lady.'

'They told me you were ill, my daughter.'

'It's all right now.'

She stretched her hand to my brow and felt it.

'You've certainly no fever.'

I didn't leave her room all day but sat watching as remorseless death grappled with her. My time in this house now depended on this old woman's dwindling life.

I was suddenly afraid for the money I had entrusted to her. Who would know to give it to me when she was dead? So I lied to her, said that a man had come from my village bringing news that my mother was ill and needed it.

'Mabruka – you aren't going to give all this money to your mother?'

'What else can I do? It's God's will.'

So I got the money back.

All this time I did not set eyes on Midhat or hear a word from him. I would often wait at the top of the staircase when he got back from college. One day, I hoped, he might run upstairs and kiss me and fondle me as before. He was my only hope once the old lady died. He would look after me because he loved me.

My chance came when Rateb Bey and his wife went to visit Suad in her new home. The whole house was quiet. My old mistress lay stretched out on her bed unaware of what was going on around her. I went downstairs, taking care to make as much noise as possible and stood waiting at his door. He did not come out. Tired of waiting, I let out a great cry and collapsed on the floor.

This brought him out. I told him I had had a fall. I rubbed my leg, pretending to grimace with pain. I tried to get up but fell down again.

Midhat looked on in dismay, then stooped to help me to my feet. Suddenly, as I put my arm round his waist, I was seized with hatred for him. 'Don't come near me,' I shrieked at him. 'I swear I'll tell my mistress. I've had enough from you already.'

He shrank back while I staggered to my feet and hobbled down into the basement.

Thenceforth I spent every day sitting in silent tears at the bedside of my mistress. Everyone in the house thought I was weeping for her, but I don't know what made me cry. Some of my tears were for her, but I think most of them were for myself.

Rateb Bey scolded me when, coming one evening with the doctor, he found me weeping.

The consultation over, he stood by my mistress looking down at her, suffering in his eyes. She was now unconscious. He himself began to weep.

Early next morning she died and the doctor closed her eyes and covered her face. I screamed like a mad woman. I beat my face and tore my hair. And when they carried her out in her coffin, I lost all control and rushed into the street where I found a huge crowd and a large funeral tent. Hands seized me and dragged me back into the basement.

Days passed; I watched the ladies who came to condole with my young mistress. More days passed and all was silent in the house; it was as though no one lived there any more.

Then my mistress called me and said in a low sad voice:
'What are you going to do now, Mabruka?'

I was frightened.

'What can I do, my lady?'

'We are very sad to lose you . . . but your old mistress . . .'
She spoke more loudly. 'Look, my girl, if you've no other job
ready, the Bey has relatives who would like to employ you.'

Although I had done nothing during these last days except
prepare myself for a future outside the house, I now felt lost: I
could not believe what I heard. How could I leave this house?
What right had they to get rid of me? I thought how Awad
had compared the luxury of this house to a palace. I thought of
imploring her to keep me, of falling to the ground and kissing
her feet, but pride held me back, and I said nothing.

'You know the people,' she went on. 'Abdul Hamid Effendi,
the schoolmaster. He's an old man and has no one to look after
him. His wife is dead.'

She looked at me piercingly. 'He has no one but his son Yusif.
You know him – he's a sensible boy.'

I heard all this without taking it in. She said quietly: 'Abdul
Hamid Effendi's coming to fetch you this evening.'

Abdul Hamid came as she had said. Rateb Bey was asleep and
did not receive him. But she sat with him a short while, then
called me. 'You're not yet dressed,' she said angrily. 'Abdul
Hamid Effendi is in a hurry.'

He said with great kindness: 'It doesn't matter. Let her take
her time.'

She laughed sarcastically.

'Oh no, Abdul Hamid Effendi. If you spoil her you'll wear
yourself out. If you don't stand over her, she'll never do any
work at all.'

Turning to me, she shouted: 'What are you waiting for? If
it's this month's wages, I'll give you them in a minute. Be off!'

I ran down to the basement and put on a blue dress which
Suad had given me before her wedding; also a pair of old shoes.
I wrapped my money in a handkerchief, pinned it to my bodice
strap and hid it between my breasts. I wrapped my possessions

30

in a big cloth, then tried to find the cook and Ismail, but they weren't anywhere about. I went upstairs. Abdul Hamid Effendi prepared to take his leave of my mistress. 'Let's go, Mabruka.'

My mistress said to me with unexpected tenderness, 'Visit us, Mabruka, don't forget.' Then added, 'I'm giving you an extra ten shillings.'

I did not know what I was saying; I was utterly confused; how could I leave without bidding farewell to Rateb Bey, Midhat, the cook, Ismail? Where had they gone? Why was my young mistress the only person left? I raised my eyes to my old mistress's bedroom and uttered a silent protest at this manner of farewell.

I walked into the garden and shook Uncle Osman's hand. He did not understand why I was doing this. I tried to tell him that I was leaving for ever but he still did not understand. I followed the schoolmaster to the bus-stop.

4

MAN IS A STRANGE CREATURE. . . .

Within minutes, seconds even, of my leaving, my hatred for the family had evaporated. No sooner had we got on the bus than I even felt tenderly towards it. With tears in my eyes I remembered my old mistress as she was when alive, sitting in her room at the top of the house, myself squatting at her feet. I remembered the nights we spent waiting for air raids in the basement, Rateb Bey sitting as though one of us, I sitting as though one of them.

My young mistress no longer seemed responsible for my departure, Abdul Hamid had taken her place, was the villain. It was he who had dragged me from my previous life.

I disdained him, I felt as though I came from a higher class. Rateb Bey must despise me, I felt, for agreeing to work as a servant in his house. I would pay them all a visit, a long visit, before long.

We alighted in a square packed with cabs, trams, carts and cars jam-packed with people. There was a terrific noise, but it was drowned by Abdul Hamid's voice as he stood on the pavement haranguing me as though I was a crowd.

'Listen, my girl . . . take heed, now . . . this square . . . what's its name?'

He fixed me keenly, waiting for my reply, which did not come.

'So! You don't know. I'll tell you. The name of this square is Al-Azhar! Repeat it: Al-Azhar!'

He stooped to hear my answer.

'Al-Azhar,' I repeated after him. I had been surprised at the contrast between his way of speaking and Rateb Bey's. But his face lit up with boyish pleasure when I repeated his words. Then he frowned as though he might have forgotten something important.

'But it has another name, Bab al-Louk. Repeat it. . . .'

'Bab al-Louk.'

'Bravo!'

He continued to shout as he led the way through the vegetable market. He warned me against buying anything here: prices were high, since this market was frequented by foreigners. Everything was a piastre or two dearer than elsewhere. He led me down the road out of the square. 'Follow me, I'm going to show you the best place for marketing.'

This road was jammed with hand-carts. You could buy anything: cucumbers, tomatoes, beans, marrows, pickles, kitchen utensils down to clothes-pegs. On the sidewalk were crates of sweet lemons, oranges and tangerines. Everything here was a farthing or so cheaper. He then took me back to the vegetable market where we had begun our tour, repeating the names of street and square, to make sure I would not lose my way if I came here alone. He next showed me a road near the market, 'This is the most important name of all: this street is called the street of the Astrologer, Sharia al-Falaki. In this street we live.' Again I repeated the name. His anxiety for me to get things right had made him short of breath. We passed a main road which he pointed out as leading to the Helwan Station, and then reached a coffee-coloured building.

'Journey's over: we're there! We live on the first floor. You won't have to tire yourself with stairs – there are only fourteen.'

He shouted: 'Mustafa! Mustafa!'

A door-keeper emerged from the gloomy entrance.

'Mabruka is going to work for us, Mustafa.'

We climbed the stairs and Abdul Hamid opened the door with a small key from a full key-ring.

At the door of the small sitting-room stood Yusif, a ghost. He was in pyjamas, his hair untidy, in his hand a book. We exchanged glances; his expression changed; he lowered his eyes. His evident shyness heightened my self-esteem. I surveyed the flat – it was a dismal place. One room at Rateb Bey's could have swallowed the whole flat. Our basement had been better than this mouse-hole.

Abdul Hamid Effendi apologized for the mess: 'It's not the house you're used to – but we're plain folk: you must take us as you find us.'

I inspected the three main rooms in turn, guided by Abdul Hamid. His bedroom contained a large brass bedstead with four pillows, an ancient wardrobe, a chair with torn upholstery and a table where little statues stood on black and white squares.

Pointing to the little statues he said with emphasis:

'Look girl, do anything you like, but don't touch these chess-men. To me they're the most important things in the flat.'

I wasn't surprised; after my tour of the market I felt he could attach importance to anything.

In Yusif's room I saw a narrow white bed like the one in the basement where Ismail used to sleep. On a table were books, a mirror, a brush, a comb, and a plate with crusts of bread and *halawa*. His clothes hung from nails driven into the walls. I suddenly pitied him; I remembered that I was wearing Suad's dress. The sight of it must be painful to him.

I followed Abdul Hamid into the third room. There was a dining-table covered with a shiny cloth. Round it were five chairs with torn leather seats. By the window a marble-topped sideboard had a wireless on it and some books. To the side was an old-fashioned sofa covered with dust; boxes were stuffed with old clothes, rags, papers, other rubbish.

We went into the kitchen. I groaned. Cooking things were scattered on the floor. In the basin, dirty plates were awash in an upflow of filthy water from the blocked drain. A rickety stove was black with paraffin. From the dustbin came a stale odour.

Could I live here? Death would be better than life in this stable. Did they want me to put my hands to this filth? There was nowhere for me to put my clean clothes. Everything was filthy.

For the first time in my life I felt a genuine spirit of revolt. I liked it. After years of submission at Rateh Bey's, I felt that for once I was on top.

Abdul Hamid Effendi asked: 'Where do you want to sleep, my girl?' He glanced in the direction of the kitchen.

I said I would prefer to sleep in the dining-room.

He frowned.

'That's where Yusif studies.'

For the first time since I had come into the flat, Yusif spoke.

'It doesn't matter, father, I can study in my own room.' He lowered his voice as though he did not want me to hear. 'Really, there's nowhere else for her to sleep.'

His father again glanced at the kitchen and muttered: 'The radio . . .' Then he gave way. 'As you think best. Who listens to the radio anyway? I go to bed early, you study.'

Father and son exchanged glances, then each went to his own room and shut the door.

I stood alone in the sitting-room, not wanting to move. I felt that if I took off my dress I would have surrendered some of my pride. I thought of sitting with one leg over another, as Suad would do. I would go to the dining-room and turn on the radio and open windows.

Why on earth did they live in this horrible gloom?

From the dining-room window I peeped through the slats of the shutters. There was another house only three or four yards

34

from ours. Its shutters were closed, too. If somebody opened the shutters, his neighbours would swear at him.

So I moved from the window, not knowing what to do. I turned on the light. It was fast getting dark.

It was no use; I could not resist. I took off my dress and laid it on top of Yusif's books. I put on a *gallabya* from my bundle, and my slippers.

I went back to the window. One side was covered with blue paper to prevent the light showing outside. I used the other side as a mirror. How would my face look, living in this place?

I saw a face that was beautiful but sad.

I smiled.

5

I DON'T KNOW WHAT CAME OVER ME DURING THE NEXT few days. I would not have worked harder if it had been my own house: sweeping, cleaning, polishing, trying to make this dingy hole more like the house I had been used to.

Abdul Hamid Effendi was amazed at my work. He would help me carry the carpets to the window and shift furniture. He would not let me go shopping but would himself buy the meat and vegetables from the market, then come and stand by me in the kitchen, helping me to peel potatoes or chop onions.

'I once ate a most delicious stuffed marrow at Rateb Bey's,' he said. 'I've never eaten one like it in my life. Do you know the recipe, Mabruka?'

He was delighted when I said I knew how to cook this dish. He helped me prepare it, watching with such hungry eyes it looked as though he had eaten nothing for years.

We became close friends. There was no formality, I did not call him Sir, or feel shy with him. I'd go into his room at any time, to sew a button on his shirt, mend his socks or clean his suit. Although he called me 'My daughter,' and although he was as old as my father, he had the mind of a child. He would chatter with me for hours – for we both liked gossip. He'd ask me all about Rateb Bey's house: how they lived, what they ate for breakfast, lunch and dinner; what was Rateb Bey's favourite food, what was his wife's. He told me secrets I didn't know – that Rateb Bey had inherited fifty-four acres from his mother as well as a house in Abbasiya. He spoke of the days when my old mistress had been young. When he spoke of her beauty and the crowds of suitors who had demanded her hand, I was incredulous. According to him, she used to take her slipper to her husband – Rateb Bey's father – because he was always drunk.

'How can you say such things,' I protested. 'My old mistress was a good and pious woman. God's taken her to heaven.'

He laughed.

'Did I say anything bad? I was talking about her youth, before she went on pilgrimage.'

'Why don't you pray, Abdul Hamid Effendi?'

His face reddened. 'Mabruka, I do pray: but what can I do about this cursed chess? It consumes my mind, my time, my health, my faith and my money.'

'Why not give it up!'

'Impossible. It's possessed me.' His eyes flashed. 'Chess is a game for clever people – it needs brains.'

'Do you think I have enough to learn?'

'You can use them differently.'

I found him excellent company; I relaxed with him, feeling for him a mixture of indulgence, affection and maternal love.

Our time for gossip was the morning when Yusif was at the university. I didn't sit on the ground as I had with my old mistress. Standing was tiring and one day he noticed. 'Why don't you sit down?' I did so and he made no comment, as though it was the most natural thing in the world. But for me it was a triumph and my heart beat with excitement.

But I never felt comfortable sitting if Yusif was present. The moment he got back I'd leave Abdul Hamid and busy myself about something. Abdul Hamid helped by going out in the evenings to a café. When he got back I'd bring him his dinner and then prepare the chessboard and watch him moving the pieces, his eyes on an open book. I would sit beside him, one ear on the radio, the other on Yusif's door.

If I heard the door open, I'd leap up and get busy so that he shouldn't find me sitting with his father. The evening hours when I was alone with Yusif in the flat were strange. I was conscious all the time of his presence. His few words seemed strained. What a contrast, I thought, with Midhat, and how differently Midhat would have acted! Yusif never once tried to flirt, though I was sure he was very conscious of me as a woman, sneaking looks at my face and breasts. When our hands happened to touch, he would snatch his back in sudden recoil. When he spoke, his words were sharp, in quite another tone from what he used to his father. He never smiled, even if I tried to tease him or smile at him. I felt that his shyness was not because I had come from a house which had sentimental memories for him, but because I was a woman. I despised him for his weakness; Midhat was the kind of man I dreamed about. Yusif's weakness made me eager to challenge him.

One evening we were alone together and Yusif turned on some foreign music. The radio crackled and whistled with interference, but he sat as absorbed as if it was Um Kalthum. The noise irritated me.

'Do you really like this ghastly row?'

He looked up.

'What business is it of yours?'

'Can't you find an Egyptian station?'

He said angrily: 'I told you to mind your own business. Get on with your work.'

I looked at him defiantly.

'No need to get worked up – do as you like.'

He flushed with rage.

'How dare you speak like that! Remember what you are – a servant here.'

I said nothing but left the room, astonished at my own boldness which had provoked his shout of rage. The fact that he called me 'servant' did not worry me.

37

I had a bath, dressed and, as I combed out my wet hair in front of the bathroom mirror, I opened the door.

He came to the bathroom and glared at me.

'Stop singing – I'm trying to study.'

'Why? Don't you like my voice?'

I smiled.

Trembling with rage he said he couldn't concentrate.

'Shall I make you some tea?'

'No need,' he replied.

But I pushed him aside on my way to the kitchen.

'Yes, I'll make it for you, to help you study.'

I had a sudden wish to arouse his desire. I wanted to excite him to the point where he would make advances, which I could refuse. In this way I could get the better of him.

I handed him the cup of tea while my other hand played with my still wet hair. He was crouched over his books, silent.

'You think it's a disgrace to be a "servant"? That's a word I never heard in Rateb Bey's house, not from anyone.'

He shook his head. He wanted to look at me, but couldn't.

'I didn't mean to . . . but you had no right to speak to me as you did.'

I was angry. Why wouldn't he look at me, why wouldn't he look at my hair and smiling lips?

I said flatly. 'You're right . . . I'm sorry.'

I left the room, feeling I had lost.

Next morning Yusif went out and I was alone in the house with Abdul Hamid Effendi. When he came out of the bathroom he found me crying.

'What's the matter, girl? What's gone wrong?'

My tears increased and he sat near me, patting my shoulder. But my tears continued. He was very upset and wanted to know what had happened.

'Yusif swore at me.'

'Yusif, my son?'

'Yes.'

'But it's impossible. He doesn't know how to swear. What did he say?'

'He called me a servant.'

'That was very wrong of him. You're in the right.'

I went on crying and, flustered, he blurted out: 'Enough, for my sake please stop.' He caressed my head and kissed my hair. I felt a sudden satisfaction as his arms enfolded me. After long minutes I felt his lips on my cheek. I let him kiss me and then stood up abruptly. I went to the kitchen and wiped away my tears.

6

WHAT DID HE HAVE IN MIND WHEN HE KISSED ME? What would his next move be?

For several days he made no move at all. I came to the conclusion that he must be frightened. His eyes still glinted with what I knew was desire when we sat together in the morning; but he seemed tongue-tied. Despite his homely speech, despite his jokes, I sensed an inner struggle. I did not want to hurry him but I knew the moment must come when he would declare himself my slave and me his mistress.

Suddenly one morning he asked what I thought of his moustache. He was serious. I was his mirror.

'What's wrong with it?' I said, hiding my amusement.

'Tell me the truth. I'm thinking of getting rid of it.'

I shrugged my shoulders.

'Why not? It's useless.'

'Modern youth attaches no importance to moustaches. They don't appreciate them.' He suddenly wished to show me his picture of long ago. 'Then you'll see a moustache! I used to twist and grease it. It was strong enough for a hawk to perch on.'

'You stay put,' I said, 'I'll fetch your pictures.'

'No,' he said, excitedly, 'I'll get them.'

He pulled from his wardrobe a box stuffed with papers and photographs. Among them I spotted a stout woman with bulging cheeks and cowlike eyes. It must be Yusif's mother. Despite myself, I blurted out, 'Who's that?'

'My late wife,' he replied solemnly. He tried to push the picture between some papers but I snatched it and scrutinized the woman. He looked nervous.

'You like fat women?'

'Never – who gave you that idea?'

'She did. Look how plump she is.'

He raised his voice. 'That was fashionable in those days. You don't know about such things now . . .'

'What things?'

'Love's changed nowadays.' He smiled, adding, 'I used . . .'

I knew what he wanted to say: I understand love and I love you!

He hunted through his papers and found what he wanted: a full-length portrait of a young man in a high tarbush. A bushy moustache divided his handsome face; one hand was on his hip.

'That's a virile youth for you. Look at that for manliness! Not one of your modern weaklings.' Perhaps he felt that his youthful good looks could wash out old age. 'In those days I was a devil. I was up to every mischief, never out of it. What do young men today know of mischief? They're good-for-nothing cissies.' His old eyes showed that he was eaten by desire and I was pleased.

His habits altered. He began leaving the café before sunset. Then stopped going to the café altogether. His constant presence in the house affected his relations with Yusif, whom he would nag on every occasion. If Yusif suggested that the old man should go out for a walk for the sake of his health, it only provoked the retort: 'What business is it of yours? My health's first class. Do you want me out of the house?'

Abdul Hamid was so jealous of Yusif's youth that it made him afraid of leaving me alone with him. At last he hit on an ingenious solution and retired to bed, pleading exhaustion. He asked me to stay with him, getting me to smooth his pillow and stroke his forehead. If I tried to leave he panted as if short of breath. If I tried to leave he'd call, 'Don't leave me, Mabruka.'

Abdul Hamid asked me to put the chessboard near his bed. He was going to teach me how to play. He arranged the pieces and told me the names of each. 'This is the knight . . . this the elephant . . . this the king . . . this the minister . . . this the castle . . . this the pawn, or soldier.'

He turned to me. 'But you can't play like that! Sit down beside me.'

I wanted to stand where I was.

'Impossible! You have to be comfortable to play chess – it is the game of kings.'

He was playing into my hands, but I was uncertain of my next step. How far should I let him go? I wanted him to propose. Were kisses enough meanwhile, or would he want more? If he wanted more, should I give it, or refuse? I had concentrated on my final goal, but had neglected the steps between. I got up on the bed beside him. His hands trembling with excitement, he showed me the moves. I didn't understand a word. I was happy to be on the soft bed which symbolized comfort and security; at the same time I was frightened what he might do, seize my hand or ravish me like an animal. I was also frightened that Yusif might come in.

I got up. 'I'll make you a hot drink.'

He looked very sad. 'I can see you don't want to learn.'

I went and heated an aniseed drink. I thought of poor Yusif, and poured him a cup too. But he was nowhere in the flat. I hurried to his father. 'Yusif's gone out.'

'Good.'

I sprawled on the bed and we drank our drinks together. He gave me his cup to put down, then said in tones that demanded obedience: 'Don't leave the bed.' He lowered his voice. 'You're sure he's gone out?'

I returned his sly smile. He reached his hand to my neck and enclosed it. 'You're as sweet as sugar.' We were both silent. After a long moment, I let him seize me in his arms and do what he wanted.

41

7

FROM ABDUL HAMID I LEARNT THE MEANING OF EX-
haustion. Morning and evening he could not keep his eyes off
me, nor his hands, which were often cruel. Sweat bathed our
bodies. His breath puffed; I almost suffocated under flabby
flesh. Our relations tired me more than housework. It wasn't
love. It was hard work that jangled my nerves and drained
away my youth. Instead of the delight of love I had to wrestle
with a worn-out body. I found myself remembering Awad's
laugh and wicked eyes, Midhat's youth. I lamented my lot. I
had abandoned youth and youth had abandoned me. For
nothing. There was no point in being a woman without a
husband, the mistress of a house whose master daily displayed
his impotence.

Yusif had taken to studying outside, with a friend as he
claimed. I worried no more about him.

My only relief came when Abdul Hamid would desist and
fall into a stertorous sleep. But even when I put my head on the
pillow I found it hard to sleep. In the morning I would awake
to a corpse beside me. The corpse would wake and again try to
possess me, to suck my life and youth.

I would leave the room very early to make sure Yusif had not
returned to his room during the night. I knew the day would
come when he would discover. And eventually it did.

I laid the breakfast as though nothing had happened. When
Yusif came out of the bathroom, I greeted him as normally as
you please.

Obviously embarrassed he said: 'Is Father still asleep?'

'No, he's up and about as usual.'

'Can I go into him?' He spoke sadly, then his eyes took fire
as if he felt the irony of the question. He went straight to his
father, without waiting for my answer. He guessed. I followed
and stood by the open door, listening.

Abdul Hamid pretended to be unwell, complaining of rheumatism and headache. 'I felt I was going to die. The girl Mabruka hasn't had a wink of sleep. She lay on the ground beside me all night.'

I was almost mad. My mind exploded. I wanted to rush into the room and call him a liar. After all that had happened, was he so afraid of his son that he spoke of me as a servant? Did he dare to talk of me as 'the girl Mabruka' – me whom he had entreated, on whose breast he would weep his defeat, whose toes he would kiss, who would slap him on his neck and push him off when I had had enough? He gave me his pension every month – £18 and 17 piastres and 2 milliemes; he told me to spend it as I liked, to dress as I liked, for he had nobody but me, no child, no family, nobody in the wide world except me, his darling!

I ran out into the street. I walked aimlessly, looking for somewhere deserted to cry. Tears were the only release: but I didn't want anyone to see them. For months I had acted like a lady, and I was determined that I would remain a lady, whatever people said or did.

I stood at the bus-stop, in the square where my misery and battle had begun. I thought of going back as a servant to Rateb Bey, of going back to my village to live with my mother, to my old mistress, to my childhood which I had forgotten, of going back to my mother's womb.

But I dried my tears. My feet knew only one road, the road to the flat, the road to Abdul Hamid Effendi.

When I got back I found they had both gone. I was frightened. Had they left the flat for ever? Abdul Hamid might have feared I would disgrace him publicly. I cowered in a corner of the kitchen, very afraid.

8

ONE EVENING YUSIF CAME IN WHILE I WAS AT SUPPER with his father. He rushed into his room, slammed the door, ignoring us. I insisted on the rights I had so dearly won: I would not be treated as a servant after all I had put up with from his father.

'I'll go and speak to him.' Abdul Hamid pushed back his chair. 'How dare he come in without saying good evening?'

I heard his steps going outside, then his voice at the street door: it suddenly sounded frightened.

'Something wrong? Who do you want?'

A gruff voice answered. 'I came with the Effendi.'

The voice dismayed me. I heard Abdul Hamid's voice continue. 'What's he been up to?'

'The superintendent sent me with him.'

I went to the door. Abdul Hamid was asking a policeman: 'What does the superintendent want?'

'I don't know.'

Abdul Hamid pushed past me and into Yusif's room. Yusif was scattering books and papers all over his bed.

'What's happened?'

'Nothing, father. They just want my university card.'

'What've you done?'

Yusif sounded indignant. 'I told you – nothing. The superintendent wants my card.'

'Why does he want it?'

'It's his wish, that's all.'

'You're hiding something. I'm coming with you.'

He hurried to his room and I followed to help him dress. He muttered under his breath, 'Disaster! Disaster!' They both left with the policeman; I was left alone to brood on what had happened.

Perhaps they would keep Yusif in prison. I tried to think

what reason they could have for arresting him. It was impossible to imagine Yusif stealing or committing murder.

I raised my voice in the empty house: God help him! God save him from his enemies!

But then I suddenly thought: Couldn't I inform against Yusif, denounce him to the police, trump up a charge against him if he opposed my marriage to his father? This would certainly be one way of getting rid of him.

At once my conscience pricked me. It was impossible that I should harm Yusif or anybody else. That was sin.

Then an evil voice whispered: But you're pleased, Mabruka. They've taken him away. You can breathe freely at last. You'll be alone with Abdul Hamid. You'll take the place of his wife, his son, everything!

I sat on Yusif's bed, looking at his books and papers scattered all over it. I'll sleep here, I said. This will be my room. How long would decency require me to wait before I could bundle his things together. . . ?

I thought of Yusif as one already dead. I prepared the words in which I would condole with Abdul Hamid when he got back. I thought of a sure way to help him forget. I would not let his misery postpone our wedding.

Suddenly the door opened. Abdul Hamid came in with Yusif. I looked at Yusif as if he was a phantom. But my heart rejoiced. And I rejoiced even more that evil thoughts could not stop me rejoicing. I ran to Yusif and all but embraced him. I felt as tender as I could have done to a brother or son. I said to him, kisses in my eyes: 'Praise God, you're safe. I was so frightened.'

He seemed embarrassed. 'I told you it was nothing: they wanted to see my card; that was all.'

Abdul Hamid Effendi strode, glowering, into his son's room as if he was going to attack it. I followed with Yusif. The old man seized the books and papers, reading what he saw.

'What are these books, Yusif?' I looked in terror at some papers in Abdul Hamid's hands: as if a snake might jump from them. Yusif stepped forward: 'That's a story.'

'*First Love.*' His father read the title and turned to Yusif, his

45

hands and lips shaking with rage. 'Your Excellency,' he screamed, 'writes a love story instead of studying? You've been fooling about this whole year.'

I remembered Suad and Yusif sitting together in the twilight. I thought of the day Yusif had come early in the morning, after she was engaged to the doctor. He must still be in love with Suad. I pitied him. I wished that his father would read the story aloud so I could know what Yusif thought of Suad. But Abdul Hamid threw the pages on the floor and glared at another handful. 'Another story! Splendid.' His rage had turned his cheeks scarlet; his eyes were popping out.

'I swear to God,' he finished, 'if you fail your exams, I'll throw you out. You'll no longer be my son; I'll not know you.'

In his room I helped him undress. He lay on his bed trembling with fury. I did my best to calm him.

From that night Yusif kept to the house, imprisoned in his room. If he came out, he saw me sitting and joking with his father. I behaved like a wife. He must have understood the situation now, if he hadn't before.

Yusif scraped through his exam and I was delighted. Neither Yusif nor Abdul Hamid shared my excitement.

'A pass is normal,' said Abdul Hamid. 'He needs more than that to get a job in the Prosecutor's Office. A pass degree is virtually worthless.'

When Yusif asked his father for £1, his father refused even a farthing.

'I've done my part; now you must get a job. I can't pay out on you. Sleep here, eat, drink at my expense, that's all right. But I've no money for you to amuse yourself on.'

All the same he did his best to find Yusif a job. Every morning he went out to visit Rateb Bey and try to get him to use his influence. I meanwhile offered Yusif the money he'd asked for. He refused my pound note.

'Why are you shy? This is your father's money.' I put it on the table and laughed. 'And please read me your story.'

'Why do you want me to read it?' he stuttered.

'I like the title – *First Love*.'

46

'Just empty words. . . .'

I gave up and cursed the fact that I could not read it myself.

It was summer. The weather was stifling. A curious sluggishness overpowered me. My usual energy had gone. I would clean half the house, then feel too lazy to do the rest. I had no wish to go to the kitchen or do any work. I would sit dozing at the table, then stir myself to do some job, then feel tired again and lie down.

Perhaps the reason I felt like this was hunger. I ate more. At every opportunity I'd go and snatch some cheese or olives from the kitchen. But the energy I hoped for did not come; I just felt more tired. One morning I woke feeling sick and went to the bathroom and vomited. I returned to bed. My sickness kept coming back throughout the day. Abdul Hamid wanted to take me to the doctor. I refused. 'It's only a chill. Tomorrow it'll have gone.' But I didn't get better. I would have to see a doctor if I wasn't better by the end of the month.

After days of waiting, my worst forebodings were proved right: I wasn't ill – I was pregnant.

I stayed in bed and wished I could die, and so avoid disgrace. I was afraid of myself, of my mother, of Abdul Hamid Effendi and of this thing in my stomach. I was fated to bear a child in sin. God frightened me most, whose stern regard I felt upon me. I cowered in bed wishing that by shutting my eyes I could escape.

In the evening I waited till Abdul Hamid turned out the light, and amorously reached for me. Then I whispered: 'I've something to tell you.'

He said, caressing me. 'What is it, my darling?'

'I'm pregnant.'

He pulled back his hand as if I had pricked it with a pin. Not believing what I said, he kept asking me questions. Then he left the bed to turn on the light. He stood looking at me like an idiot, while tears poured down my cheeks. If only they could wash away my shame.

He tried to calm me. 'Tomorrow I'll see a doctor who'll fix things.'

47

'For God's sake, save me from disgrace – I would prefer to die rather than be disgraced.'

In terrible depression I thought next morning of telling Yusif. He was more sensible than his father. But I hesitated to confide in him.

When Abdul Hamid came back at noon, he took off his clothes. 'What have you done, Mabruka?'

'What have you done is more to the point.'

He admitted, 'Nothing. I went to the café where the doctor goes, but he didn't come . . .'

I should have asked him to marry me. But I was terrified he might say no.

Yet my attitude changed. I no longer wanted to have an abortion. At first I had regarded pregnancy as so shocking that I wanted to end it. Now I thought I'd see what Abdul Hamid would do.

After a few days he again went to the café. Again he failed to meet the doctor. I was pleased. I knew he would never go to another doctor. His reluctance might show that he was thinking of marriage.

The next time he went to the café, the doctor was there. But he didn't have the courage to approach him.

I concealed my pleasure.

'I thought of saying it concerned a friend of mine. But it was too embarrassing.'

'You'll leave me like this, then?'

His head slumped forward. This was my moment.

'The best thing would be for us to marry.'

His head hung motionless.

I pressed on. 'I'll not go to the doctor and let him kill me. What's in my belly comes from you. It's up to you to put things right.'

I changed my tone. 'I swear, if you don't marry me I'll go to Rateb Bey and cause a scandal. I don't care a fig what happens.'

He was trying to wriggle out.

I shouted: 'Yes or no?'

Hopelessly he gave in. 'All right, all right: but let me choose the time.'

I was enraged. 'Choose the time – why?' I felt suddenly strong enough to overpower him. I would go to the police that very moment if he didn't accept my terms. I'd tell them what he'd done unless he promised to marry me at once. As I reached the door, his face was the colour of washing blue.

'All right, Mabruka, I agree.'

'Go and bring the notary.' It was an order.

'All right, but be patient. . . .'

At that moment the key turned in the door and Yusif came in. He noticed the strain in our unusual silence. He went to his room and I saw panic in his father's eyes.

'Now's the wrong moment. . . .'

'You're frightened of Yusif?'

He whispered: 'Be patient and God will reward you.'

'But aren't you going to tell him?'

'There's no need.'

'But there is.'

Again he yielded. But this time as he staggered to the table and sat down chalky white, I realized that he was serious in needing a respite. He might otherwise die. He refused a glass of water. He wanted to rest. So I guided him to his room and spent the day being tender to him. That night I squatted on the bed beside him, chatting, joking, making no reference to marriage.

But next morning I told him that Yusif was dressing and about to go out. Now was the moment to tell him.

'Send Yusif to me.'

As I went to the door he called me back. 'Have you got £5?'

'Why do you want them?'

'To give to Yusif.'

'You're welcome.'

I gave him the notes and he pushed them under his pillow. I followed Yusif into the bedroom ready to scream at the father if he broke his promise or at the son if he opposed my marriage. But Abdul Hamid asked me to leave them alone. My long look

49

warned him not to go back on his word. Yusif shut the door behind me and for several minutes there was silence. Then I heard Yusif's voice raised in protest. 'Impossible, father! You're insane. Rather than that, I'll kill her. I'll show her what's coming to her.'

I would have burst into the room but Yusif came pushing past me. I shouted in his face: 'So you want to kill me, do you?' I screamed hysterically: 'I'll show you and your father what's coming.'

Yusif stared at me in terror then fled from the flat.

9

THAT VERY EVENING THE NOTARY CAME TO DRAW UP the marriage contract. We sat at the dining-table. The notary opened his ledger, Abdul Hamid on his right, myself on his left. Nearby stood Mustafa the door-keeper and one of his relations, as witnesses.

There was nothing festive in the atmosphere. It was a bitter contrast to Suad's wedding: there were no guests, no glasses of sherbet, no rowdy rejoicing. Our witnesses looked grim: it was impossible to guess what they thought of Abdul Hamid's action.

The notary was old and hard of hearing. He insisted on clear, loud answers to his probing questions. He showed no pity for Abdul Hamid's whispered answers. He looked incredulous at some of them, repeating them loudly: So Abdul Hamid was sixty-one, a widower, a pensioner, he shouted, to Abdul Hamid's discomfiture. It was then my turn to be shouted at: what was my age? Abdul Hamid replied for me, that I was nineteen. The notary scrutinized my body as though suspicious that I was not ready for marriage.

After these painful moments, when it was all over and every-one had left, I felt wretched. All I wanted was sleep. I did not want to see Abdul Hamid, and he, for his part, sat away from me. We were both conscious of having sinned.

A new situation now existed between us and I did not know how to meet it. Until a few minutes before I had been servant and he had been my master, however informally I had treated him. But now I was a wife and he was my husband. I didn't know how a wife should treat a husband, even how she should ask such a simple question as whether he would like a cup of tea.

I decided to wait till he spoke first. His manner would suggest the right way for married people to converse.

He called me into his bedroom. He had taken off his jacket and stood in his shirt and trousers.

'Why were you sitting alone? Why didn't you come here?'

I had no answer.

He said without conviction: 'You'd like to go out . . . and have some fun.'

His words were empty of emotion.

There was nothing I wanted to do; I was exhausted. So was he. 'Is Yusif still out?'

He was, I said.

That was my wedding night. We dined off white cheese and slept side by side as if we were sick.

In the morning we found that Yusif's bed had not been slept in. Very worried, Abdul Hamid went out to look for him and returned with the news that henceforth Yusif preferred to live with a friend and not with us.

'He came to me in the café, as I felt he would.' He tried to pull himself together. 'He sat with me. I saw he knew we were now married. He was quite calm, he said nothing.'

'And then?'

'Before he went, he diffidently asked me if I still had the £5. I asked him how I would see him. He said he'd come to me.'

His words cut me. I had not foreseen I would feel like this after my triumph – as though I was defeated. I thought of hunting for Yusif myself, of telling him I wished him no harm, that all I wanted was reconciliation: I wanted to break the wall of servant and master, so that we could be friends.

This desire for a reconciliation lasted until it was driven out by a new concern – the thing moving inside my stomach. This now seemed the one thing of importance. I longed for the day when my baby would be born. I paid no more thought to Abdul Hamid than to washing my face in the morning. We would chat as usual, but his words meant nothing. It made no difference if he was at home or in the café.

Days passed while I waited for my child.

Then I took a step I was to regret.

In my loneliness I had thought how much I would like to see my mother. I wanted to see the joy in her eyes when she saw how I had got on in the world. I asked my husband to write a letter to my village. I said I needed a servant to help me. Looking at my swelling stomach, he agreed.

How wonderful it would be to sit at her feet, telling her how I had missed her all these years, telling her how all I had done had been for her sake, how she could now leave the village and live with me.

A few days later I heard a noise at the door. Outside I found my mother with a basket on her head, Sheikh Dessouki grasping a bundle, and with them a dirty little girl. I recoiled. This was the moment I had waited for. . . . I kissed and hugged her, then watched with astonishment as she squatted on the floor. I insisted that she sit on a chair. I kissed her again, noticing how coarse and brown her cheeks had grown. Her eyes were dim, her body weak and worn. But her eyes smiled with excitement at my marriage. At the same time she began to tell me of her troubles, raising her voice in complaint. Sheikh Dessouki supported her, seeing in my marriage a good reason for me to give my mother a lot of money. Quickly my dream of welcoming my mother dissolved. I had nothing in common with this person; her talk oppressed me. I couldn't see myself eating with her or talking to her. My exasperation increased when I saw Abdul Hamid's reaction when he got back. I was ashamed of my mother. I was sorry she had come and wished she would leave for the village that very night.

I turned my anger against the little girl servant. I scolded her for being dirty, ugly and ignorant. I told my mother she would not do for me.

'But you were just the same when I brought you to Cairo.'

Horrified, I realized that any link with my mother and village was broken. This meeting proved that I must love them in memory and imagination, but never see them as they really were.

My mother left a few days later. I gave her £3.

She wasn't pleased. She supposed my marriage had opened the gate of heaven. She wouldn't believe that this was all I had.

Abdul Hamid wanted to keep the girl till he could find a better one. I agreed, reluctantly.

The girl cried. I did my best to clean her up and teach her, but my repulsion overcame me. I wouldn't let her sit in my presence. I feared her ugliness might affect my unborn child.

When my time drew near, Abdul Hamid was strangely kind. In the evening we would go out walking as far as Kasr al-Nil bridge together. Yusif sometimes called on him.

'Can't you persuade him to come back to us?'

'No use; I've tried the impossible.'

'Have you found him a job?'

'No one's helped at all. They all make promises, but do nothing. Even Rateb Bey hasn't lifted a finger.'

I was worried about my own child: would he have such problems, too?

That evening, labour started. Abdul Hamid brought the midwife, and at dawn I heard the cry of my son, Ibrahim. I was deliriously happy. I felt I was greater than everything, stronger than everything. My room was a palace, more beautiful to me than Rateb Bey's. Abdul Hamid's happiness could only be a fraction of mine.

After days and nights in which I thought only of my baby, Abdul Hamid came to me, beaming: 'Yusif has found a job!' My baby had brought his older brother luck, I exclaimed. Yusif had been taken on by the newspaper, *Al-Ayyam*. It was the paper Rateb Bey used to read: I remembered it well.

'Make a note to buy it every day, Mabruka.'

'What does Yusif write?'

He said vaguely: 'All the news.'

How I wished I could read! I gazed at the hieroglyphics on the pages but all I could understand were the pictures. Even so, I valued the incomprehensible pages, since they made me feel nearer to Yusif. I scolded Abdul Hamid Effendi if he took the paper into the bedroom or forgot it in the café. He asked me why I cared, who could not read or write? Why didn't I use the paper to clean glasses?

'Because,' I said, 'I want to keep all the copies till Ibrahim grows up. Then I shall show him what his brother Yusif wrote.'

10

IBRAHIM COULD NOW CRAWL ON HIS HANDS AND KNEES, could point at things, could with some difficulty manage 'Papa!' and had three teeth. Abdul Hamid doted on his son, using baby talk and making funny faces till I sometimes thought he must have lost his reason.

One morning I was alone as usual. Ibrahim was crying without pause and nothing I could do would stop him. I waited anxiously for Abdul Hamid so that we could go to the doctor.

Suddenly I heard a loud knocking. The door-keeper was talking to someone whose voice I did not recognize. Outside stood a thickset stranger.

'Is madame the wife of Abdul Hamid Effendi?'

'What's wrong?' My heart beat as loudly as Ibrahim's screams.

'I'm very sorry . . . Abdul Hamid Bey . . . in the café.' His voice faltered; his eyes would not meet mine. 'You're still living . . .'

Everything whirled before me. I didn't know what I was doing, where I was, or what I was saying. All I remember is the thickset man trying to keep up with me as I ran like mad through the streets, carrying my baby. I pushed through cars and trams, unaware what they were. I fell and the man picked me up, trying to relieve me of Ibrahim. Frightened that he would kidnap him, I kept him in my arms. Again the man took my hand and pushed me into a taxi.

When I try to think of what happened in the café, all that comes back is a nightmare of pictures: bodies, eyes, voices and Abdul Hamid lying on a bier improvised from marble-topped tables. His eyes are closed. A rough hand seizes me and I slump on a chair. People question me, I answer, Ibrahim bellows. People swarm. Suddenly I see Yusif. I scream to him. He turns his back. 'Your father, Yusif. . . .' I see men carrying Abdul Hamid. I want to get to my husband. They push me aside and take him out. It is my right to take him! But Yusif stops me roughly: 'Go home. What are you trying to do here?' I try to reach Abdul Hamid. In vain. A large car with two doors at its back swallows my husband, then Yusif.

The car drives off and I run screaming after it, hoping that Abdul Hamid will hear.

How I reached the cemetery I don't know. But I found myself in a crowd, some wanting to send me home, others arguing that I had the right to be present at my husband's burial. These must have taken me with them. I stood near a little mosque with huts and small houses clustered near it. Village women in black sat on the ground; screaming children played near by. Groups of women mourning and screaming passed continually. We were waiting for Abdul Hamid. I stared at the people who passed, hoping he might be among them. I peered at the huts and the children. Men glanced at their watches.

In terror I screamed, 'Are you leaving me like this, Abdul Hamid?'

I hoped someone would react to my scream and bring me my husband. But everyone looked away.

Suddenly a motor horn was followed by a cloud of dust. Children welcomed it with screams. The car stopped and out stepped Rateb Bey and Midhat. Left alone for a moment I pushed in front of Rateb Bey.

'Rateb Bey, please, Sir, they've taken my husband.'

He turned to those near him.

'What's she doing here?'

At once rough hands pushed me from him. I found myself going down a sloping path. Everything was confused. From the hall of the tomb, they dragged me into a dark room and kept me shut up there till the coffin arrived. I saw it from the door and ran to it. That is the last I remember, except for a grief that seared me like fire. Then nothing.

When I came to, I was at home with Ibrahim alone. I thank God for my confusion. For automatically I undressed the child and put him to bed. It was as though I didn't realize my loss. Otherwise I might have killed myself.

I was sitting on Abdul Hamid's bed when I heard a noise outside. I opened the door to find my mother slapping blue paste on her cheeks and hair. Two other women were imitating her in anguished little jumps. Sheikh Dessouki was there, too, and with him a tall thin man in a blue *gallabya* whom I recognized after a moment as my uncle Imbabi. They pushed into the house and in a moment I found myself acting as hysterically as they were, if not more so.

II

MY ONLY ALLY NOW WAS SHEIKH DESSOUKI. HE TOLD me that the government would give me a pension of £13, and spoke of the figure ecstatically, almost as though he envied me what had happened. I heard him, but my thoughts were on Yusif; surely he would come home and help me?

Sheikh Dessouki had seen him at Rateb Bey's house – for Rateb Bey had paid for the funeral. But he couldn't tell me why Yusif hadn't come to see me and his little brother.

My mother overheard what we were saying.

'Who will look after you here? It would be better for you to come back to your own people.'

Her words enraged me. I was not going to throw away all I

had gained; I was not going to ruin my son's future; I would not leave my house. I wasn't Mabruka the poor village girl any longer, I wasn't a servant; I was the widow of Abdul Hamid Effendi, the mother of his son.

My mother's motives were clear; she wanted to share my pension.

'I'll never go back to the village,' I told her flatly. 'I don't want Ibrahim to set eyes on it.'

She raised her hands in prayer that my heart might be changed.

At this time we visited Abdul Hamid's tomb daily. I hoped I might meet Yusif. But despite hours of waiting, I never saw him. Someone told me he had visited the tomb very early on the first Thursday after his father's death; he was afraid, I realized, of meeting me.

Our meeting eventually took place in the law-courts, the day I went with Sheikh Dessouki to get my husband's death-certificate. I was sitting on a wooden bench outside the magistrate's office. When Yusif saw me, he frowned and took refuge in conversation with the Sheikh. I picked Ibrahim up to display him. 'Isn't this your father's son, your brother, your own flesh and blood?'

He glared. 'What do you want from me?'

I could hardly believe my ears. For months I had dreamed of reconciliation, that he would come home, and by his acceptance of me prove that I really had changed from a servant to a lady.

'Shame on your words!' I retorted. 'Let your father have peace in his tomb.'

'Don't you dare talk of my father. You've done enough to him already. Aren't you satisfied with driving him to his death?'

'May God forgive you!'

The magistrate's assistant interrupted us, calling us in to the office. I replied to the questions automatically. When we came out Yusif left us without a glance.

That day I wept with bitter hatred. I almost accepted my mother's advice, but I would have rather died than see Ibrahim in the village. I would stay in Cairo and educate him so that he would be a thousand times better than Yusif.

Days passed and my money flowed through my fingers. The delays continued. Daily Sheikh Dessouki asked me for money to use at the law-court and in the pensions department. I trailed behind him through government offices, one lot of employees handing us on to another. Some smiled encouragingly, saying it was only a question of time. But time passed and there was no result.

When I found myself on the way to Rateb Bey's house, I bitterly regretted that I was not going with a husband. Then I should have been welcomed in the drawing-room by my young mistress and offered orange juice by Ismail. My visit now was squalid and pathetic. I needed money for the rent.

'Uncle' Osman did not recognize me. He had aged. I went to the servant's entrance, where Ismail welcomed me warmly, taking Ibrahim in his arms and playing with him. Tears trickled down my face, I was so touched. He sat me down on a chair and treated me like a lady.

'What'll you have?'

'Nothing, I only want a glass of water.'

'I insist,' he said, 'I'll bring you cold lemon juice.'

He brought me the drink, then went to tell my young mistress I was there. Minutes passed, perhaps an hour, before I heard her footsteps on the stair. I was afraid. She looked at me questioningly. 'My condolences, Mabruka.' Her kindly tone at once changed. 'But what do you want?'

Her dry voice held no welcome. It silenced me. My embarrassment was increased when Ibrahim began to cry and she stared at him with dislike.

'Tell me what you need. I haven't got all day.'

I wanted to say what I had to say quickly but my words were drowned by Ibrahim's crying. Before I could finish, she said: 'Take this.'

There was a £1 note in her outstretched hand, and without thinking I took it and thanked her.

On my way out, Ismail saw I had been crying. He asked me sympathetically what had happened, but I did not tell him.

In a few days Ibrahim and I had eaten the £1. The house was empty and the rent was still to pay.

I decided to go to Yusif and try to soften his heart.

I found the street where the newspaper was. The doorman would not admit me. He stared at the child at my breast and asked what I wanted.

I told him that I wanted to see Yusif Effendi.

'Visits are not allowed.'

'I must see him. He's my relative. This is his brother.'

The doorman, perplexed, led me into a large hall where a man with a telephone sat at a desk.

'Ask the effendi.'

The official looked at me, spoke into the telephone, then told me Yusif would be right with me. Hardly had he finished than I saw Yusif running downstairs, puffing as if out of breath.

'What's brought you here?'

I was in tears. He took my arm gently and led me into a corner of the hall. 'Stop that crying. What do you think people will say?'

It was clear how embarrassed I made him. I told him of our hunger, of the pension that had not come through, of the rent. He said quickly: 'All right, all right. I'll see to the pension myself.'

Hope returned to me. 'When, Yusif?'

'Tomorrow.'

'Shall I come to you here?'

'No,' he said hastily. 'I'll come to you.'

I was overjoyed. 'May God reward you. But don't forget?'

'I'll not forget.'

Before he could leave me, I added: 'I have no money. I came here on foot.'

He took ten shillings from his pocket and gave it to me. Before I left the hall I saw him rushing upstairs.

I waited next morning, then noon, then evening. But Yusif did not come. I feared an accident. I went to a tobacconist in Bab al-Louk and asked the owner to get me Yusif on the telephone. Someone asked me my name. A moment's silence, then he said Yusif wasn't there. I told him I had waited all day. There was no cause for worry, the man assured.

I decided to try again next day. This time the man in the hall told me Yusif was out.

'But it's urgent,' I said.

He smiled. 'All right. When he comes in, I'll tell him.'

'When will that be?'

His quick answer reminded me of Yusif's way of speaking. 'I've no idea. I'm not *au fait* with his appointments.'

'Then I'll wait.'

His smile vanished.

'That's forbidden, I'm afraid.'

'I'll just wait here in the corner.'

'No, please find somewhere else.'

I went out and waited on the pavement. The doorman was furious and told me it was forbidden. I refused to move and we began to scream at each other. At this moment a thin young man with a dark complexion came up and asked good-humouredly what was the matter, then offered to go in and investigate. When he came back and told me he couldn't find Yusif, I felt he was telling the truth.

'There's no point waiting. Perhaps you can tell me where you live?'

'In a flat near Bab al-Louk.'

'What's the rent?'

'£5 10s a month. I'm two months behind.'

'Couldn't you find something cheaper? You could sell your present lease at a profit?'

He seemed an angel sent to help me. I warmed to him.

'I'm Showki Mahmoud.' His smile thrilled me. 'I draw,' he said, 'for the paper.'

His lower lip trembled in a way I had already noticed. I did not know how to answer his suggestion. 'What if I don't know how to let my flat?'

He spoke as though he was in charge: 'You must sell your lease.'

His confidence pleased me but at the same time I felt he was making me do what he wanted. I resisted, saying that I would think things over.

'Think things over?' He said in a strange tone, 'You don't have time. We'll go together now! I'll settle things.'

'Perhaps tomorrow I'll find the money. Things will work out.'

Again his lip trembled and he seemed angry.

'Do you really think the government will give you your pension?'

'It's my right.'

'Your right!' he said sarcastically. 'Are there rights in this country?'

'But how do you want me to feed my son? Shall I let him die?' I added emphatically, 'Yusif knows everything. He's promised to get me the pension.'

He looked up, seeming to struggle free from something that oppressed him. Slowly raising his eyes to mine, 'Listen to me. I can't lie to you as others have done. Yusif was in the newspaper office when you called.'

'Why wouldn't he see me?'

'Because he knows you haven't a chance of a pension.'

12

A FEW DAYS LATER, OUR DOOR-KEEPER HANDED ME £50, paid by a new tenant; the rent overdue had been deducted.

Wrapping the money in a handkerchief, I hid it in my bosom. I then put Ibrahim on my shoulder and went with Showki to look at my new home.

We left the wide streets behind us and entered a narrow, twisting road, crowded with men in *gallabyas* and women wrapped in black. There were small shops on both sides. The hubbub was not unpleasant. Sometimes a car would block the road, almost knocking people over. I pushed through hands which seemed ready to push me down the wrong lane – from which I would never find my way out. I felt that among these hands Yusif's might be just behind me.

We reached a huge gateway. Showki told me it was Bab Zuweyla. I shuddered at its secrets as I passed beneath. We entered a narrow lane, covered and dark. Before we reached the end, Showki stopped by a large door in front of which sat three yawning men. They looked at me through half-shut eyes. As if to wake them, Showki greeted them loudly. Their reply, though sluggish, was friendly.

Crossing the threshold I saw a large courtyard, in one corner of which was a carpenter sawing logs.

At the end I saw a shop for dyeing leather. Beside it, over a hole edged by stones, squatted a boy, excreting, at the same time staring at me inquisitively.

Showki stopped at a door by the dyeshop – a thick door of ancient wood. Above I saw two storeys, each with two large windows.

The first floor was my new home.

'And you live above it?'

I was right, and his smile increased.

He then shouted to the squatting boy: 'Where's your mother, boy?'

'Inside,' and the boy pointed to the left of the door.

Showki knocked. 'Um Hanafi!'

'Ready,' answered a broken, weak voice, 'I'm coming.'

A large fat woman, swaying as she walked, approached us, puffing and panting.

She welcomed me in a kindly manner and, waddling to the door, unlocked it. We climbed four stone steps and came to another door on creaking hinges. A narrow wooden stair led to the first storey. A little room gave on to a larger one. The stone floor was covered with dust. Spiders had spun their webs over all the woodwork. Had it not been for the light from the two windows I should have thought it an abode of demons. I did not like this room: it frightened me. Showki tried to cheer me up, saying how different it would be once I had cleaned it and brought my things.

As if to celebrate my arrival, he asked Um Hanafi to make us tea.

Showki's home had two similar rooms, but scattered all over the first were lots of pictures, one on top of another. Dust was over everything. Paper was everywhere, empty bottles, torn, colourless curtains littering the floor. But the second room was tidy: matting on the floor, two large backless divans, wooden chairs with two tables and a wardrobe painted red. The distorted pictures on the walls astonished me: the only normal picture was that of a white dove. On an easel in the middle of the room was a canvas whose crude black lines looked as though a child had been playing with paint.

The staircase creaked. Um Hanafi brought the tea, and then two brooms – and this was the start of my spring-cleaning. I could never have imagined someone as fat and short of breath as Um Hanafi being so active. She had the strength of three ordinary women. I helped her, while Ibrahim played with Showki. Next day the rooms were ready to take my things. By nightfall I was so exhausted that I could not be bothered to light the lamp but sat mindlessly in the dark, until Showki's calls for light pulled me together.

He was climbing the stairs with three men behind him. They looked like ghosts, each greeting me as he passed. To each other they seemed to be talking in a strange tongue. I couldn't understand what they said, but I heard them call each other 'comrade'; Comrade Showki, Comrade Lutfi, Comrade Subri.

I sat the whole evening in my room listening to steps coming up and steps going down. I wondered at the secret purpose of these strange people.

13

AS THE MONTHS PASSED, SHOWKI'S FRIENDS CAME TO trust me. On their way up to him they would stop and joke, ask after Ibrahim or play with him, even. Sometimes they seemed jubilant, sometimes downcast. They used to pool their money for me to go and buy them a snack. I'd fetch cheese, *halawa*, *taheena* and Hollywood cigarettes and then come and join them in their supper.

They no longer minded speaking in front of me about the demonstrations they were planning. I was astonished at their schemes. Towards the end of the session they would stop chatting, and Showki would tell each of them where to go: Subri to Al-Azhar, Lutfi to the University, Muhammad to a school. They would be the leaders of the demonstrators, responsible for the slogans.

I thanked God that Showki went nowhere. He was the thinker; at night he planned the route for the demonstration; in the morning he went to his newspaper and waited to hear how things went. When in the evening he told me the news, I admired him as the master-mind of Cairo – behind the over-turned trams, the smashed lamps, the stones hurled at the police.

I was thrilled when he told me these things: I felt that I was his partner, that I was strong like him. Showki repeated emphatically: 'All this is on your behalf, Mabruka, and on behalf of others like you.'

'When will it all come to pass?'

His answer to this question was in long phrases whose meaning I did not understand. But even so I could not resist his eyes.

One night I heard him tell his friends a piece of news he had picked up at the newspaper. One asked him: 'Are you sure that's true?'

'Absolutely,' said Showki. 'I heard it from Yusif.'

I went to my own room, disturbed at heart. Though Showki and I tried to put Yusif from our thoughts, I for one had not succeeded. I would sometimes wake up with a vision of the last time I saw him, when having given me the ten shillings (and having promised to come to me) he had run upstairs. I tried to imagine where he was now. Was he thinking of marriage? I imagined he might suddenly arrive, imploring my forgiveness with his shy eyes, then ask me to go and live with him where he could look after me and help with Ibrahim's upbringing. I wondered whether I should agree and go with him, or stay with Showki where I was.

When at long last Showki's companions had left, I could contain my curiosity no longer.

'I heard you talking about Yusif, you and your friends. What is he doing?'

He seemed reluctant to explain. 'He's become an important person in the paper.'

'How?'

Still seeming reluctant, he said: 'What do you think of him? He seems good. He treats people correctly. Little by little . . . he profits from that. His salary goes up; his name appears in the paper. The truth is, though, I'm dubious about him. Is he good, do you think, or bad?'

I rushed to Yusif's defence. 'He's good. He's as bashful as a girl.'

'You say that, after what he did to you?'

'Why not? He changed towards me because I married his father. But he remains Ibrahim's brother.'

He seemed perplexed. 'I don't know. . . . I distrust good people when they profit from their goodness.'

I gleaned all I could about Yusif: his salary was now £70 a month, he lived alone in a flat in Midan Ismailia. When I asked if Yusif had any girl friends, Showki got angry. Dawn was breaking.

Then one evening Showki returned looking very anxious. The police had arrested his friends.

That moment I seemed to wake up and see things in their true light. This was not make-believe, his friends were not playing. Stupidly, needlessly, they were rushing to do battle with terror, the police, prison, even death.

I feared for Showki, not for his friends.

'By the Prophet, give up this stupid game.'

I knew, if he persisted they would gaol and torture him. I was worried for him, as well as for my child and for myself.

Now when he left the house I could not bear sitting alone. So I would go and sit with Um Hanafi while Ibrahim played with her little boy in the yard. She was delighted to have an audience for her endless stories. But my thoughts were on the days to come. I would grow like her, but worse. I watched Ibrahim filthying himself from head to foot. I would scream at him, he would scream back, and we would make the yard ache with our shouts until, tired out, we slumped into a heavy silence.

If only God would turn Showki's mind from what he was doing. . . . In my mind I saw the events of my life: Awad's thefts and imprisonment, Midhat's desire to possess me, Abdul Hamid's sucking of my youth, Showki's desire to burn everything, including all of us. O Lord, I asked, why has my fate always been like this? Yusif was the only clever one. In his cleverness he fled from me so that my luck would not infect his. Now he was going up and up, while I was going down and down. My role in life was to be defeated. I had wanted him to recognize that I had become a lady. I hated him.

And I longed to provoke Showki into changing his own way of life, to break his pride so that he would no longer feel strong enough to challenge the police, for he was now receiving new secretive visitors who came for brief discussions, then vanished like ghosts. I saw lots of papers stuffed under the divan reminding me of the time Abdul Hamid had gone through Yusif's things, looking for pamphlets.

'You've brought these papers for the police to find?'

My shout surprised him. 'What do you know about them?'

'They're leaflets.'

I told him what had happened to Yusif and threatened to chase his friends away, next time they came.

His lips trembled and he snapped that if I did such a thing, I, not they, would leave the house.

I went to my room and cried like a madwoman. Then I heard him call me. Was he going to turn me out then and there? On my way to him I felt as if I was again a servant.

I trembled, lowering my head; I did not want him to see my tears and curse me as Rateb Bey would have done.

But he sat me down on the divan beside him, whispering: 'Mabruka, I don't know how I could have said what I said.'

My tears increased, but a new strength flooded my heart. I heard him say, 'This is your house. I apologize.'

'Do you want me to leave?'

He exploded: 'You've punished me enough, Mabruka. This is enough. Let me kiss you.' He kissed my hair. But I was still not sure of him. I implored him once more not to throw me out. 'Enough, Mabruka, enough!' But I went on weeping. 'Let me stay here – I'll do whatever you like. I'll kiss your hand, I'll kiss your feet.'

If he was deceiving me, I would not forgive him as I had forgiven Yusif.

14

SHOWKI'S MANNER TOWARDS ME CHANGED. EVERY word and action seemed calculated to apologize for what had happened. When his friends came he looked at me in embarrassment, as if asking my permission to let them stay, and the moment they left, he would rush to humour me.

Once when he was painting at his large canvas, he told me that Yusif was in love with a girl who worked as a cinema extra. Her name was Samia Sami.

'Will he marry her?'

He smiled at my anxiety. 'Who can tell?'

I exploded: 'But you must warn him!'

'Believe me, Yusif's shrewder than me, or you.' He waved the brush in my face. 'I'm sure he won't marry her. He'll fear for his position on the paper.'

'What is an extra?'

He returned to his painting. 'A minor actress – not a Layla Murad.'

I was astonished at myself for being so concerned whether or not Yusif married this extra. My hatred suggested it would be a good thing if he did marry her and wreck his career. But my tender memories of the days with Yusif outweighed my hatred.

I could not hate the days when I had lived as a lady, nor the hope which I had lived for and nearly achieved.

One evening Showki invited me to the cinema. With a cunning look in his eyes he explained, 'Then you can see Samia.'

I put on my prettiest dress and stood for a long time in front of the mirror making sure of my appearance. I felt that I was going to meet Samia in the flesh and that she and I would be locked in a contest which would show which of us was the most beautiful. I was full of confidence. She would look at me from the screen and acknowledge her defeat, then die of sorrow.

My mental picture was of someone like Suad: a white oval face, beautiful foolish eyes, a tall body offset by plump flesh. But the new Suad was only a third-rate actress: I felt sure I could defeat her. I pitied Yusif and smiled at the catastrophe which would shortly befall him.

I fidgeted in my seat next to Showki, asking him each moment if this actress, or that, was Samia. I got impatient. The comedian – Yusif's namesake as it happened– Yusif Wahba was passing down a narrow lane followed by thieves out for his blood. A girl suddenly appeared swathed in a black veil. Showki nudged me. 'That's her.' I was astonished; my hopes were dashed. She was totally different from what I had imagined. She had nothing in common with Suad. Thin, even skinny, she wasn't tall and her eyes had a cunning, evil look. Her wide mouth almost cut her face in two; her lips were large, almost swollen. She slunk down the lane casting langorous glances at Yusif Wahba. She stopped and asked huskily: 'What do you want of me?' As Yusif stuttered in confusion, one of the thieves attacked him from behind, knocking him to the ground with a cudgel. Smiling, Samia moved off, prancing as though her body had springs.

I turned to Showki and whispered: 'She's a bad lot. Can't he find anything better than this bitch?'

'Don't blame her: blame the role. She's not bad.'

I was irritated. 'What do you like about her?'

He shrugged his shoulders.

I sat in silent anger. I waited for her next appearance, but there was none. After the film I asked why this was.

'What?'

'That rubbish Samia didn't appear again.'

He laughed.

'She only had a small part.'

'She's not worth sixpence. I'm better than her.'

He seemed surprised. 'Would you like to be like her?'

This suggestion enraged me. All the way home and long into the night, I raged at him: I was important to no one – not even to Showki; his yawns did not mean that he wanted to sleep: they meant he was tired of me; if Samia had been there, he wouldn't have yawned.

Words came beyond my control.

Two days later Showki knocked at the door.

'Mabruka, something urgent.' – He and his friends had decided to buy a printing press. He suddenly added, 'I want £20 from you.'

He had to repeat his request. I could not believe my ears. I only had £37 left. This money wasn't mine – it was my child's. He was growing. Every day he wanted more. I had need of every piastre, and Showki knew it. My mind screamed: Refuse! Don't give him a single millieme. He wants to waste it all on a press which will do nothing to feed your child. But I could not refuse. All I had, I owed to him.

Instead I asked: 'Isn't £20 a lot?'

'Yes,' he said, 'but I need it.'

So with trembling hand I gave him the money and, with a curt word of thanks, he took it and left.

For the next few days he was too busy to speak to me. Then one evening I heard the noise of many footsteps on the stairs! From my door I saw him and his friends carrying up the press. Because I had given the money, I was allowed to watch as they printed their leaflets.

At dawn, when they had carried off their bundles to distribute, I wanted to go to bed. But Showki put his arm round me, his face beaming with delight: 'This time I'm going to keep you awake. I don't know how to repay you, Mabruka.'

He kissed my cheek and held me tighter.

I felt my body go soft between his arms. Unconsciously I returned his kiss and put my arms round his head. 'How shall I repay you, Showki . . .?'

His lips silenced me. A feeling of physical desire swept over me; I desired him with everything in me. I took everything from him: I gave him everything. I devoured him; he devoured me. We were in a world high above this one, remote from sorrow, memories, even from love.

A pleasant numbness possessed me and I let him talk of his feelings for me till he fell asleep, and I slept by him. It wasn't till I woke up in the morning that I remembered I had left Ibrahim alone all night. I ran downstairs, very upset. He met me with a strange, suspicious stare, which pierced and hurt me. When I pulled him to me, his little hands pushed me away in disgust. It was almost as if he smelt Showki's smell on my flesh. All day I felt desperate. When Showki came back, I ran to his arms.

'Ibrahim doesn't want me to touch him.'

He pondered a moment. 'We must take care. Little children understand a lot.'

From that day we both did all we could to please Ibrahim. I succeeded in convincing him that Showki was his father. Nor did I feel that I was being deceitful, now that I no longer thought of Abdul Hamid. Showki, for his part, brought Ibrahim sweets and played with him. He would never embrace me or talk till Ibrahim had gone to bed. Only then would I go upstairs, watch Showki paint, then chat till love overpowered us. For I felt increasing desire for his love as though it might wash out Abdul Hamid's pathetic attempts. I was angry when his friends' visits kept him from me. I wanted to turn them out. He knew this and would take any opportunity to get rid of them early and then come to me.

Why wouldn't he ask his friends to choose another meeting-place?

But this place was safe, he said; the police didn't know about it.

His folly enraged me. 'You want to go on using this place till they do know about it and arrest the lot of you?'

'Listen, Mabruka,' he said gravely. 'You must realize that the police can lay hands on me any time they want.'

I was sarcastic. 'That does relieve me, I must say!'

I felt I must fight for my happiness. I could not rest till I had rescued him from his friends.

I rubbed my cheek against his hair.

'If anything happened to you,' I said tenderly, 'I should die.'

'You want me to give up everything?'

I kissed him on the throat.

'Don't ever leave me. What would I do without you?'

When he protested, I kissed his lips silent. But despite his apparent submission, he let his friends go on visiting him. This was the one request of mine, he said, which he could not grant; he considered me his partner in all he did. But he would not be able to respect himself or love me unless he remained true to his beliefs.

Over the following months all my efforts failed.

Yusif was cleverer, I told Showki. He knew better than to put himself in danger. His position therefore got better, his salary increased.

'But you, I suppose, are prepared to go on earning £30 a month all your life? While he lives in a palace, earns £100 and rides in a car.'

He was angry. 'You don't estimate people by their money.'

He spoke at great length about my errors.

15

WHEN I DISCOVERED THAT FOR THE SECOND TIME I WAS pregnant, it did not upset me like having Ibrahim. Showki would take the news calmly and marry me at once.

But I was wrong. His face went yellow, he trembled as though at a disaster and beat his head against the wall. Pitying him, I tried to calm him. But he laughed in a strange, sarcastic manner and screamed at me bitterly:

'Now show your cleverness, Mabruka!'

I didn't understand what he meant, till he said: 'You want me to marry you today, and go to prison tomorrow?'

I raised my eyes to his: they said, Yes, I would like to marry.

'And bring up two children instead of one?'

I whispered: 'There's always God.'

'If there was God?' he shouted, his body trembling, his face bitter, 'why doesn't he feed the beggars who crowd the streets, why doesn't he heal the sick, why doesn't he let us live in peace?'

His words frightened me.

'Don't blaspheme, Showki.'

'Blaspheme? Don't talk like an idiot.' He laughed at my fears. 'I'm a coward . . . understand . . . a coward.'

He raved on insanely.

But the day came when he brought me back from the doctor who had aborted me. He sat beside me and started crying. In all my life I had never seen anyone cry like this. It was as if he wanted to kill himself with tears. Despite my own pain, I did my best to calm him. But he beat his fist on his knee and said with violence, 'Look at me, Mabruka, and what a cheap swindler I've been. I took you in, just as I took my friends in, and myself, too. . . . There I was preaching about humanity, brotherly love, communism, and look what I've done. I'm a swindler, nothing more.'

This was the first time in his life that his revolt was against himself and his thoughts. It was a miracle from God. I had been enabled to triumph over his comrades.

I persuaded him that what had happened had not bothered me. I poured out my love in looks and words, in the food I brought him and in the way I cleaned his room. I wanted him to be mine only, and me to be his. I sensed the moment as near when I could rescue him from danger. He yielded to me, although at times his thoughts seemed to be wandering.

Meanwhile, though his friends continued to visit him, I noticed he did not argue so much with them. I felt that soon they would break with him. Then he and I could live at peace, safe from risk.

But whenever I worked round to this subject, he was evasive, I knew he was still reluctant to take the final step.

So I gave him more love, till a sudden change took place. He began fighting with me over trivial things. Once I brought him a cup of tea which he said had no sugar in it. He threw it on the floor and smashed it.

His fury made me anxious for him, not myself. I wanted to soothe his angry head against my breast. But when I stopped to pick up the bits, he raged at me to leave them alone. After a few moments he came and knocked at my door. His eyes showed that he was sorry. Ibrahim threw his arms round Showki's legs. 'A piastre . . . a piastre!'

He picked up the boy and kissed him, his eyes on me. He gave the boy his piastre and Ibrahim ran out into the street.

'Make me tea.'

'So you can break another cup?' I laughed good-humouredly.

'Yes,' he came towards me, 'and your neck, too.'

He embraced me, whispering: 'Are you angry?'

'Because of a cup?' I asked. 'Your ransom is sixty cups!'

I put my hand on his chest, wishing to banish his worry and regret. But he explained that what had upset him was what had happened to our unborn child. Since my abortion he had lost his bearings.

'All my principles were against the murder of our baby. He might have grown up like Ibrahim . . . laughed . . . cried . . . asked me for money . . . grown into a man . . . a man better than me, a man with principles.'

'But I'm not angry,' I broke in.

'Because it was for me?'

'Yes.'

'So I'm the reason. . . . I wish you had defied me and kept the baby. Who was I to deserve all this?'

73

I was perplexed. I could not understand why he tormented himself like this.

'I'm a fraud. You must have seen me arguing with my friends, pretending to be a good communist, criticizing them for not being real revolutionaries – all this to hide the lie that I am living.'

He seemed now to be talking to himself.

'I've a good mind to tell them everything . . . and then resign.'

It looked as though the final step was near.

16

ONE EVENING SHOWKI LOOKED VERY PERTURBED. THE story he told me alarmed me. For months, he confessed, he had lost all control over his tongue. He had spoken about communism overtly and in long conversations with the other people on the paper. If anyone defended the Government, he would turn and curse first him, then the Prime Minister. If the man protested, he would curse King Farouk, too. He knew such frankness was dangerous. But he was possessed by something beyond his control. He felt on fire. He thought of his friends in prison and despised himself as a coward for being free. They were better than him, more loyal.

Until one morning. Then Yusif summoned him to his office. He greeted him, offered him a cigarette, with his gentle, embarrassed smiles that concealed cunning and prudence. They spoke of commonplaces for a moment. Then suddenly Yusif said: 'I must ask you, Showki, not to discuss politics in this building.'

That gentle apologetic tone enraged Showki. He would have preferred a direct attack, to a threat wrapped up in kindness.

'I'm free to speak as I wish; I can say whatever I want to say.'

Yusif countered his explosion with a calm voice. 'No, you can't.'

'Why not? Do you think I'll be bossed by you, or by any one bigger than you?'

Yusif abandoned his normal manner. In a tone that no longer concealed its menace, he warned him that one more word about politics and he'd be sacked on the spot. Showki kicked his way out of the door.

He had not gone a few paces before he felt very afraid. Although he tried to keep cool, by the time he had reached his desk, fear had turned to panic. Almost unaware of what he was doing, he found himself back at Yusif's door, hardly seeing the man he was addressing, babbling apologies for what had happened. He protested his innocence of the charge: he hated the communists; he cursed them; he despised them.

Having told me this, he beat his fists on his knees as if he wanted to break them; he looked as distorted as one of his own pictures.

'I told you,' he muttered feverishly, 'so you can see how contemptible I am.'

I kept back my tears. This was not the Showki I knew, the man whose fearless glance had strengthened me that day outside the newspaper. This sick man, infected by an illness I could not understand, was no longer Showki.

'What on earth made you do that?' I was disappointed that his collapse had come just at the moment of my victory.

His answer was spiritless. 'I don't know. But I fear Yusif.' He laughed bitterly. 'Yes, I fear him. And I tell you, so you can despise me. I'm not even a man.'

If this continued true, I would despise him, I knew.

'Don't say that again. You're worth a thousand Yusifs.'

I did not fear that Yusif would carry his threats to the point of denouncing Showki to the police. What upset me was that Showki, usually so manly, had been so weak in front of Yusif. Showki was the man I relied on, a counterweight in my mind to Yusif. It distressed me that he had demeaned himself in front of him. A crazy impulse seized me. I would rush to the newspaper and hit Yusif over the head with my shoe: I'd tell him Showki was the better man; that Yusif was contemptible beyond contempt.

The following days were heavy. Showki avoided me.

Then one night very late, when we were not sleeping because of the summer heat, he suddenly said: 'By the way, Mabruka, I congratulate you for your relative.'

I knew who he meant; I did not want to hear. But he told me Yusif had been promoted yet higher; his monthly salary was now £200. I wanted to choke him off. 'Aren't you tired?'

He yawned, 'Good night.'

This latest news upset me finally. I had no more hopes where Yusif was concerned. His wealth had put him beyond my reach. Money was flowing uncounted between his fingers; he was probably richer than Rateb Bey. How happy he must be! But I was wretched. While he was rich, I was poor. This money of his was stolen from me and Ibrahim, his little brother. Running forward to the goal of wealth, he had abandoned us.

My love for Showki withered; so did my love for my child; so did all tender thoughts. I raised my hands to heaven to curse Yusif the thief. The bitterest was that Showki had Yusif as his boss. Showki was working as his servant, just as I had once worked as a servant for his father.

Showki must leave. My chance to suggest this came when a raise was given to everyone in the office except him. When Showki had protested, Yusif had kicked him out of his office, shouting that his communism was endangering the paper.

I said: 'Look for another job.'

He turned to me gratefully as if he had wanted to hear this advice. 'I'll do just that.' Then he added, his lip trembling. 'But I'm afraid he may do something.'

'What more can he do?'

'Denounce me to the police?'

He laughed ironically. 'It's strange, isn't it, that the very moment when I'm turning against communism, they'll probably arrest me as a communist.'

76

17

ONE NIGHT AFTER WE HAD MADE LOVE WE WERE wakened by knocking. It was the police. They muscled their way into the room, searched every corner, confiscated the printing press and the pamphlets and took Showki with them.

I was left alone. My body felt deflated. I could still smell Showki, his shadow still seemed near me.

But everything was over. All I had striven for was gone; my life was like the public lane, trampled on by heedless feet.

Why, I asked God, have you shut every road? Did I sin when I left the village? But I did that despite myself; I was so hungry I could have eaten mud. I saw the life which city people enjoyed and wanted to share it. Was that a sin?

And now the axe had fallen.

Everything was over.

Could I live when things were over? I had no tomorrow. Showki . . . my dear Showki . . .

Why didn't you foresee this? I was insane to think you could make mankind happy: you couldn't make me happy. All you did was kill my baby. Don't be angry at what I think, Showki. I'm just as crazy. I love the way your bottom lip trembles.

You and I, both lived for a dream, for a secret whisper from our hearts. My ambition was the dream of us two living happily together. Your ambition was greater: you dreamed of happiness for everyone.

The carpenter and I went to ask about Showki at police headquarters. They glared at us and asked Taha for his name and address. We fled from their questions and suspicious stares.

I sat with Um Hanafi. She told me in her weak, faltering voice that our only hope was in God . . . in our present Lord.

18

ALL I COULD DO NOW WAS TO TURN TO YUSIF: TO VISIT
this little lord who was rising higher and higher. He was the
one person who could restore Showki to me.

I went to the newspaper building. It had not changed at all
despite the passage of years. There was still the same man on
the door. But he did not recognize me.

'Where are you going, madame?'

'To see Dr Yusif.'

He raised his voice. 'Why do you want him?'

'I'm his relative.'

His eyes showed that this reminded him of something, but he
still could not place me. Perplexed, he asked me to go up to the
official in the outer hall.

The official heard Yusif's name with great deference. When
he picked up the telephone it was as though he was waiting for
inspiration from on high. Then he replaced the receiver and
looked at me hostilely.

'Dr Yusif can't receive you.'

I didn't argue; I didn't try to resist. Feeling utterly weak, I
made my way home.

When I told the carpenter in our yard what had happened, he
said: 'You must send Ibrahim to intercede.' When dispiritedly
I said that Yusif would not admit him, Taha thought for a
moment, then said: 'He should wait at the door. When Yusif
comes out, he can approach him.'

Usta Taha drafted a letter for me:

To the respected Lord, Yusif Bey Abdul Hamid :
  Peace be unto you and the Mercy of God and His Blessing.
Ibrahim Abdul Hamid al-Suefi, the son of your lamented
father, your obedient, faithful brother, presents his respects.
He invokes God's blessing upon you and implores you of

78

your goodness to help and guide him. Being an indigent orphan, lacking even food, he turns to you as his only relation. The holy laws of religion and the Koran have alike recommended the care of the orphan and the outcast. I invoke God in requesting you give me of what He has given you, for you are good and generous. Peace be with you and the mercy of God.

Your brother, and servant, *Ibrahim Abdul Hamid.*

As I tearfully stowed the paper in my bodice, Usta Taha said: 'If he doesn't help you after this, you must ask the court for a maintenance order. That's the advice of the sheikh who wrote this letter.'

I went in the morning with Ibrahim and stood outside the newspaper while people came and went. It was exhausting. Ibrahim crouched beside me on the pavement, while I tried to reassure him: Yusif was his brother, there was nothing to fear. I told him what he was to do.

Suddenly Yusif came down the steps, walking briskly and smiling. Two men followed him.

'That's him,' I said to Ibrahim, pushing his shoulder. 'Run and give him the paper.'

The boy hesitated, so I screamed at him to go.

Yusif reached the bottom of the steps; the doorman saluted; a large white car drove up. The horn blared out and everyone stared at Ibrahim as he just managed to avoid being run over, his hand holding the paper in Yusif's face.

I stood watching, bemused.

Yusif stared closely at his brother for a long moment. The two men tried to push the boy away. Yusif took the paper. It was as though his hand touched me and woke me from my dream. I rushed towards him, forgetting all the evil he had done me, eager only to smile at him and have him smile at me in return.

'How are you, Sidi Yusif?'

He lifted his eyes from the paper to my smile and smiled back, the same embarrassed smile, the same kind, rather sad look I remembered from of old. He put the paper in his pocket.

'How are you, Mabruka?' His tone was warm. He held my hand a moment but, when I stopped to kiss his, he drew it back in a way that reminded me of the time my old mistress had withdrawn hers when I first came to Cairo. He ran his fingers through Ibrahim's curls.

'You see how he's grown?'

'He's a man already.'

I smiled as though Yusif had been the one who helped me bring him up all these long years.

His smile vanished. I said eagerly, trying to bring back his smile; 'What'll you do for him?'

He fumbled in his pocket and pulled out £1.

I screamed as though the money was a snake. 'I don't want money.'

'Then what do you want?'

'You think you can get rid of me with £1?'

He took no notice but handed the note to Ibrahim.

I was in despair, needing someone to turn to, but I saw that everyone was against me. I heard Yusif mutter: 'I'm busy now.'

'I'm busy now.' One of his friends prevented me from approaching Yusif. 'Now don't be greedy. He's given you £1. Be grateful for it.'

Yusif got into the car. I pushed past the man screaming: 'Where are you going? If you leave me, what can I do? I'm a poor woman.'

The car shot forward.

19

MY LIFE CHANGED. THE MABRUKA WHO LIVES TODAY is a creature without heart, ruled only by hatred. She knows neither sadness nor joy; a cold mind rules unfeeling flesh.

I come and go only for the sake of bread. Without hope,

without anger, without dreams. For my dreams have faded; the voices I heard in my heart are stilled. All that remains is hatred and food. Food. . . . Food. . . . This is all I think about. By day I hunt for food which Ibrahim and I then eat. By night hatred hunts for me and eats me. The hunt for food is my obsession. Sometimes I remember how my mother would slap me when I complained of hunger. I feared her so much that rather than complain I would go to bed hungry. I do not want to treat Ibrahim this way.

Hunger drove me back to Rateb Bey's. I entered the house as a stranger among strangers: simply a place where I could eat. My young mistress frowned when she saw me. It did not worry me. I pretended to be weeping as I complained about Yusif.

To my surprise she seemed moved, and called Rateb Bey. He tottered slowly into the room, his back bent, his face fallen, his hands trembling. He listened while I repeated my story. I hated the smile on his lips and the delight in his eyes. My young mistress looked at me kindly. She would give me some washing to do.

Doing his best to speak firmly, Rateb Bey said: 'We're not heartless like some people, Mabruka.'

They shared my hatred for Yusif; but this gave me no pleasure; all I wanted was to eat.

So I went once a week to Rateb Bey's and washed, swept, cleaned till I was exhausted. I'd then go to the kitchen and eat and eat. Then I'd wrap food for Ibrahim in a cloth and take it home.

I washed for other houses. Suad had great need of me; she had two children herself.

She too enjoyed hearing what I had to tell about Yusif. She laughed when I told her about my last meeting with him outside the newspaper.

'You certainly showed him up, Mabruka!'

Seeing her sympathy, I imitated Um Hanafi's broken voice and enjoyed bringing tears to her eyes.

'Why don't you try Yusif again?'

I told her truthfully that if he suggested I should wash for him, I'd accept.

She laughed. 'Why not try him?'

'He'd not accept.'

Her laugh died; I was robbing her of a good story.

Going to her house like this, I forgot the time when I had compared myself with her. The old Suad was as dead as the old Mabruka. She was just a strange woman whose sympathy I could play on for money and food.

Suad sent me to Midhat's house. He had married a woman much older than himself. She received me in a dry, brusque way and left me in front of piles of washing.

Months passed and I did not set eyes on Midhat. But I did his washing and was astonished how dirty his underwear was, and how full of holes.

One evening he passed me as I was leaving the building. He noticed my stare and turned.

'Mabruka! What are you doing here?'

Trying to make myself as pathetic as possible, I told him I did his washing.

'Why didn't I know?'

His face looked strained; there were dark bags under his eyes; but though he looked worried and anxious, his smile was sweet.

I told myself that if he wanted me now I'd not resist. I might get more than from washing.

But he did not read my smile. Instead, as though thinking suddenly of something important, he asked: 'What news of Yusif?'

I smiled as though his question did not affect me. 'I never see him.'

'But he shouldn't let you work.'

'He doesn't bother with me, Sidi Midhat.'

'I must talk to him,' he said earnestly, but nothing came of it.

One evening as I was carrying my bundle of food from Rateb Bey's, I saw that the city was on fire. People were running into flames and out of them. Glass littered the ground under my feet.

Shouts came nearer. Children carrying lengths of cloth chased each other down the middle of the road. Destruction was everywhere. The sky was black. I saw a huge shop in front of me with men bringing out every kind of cloth. I bumped into other people, was jostled, but felt nothing. I threw away my bundle of food, filled my arms with as much cloth as I could carry and fled from the shop towards my home.

I panted up Muhammad Ali Street. I could not believe what I had seen; I was not sure if it was reality or not.

Suddenly a voice called my name, a sad, warm voice.

I did not turn to look but the voice followed me and turned into a man who blocked my way. He wore an overcoat over his *gallabya* and a scarf round his neck. Crinkly black hair stood up on his head.

I was about to abandon the cloth in panic when the man smiled. He repeated my name tenderly.

Who could he be?

Before I could escape he said, 'How are you, my girl? Where are you nowadays?'

I knew his voice: it was Awad.

I remembered that he had been in prison.

'Have you left the house in Giza?'

I thought of Showki: he was in prison, Awad was free. What was happening in the world?

Awad repeated his question. 'You don't answer. Are you still in Giza?'

'I go there sometimes.'

His eyes spotted my burden. He smiled happily.

'By God, you're the smart one. You knew how to make the best of the riot.' He asked again: 'You go to them sometimes. . . You don't live with them?'

'No, I live with my son near Bab Zuweyla.'

He was surprised. 'And you're married, too?'

I told him as we walked of my marriage to a teacher, of how he had died and left me a son to bring up.

His sharp eyes showed he did not believe me.

83

'Right. . . . You marry a teacher . . . and then work as a washwoman. Good . . . I like you.'

He eyed my figure. 'I want someone like you to work with.'

At Midan Bab al-Khal he pointed at what I was carrying.

'There's no need for you to pinch things. Use your brain and listen.'

He told me of the money which could deluge me, of the beautiful furnished house that I could live in, and the comfortable life that could be mine.

His voice was as sweet as when in the cleaner's, long ago, he had sung songs. I listened and gave way. My mind told me: You're tired out, Mabruka. The houses of Rateb Bey and Suad and Midhat . . . they are tombs. Remember that Mabruka has died. Listen to Awad's words. Follow him. Rest, Mabruka, from Mabruka.

BOOK TWO

Samia

I

I AM SAMIA SAMI, THE FILM ACTRESS. I MUST ADMIT my name is not well known, but I'm ambitious and I have the talents which could still make me famous. I also have something more important than talent – I have beauty. I know I'm attractive; I know men get excited when they look at me. God must have fashioned my lips when he was feeling happy. . . . How can I put it? I realize that every part of my body is attractive: my hair, my hands, my legs, my voice, the way I speak. I've got sex appeal to the point of madness. Funnily enough, this doesn't make me conceited. In fact, I'm often driven desperate. I sometimes think God would have done better to make me ugly. For in my innocence I imagined that looks would help me in the cinema. But the cinema is a jungle; all the people in it, producers, distributors, directors, actors, photographers – all are wolves. Even the journalists who hover round us in the studios for their little bits of news – they are wolves too.

And one of them has been my ruin. He is now a famous editor. But none of the people who talk about him know the truth. I am the only person who can reveal what Yusif Abdul Hamid really is.

How mad of me to have trusted him, to have imagined that he and I could mount the ladder of glory side by side, he to be Egypt's biggest journalist and I the best known actress! Because of him I lost my chance to be a star. When his hour struck, he kicked me down the ladder and climbed up, alone.

I can't deceive myself. I still love him, despite all. If only I could wipe him from my life. . . . But even his name obsesses me. Everywhere I go, people talk about him. He is famous; I am a failure.

Where did I go wrong?

What is the secret of a man like Yusif, who could throw

himself at my feet, saying how much he loved me, how I was his world and his life, then suddenly step over me and climb upwards, leaving me lying at the bottom rung?

If I am to stay sane I must dredge up the answer.

2

I FIRST MET YUSIF YEARS AGO. EIGHTEEN, FULL OF *joie de vivre*, I felt the world was at my feet. It was my first day in Cairo Studios. I was one among a crowd of girls in evening dress under arc lights. In my hand was a cigarette-holder. The cameras looked like the eyes of a giant – but a giant that did not frighten me, for I was sure I would infatuate him, too. Exactly what I expected happened. The director shouted, the shooting stopped; more orders; the girls were told they could go. I was left alone in the glare of the lights. Puffing smoke languidly from my lips I was photographed.

When the cameras stopped, I felt surrounded, devoured even, by the eyes of jealousy and envy.

The director's name was Helmi Kamil. He pinched my cheek.

'Well done, Bahia. You have a future.'

Blood rushed to my head. I could not answer as, taking my chin and staring into my face, he added: 'You wait while I finish and I'll run you home.'

'I'm sorry,' I said, 'but tonight I'm visiting a girl friend.'

Outside the studio door Midhat was waiting for me in his Citroën. As he turned into the road that leads back into town, I asked where we were going.

'I'm afraid there's some silly business I must attend to. . . .'

'Business, now?'

'A friend of mine, blast him, lost his father two weeks ago. I must take him out.'

'What on earth! Are you going to join your tears with his? Or are you turning into a baby-sitter?'

He was apologetic.

'We'll only stay a moment, then leave.'

Then he added. 'By the way, this friend, Yusif Abdul Hamid works on *Al-Ayyam*. We'll make him write about you.'

The high newspaper building was ablaze with lights that seemed right for my dreams. One day the journalists would jump up from their desks when they heard I was coming. They would throng round me for statements and pictures. 'What do you think of Abdul Wahab?' 'Which of Um Kalthum's songs do you like best?' 'Which actor would you like to play opposite?' 'Why aren't you married?'

Midhat blew his horn.

'Aren't we going up?'

'You'd like to?'

His surprise annoyed me.

'Not particularly.'

He glanced at my frock.

'If they saw you up there, the paper wouldn't appear tomorrow.'

The doorman saw Midhat and rushed out smiling.

'Shall I call Mr Yusif, Midhat Bey?'

'But tell him I'm in a hurry.'

At that moment a large black car drew up. The chauffeur quickly opened the back door for a tall man with a cigarette in his mouth. I was delighted to recognize in his handsome, melancholy good looks Muhammad Nagi, my mother's hero. She read every word he wrote – his political articles, his anecdotes, his column. I liked him too. He was known to be the friend of all the famous actresses and singers. They attended the parties he gave for ministers and pashas. The parties would then furnish material for his column.

My mother would be delighted to hear I had seen him. According to her, he was a wonderful poker player, losing hundreds without the quiver of an eyelid. She claimed to speak from experience, having played with him once during the war, at a friend's house. She now dropped his name on any occasion. If she was annoyed about anything, she'd threaten to telephone

Muhammad Nagi and get him to write on the shortage of sugar in the shops: or about the telephones which don't work: or the rascal who sold her these dreadful shoes. Once when she was angry with me, she threatened to get him to write an article against emancipated young women. I countered:

'But he's enjoying himself fabulously. Isn't he in love with Dalal?'

He was at that time having a mad affair with the singer, who is now dead.

But my mother never telephoned him. Why should he remember her from among the hundreds of women he met at the hundreds of soirées which composed his life?

I was eager to meet Yusif. Perhaps fate wished me to reach Muhammad Nagi through Yusif? It was a night of miracles. Lights flaring, cameras whirling, Midhat in love with me, Yusif going to write about me and introduce me to Muhammad Nagi. My dress, my car . . . for the car was Midhat's no longer, he was just my chauffeur. I was desperately happy.

Someone came out of the building. I knew that it was Yusif before Midhat whispered:

'Here he comes. . . . Please be patient till we can escape.'

I smiled at my secret thoughts.

'He doesn't have a car.'

'No.'

'Then he must be hard up?'

I had to stop. Yusif was leaning down and talking to Midhat through the window. He did not look at me: almost as if he did not see me. But I noticed his pale, oval face, his thin lips, his nervous eyes and embarrassed voice.

'Jump in,' Midhat said.

Yusif asked as Midhat reversed:

'Where are you two going?'

The fact that he spoke of 'you two' showed me he had seen me: but he had not said a word in my direction. I was furious.

'Just get in. . . . We'll drive anywhere.'

Midhat took the wheel and drove a few yards, then asked:

'Why haven't you said good evening to Mademoiselle Bahia?'

'I'm so sorry . . . but we haven't been introduced.'

He turned to me – to my back rather, since I would not look at him – and half-laughed in his nervousness: 'I'm so sorry. You must blame Midhat.'

'Blame me for what? Are we foreigners that you have to be introduced before you say hallo?'

'Perhaps,' I said, 'he doesn't want to say hallo to me. Why bother him?'

Yusif's hesitant manner made me feel sorry for him. At the same time I scolded myself for wanting such a useless person to introduce me to Muhammad Nagi. I said:

'Midhat, let's go to the pyramids.'

'You write,' I asked Yusif coldly, 'in the paper?'

'Yes. . . . I try.'

'I don't seem to have read anything by you?'

'I turn my hand to anything . . . now crime . . . now news about art.'

Midhat broke in. 'I want you to write about Bahia. She's an actress.'

I could hardly prevent myself turning round to see his reaction.

But all he said was, 'Is that so?'

I was so angry at this, I decided when we got as far as the Cairo Studios I'd get out and go back to town with the producer.

I said abruptly:

'I love reading Muhammad Nagi. . . . I'm mad for him.'

'I too,' Yusif answered quickly. 'He's my teacher.'

Compulsively talking to him about Nagi, I passed Cairo Studios without noticing. We reached the pyramids. We stopped by the big one. Yusif got out:

'I want to walk by myself a little.'

And he walked off between the rocks.

'Your friend's a *strange* one,' I said to Midhat.

'Not at all . . . His trouble is that he's so shy.'

'He doesn't say a word.'

'What nonsense! He didn't stop talking about Nagi the whole way here. . . .'

I peered at the darkness.

'Where's he gone?'

'Didn't I tell you his father died?'

'Who was his father?'

'My tutor.'

I laughed mockingly.

'Anyone who saw him walking in the dark would think his father was a minister . . . or a pasha.'

His eyes glinted. 'Yusif has a tragedy in his life.'

He searched the darkness to make sure Yusif was not near. 'Imagine, Bahia, his father married a maid who worked in our house.'

I hadn't expected something as rich as that.

I laughed aloud.

'Confess! You had doings with the maid?'

'Alas! And Yusif knew all.'

'How? Who told him?'

'I did. I had no idea his father would marry her.'

'How did Yusif take that?'

'It was fantastic! He walked out, for keeps.'

I felt a sudden pang for Yusif.

'I don't want to listen,' I shouted. My own father had died two years ago . . .

I wanted to open the door, to run into the darkness, but I saw Yusif coming back.

I forced myself to appear as merry as usual, with no experience of grief.

All my life I have had sudden changes of feeling.

I now shouted to Yusif as if he was an old friend:

'Where did you get to? Weren't you scared of ghosts?'

He got in the car with his timid smile.

'Are ghosts dangerous?'

Our eyes met. Quickly he turned his away. He was not scared of ghosts. He was scared of my beauty. I liked this. I wondered if he had ever had an affair. More probably he was still a virgin.

I felt an urge to tease him.

As we drove back towards Cairo I said:

'By the way, I'd like both your help in choosing a name. It must be for a girl as lovely as the moon.'

Midhat was puzzled.

'Has one of your friends had a baby?'

I watched the effect my words would have on Yusif:

'No, the baby's mine.'

'Impossible!'

Yusif's eyes begged me to explain.

I asked: 'Anything wrong with having a baby?'

'No.' But he sounded embarrassed.

'But you're not married.'

I laughed at Midhat.

'So what?'

Yusif's expression was of pity mixed with fear. But Midhat shouted:

'You've gone mad. I don't believe you.'

I repeated my question to Yusif: 'What do you advise me to call her?'

'She's already born?'

Midhat shouted: 'Don't you believe her!'

'No, she's due in seven months.'

Midhat greeted this news with hysterical laugher. Yusif frowned.

'Then it might not be a girl. . . .'

'I am sure it will. What do you think of Muna Munir?'

Midhat screamed.

'If Munir is her father's name, who is this Munir?'

I laughed.

'Perhaps you'd prefer Madiha Midhat?'

He was now terrified.

'But I'm not the father.'

'Or Yusifia Yusif?'

Midhat shouted in relief.

'You are joking. . . . I'd almost taken you seriously.'

'Seriously, I am searching for a name.'

Yusif's face suddenly lit up and his eyes triumphed. He understood.

'You are looking for a film name.'

'Bravo!'

I turned to scold Midhat.

'Mr Yusif is brighter than you are.'

Yusif said: 'I almost believed it, too.'

'You think I'd be capable of something like that?'

'I didn't mean it that way.'

He was embarrassed.

'The one thing I hope is to become an actress. The directors who have seen me all agree I have talent. That's why I must push away all thought of love, marriage all that rubbish.'

We had reached the road leading to Cairo Studios. I asked Midhat to take it. The director, was waiting for me, I said, to announce my new name. He had to know it tonight or else it would be too late for the morning's papers. Yusif was now suspicious.

'Are you joking again?'

'Not this time.'

'You know, I didn't believe Midhat when he told me you were an actress.'

'Why not?'

'I'm not sure . . . ' With a nervous laugh he added: 'You don't look like one.'

I was not sure if this was a compliment, or the reverse. I was ready to lose my temper and insult him back.

'What do you mean, sir?'

'I don't mean anything.'

But after a moment's thought he added: 'I meant, I hadn't realized you were such an important actress. I didn't know you were a new star.'

He was reading my thoughts and retreating in fright, bribing me with insincerity. I said coldly:

'Now you do.'

Midhat dropped me at the studio entrance. I turned to say good-bye to Yusif but to my surprise he offered to keep me company. He said he had some work to do, too. Perhaps he would write about me.

Helmi was preparing to shoot a scene between Anwar Sami and Huda Murad. Though Helmi saw me, he did not return my smile. He was too busy gesticulating to Anwar. I hoped desperately that Yusif had not noticed. I turned to see Yusif calmly advancing in Mr Helmi's direction.

The warmth with which everyone greeted Yusif amazed me. Anwar Sami pounced on him with a kiss for each of his cheeks. Helmi shook hands, shouting: 'Where've you disappeared to? I've been shooting a week and haven't set eyes on you.'

Huda Murad gave Yusif her warmest smile.

From my distance I watched him with surprised regret: Yusif had said nothing to me about knowing these celebrities.

He was plainly not as innocent as he pretended. He was sly. I remembered his earlier words about not believing I was an actress. Had he thought Midhat had picked me off the streets?

In my fury I felt like shouting: why can't you recognize a great actress when you see one? Aren't I a thousand times more beautiful, more talented, than Huda Murad?

Time would show Yusif what a fool he was – I shouldn't be accepting any invitations from him. Muhammad Nagi only for me, and no less!

Anwar ordered coffee for Yusif. Helmi offered him a cigarette despite the studio rules against smoking. They treated him as if he were already a famous journalist, as if he were Nagi himself. He must be writing about them and printing their photographs.

Suddenly Yusif shouted in my direction:

'Bahia . . . Why don't you join us?'

I was overcome with confusion. He was so brave to shout for me like that, while in the company of people like Anwar and Huda. For after all, I was still only an extra. But I felt proud as I approached them; my shyness vanished.

Helmi was plainly surprised that Yusif knew me.

Yusif smiled at him. 'I've just been thinking of possible names for Bahia.'

'Nothing is secret from you,' Helmi burst out. 'You even know her name.'

I felt the probing eye of Anwar Sami playing over my body. 'Is Mademoiselle a new actress?'

Helmi took my face in his hands.

'What do you think of her, Anwar? Pretty?'

Anwar kissed his finger-tips and blew a kiss in the air.

'Madly! Where did you find her, Helmi?'

Helmi shouted with a laugh: 'You keep away from her. She isn't your type.'

Blood rushed to my cheeks. My eyes met Anwar's. They had a strange attractive glitter. He was handsome. I had long admired his soft black hair and also his acting. He had a sense of humour, too. His words carried a delicious warmth. He was evidently flirting with me, perhaps even contemplating an affair. He might fall in love, marry me, let me act with him. This was my chance. When I got home I'd consult mother. She understood such things better. But now I must pull myself together so as not to make any false moves.

'What is your name, darling?'

'Bahia Abdul Rahman . . .' I whispered.

Huda Murad, who had been staring expressionlessly in my direction, remarked: 'Bahia . . . a pretty name.'

Helmi shouted back. 'Bahia Abdul Rahman would be hopeless of the screen. It's so unmusical.'

I felt that the star wanted me to keep my unmusical name out of jealousy. Anwar voiced my thoughts.

'Bahia Abdul Rahman . . . you can't be serious, Huda.'

To me he apologized with a smile. 'Don't be angry: it's because I like you.'

Helmi said he wanted a name with two similar sounds, Muna Munir, Samira Samir, something like that.

Anwar suddenly burst out: 'I have an idea. Call her after me.'

Clutching Yusif's hand, Anwar asked enthusiastically:

'What do you think of Samia Sami as a name?'

'It's nice.'

Helmi was doubtful.

Yusif added: 'It will make a good news story. "Anwar Sami adopts a new actress, calls her after him."'

Huda objected, 'I don't like the name.'

I knew it was the right name then. Her jealousy was obvious. Anwar told Yusif to write it up for the paper. To me he said:

'The doors of Heaven have opened before you. What glory, my dear, to carry my name!'

3

IT WAS AFTER 10.30 WHEN HELMI KAMIL DROVE ME home. I was in luck, he told me, to be a friend of Yusif's. If my picture appeared in the paper several times, I'd be famous before I ever appeared on the screen.

He laughed.

'I'll have to sign you up before you get too famous.'

'How much will you pay me?'

'You're just like your mother,' he complained. 'It's stupid to talk of money before you've been in two or three films.'

'Muhammad Nagi is Yusif's boss?'

'Of course. Nagi's the editor in chief. Yusif's one of his boys.'

'What's Yusif's pull, then? I've never read anything by him.'

He gave a knowing laugh.

'It's the small fry who get the news. Nagi will only publish things if we pay him – like an advertisement. But we need only embrace Yusif for him to write about us.'

I smiled, wondering if I would have to embrace Yusif to get publicity. If there were embraces to throw around, I'd prefer to throw them in the direction of Nagi. I didn't want to be just another actress.

When we got back, mother was at her usual game of poker.

'How did things go, darling?'

She didn't wait for me to answer but immediately turned her attention to Helmi.

My stepfather Mahmoud – a kindly idiot – asked if I had eaten: he would bring me a ham and cheese sandwich if I liked.

Our house – you could hardly call it home – only comes alive at night. Everyone is cheerful when mother welcomes, I won't say her guests, certainly not her friends: her clients. They come to play poker. My stepfather does not play but waits on the clients, running out to buy whisky or snacks; he fetches cigarettes. He pours out drinks, pops in the ice and hands round olives.

Mother receives every kind of client, even British officers.

I well remember the first night they came. Mother came in a panic to my sister Insaf and me. 'Girls, keep to your rooms.'

My stepfather got the officers drunk and they lost £20. My mother sighed with relief when they left without incident. Never again, she declared.

'But they were polite,' my stepfather protested.

'I don't care. I was terrified they might draw a gun and take all our winnings.'

But my mother's other guests insisted that Englishmen were sporting losers; they were polite and stupid. Mother became converted to having English players. I used to hear her laughter as she tried out her few words of English on them when they came to the door.

I would go out when mother was playing. She never minded. But next day at noon, as she lay in bed lighting her first cigarette and sipping her black coffee, she'd call me to come and lie beside her. From her exhausted face would pour words of advice. A boy friend was all right, she'd say, if he was rich and I could get him to marry me. But love was a weakness, a source of humiliation; a woman had to overcome that disease. Even if one loved a rich man, it was disastrous. For love blinded a woman to the right way of exploiting his wealth. First find your man and catch him; think about love later. The vital thing was to get money from some rich simpleton.

'If you haven't a penny,' my mother would repeat, 'you're not worth a penny.'

Mother had been pleased when I told her about Midhat.

Not that he was my first boy-friend. I had had several, including the brother of my best friend, Yolanda Grazia. Marco was well over twenty and had a Lambretta. He was a mechanic in a workshop near Shubra. I was fourteen. He treated me like his sister or a younger child, and took us to the cinema on Saturdays.

Then we moved from Ghamra to our new home in Giza. After spending a couple of days helping to clean and arrange the house, I decided to have my hair done at Rameau's in Rue Kasr al-Nil.

I waited for the bus in Giza. I noted a dark young man eyeing me hungrily. This wasn't the first time this had happened at bus-stops. I didn't even mind – such looks were tributes to my beauty. In Ghamra I had had several such admirers of all ages and types. Depending on my mood I would give them a sidelong glance, or ignore them completely. But I never allowed myself to get in conversation with such people. They travelled by bus, which meant they had no car; they were poor – in other words, useless.

This dark young man was my first Giza admirer. I didn't encourage him; there would be many more, I knew.

But suddenly a Citroën drew up, driven by a pale young man who looked as though he was of a good family. The dark young man jumped into the car, having first flashed me a smile. I pretended not to notice. They drove off. To my surprise, a few minutes later, they were back again. I put on a haughty look, while inwardly smiling. A few moments later and they had returned. I frowned. I saw them talking to each other. They were arguing which one should invite me to join them.

My bus drew up and to my amusement the Citroën slowly followed, keeping pace with us, stopping when we stopped, then starting again. I got out at the Place de l'Opéra and walked slowly down Rue Kasr al-Nil. I knew they would follow and it amused me to be pursued. I kept looking in the shop windows.

I sensed they were behind me, having left their car. Suddenly I turned on my heel and frowned angrily at them. (Inwardly I was delighted by their interest.) When I reached Rameau's, I turned and gave them a fleeting smile. I had a feeling they were people I should meet again. I have this presentiment with people. Some people you see once and never again; others you are sure to rediscover. My presentiments are usually right.

When I got home, outside the villa next to our block stood the Citroën. The people who owned the villa were obviously rich.

I consulted my mother who already had the whole neighbourhood at her finger-tips.

'Why do you want to know?'

I told her matter-of-factly:

'Their son followed me.'

'Midhat? He's their only son, an engineer.'

She sighed. 'If only you could marry him.'

That was how I met Midhat.

4

'What's all this about a new name?'

I told her about the meeting with Anwar Sami.

She said crossly:

'Helmi told me that.'

'What do you think of the name?'

'He'll ruin your reputation. People will say you are Anwar's mistress.'

'Does it matter?'

Her voice rose to a scream.

'Don't be insane!'

I raised my voice too.

'If I work in the cinema, people are bound to link my name with Anwar, or someone else.'

She clasped her head in her hands. Her headache had got worse – she must have had a bad night at poker.

Reading *Al-Ayyam* from cover to cover, I imagined my picture instead of Churchill's, instead of Ginger Rogers', instead of a murderer's called Basyuni whom the police had just arrested, instead of the pretty girl's in the tooth-paste ad.

But it did not appear until the day after, when bemused I saw a small picture of myself next to another of Anwar Sami. I just managed to read 'Anwar Sami adopts a new actress,' the sentence Yusif had used in the studio.

The article went on: 'Samia Sami is the new name of an actress who will star opposite Anwar Sami in "Forever With You". Anwar, who chose the name, foresees a great future for her. This is why he gave her his name.'

I looked at the picture again. It was not as beautiful as I was. Yusif must have got it from the studio.

I looked in the mirror and compared myself with the picture. I then glanced at my fellow celebrities: Stalin, Vyshinsky, Anwar Sami, Muhammad al-Gindi, the National Club Soccer star, Um Kalthum and Charlie Chaplin.

It annoyed me that mother was still sleeping; she would have to understand, I was no longer Bahia Abdul Rahman. I was Samia Sami. I would need plenty of new dresses. I would go to Rameau's every three days. Or perhaps Socrate? I would have to look after my looks. And could we go on living here? It was a cheap flat. And how could I go on sharing a room with Insaf? If Mother was wise she would give me lots of money. My make-up was more important than Insaf's university fees. She would merely be a doctor. I should be the one to be rich and famous and pay for everything. I'd buy a villa on the road to the pyramids. I would let them share it. I would buy a Cadillac. . . .

If Mother didn't give me money, I'd leave the house and marry Midhat.

But Midhat's father was still young. Midhat was lazy, and at that moment probably still asleep.

Perhaps I should telephone Yusif . . . handle him prudently, say nothing about the badness of the photo. . . . I'd have a new picture taken. I'd go now to Socrate and have a new hairstyle made.

Mother must give me money.

When would Yusif reach the paper? It was only nine o'clock.

I looked out of the window. Only a few cars. No one had read the paper so far.

If I went to Socrate would people recognize me?

'That's Samia Sami. She's far lovelier than her photo.'

I couldn't take buses any more. From now on I must only go in taxis or cars. Mother must give me money for taxis. She must understand my new status.

Why wasn't Mother awake?

5

THE TELEPHONE RANG AS I WAS MAKING COFFEE. BUT before I could answer, it stopped.

My patience collapsed.

I dialled the number of *Al-Ayyam*.

Then, as the operator answered, a strange impulse forced me to ask, not for Yusif, but Muhammad Nagi.

'Who wants him?'

'Just put me through . . .'

'I'm sorry. I must know your name first.'

I said sharply: 'Tell him it is someone who doesn't want her name revealed.'

A moment's silence and the voice answered: 'Nagi Bey will speak to you.'

A tender voice whispered down the line: 'Hello . . . who's speaking?'

'Mr Nagi?'

'Speaking. Can I help you?'

'I am one of your admirers.'

'Thank you for saying so.'

I added, 'I read everything you write.'

'I'm delighted.'

'I hope you're not busy, but I want you to know how dear to me you are.'

He laughed. 'If you're pretty, then I'm not busy.'

'Oh, you can rest assured that I'm pretty.'

'How can I be sure?'

'I'm eighteen.'

'Impossible . . .'

'You don't like young girls?'

'On the contrary.'

'Medium height, good figure, sparkling black eyes, full but small mouth . . .'

'Who put you up to telephoning?'

'No one.'

'Tell me; I'll keep it to myself.'

I laughed. 'Who are you frightened of?'

He sounded confused. 'Only you.'

'Why, are you attracted?'

'You seem mischievous. What's your name?'

'Not so fast . . .'

'But the time will come?'

'Yes, but don't rush things.'

'We live in an age of rush . . .'

'Except that . . .'

'Except what?'

'The thing you're thinking of . . .'

He said brusquely: 'What a filthy mind you must have . . .'

'It's yours, not mine.'

'But help me a little. I don't know your name, your number, not even what you look like.'

'How about my voice?'

'It's lovely.'

'As good as Dalal's?'

'Can you sing?'

'No.'

'I'll have to see you . . .'

103

I suddenly pretend to be panic-stricken.

'I'll ring later . . . My husband's got up.'

'Then I'll give you my private number.'

I wrote it down and put it in my handbag.

All men were alike! Muhammad Nagi was as easy to catch as any one else. Older men were if anything easier. *Al-Ayyam* would be at my disposal. Poor old Yusif, little did he know that I'd soon be able to have him sacked, or promoted.

As I moved away from the telephone, thinking I'd ask Midhat to take me to the Auberge des Pyramides, it started to ring. It must be Yusif. Instead a strange voice spoke.

'Who were you talking to behind my back?'

'Who on earth are you?'

'Shame on you! Don't you know me?'

'No I don't.'

'Not your own father?'

It must be Anwar Sami; but I wasn't sure.

'If it's my father, you must be ringing from Heaven.'

'Surely you know who I am? Tell me, where are we going tonight?'

'I have a previous invitation.'

'How dare you accept an invitation without consulting your father?'

He changed his tone. 'I have some business to discuss.'

'If it's really business, I apologize.'

'Of course it's business. What time shall I call for you? Is nine all right?'

'Make it half past.'

'Fine.'

'Where are we going?'

'Nowhere. The party's at my house.'

'Who'll be there?'

He raised his voice.

'Are you frightened? Lots of people . . .'

'Why should I be frightened?'

He swore, then softened his voice to a whisper.

'Right, then. Half past nine, my pet. I'll blow my horn.'

Mother had got up at last and was slouching bleary-eyed towards the bathroom.

'Mother,' I said, showing her the paper, 'look, my picture.'

She glanced at it with tired eyes but made no comment.

The telephone rang. Not Yusif, but Helmi, congratulating me. My mother snatched the receiver from me. She began a terrific attack on him for endangering our reputation. Here I was with my picture all over the press, and no profit to us . . . Unless he signed a contract at once she would telephone Muhammad Nagi and get him to deny the whole story.

She rang off, smiling, all trace of anger gone.

'Everyone who works in the cinema is a crook. We must be on our guard.'

When I protested, she started a self-pitying monologue about the money she had wasted on me, the food and the clothes she had bought me, till I was mad with rage. I thought of getting money from Anwar Sami and moving to a hotel. I thought of appealing to Midhat. At the same time I didn't forget to think of getting Socrate to design me a new hair-style.

Midhat rang at his usual time.

'Please,' I implored him, 'come and rescue me.'

'I'll be right over. Where do you want to go?'

'Anywhere to get away from home.'

He had an idea.

'Why don't we go swimming at the National Club?'

'But I wanted to see Yusif, to thank him.'

'I'll ask him to join us.'

6

AN-HOUR LATER I WAS LYING ON THE GRASS BY THE pool in my yellow bathing suit. Beside me Yusif turned his chest to the sun. Midhat was in the water, waving to us every time he passed.

I had forgotten my quarrel with mother. All I thought of was my picture in the paper. I wondered if any of the people in the Club recognized me.

Everyone I looked at stared back at me, except Yusif. There were no pretty girls; all the members seemed to have fat faces and big bellies. A trainer was giving them exercises. It was amusing to see them bend their obese bodies at his command.

A waiter brought us two Coca-Colas. Mine overflowed on to my bathing suit and Yusif offered his handkerchief to wipe the froth away. I caught him looking at my body in a way I understood.

I asked:

'Have you ever been in love?'

His voice sounded remote.

'Yes, once.'

He was gazing at the fat old people stretched out on the grass like corpses.

I sighed.

'I wish I knew what love was. . . .'

'You really want to?'

'Yes, really.'

'Love is . . . love.'

I laughed.

'No, I mean it,' he insisted. 'The feeling cannot be explained.'

He suddenly looked tired as though he had been thinking about this for years. I was used to hearing love discussed in a lighthearted way, almost as a joke, but suddenly he said very seriously:

'Love is like a mirror. . . . You see yourself in the mirror, the colour of your hair, the clothes you are wearing. . . . When a man loves a girl, she is like a mirror. In her he sees himself. But other things, too.'

I had never heard such weird talk in all my life.

I whispered.

'What else does he see?'

'He sees his real life, his depth, the things that are hidden from himself. He sees his strength and weakness, the things he wants to do, the things he fears. This makes him unhappy – and

106

happy too.' Then he said with warmth as though remembering something important: 'When someone loves, he lives. Do you get what I mean?'

I understood what he was driving at, but did not know how I understood. A question occurred to me:

'Which do you think is more important, love or tenderness?'

'They are the same thing.'

Then he added, as though to himself: 'Or so I think.'

'I want tenderness.'

'You haven't ever fallen in love then?'

I remembered Marco.

'Once when I was a little girl.'

I suddenly felt near tears. None of the boys I had known had ever shown me tenderness and that was what I wanted, what I felt Yusif could give. I could not imagine how the girl Yusif had loved could have abandoned such a love.

7

THAT EVENING ANWAR SAMI DROVE ME ROUND CAIRO IN his white Lincoln. We were doused in scent; we laughed like mad folk. He told me dirty stories, glancing at the same time at other drivers and pedestrians to see if he was recognized. When he was, he would try to get away, and would then slow down for more admirers.

I was haunted by the memory of Yusif and what he'd said. I enjoyed being seen with Anwar, but I disliked his vanity.

'Let's drive a little before going home.'

'But the people you invited . . .'

He laughed.

'The party.'

He laughed louder.

'I'll let you in on a secret – there is no party. '

'Then why do you want me to go home with you?'

'Don't act the innocent.'

'I am innocent.'

'I'd rather say stupid. The moment we get home I'll curb you.'

'I'm not going home with you.'

'Listen here, my girl. I don't like complications.' He stopped the car. 'If you are pretending to be innocent . . . now's the time to get out.'

But I couldn't. We were among the crowds in Rue Kasr al-Nil and I felt thousands of eyes on us.

His arm jerked me towards him.

'Now, are you going to act like a big girl?'

I thought of the contrast between him and Yusif, as his boastful voice continued: 'Any other woman in this city would be proud to have her name coupled with mine. Your picture's been published next to mine, you've been seen next to me in public. What more do you want?' Suddenly his voice became gentle. 'Have I annoyed you?'

'Yes, you have.'

'I know I must sound mad. But I am mad.'

We had stopped by the Immobilia Building and in a moment we were in his flat on the fourteenth floor. It was a charming prison, beautifully decorated, skilfully lit, the furnishings simple but good. It was all one room divided into separate areas – a place to sit, a place to eat, a bar and, in one corner, bookshelves crammed with books.

'Whisky with soda or water?'

'Soda.'

He pulled me down on to a sofa and we drank, his arm still round my waist. He got up to refill our glasses.

'Why are you frowning?'

He began to caress me. Suddenly he gave me a brutal kiss to which I responded only with my lips. They felt separate from me.

Then he began teasingly to question me about mother, saying nice things about her in a nasty way, ending up by saying he knew her better than I did.

I wished I had never come. I even wished I had told mother where I was going; she would have used force to prevent me.

Then I remembered a night before mother remarried. The lawyer who was arranging the divorce had come back with her late. At least she said it was the lawyer – a tall, square-faced man with a flat nose and a small moustache. He had a disgusting laugh. He asked me about school and tried to flatter me by saying how bright I was. Mother kept trying to get me out of the room, but for some reason I refused to go. They went on chatting. He complimented her on her legs. I heard mother whisper . . . 'Not tonight . . . some other time.'

I now wondered how well Anwar knew my mother. Did he know things about her that I didn't know?

Anwar brought another whisky.

As he kissed me, he asked. 'Do you like my flat?'

'It's lovely.'

I answered automatically. I returned his kisses, too, with automatic warmth . . . His chest was against mine . . . What scent did he use? . . . There was no time to ask . . . His nose hurt mine. I pulled his hair, hard, but he did not cry out. His teeth bit into my lips. His hands roughly squeezed my breasts. I tried to fight him off but he clasped me round the neck as if to throttle me. His teeth on my neck . . . his fingers over my eyes . . . his hands trying to pull up my dress . . . I stood up . . . He tried to unbutton me.

'Anwar, I can't.'

He didn't stop.

'Please, some other time.'

'No, now.'

'I promise I'll come another night. But tonight there's a reason . . .'

'Why didn't you tell me from the start?'

'I was too shy . . .'

'You'll kill me if you go now.'

I left him, wondering if what I had saved from him outweighed the indignity I had suffered.

Next morning I telephoned the newspaper and asked for Yusif. I heard him answer:

'Hallo . . .'
I stayed silent.
'Hallo . . . Hallo . . .'

8

MY TELEPHONE TALKS WITH MUHAMMAD NAGI BECAME
more and more frequent. But I let him feel my power by keeping him waiting before I rang him up. He would then talk to
me for ages as if he had nothing else to do. When the other
'phone in his office rang he would ask me to wait while he talked
to ministers or millionaires. And there I was at the other end of
the line, listening inquisitively, disappointed when someone
whispered and I missed what was said. The sense that Nagi was
more interested in gossiping to me than talking to important
people made me feel proud.

Sometimes I heard him talking to Yusif. He would tell him
to write a story about the composer Abdul Wahab or would
pass on the irritation of the famous singer, Um Kalthum, at
some item that had been published about her. I felt an insane
urge to tell Nagi I knew Yusif, but resisted it, for by this time
Nagi was persuaded that I was unhappily married. Every day I
would invent some new quarrel between myself and my ficti-
tious husband; I enlarged on his stinginess, his stupidity, his
cruelty. After my night with Anwar Sami, I read in the paper
that he had gone off to Beirut. I immediately rang Nagi and
described all that had happened between me and Anwar, pretending it had happened with my husband. I told him how
brutal he was and how I could no longer bear to make love with
someone who was only interested in my body, who used foul
words to accompany his obscene acts. My words obviously
excited Nagi, because he hungrily probed for details: how did
he kiss me? what kind of night-dress was I wearing? how did I
react? Cunningly he tried to use sympathy to get me to meet
him. I refused but always let him keep a little hope.

'I must see you today,' he said. 'I have an idea for a new story. I want your opinion.'

'Is it about me?'

'Yes.'

'Suppose someone saw me entering the building and told my husband . . .'

'Who said I wanted to see you here? I meant my house.'

'The one in Zamalek?'

'No, I have another which no one knows about, in Maspiro Street.' He added simply: 'Four o'clock suit you?'

'What shall I tell my husband?'

'Can't you have a tooth-ache or a visit to the hairdresser?' I whispered. 'Good. I'll be there. Four sharp.'

He sounded very happy. 'I'll be waiting.' He explained where the building was. I should take the lift to the fifth floor. The flat was number 45.

I went to my room and locked the door. I felt terrified. My experience with Anwar came back to me. This was a new Anwar, perhaps in a gentler style, but the same thing. He would not marry me; he was almost fifty, elderly. His way of talking was charming. But could I put up with more than that? Could I let him kiss me? If he found out I was Samia Sami the actress, not the injured, faithless wife, his rage and disappointment might prompt him to destroy my career. I rushed to the telephone and told him my husband had forbidden me to leave the house.

To my surprise one morning I found Nagi's column in the paper had been built round our conversation. I skimmed rapidly to the end where he humorously advised the wife to be patient and prudent, not to do anything she would regret later. I rang him up.

'If only your readers knew the truth! That your real advice is for women to come to you for counselling.'

He laughed. 'Eventually they'll all come. I can't keep them from me.'

His conceit was more amusing than Anwar's. I heard the phone in his office ring. It was Yusif. Nagi shouted at him, as editor to subordinate, then said to me: 'I'll not let that boy print anything in future. You saw the piece he published today about Shohdi Pasha? I'll sack him, I'll have him gaoled, the communist!'

When he stopped screaming, I said: 'Heavens, you're in a tough mood. What's the row?'

Quite calm, as though he had never shouted in his life, he remarked: 'These filthy communist thieves . . . Shohdi Pasha, my friend for years, has been attacked in my own paper. It's unforgivable.'

'If I was a communist, would you denounce me?'

He laughed. 'No, I'd become one too.' He suddenly sounded worried. 'You aren't one by any chance?'

'What is communism?'

'Don't worry your head with such things . . .'

'And who is this Yusif?'

'Someone who works here.'

'Is he a thief too?'

'I've not caught him out yet.'

I laughed.

Then I changed my tone. 'Which is more important, love, or tenderness?'

'Love, of course.'

'A pity.'

'Why?'

'I'm not interested in love.'

'You want tenderness?'

'Yes.'

'Why? Are you sick? It's only invalids who think about tenderness. Or perhaps you're ugly.'

'My God, I wish I was sick or ugly, if only I could find tenderness.'

'You really mean that? Then come to me, I'll give you all the tenderness you need.'

'No, I'll never find it from you.'

He could not know that I was almost crying. After my talk with him I fought back my tears and began to think I might contact Yusif after all. But I thought I might sound Midhat first if he had seen him recently. Over drinks in 'Covent Garden' I said: 'Did you know your sly journalist friend was once in love with someone who got married?'

'When did he tell you that?'

'In the club.'

'He never told me – when?'

'Long ago, before the marriage took place.'

He shrugged: 'It must be the maid who married his father. Mabruka – didn't I tell you about her before?'

We decided over our beers that his love for the servant must account for why Yusif seemed to make himself so scarce.

'What's Mabruka like?'

He paused as though trying to recall her. 'Attractively plump: big black eyes, very pretty, her only bad points her hands and legs.'

'Were you in love with her, too?'

He gave an embarrassed smile. 'That was long ago . . .'

'You put up with her hands and legs?'

'The truth is, this Mabruka never acted like a maid. She had great dignity. She acted as though she considered herself one of our distant relatives.'

By now I was resolved to see her. Was this idiot Yusif avoiding me for love of a maid? If so, I'd tell the world.

Two days passed.

The idea occurred to me of telling Nagi all about Yusif. My conscience revolted, however, at such a mean trick. It was none of my business whether Yusif loved a princess or a servant.

I found myself blurting out everything, all the same.

'Do you want to know something peculiar about the man near you? The one who's not a thief.'

'Ah, Yusif. What about him?'

'One of my girl-friends tells me he's in love with the servant who married his father. When his father died, he lived with her.'

He was incredulous.

'Her name is Mabruka,' I insisted.

'I don't believe it.'

'Ask him.'

I have never despised myself as I did that night.

Next morning I asked for Yusif. The operator asked me my name. Disguising my voice I said, 'Mabruka.'

The operator shouted, 'Madame, haven't I told you a hundred times he's not here?'

He cut me off.

If Yusif had broken with Mabruka, did it mean that Yusif – so good, so easily embarrassed – had seduced her, then got rid of her?

I called him again under my own name.

This time he at once answered. He spoke with emphatic warmth.

'How are you, Samia? I've been longing to see you.'

9

A WEEK PASSED, PERHAPS MORE. I RANG YUSIF EVERY morning. Every time he was as welcoming: 'Samia?'

The tender tones in which he greeted me filled me with self-contempt. How could I have treated this voice so meanly, I who claimed to love everything tender? What evil prompting had made me tell Nagi that tale! I felt I had to do something to make up for my cheap treachery; to prove to myself that I was not wholly corrupt; that I had acted merely on an impulse. He was quite different from Anwar and Nagi, good to the point of silliness, soft to the point of respecting me for myself. His voice could not have been warmer or more respectful if I had been his sister or daughter. I had never imagined knowing a man who would treat me in this way. Could it be because he loved another?

When I spoke to him now I no longer teased or joked. I was all tenderness. I felt a strange confidence when I spoke to him, a trust that nothing, I hoped, could ever spoil.

'How are you? What are you doing? Where were you yesterday? What time did you get to bed? You work much too hard, Yusif.'

I lived with him for ten minutes every day. These ten minutes left me feeling faint with happiness. Sometimes I'd shut my eyes and almost sleep. Then I'd pull myself together, ring Muhammad Nagi, meet Midhat, go on with normal living.

Yusif never asked to see me; he never asked me for anything. I felt that he ascribed my frequent calls to eagerness for film news, particularly my own. He told me of a new production company to be formed. He had heard that Helmi was going to put me under contract for three pictures as soon as Anwar came back from Beirut.

'How much will they give me, do you think?'

'I don't know. They're bound to try and cheat you. But it doesn't matter. The important thing is for you to act well.'

'You mean I should accept anything?'

'Yes.'

'What peculiar advice!'

'Now's not the time to think of money.'

'Don't you think about it?'

'Never. I just work hard. They increase my salary of their own accord.'

'Do you think I'll become a famous actress?'

'Of course.'

'And you will be a famous journalist?'

'Perhaps.'

'We'll grow famous together.'

He laughed. 'You'll leave me far behind.'

He seemed to lack ambition. Could this be the result of loving a servant? If I loved him, I'd push him forward till he became the equal of anyone – richer than Midhat, with a bigger car.

When Helmi Kamil eventually called on Mother to negotiate my contract, he was businesslike and peremptory, and hardly so much as glanced in my direction. He would pay her £100. She screamed in indignation. There was a good deal of haggling. I sat listening in silence. My heart trembled as he said in dry final tones:

'More than that I'm not prepared to pay. She's a mere beginner. To launch her will cost me far more. It's a gamble. I'll be out of pocket.'

More screams and threats from Mother.

'We're the ones who are gambling. It's easy for you to talk of turning her into an actress. But who'll marry my actress daughter? You're afraid for your money. We're afraid for our reputation, Mr Helmi.'

He laughed sarcastically.

'Who marries anyone but actresses these days? What's a reputation that £10,000 of publicity can't put right?'

He handed his cheque to my mother who grabbed it, then exclaimed: '£50! We spend this in one evening.'

She accepted the cheque, however.

When he'd gone, I said: 'Mama, the cheque.'

'Why do you want it?'

'That cheque's mine.'

'Hold your tongue!'

'I want my money.'

'Your money? You ill-bred girl. Get out of my way. . . .'

My sister came in, drawn by our voices. She tried to quieten me. I said through my tears: 'Mother has robbed me.'

I heard my stepfather's voice: 'Shameful to address your mother like that . . .'

'Is it your money?' I shouted back. 'I suppose you want Mother to spend it on you.'

He went out muttering: 'God forgive you for speaking like this after I reared you.'

'You reared me?' I screamed. 'It was my father who reared me, not you.'

All I wanted was to die, like Father.

I felt besieged by their angry eyes. I went to my bed and soaked my pillow with my tears.

I must contact Yusif.

When I had pulled myself together, I rang his number.

'How are you, Samia?'

'The contract's signed.'

'A thousand congratulations. Are you content?'

'There's something I want to talk to you about. Can we meet?'

'Of course. I'm under your orders.'

He seemed a little reluctant. But there was no one else I could turn to.

'The Garden Groppi's?'

'I'll be there in an hour's time.'

I found him waiting in a corner, under a tree. It was like seeing him for the first time. He smiled at me in his shy way. His suit was badly cut, his tie was badly knotted. He did not know how to tie it. There was some bird-lime on the shoulder of his suit.

'Look what the birds have done! Why sit under the trees?'

He took out his handkerchief looking very embarrassed. I took it from him and rubbed his shoulder. I made him move to the middle of the garden, among the people. We ordered tea and gateaux. I waited for him to ask why I wanted to meet him. But he continued to look round him in embarrassment. Drops of sweat formed on his brow. He did not look pleased about our meeting.

His first question, 'How's Midhat?' enraged me.

Why was he asking me about Midhat? Did he think that by asking to meet him alone I was letting his friend down?

'Why do you think I want to see you?'

'I don't know.'

'Because I want to flirt?'

He looked at me in panic.

'I told you there was something important. And the first thing you ask about is Midhat.'

'You've got me wrong . . .'

'No, I know exactly what you're thinking – that I'm one of those girls who play around, that go with anyone.'

His eyes implored me to stop bullying him, but I couldn't control myself.

'You've misunderstood my relationship with Midhat. We're

117

just friends. There's nothing between us. Or did he tell you something else?'

'No.'

'If he did, he's a liar. I won't see him again.'

He shook his head, then raised his eyes to mine. I saw his expression seemed very tender all of a sudden.

'Is there something wrong?'

I nearly put my head on his shoulder and wept.

'I'm so sorry, Yusif. I'm all mixed up.'

'Tell me.'

What should I tell? That I had quarrelled with my mother no longer meant anything. I wasn't thinking about money; I didn't even want it. The tenderness in his eyes was all I wanted. If only everyone was like Yusif, how at rest I should feel! At the same time I felt ashamed.

'I wanted to know your opinion: should I work in the cinema or not?'

'You're a strange girl!' He laughed. 'You think of this after signing the contract.' His tone was sincere. 'But I understand your feelings exactly. I felt the same about working for *Al-Ayyam*.' He leant on the table, putting his fingers together; how I wished I could have touched them. . . . 'The man outside dreams. He imagines so much. But the moment he steps inside and works, it's finished. No more dreams. From now on it's only work.'

'But the cinema's not the Press . . .'

'It's all work.'

'You have no one like Anwar Sami.'

He did not understand.

I almost decided to tell him what had happened between me and Anwar – not the details, naturally, it would be enough to tell him that Anwar pursued me. Instead I said, Anwar had told me before he left for Beirut that my future was in his hands. If I gave in, he would raise me. If I refused, he would block my path.

Yusif's eyes blazed; he breathed deeply.

'Can he do what he threatens?' I asked.

'Don't be afraid. If he tries anything,' Yusif said reassuringly, 'tell me and I'll stop him.'

'How?'

'I know how.'

'When does he get back?'

'Anwar's been back these last two days.'

I felt a sudden panic. If Anwar rang me up, would I be able to resist him, would Yusif be able to protect me? I was no longer the same Samia as had gone with Anwar to his flat. I was a new Samia, perplexed, afraid, conscious only of tenderness.

'I must go now.'

'It's early,' he protested.

'But I mustn't be late.'

If he had pressed me a little harder, I would have stayed with him, gone to the cinema or just walked in the streets with him. I had no desire to go home and hear Anwar's voice.

'I'm rather pressed for time, too.'

It was no use. He would leave me. He looked at his watch, called the waiter and paid the bill.

I would become the old Samia again.

'Where are you spending tonight?' I asked.

'At the paper.'

'Truthfully? You're not going out . . .'

'I wish I could.'

'And the married woman?'

'Who?'

'The one you loved. . . . Look me in the eyes: don't lie. Do you still love her?'

'Not any more.'

Perhaps he meant that I had driven her from his mind. But when I asked him what he meant, he blushed and lowered his gaze. When I persisted, he stayed silent, then muttered: 'I've no time to think of her.' This was not the reply I wanted. As we were saying good-bye, he asked what I was going to do. I told him I would do nothing, just be Samia.

Next morning I rang him up.

'Tell me, Yusif, what colour is your tie?'

'Why do you ask?'

'Tell me!'

'Grey with white dots.'

'And the suit?'

'Grey.'

'I hope it's not the same as yesterday's.'

'I'm afraid it is.'

'For God's sake, get rid of it. It's too big, it doesn't fit you. Who chooses your ties?'

'I do.'

'I don't like your taste, then. May I choose the next? Fancy wearing a grey tie with a grey suit!'

'I put on what comes to hand.'

'I like men who are chic.'

'But I'm not an actor.'

'No, but you can still be chic. You're attractive. . . . No, I mean it. You could be much smarter if you tried. Your girl-friend – what was her taste like? Didn't she tell you how to dress?'

'It meant nothing to her. She was used to seeing me wear anything.'

'Naturally. Wasn't she . . .'

But I pulled myself up before adding 'a servant?'

'Wasn't she what . . . ?'

'Rather common?'

'On the contrary, she came of an important family.'

'You liar. I don't like liars.'

It was I who was lying. I was delighted that he was lying. His pretence that Mabruka came of a good family showed he was ashamed of her – and I would make this shame increase.

10

'WHEN DID YOU LAST SEE YUSIF?'

'Two days ago.'

'Why didn't you tell me?'

'Do I have to tell you everything? I wanted to see him about my work.'

'What work?'

'The cinema.'

Midhat was interrogating me as though he didn't trust me; at the same time he was looking for a dark place to park the car. We stopped under a shady tree by some iron gates leading down to a deserted houseboat. It was a stifling night, humid and hot as hell. I felt so bored, I was glad that we were going to quarrel. I preferred an argument, to having him slobber over me while he pressed his damp body against mine.

'Yusif informed me . . .' His voice was not as usual, and I wondered if Yusif had mentioned the affair with Anwar.

'What did he tell you?'

He stared into the distance. 'Aren't you ashamed to have spoken as you did?'

Yusif went down in my estimation. How could I have trusted such a child? I felt I had lost him, and this saddened me. Midhat's voice got louder.

'You think this is the way to trick me into marriage?'

'Marriage?' He spoke as if he was in charge of me, my father, almost.

'He told me you met him at Groppi's. I understand everything.'

I screamed: 'I told him nothing. Only about the cinema and my work.'

His smile showed his distrust; his voice was threatening.

'Listen carefully, Samia. This is not the way to get married.'

I was almost weeping with rage.

'Do you think I'm such an idiot as to marry you?'

I used every insult that came into my head. I told him to drive me home immediately. On the way I saw a tobacconist with a telephone and asked him to stop. I wanted him to ring Yusif up and confront him. But he refused. I was determined to see Yusif by any means. I needed him. I got out with Midhat and dialled the number for myself.

'I'm sorry, Mr Yusif's not in.'

'Where's he gone?'

'He went out with Nagi Bey.'

I wanted to pursue him anywhere, to intrude on any gathering, if he was in conference with Nagi Bey, the Prime Minister, or even the King. I must see him at any price.

'Thank God,' I said to Midhat, 'we've reached this point.'

I didn't want to see him again, nor Yusif, nor anyone else in this disgusting world. I ran into my building and found the porter standing by the lift with a note for me. Tomorrow morning at eleven I must be at Cairo Studios with a black evening dress.

I I

I WAS TERRIBLY EXCITED WHEN MR HELMI TOLD ME OF a big scheme for a co-production with an Italian company. It would be in colour. Sylvana Mangano was to star with Anwar Sami. He had chosen me for the important role of Fatima. This would give me a world reputation. Helmi meanwhile wanted to send a coloured picture of me to the producer in Rome.

My head swam; the world seemed to turn round me. I remembered Yolanda, Signora Grazia, and Marco. I felt I was already in Italy. The producer would love me as they had loved me. I wished I could shut my eyes and open them on fame. If only it was the first night now. . . . People clapping me. . . . My picture in all the Italian papers.

My anxiety increased each minute.

The set was busy. Anwar Sami was filming. I thought of going in and watching him act. But I hesitated. I was afraid he might see me. But I finally tired of waiting and went in. Anwar noticed me from where he stood in the middle of the set. He pinned me in my place with his penetrating stare. But he made no sign that he had ever seen me before.

Shortly afterwards I was called to the maquillage room.

Suddenly Mursi, Helmi's assistant, burst in. 'Mr Anwar wants you in his room.'

'But I'm being made up.'

'That can wait. Go to him at once.'

I appealed to the make-up man, who shrugged his shoulders with indifference.

I found Anwar lying on a sofa. He was holding a magazine with his picture printed across an entire page. He did not stir, and addressed me with a cigarette hanging from his lip.

'Why didn't you greet me?'

'You were busy.'

'Haven't you missed me?' He laughed at my embarrassment. 'You do look funny.'

He gestured to the sofa.

There was so little room my back touched his chest.

He said calmly: 'Get ready for tonight.' His arm was round my waist. 'Why have you made me think of you so much?'

I said politely: 'But tonight I'm not free.'

I wished I could smile and speak normally.

'Now – please – not that old record.'

He flung his magazine on the ground.

'Listen to me and grow up. Let's understand each other properly. You've nothing to gain by opposing me.'

I spoke as through a nightmare. 'But there's nothing between us.'

His eyes flashed surprise. 'Really? Are you trying to have a laugh on Anwar Sami?'

He began to swear at me till I interrupted indignantly.

He now screamed: 'If you don't come with me tonight, you have no future in the cinema.'

'All right. I don't want anything from you.'

He was incredulous.

'Don't I attract you?'

I said nothing.

'Don't you want money?'

Tears started from my eyes. He exploded, standing up in the middle of the room. 'What are you crying for?'

'No one's ever spoken to me like that before.'

'I am sorry. I didn't realize that I had to follow etiquette when speaking to Mademoiselle la Princesse . . .'

'Don't mock me.'

But he went on: 'Did you imagine I was a gentleman? I am the son of a dog. I have rolled in filth. I have eaten pebbles. I have walked barefoot. I have worn torn shoes. I used to beg for sixpences. I robbed the bus-conductor. I'd walk from Shubra to the Opera. The world was my education, not a school. I don't know how to speak like well-bred people. I only act like them. I swear at whoever I like – even my mother. I don't like dealing with nice girls . . . girls who want me to get up when they come into the room, to bow and kiss their hand.'

His bitterness turned to anger.

'Who do you think you are? You are just an extra in my company. You'll do what I tell you. I am Anwar Sami, and don't forget it. I have £100,000 in the bank. I can buy you or your mother. . . . or a hundred like you.'

The door opened on staring faces.

I covered my face.

'What do you want?' he screamed. 'I'm just having a row with my girl. She doesn't want to go out with me tonight. She'd like me to bow and scrape and talk French to her. The young aristocrat!' He then screamed at them: 'Get out of here, all of you.'

A moment's silence, then he turned to me again.

'You're ridiculously naïve. You'll never make an actress. You're far too wooden.'

I pushed my fingers into my eyes. I didn't want to see him. All I wanted was for the earth to swallow me.

I shivered at his touch. 'You're wrecking your make-up,' he said. 'Go and repair it.'

I saw through my tears his white teeth as he finished. 'All right, I'll see you tonight.' I said nothing. 'I'll pass by at nine-thirty, like the last time.'

I whispered, 'Please don't come.'

'Grow up.'

I went back to the make-up room and when the filming was over, Helmi came and asked me anxiously what I had done to make Anwar so angry.

'But I can't stand him . . .'

He was irritated.

'You want to involve me in your row?'

'You back him up, then?'

He said coldly, 'But you didn't object to going with him before.'

'Who told you that?'

'He did.'

I went home in a rage. My only hope was Yusif. But I could never tell him what had happened between me and Anwar.

But why was I so worried about Anwar? I could always give way, and profit. I had thought nothing of doing this before.

But Yusif – the only one who showed me any tenderness – was the only person in my thoughts.

When I telephoned Muhammad Nagi, he noticed that I was crying.

'What's the matter?'

My sobs increased.

'You mustn't go on like that . . . There's nothing in this world to deserve such tears.'

His voice combined sympathy and curiosity.

'I told you a lie.'

'How?'

'I'm not married.'

'You're not?'

'Are you angry?'

'Why should I be?'

'Don't be. I'll tell you everything. You're my only friend.'

'Calm yourself: I can't bear to hear you cry.'

'I'll tell you who I am, so you can rescue me.'

'Rescue you?'

'I'm still frightened you'll be angry . . .'

'Of course I won't. Tell me . . .'

'You may have forgotten, but my name and picture appeared in your paper.'

'When?'

'My name is Samia Sami.'

'Of course! I remember you well. You are very pretty. I remarked at the time: we have no one pretty in this way on the screen. How are you, Samia? Why have you been hiding from me?'

I told him about Anwar.

He laughed.

'It was to be expected. Surely you know Anwar? He's mad.'

'Mr Helmi wanted me to humour him. What do you advise? For myself, I'd rather die.'

He answered as though the whole matter was trivial.

'Forget about him.'

'But if he harms me, if he attacks my reputation, he might ruin me.'

He laughed. 'I can deal with him.'

'How?'

He told me to trust in him. He would know what to do.

Then he asked: 'Tell me truthfully, are you in love?'

Thinking of Yusif I replied, simply, 'Yes.'

'He's a lucky man, then; but my luck's out.'

I said quickly: 'But I love you, too.'

'I hope it's not another long-distance love?' He laughed. 'You're still very young.'

12

ONE MORNING YUSIF RANG ME: WOULD I MEET HIM IN Groppi's?

He apologized for being fifteen minutes late – he had had an interview with Shohdi Pasha.

I expected him to ask me about my quarrel with Midhat. But instead he chatted normally and then invited me to lunch.

I was happy to have a few hours alone with him.

Perhaps he would now throw off his shyness. Perhaps he had learnt of my quarrel with Midhat and would feel free to go out with me.

As we walked side by side in the street, he said shyly:

'I'm sorry I have no car.'

He was still comparing himself to Midhat. This annoyed me.

'How absurd? Do I have a car?'

We stood window-shopping, looking at shirts and ties.

'When you've got some money we'll come shopping together.'

We went to a small restaurant in Rue Sherif.

It pleased me the way the other people looked at us, taking it for granted that we were lovers.

Lunch over, he pulled out an enormous cigar, lit it and began coughing.

'Shohdi Pasha presented me with this,' he laughed. 'I've never smoked one before.'

'Is the Pasha still angry about the thing you published?'

I bit on my words.

'How did you know about that?'

'We had some guests,' I said in embarrassment, 'yesterday, and they were talking about it.'

'What did they say?'

'That Nagi had allowed his friend to be insulted in his own paper.'

He looked distrustful of my explanation.

'You read the item?'

'Yes.'

He smiled, called for the waiter, paid the bill and as we went into the street asked where I was going.

We neither of us had anything to do.

'Good. Where shall we go?'

'Anywhere you like.'

His voice trembled as he suggested, 'What about my place?'

'That's a good idea.'

Drops of sweat stood on his forehead; he looked round for a taxi. It seemed as though he already regretted his invitation.

'Will there be anyone there?'

'No.'

I said firmly. 'But you'll be sensible? I'm trusting you.'

'Of course.'

He told the taxi to take us to Rue Maspiro.

It was the same address as Nagi had mentioned. When we reached the building, overlooking the Nile, we took the lift to the same fifth floor and Yusif produced a small key for flat 45. I told myself the first present I would buy him would be a key-ring. Strangely, I did not feel in the least afraid or worried.

The door opened on a large sitting-room full of old but comfortable furniture. The chairs were deep and large. Lamps with inlaid stands had green velvet shades. Heavy green curtains covered the windows that looked onto the Nile. My feet sank into thick Persian carpets which must, I felt, be worth at least £500. They ran from wall to wall. There was a radio, a pickup and lots of records. The walls were pistachio green outlined with lightest blue. Oil-paintings depicted rural scenes in Europe. The atmosphere was luxury itself. A narrow passage led to other rooms.

We went on to the balcony and the sun beat on us fiercely.

'Would you like a Coca-Cola?'

His whole manner was unsure. His eyes, even his feet seemed hesitant. We went into the kitchen which was neat and tidy. He opened the refrigerator, but there was only beer and lemonade.

'Don't you know what you have?'

Embarrassed, he opened a bottle of lemonade.

We returned to the sitting-room and sat, two yards apart, on facing armchairs.

He gazed at me in a preoccupied manner. I began to laugh.

'What's the joke?'

'There isn't one.'

'But really?'

'Just that I'm pleased. . . .'

I never mentioned my mother, only my father. It was as though Mother had died, and Father had gone on living.

When I went home I'd lie down on my bed and weep.

My sister was worried. 'What's wrong with you?'

'Nothing.'

'Then why are you crying?'

I answered between smiles and tears, 'I'm so happy.'

She stared at me in despair. 'I think you're going mad.'

I said nothing.

'God help you,' she muttered.

I wanted to ask her if she remembered Father.

But I could not ask her about him. The only person I could bear to mention my father to was Yusif.

14

AGAIN YUSIF ASKED ME TO GO TO THE FLAT.

'I don't want you to stay frightened of me.'

'It's not that. But what do you want?'

'There's something important I want to tell you.'

Once at the flat he was again tongue-tied. We chatted in a desultory way.

'Isn't there something important you want to say?'

'I'm afraid you'll be angry.'

'With you? Impossible,' I added firmly. 'You don't seem to realize how dear you are to me.'

He got out with difficulty. 'And you to me.'

We plunged into an exhausting silence. All I heard was his breathing and mine, as though we were mounting stairs without an end.

'Samia, I must tell you: I love you.'

Although I had expected his confession, when it came my head swam. It was as though I heard the phrase for the first time.

'I don't know what has happened. . . . I feel I have loved you for ages . . . since before I knew you. . . . My love is the reason

131

why I was born. I love you when I sit writing with pen in my hand. I love you when I am in a bus, in a hurry. I love you when I am accepting a cigar from Shohdi Pasha. I love you when I'm asleep dreaming. Or when I'm asleep and not dreaming. When I breathe I love you. When I drink, I love you. When I'm thirsty, I love you. Samia, I am worn out. I love you.'

I murmured in reply, 'I don't want to wear you out, my darling.'

I began to cry.

'Samia, please, or I'll begin to cry too.'

Tears choked my words. 'I love you too. But I don't want anything from you, not even love. Tenderness is enough for me.'

'You mustn't speak like that.'

'But you'll give me the tenderness I crave? You won't torture me? I can't bear to be hurt by you.'

'Darling, when you say things like that you torture me.'

'But tomorrow, when love is over. . . . When you leave me . . .'

I expected to feel his arms around me. But instead he sat frozen in his place as though he did not know what to do next. I got up and played with the radio, fiddling with the knobs.

'How does this radio work?'

I felt him approach. My body trembled, wanting him to embrace me. But again he stood beside me and asked:

'Which station do you want?'

'Any station.'

I turned to him. There was not more than a hand's breadth between us. Love shone from his eyes: also shyness. Desire and perplexity shone from mine. We returned to our separate seats while the radio began to play 'Symphonie . . . Symphonie d'amour.'

'Couldn't we find a different place to meet?' I said, suddenly insecure at the thought of Muhammad Nagi.

'All right.'

'You say all right, but I'm sure you'll not look for one.'

'No, I promise.'

I felt so relieved. Even if the new place was not so comfortable, it would be for us alone. I smiled.

'Do you want anything?'

He said very timidly, 'Yes.'

'To kiss me?'

He looked baffled, incredulous, burdened; I yearned for him. He came near me and I lifted my face to his, shutting my eyes. He placed a light kiss above my eyes, then for a moment pressed his lips on mine. I opened my eyes. He seemed to have blanched. He looked as though he wanted to repeat the kiss. But gently I pushed him away. I did not want another of his inexperienced kisses.

'Go and sit down,' I said smiling. 'Be sensible.'

He sat down.

'Now tell me about your first love.'

'Why do you want to know?'

I felt certain that he would protest I was his first love, although I knew all about Mabruka, and although he admitted that he had loved someone who was married. Yet I sensed that perhaps he never had loved another woman, neither Mabruka nor anyone else. This hope filled me with joy.

'I want to know if she was worthy of you.'

'It's all over.'

'I can't rest till you tell me everything.'

'I've put her out of my mind.'

I had to attack. I had come to depend so much on his tenderness. I had to know if he was like all the others.

'If you won't tell me, I won't tell you, either.'

'Tell me what?'

'About the one I loved before you.'

He paled; his eyes trembled. 'You mean Midhat?'

'Someone else.'

'Who?'

'I'm not going to tell you.'

'If you don't, I'll beat you.'

I recoiled.

133

'Never use that word with me again. Or I'll leave you and never see you again.'

He blushed. 'Samia, I am sorry.'

He soothed me with caresses, and I felt ashamed that I had given him such a false picture of my life. He had no idea what I had to put up with, nor what Anwar had done to me.

I suddenly said, 'You believed me?'

His eyes said that he did not understand me.

'I wanted to test you . . . to see if you would change.'

I took his head in my arms. 'Don't be angry.'

I kissed him on his forehead, then on his lips. Still he seemed sad.

'Samia, I can only tell you one thing: I love you. Anything you hear from me means this. If I say, *au revoir*, it means I love you. If I threaten to beat you, it means I love you. If I don't want to see you, it means I love you. Anything I do or say has this meaning only – that I love you.'

My happiness flooded back to me, but he had to force a smile to his lips, he was still sorry for his harsh words.

We left the flat and walked by the banks of the Nile, our hearts beat together, our steps and our very breath, everything was together.

We walked and walked.

15

MY MOTHER WAS DELIGHTED WHEN SHE HEARD I WAS going to one of Muhammad Nagi's parties. I would meet the most eligible men in town, she said, advising me to keep smiling and talking throughout the evening. I must let no one outshine me. For this was the chance of a lifetime. If I succeeded at the party I'd be made. Pashas and ministers would invite me to theirs. Mother showed how pleased she was by giving me money for a new dress – it was finished in two days – a red dress with bare back and bare arms. She even opened her reserve bottle of Carven's 'Rien Que Nous'.

Yusif, who had invited me, picked me up in a taxi and at nine sharp we arrived at a two-storey villa in Zamalek.

A smart doorman rushed to open the gate and we found ourselves in a small but beautifully kept garden with such neat shrubs that they looked as if they had come from the coiffeur. There was the barking of a dog. Upstairs there were lights and I imagined I heard the sound of music. The barking stopped and a dog appeared, as big as a horse.

Yusif saw my terror. 'Don't be frightened. That's Tony.' He whistled, and the dog ambled forward and began to walk round us. I edged towards the steps, not wanting him to touch me. Yusif whispered, 'He used to belong to Dalal.'

A strange creature in a white dinner-jacket opened the house door. He bowed low, his eyes on the ground. I found it hard to imagine it was a servant who ushered us into a huge, empty room brilliantly illuminated. This hall led to a large salon, also illuminated, also empty. The music I had imagined was nonexistent! Instead a strange perfume of carnations drifted everywhere. The servant disappeared behind a curtain. I looked to Yusif for help, but his eyes were gazing into space, preoccupied. The curtain moved and the servant reappeared, only to vanish through another door. There was total silence. Then I heard a subdued sound to my left, and noticed a white telephone lying on the ground. Its almost inaudible ringing stopped and I heard the voice of Muhammad Nagi from behind the curtain.

'Impossible. . . . Of course we won't eat until he comes. . . .' Then he laughed and said pleasantly: 'But of course, darling.'

The curtain quivered and Muhammad Nagi appeared, gleaming and scented as from the bath. His eyes were fixed on me while his lips curved in a smile. I tried to laugh back as my mother had taught me but I was too shy. He clasped my hand in both of his and said as if we had known each other for years:

'How are you, Samia?'

He didn't shake hands with Yusif but nodded to him in a

135

cursory manner. He sat down near me, resting his hand on my knee.

'It's good you came early . . . It gives me a chance to sit with you a little.'

Patting my nearest knee, he asked, 'What do you think of Yusif?'

I fought back my shyness. 'You know him best. . . .'

'No, you're too shy to tell me.'

It irritated me that he had noticed my shyness.

He pulled me to my feet. 'Come to the bar.'

The bar was in one corner of the salon; in front of it were high stools. He went behind the bar telling us to take a seat. He glanced at the rows of bottles behind him. 'What will you drink? I've got everything, whisky, gin . . . or vodka.'

The servant appeared unsummoned and put ice in front of us, then vanished in silence.

'Or how about a cocktail?'

He approved his own suggestion.

'Yes, we'll all drink Martinis.'

Nagi mixed gin and vermouth and shook it with ice. He popped a green olive in my glass.

'I once saw King Carol of Roumania in New York. I was staying at the Waldorf Astoria and went down to breakfast at nine in the morning. There he sat alone with six Martinis lined up in front of him which he proceeded to drink, one after another. I knew then, his marriage had been a flop. Naturally. . . . How absurd to have to give up your throne, for a love that cannot last. Your healths.'

We raised our glasses and drank.

'It tastes good, doesn't it? Why are you silent, Yusif? Perhaps you're thinking of the King. . . . In his place you'd have done the same. . . . You'd have abdicated your kingdom for the sake of love . . . and you'd have been sorry. . . . Samia's a lovely girl . . . very lovely.'

After half a Martini my courage had returned.

'Why do you talk about me as though I was absent?'

Nagi shouted: 'Yusif loves you . . .'

'Let him speak for himself.'

'I must speak as his deputy.'

'That proves he doesn't love me.'

Yusif sipped his glass and laughed irritably.

Muhammad Nagi, mixing a new round of Martinis, said: 'You've still not told me your opinion of Yusif.'

'First I want yours.'

He looked at Yusif with a sarcastic smile.

'My opinion? He's a fraud.'

Yusif burst out: 'How can you say that?' Nagi disregarded him.

'The man's unreal. Too polite . . . too frank . . . too sentimental . . . too clever . . . too everything. Nobody can really be like that. He must be a fraud.'

'Then why employ him?'

He laughed.

'Because he *is* a fraud.'

'Are journalists frauds?'

'But of course.'

'Even . . .' I swallowed my question.

He laughed. 'You wanted to say, even me? The answer is yes: even I am a fraud. Do you know what being a fraud means? It's not easy. It's a talent. You must learn to delete your real opinions, to show others the appearance they want to see . . . to make them cry when your heart is laughing . . . to get them worked up when they have no idea what for. . . . You're still young. When you've become a famous star, you'll understand.'

'Will I learn to be a fraud?'

'Certainly.'

'But I still don't think Yusif's one.'

'Yusif's a doctor of fraudulence – but in a new style. This promises him a great future.'

'To me he seems kind and honest.'

'When he's being honest he's being most fraudulent; when he's at his kindest, he's being most cruel.'

Anxiously I asked:

'He doesn't love me, then?'

'No, he loves you. But he won't abdicate for love. . . .'

Yusif whispered in an embarrassed voice.

'You do have a poor opinion of me, Mr Nagi.'

'On the contrary, I have a first-class opinion.'

Why was he needling Yusif? He must be jealous, because Yusif was young and because I loved him. But no, Nagi had everything. He was full of self-confidence. Was he inviting me to leave Yusif . . . to transfer myself to him . . . to join his harem . . . like the woman he'd been calling 'Darling' on the telephone . . . another Dalal? I remembered the dog.

'That huge dog outside terrified me . . .'

'He doesn't bite.'

'Where did you get him?'

His eyes searched my face.

'That dog was Dalal's . . . it was her only legacy. "If I die, Muhammad, look after Tony." She was sitting at this bar, where you're sitting now . . . no, where Yusif is. . . . She was drinking heavily. It was the day she tore up a contract for £15,000. . . . The producer had tried to kiss her, the cheque in his hand. . . . She tore it into little pieces and threw it in his face. . . . He had bad breath, she told me afterwards. . . . She was insane . . . capricious, impulsive. . . . You never knew what she would do, what her next mood would be. . . . She lived with me here for four months. She was on the run from Hikmet Pasha, Comptroller of the Crown Lands. The Prime Minister rang me up – if I didn't give her up, he'd not be responsible for what would hit me. That evening she tried to commit suicide at her mother's house. She swallowed a bottle of aspirin. We saved her . . . or rather Dr Zaydan did. . . . You'll be meeting him in a moment. . . . He gave her a stomach-wash and brought her to. She came back and sat here at the bar. I remember I said to her: "And next time, Dalal? Can't you come to terms with yourself and relax?" "I'll relax when I'm dead; I'll have a long sleep then, without one regret. The only thing I want you to do for me is to look after Tony. If I die, Muhammad, look after

Tony." I said jokingly, "Who'll look after me?" She just laughed. "You're a fraud, Muhammad.'"

He looked to see how we reacted to his story, especially me.

'Why aren't you drinking, Samia?'

He shouted to the servant. Then in a gentle voice he added, 'She was the first person to teach me that all artists, journalists, celebrities . . . all of them are frauds. She was a fraud herself. She wasn't at all satisfied with her voice or her songs. But she'd fly into a rage if people didn't applaud her till their palms ached. She was furious if any journalist implied that her singing was less than perfect.'

He fixed me with his eyes and asked:

'Do you think you can develop like Dalal?'

I murmured: 'Her story frightens me.'

He said quietly:

'If you're afraid, you shouldn't start. Just stay an extra.'

I protested:

'You mean, to be something, I've got to be like her?'

He considered.

'Not necessarily. But you'll lack something otherwise.'

He emptied his glass.

'When I know you better I'll tell you what it is.'

A man's voice shouted: 'Where is everybody?'

A short, stocky man with curly hair rising from a dark complexion came in, smoking a large cigar. He looked thoroughly pleased with himself, almost making a stage entrance.

'Here's the villain,' Muhammad Nagi shouted.

The doctor puffed smoke in my face.

'The villain's the one who cures you.'

Nagi introduced Dr Zaydan to me, then to Yusif.

After a quarter of an hour the house was awash with guests. The men either wore white shirts, shark-skin jackets, or ordinary dinner-jackets. The ladies all had bare backs and bare arms like me. They were heavily perfumed. Rouge was smeared over the wrinkles of time. I was by far the youngest woman present. There was one woman of about thirty-five who was still quite attractive; she had a drawling voice and amusing

139

gestures. The rest were all over forty-five. They either had dyed hair or wore their white locks as crowns of dignity. There was nothing dignified, however, about their talk, nor the way they smoked and drank incessantly. The one thing they all had in common was their age. The only young people were the strangers, islands in an ancient sea. The guests exchanged insincere smiles. They puffed smoke into each other's eyes.

I no longer felt shy. The Martini had done its work.

Forcing a smile onto my face I plunged into the throng. Nagi introduced me to a huge lump of flesh. This was Qadri Pasha, Minister for Religious Endowments. He was like a puffed up balloon which might burst at any moment. The features hardly projected on his round face, so that even his nostrils looked as though they had been pencilled on; his face was like a small balloon linked to a larger. His eyes were askew, one squinting to the right, the other to the left, but they managed to focus on me. They were ice-cold. He said in a high-pitched, childish voice: 'How are you, Mademoiselle? Everyone who's seen you act predicts a splendid future.'

I said shyly, 'But I've not yet acted, Pasha.'

Perplexed he turned to an athletic young man standing beside him. He had the face of a wild animal; the muscles bulged under his suit. 'Surely she's an actress?'

'Of course, Pasha,' said the brute, with a threatening glance, 'she's an actress.'

'As God wills,' said the Pasha. 'And she sings?'

'No, only acts.'

The brute with the muscles said: 'The Pasha has taken to you, Mademoiselle. You are indeed fortunate!'

I took the first opportunity to escape from the Pasha. I found Yusif talking to Dr Zaydan. But before I could reach them, Nagi called me. 'Where are you off to? Aren't you enjoying yourself?'

He led me to the bar.

'What news of the new film?'

'We're still waiting.'

He said quietly: 'When am I going to see you alone?'

'Why?'

'Afraid?'

'Not at all.'

'D'you want to be remade? Do you want me to mould your future?'

He poured me a Martini.

'How?'

He said emphatically: 'First I'd change your attitude.'

'In what way?'

His eyes wandered over my body.

'You must become a little silly. . . . All successful actresses until now . . . all of them common, silly. . . . Thick lips, eyes glittering with stupidity. . . . That can't be your line. But a certain silliness would suit you. It would make you madly attractive. . . .'

'But if I'm not silly?'

'Then no one will employ you. They'll be scared of you. Conceit is no drawback. All famous actresses are conceited as well as stupid. Your trouble is that you're too clever. You're always thinking, always planning how to get famous, how to arrive. That's not as easy as you think.'

'You're talking like Anwar Sami.'

He said quickly: 'Talk of the devil . . . here is Anwar! How are you?'

Anwar embraced him, then turned to shriek at me.

'Keep out of my way. . . . You're always under my feet.'

He turned to demand of Nagi:

'Who brought her here?'

'I did.'

Anwar shouted:

'Congratulations, my girl, you've arrived. . . . No one can stand in your way.' He raised his hands in mock salutation. 'I'm going.'

'Where?'

'I'm fed up with this city.' To me he shouted with a smile, 'Now I realize why you disdain me. You're right, I'm not good enough for you,' and he made a theatrical gesture. 'We are your ladyship's servants.' To Nagi he winked: 'Her ladyship disdains us.'

Yusif, standing near the door, stared towards us. But when our eyes met he turned on his heel and vanished. Meanwhile an old woman came screeching up to Anwar. 'Anwar, where have you been hiding?' Anwar whispered in my ear, 'Don't leave me at the mercy of this hag. . . .' To her he turned and said: 'Just a moment, darling.' He took me by the arm and led me to a group of old people. We sat down side by side.

'You all know my daughter, Samia Sami?'

There was more than one sarcastic laugh.

'Please insult her since she's defeated me.'

I sat in silence. Anwar continued to rattle on:

'No one pleases me. My whole life is trash piled on trash. No one cares about me. Who takes any notice of an urchin with torn shoes? No one wants me. I know this. That's why I worked and worked to make myself rich. Now some people say: Look at the *nouveau riche* guttersnipe . . .'

A drunken voice answered: 'God help you, Anwar. . . .'

He looked at each of them. 'Even my mother would like me to die to get my cash. . . . Yes, even that toothless coughing old woman. . . . If I died the thought that would plague me is my money. I'll leave directions for my money to be buried with me. I'd burst out of my shroud if I thought other people were spending it. It would be worse than a second death.'

He whispered while everyone strained to hear:

'You'll come with me tonight.'

'No.'

He raised his voice: 'Then I hope you die first, Samia. . . .' He again whispered, 'Don't tell Nagi, or I'll kill you.'

Just as I was laughing, the athletic brute approached and Anwar warned him: 'Beware of this bitch, she bites.'

The athlete disregarded him. 'Could I have a moment, Mademoiselle?'

He took me to a corner of the room.

'I am Basyuni, the Minister's secretary.' He scratched his neck and tapped me on the shoulder. 'His Excellency's giving a party tomorrow, at 4 p.m. An intimate party. I'll fetch you myself.'

I shook my head angrily. I wanted to call to Yusif but when I looked at him, he turned away. I was frightened of this brute.

'I can't come.'

'Don't dare to anger the Minister. He can be dangerous. If he knew you weren't coming, he'd leave this party now.'

'All right,' I said, to gain time, 'call me tomorrow.'

'I'll call you,' he said in a brutal whisper. 'I have your number.'

I ran to Yusif. Dr Zaydan lit a new cigar, 'I can see you're having a good time, Mademoiselle.'

Yusif left us.

What was wrong? Had I done something to annoy him?

The doctor began to ask me what I had done in the cinema. As he puffed at his cigar he suggested that I should try working as a nurse in his clinic. I'd make just as much money as in films. The presence of someone as beautiful as I would attract so many elderly clients, eager to become young and beautiful once more.

I felt as though I would burst. 'They're all frauds.'

He puffed smoke in my face.

'Don't say that. They're the leading personalities of our country. You're only a beginner. Tomorrow you'll understand. They're all tired from their heavy burdens. They need to relax a little.'

Then he suddenly exclaimed: 'Shohdi Pasha's arrived!'

A change had come over the party. Men and women alike stood up, all gazing at a pale-skinned portly man with rosy cheeks and carefully waved hair. He was smoking a much bigger cigar than Dr Zaydan's. Everyone greeted him with deference except Anwar who shouted:

'Give me a piastre, Pasha. . . . God prospers the alms-giver.'

Shohdi Pasha handed him a florin which Anwar took, kissed and raised to his head. He then scrutinized it while, without knowing what I was doing, I walked towards Shohdi Pasha as if under a spell. His eyes seemed to see through mine. I heard Nagi's voice: 'Mademoiselle Samia Sami, one of our new stars.'

A soft white hand shook mine.

'*Bon soir*, Mademoiselle.'

He wore a diamond ring; a large red stone was stuck in his tie. He noticed Yusif and said with an enthusiasm that lit up his face:

'How are you, Yusif? I haven't seen you for ages. How are you doing, my boy?' He flung his arm round Yusif's shoulder and led him to a corner where they sat down side by side. I noticed a puzzled look on Nagi's face as we watched them. But Anwar shouted:

'Pasha, why are you deserting us? We want to play roulette.'

'After we've had our buffet,' said Muhammad Nagi, going up to Shohdi Pasha. 'Please lead the way, Pasha.' Turning to one of the ladies, Shohdi Pasha took her arm. All the guests followed them towards the buffet supper. I was among the last, with Yusif.

'Aren't you going to eat?'

'I have no appetite.'

'Nor have I!'

His eyes wandered round the room. 'I'd rather leave.'

'Let's leave, then.'

I took his arm and before anyone noticed us we had passed the garden and reached the street. The only one who had seen us leaving was Tony, who gave one bored bark and then fell silent.

16

DESPITE ALL MY MARTINIS, I WAS WIDE AWAKE. MY head was surprisingly clear. But Yusif, pale and silent, looked worn out. Even after all the glitter, I felt in the strength of my youth and beauty that I would have chosen no one other than this young man walking beside me. Though he was not famous

I wanted no one else. He was the only one who showed me tenderness.

'Why so silent?'

'I'm tired.'

'Has something upset you?'

'Of course not.'

'Then talk to me.'

'About what?'

'You *are* hopeless!'

He sighed. 'That's right, I'm hopeless.'

We picked up a taxi at the corner of the road.

'Where are we going?'

'I'll drop you home.'

'I don't want to go home.'

I whispered:

'Let's go to the flat.'

'Now?'

'I want to be with you awhile.'

In the flat Yusif tried to sit away from me, but I put my arms round him and dragged him on to the sofa.

'Yusif dearest, your silence is unbearable. What's wrong?'

'I don't know myself.'

'I know.'

His eyes probed for what I knew.

'The other guests . . . what a strange lot. Isn't that the reason? They're mad.'

He smiled sadly. I continued:

'Muhammad Nagi . . . he doesn't like you as much as you imagine, either.'

'You think so?'

'You saw how he attacked you? When Shohdi Pasha sat with you, you should have seen the look in his eyes! It was ferocious. He seemed to suspect something between you.'

He brushed my suggestion aside. I was imagining things, Muhammad Nagi was his best friend.

'Yusif, I'm upset. You let them treat you exactly as they want. You're a toy in their hands.'

As I said this I felt I was describing my own predicament too.

'They treat you like a child.'

My frankness made him flush. He sighed deeply.

'What do you want me to do? There's nothing between me and them but work.'

I cut him short.

'What do you want to become?'

He looked puzzled.

'Do you want to end up like Muhammad Nagi?'

'No,' he said quickly, 'I don't.'

'Then what?'

'I don't want anything.'

I kissed him on his forehead.

'But I do. I want you to become better than all of them. Didn't we agree on that? You're to be the best journalist and I'm to be the best actress.' I whispered in his ear. 'Tomorrow you'll have your own paper and I'll have a film company.'

He smiled bitterly.

'You're dreaming.'

'Why? Are such people formed from a better clay?'

'It's almost as if they were . . .'

I was firm.

'You'll see – tomorrow.'

A strange look came into his eyes and seizing me in his arms he kissed me. I surrendered to his kisses. I knew he needed me. I knew that I must give . . . and give. His lips prowled over my face and I seemed to be floating in the air, far from people, far from the world. My eyes were closed and I thought of nothing, not even Yusif. I felt alone in a strange magical world, where there were no feelings and no thoughts, but only tenderness and warmth.

I opened my eyes to find Yusif lying beside me, his eyes bright with a lazy and tender love.

I smiled. He smiled. It was as if we were meeting for the first time and conversing without words.

That night I felt I had been linked to Yusif all my life, he was

146

my life. I would do all I could to keep him. I would give up my career and marry him. I would give up everything to marry him.

Then for some reason I remembered when we lived in Abbasiya. I was proud of my father's uniform, his crown and a star. Soldiers saluted him when he passed.

One morning my mother left us in the flat without any food. I thought my father had left for his land near Tanta.

Hours passed and Mother didn't return. I felt more afraid than hungry. But my sister cried with hunger and this increased my fear. I kept going out to the stairs looking for Mother. Or my father. Neither of them came. My sister cried: I want Mummy! I want Mummy! I cried too. Evening came and I saw a cab drawn up and my mother get out. Her face was sad and stern.

'Where's Father?'

'Never mention that name,' she said brusquely.

'Why not?'

'It's all over. Your father's left you and never wants to see you again.'

When I was fifteen Mother called me one morning. She showed me a letter, clicking her lips.

'Do you want to see him after all these years? Your father is staying a couple of days at the Nile Hotel. He has asked for you. If you and Insaf want to see him, ask for him there.'

After some hesitation and despite Mother's disapproval, I decided to meet him. Insaf refused to come with me.

By this time my father had retired and no longer wore uniform. His hair was white. He met me in the lobby of the hotel and we sat on two shabby chairs among the people coming and going. We chatted meaninglessly. He was embarrassed. He kept smoking as he asked about my stepfather and heard my replies without interest. He asked me if I would like to go and spend a few days with him at Tanta.

'I must ask Mother,' I said, fumbling for an excuse not to go. He was no longer the father I remembered.

And I went on holiday with Yolanda and a friend who owned

a large red Chevrolet instead. A telegram announced his death
soon after. He had thrown himself, lonely and hopeless, from a
third-floor window.

17

WE FOUND A SMALL TWO-ROOMED FLAT ON THE FOURTH
floor of a new building near the Paradise Cinema. The balcony
overlooked the open-air screen.

After Yusif had paid the rent and the caution money he gave
me all he had left – £5. I went to the second-hand furniture
shop in Ataba and bought an iron bedstead and a straw mattress.
A horse-drawn cab carried it to the flat and we passed our first
evening by the light of a candle. We got sandwiches from the
Excelsior and a melon and laid the mattress on the balcony and
watched a Technicolor film called 'Sally'. The stars were Rita
Hayworth and Victor Mature. We devoured the melon with our
fingers. We were very happy.

Yusif's poverty did not worry me. When I was with him I
did not think of money. I wore any old dress, any old shoes.

We would wander in the streets and then go home as if we
had everything.

I would lie to Mother, saying I was needed at the studio. If
she gave me the money for a taxi, I'd invite Yusif to supper
at the 'Americaine'. After ice-cream we'd return to the flat
and watch the film, even if we had seen it four or five times
already.

On the first of the month Yusif gave me £63, the balance
from his salary after paying the newspaper canteen.

I had not expected him to give me so much.

I accepted it with trembling fingers. It was an omen that we
would get married.

Laughing I said: 'When we're married you must do the
same.'

I felt that I had said something dangerous. This was the

first time marriage had been mentioned. But he answered quickly:

'Of course, darling.'

I brushed his face with my lips, my eyes blinded with happiness.

From Khan al-Khalili I bought two brass lamps for £3. I also bought a primus, sugar and coffee. And for Yusif I bought a key-ring for the latch-key. It had on it a little disc which spelt, when you whirled it, the words: I love you! I also went shopping in Rue Fouad and Rue Suleiman and bought him three shirts and cloth for a winter suit. For myself I bought cloth for a new dress. I spent more than £20 in a single day. I still owed £9 for the rent . . . and there were still things to buy. There was the carpenter. I had to arrange for him to make our furniture. I needed a carpet and radio. I needed things for the kitchen. I needed towels. I needed . . . I needed . . .

I said to Yusif through tears of anxiety:

'The money's running out.'

'Then why did you take it?' He sounded amused.

'How will we manage to the end of the month?'

'Somehow.'

I went to the carpenter and ordered furniture for the bedroom as well as an American sofa and two armchairs. I agreed on the price of £150 to be paid in instalments. Every month £20.

I had promised Yusif I would not talk to Muhammad Nagi any more. I kept my promise and weeks passed without my thinking of him. I had forgotten him almost.

Then one morning he telephoned me.

'Samia, can I trust you?'

'What about?'

'First I beg you to forget the past. It's true I flirted with you. I wasn't to blame. I'm unmarried and you are beautiful. . . . It's not shameful to flirt. On the contrary, it would have been shameful if I hadn't. But now it's all over. You love Yusif and he loves you. I am talking now about his career.'

'What's wrong with it?'

'But promise you won't tell him.'

'I promise.'

'Listen, Samia. Yusif's getting into deep water. You must prevent him from going too far before things boil over.'

I was alarmed. 'What's happened?'

'It's a long story. I can't tell you on the phone. Can you come here?'

'Of course not.'

'Believe me, Samia, I'm not joking. If you want, come to the newspaper. But at a time when Yusif's not there . . .'

'Yusif would be furious if he knew.'

'Yusif mustn't know.'

The serious way he spoke increased my anxiety. I didn't know what to say.

'Doesn't his career matter to you? On second thoughts, I think it's wiser for you to come to the flat. I'll wait for you there at five.' He added threateningly, 'But don't try and deceive me, Samia. If you tell Yusif one word, you'll lose everything. We'll never be able to help each other again.'

Hours passed and I was in torment. Should I tell him? Why had I got involved? What role was I supposed to play?

I could not suppress my fears and contacted Yusif. At the precise moment Muhammad Nagi was waiting at the flat, I was at home telling Yusif everything. He listened without surprise, then smiled.

'That man's going mad.'

'Are you hiding something?'

He shouted: 'He's still adolescent. Don't ask me about him.'

'But why does he say your career's at stake?'

'Don't believe a word he says.' Then he added quietly, 'But I have decided I can't work with him any longer. I'm going to resign.'

'Don't make me wish I hadn't told you,' I shouted. 'Be sensible, Yusif.'

He took no notice and left me in despair. How stupid I had been! He would resign; we would be unable to marry.

That evening when he came back a strange half-smile played on his lips.

But he said nothing.

'Tell me what happened,' I asked impatiently.

'I didn't resign.'

He seemed embarrassed.

'This is a strange world.' He rubbed his chin, and muttered, 'I went to resign. The result? I got promoted.'

'It's incredible.'

'Listen to what happened. . . . I've told you how I've never asked for anything? Yet all I do seems to get me entangled. That is my whole life-story. I don't want anything; I just want to be left alone; but I get entangled.'

What he said was unclear: but his news perplexed me. He no longer seemed the Yusif I knew.

'My salary's gone up from £70 to £120.'

He told me the good news as if it was a catastrophe.

'You'll see I'm telling the truth on the first of the month. I've been promoted to deputy editor.'

'But what happened? What did you say to Nagi? What did he say to you?'

'I told him I despised him, that what you told me had made me lose all respect for him. I threw my resignation in his face and left. I went to my office to collect my things. Not five minutes passed when he came in weeping like a dog. He implored me to remain on the paper. He almost kissed my shoes. Can you imagine that man crying real tears? I took no notice; I was mad with rage. He told me the newspaper would be ruined, that it would be closed tomorrow if I left.' Yusif laughed. 'Don't imagine I'm really so important to the paper. The paper can go on coming out for ever. If I leave or ten like me. But orders had come from on high.'

'Whose orders?'

'Shohdi Pasha's. He's the man who finances the paper. Nagi rang him up and spoke to him. "Pasha," he said, "I can't persuade him to stay." Nagi handed me the telephone. "Talk to the Pasha." Our conversation was brief. "Yusif my boy, I've asked for you to be promoted. You must accept. If you resign, I'll close the paper tomorrow. Decide for yourself. You're free."

I found Muhammad Nagi still weeping. I couldn't refuse. I accepted. In a short while Nagi was smiling as though nothing had happened and I had become deputy editor, my salary almost doubled.' He rubbed his chin reflectively, staring at some ghost in his mind. 'What do they want from me?'

I was sure Yusif was holding something back. I was not so stupid as to believe that the proud Nagi I knew had used tears to get Yusif to accept promotion. . . . I was in despair. There were secrets between Yusif and me. He was building a wall between us and to know the secret I must destroy this wall. But despite all my pleading he would reveal nothing more than that for some reason Shohdi Pasha had a down on Nagi and wanted to hurt him. What the secret of this quarrel was he could not or would not reveal.

A few days later Yusif told me that his colleagues at *Al-Ayyam* were giving a party to celebrate his promotion.

'Take me with you.'

He hesitated and I asked if he was ashamed to be seen with me. He at once said he would take me. This made me happy, as I had feared he would refuse. If he was willing to show our love in public, he would not refuse to marry me later.

The party was in a house near the Citadel. Some stone steps led up to a narrow lane between ancient houses. In one of these a gloomy courtyard gave onto a narrow stone stair. From above we could hear the murmur of voices interspersed with laughter and shouts. A mad mixture of young men and women was crowded into a big room with a high ceiling, the floor covered with rush mats and bare wooden settees. The walls were plastered with dozens of pictures. People rushed towards us clasping bottles of beer and in less than a minute I was seated in their midst as though we were all old friends. They thrust a bottle into my hand and placed a cardboard plate on my lap loaded with sandwiches and pickles. They squatted round me eating from the plate they had given me.

A thin, dark young man in thick glasses stared at me. When our eyes met he smiled. As though we were already friends he drew near me.

'How are you, Samia?'

'How are you?'

'I am Showki Mahmoud, a painter. I work with Yusif.'

So this was the man who was living with Mabruka.

When Yusif came near as if to join us, Showki shouted boldly: 'You keep away. . . . . We want to talk in private.'

Yusif smiled good-humouredly and turned his back.

'What's your opinion of Yusif?'

It was the same question Muhammad Nagi had asked.

I knew that anything I said would be repeated to Mabruka.

'The best person in the world.'

'No, your real opinion.'

'Why? Don't you agree?'

His eyes pierced mine.

He looked round and said quietly: 'Will you come outside?' Force in his voice compelled me to follow him out of the room up the stairs to the flat roof. It was a night without moon. I stumbled on statues lying on the ground like corpses. Against the darkness I could discern minarets towering in silhouette above me. He offered me a cigarette and struck a match. His face was stern; his eyes looked grim. He pointed to the houses all round.

'Is this your first visit here?'

'Yes.'

'Seriously, Samia, we've not met before, but we're not strangers. There's no such thing as strangers anywhere. We're all human beings with hearts and with brains. We all want the good of others.'

My eyes were getting used to the darkness and I could see that he was hesitant. Was he drunk or mad?

'Do my words alarm you?'

'Yes.'

'Do you know anything about art?'

His question was hardly polite but I felt impressed by his sincerity, which was not meant to hurt.

'I'm studying.'

'I'm attacking you so as to know you better. Don't get

153

upset. I don't know you; I have no right to judge you. But I know that Yusif loves you. Everyone at the paper knows this; several people have seen you together. Yusif has a high position at the paper; he has big responsibilities. For this reason it is important for me to know who he loves and what effect love has on him.'

His words pleased me because they made me feel important.

'Are you afraid I'm no good?'

'No, but I wonder if you know your role or not?'

He crushed out his cigarette with his feet.

'Will you answer a question?'

'What question?'

'Do you know how Yusif got promoted?'

I was suddenly afraid. His question was unexpected, though it was the same that had worried me.

'He deserves promotion.'

He laughed bitingly. 'You really don't know? Yusif is going through a dangerous phase. He used to be a good chap, honourable, straightforward, working to live, like anyone else. Then a rich capitalist got hold of him. Naturally you've heard of Shohdi Pasha. Our paper is almost his private publicity sheet. In a sense we all work for him . . . including Muhammad Nagi, the editor. The man who built the building . . . is Shohdi Pasha. The man who installed the presses . . . is Shohdi Pasha. Muhammad Nagi is his employee, hardly better than a servant. Shohdi Pasha wants to raise the Stock Exchange . . . we write news that sends prices up. He wants to depress the Stock Exchange . . . we write news that brings prices down. A minister refuses a request from Shohdi Pasha . . . we attack him. A minister does what he wants . . . we laud him to the skies. That's our real function. Naturally I don't keep my ideas secret. I take their money in order to fight and defeat them. My work there is like a job anywhere else: a chance for me to attack capitalism, to fight the people sucking our blood. Yusif could have joined us. But now it looks as though he's chosen another way. He wants to become a second Muhammad Nagi: a servant to Shohdi Pasha. How can I explain? Imagine that some producer wants to sign you up for £1,000. Then you realize that the contract is just for you to sleep with him. Worse things than that happen – don't they? – to half the people in the cinema. Would you agree, or throw the contract back in his face? You must either fight the capitalist and his corrupt power over you – or surrender. To my way of thinking, Yusif has surrendered.'

Remembering what Anwar had tried to do to me, I shouted:
'Yusif could never do a thing like that.'

'Then why has he taken a bribe?'

'His promotion,' I protested, 'was not a bribe.'

'Muhammad Nagi,' Showki went on, 'has had an affair with Shohdi Pasha's wife, and Shohdi Pasha found out. But like every businessman he refuses to be ruled by feeling. Shohdi Pasha needs Nagi's pen; the money he gains from it means more to him than his wife's honour. But he'll get his revenge in his own way. He is persecuting Nagi. If Nagi wants to get rid of Yusif, Shohdi gives him a raise. Shohdi Pasha is roasting Nagi over a slow fire. He's flaying him by degrees. And he's preparing his successor before his eyes. This is the vengeance of a millionaire. And Yusif is the executioner.'

'But Yusif does not know . . .'

'Or he pretends not to know. This is Yusif's way, to pretend to be simple. But what will your role be?'

'Don't forget I love him.'

He cut me short.

'If you want to keep his love, you must make him remain a man. If you let him go with the current, he'll become somebody without love, someone who tramples on his feelings in order to get on.'

Rhythmic clapping came from below, and the sound of many voices singing a song. I bitterly regretted having listened to Showki, my heart warned me something terrible would spoil my dreams. The minarets looked about to fall and crush me. The night was an obscure sea.

'Do you want to go and watch them dance?'

'Why do you hate Yusif?' I asked, ignoring his suggestions.

'I don't hate him.'

'I know there's trouble between you.'

'So he told you? But Mabruka's an honourable girl.'

'Because she lives with you?'

He was angry. 'The girl's never said one word against Yusif, despite all he's done. I myself can't tell her my real opinion of him, or she gets angry. She doesn't know what I've just told you. She still considers him her husband's son. I'll tell you the truth: I'm a communist. Yusif knows too. Today he says nothing. Tomorrow he may get me sent to prison. I accept the risk. But with Mabruka there's no risk. She gave us her savings to print pamphlets, without knowing why, without being able to read what we print. She believes in people, she likes to live with people and to have people's respect. She doesn't seek glory and fame. . . . She doesn't want a spotlight on her.'

'You love her?'

'Yes. I love her.'

His voice depressed me. I should like to have heard Yusif say this of me with the same conviction.

'I'm afraid your love for Mabruka has put you against Yusif.'

'That's not the reason . . .'

Suddenly Yusif's voice reached us.

'What are you two up to?'

'Come and join us,' shouted Showki.

Yusif climbed up and asked us what we were doing.

Showki said simply, 'Discussing you.'

Yusif turned in high good humour to Showki. 'I suppose you were abusing me?'

'Naturally.'

'What did he tell you, Samia?'

I was embarrassed. 'He said dreadful things.'

'Briefly,' Showki explained, 'she now knows everything – that I am a communist and that you've sold yourself to Shohdi Pasha, that you can send me to prison. There's nothing she doesn't know.'

'She also knows,' Yusif broke in, 'that far from seeking promotion, I had actually submitted my resignation.'

'But you accepted promotion?'

'To save the paper.'

'No, to do down Muhammad Nagi and to delight Shohdi Pasha!'

'Listen, Showki,' said Yusif firmly, 'The quarrel between those two is not our business. I don't like rumour-mongering.'

Showki looked at me. 'Didn't I tell you he'd play the innocent?' To Yusif he said: 'Why did Shohdi press for your promotion?'

'Be frank,' said Yusif. 'If you think I'm not worthy of the promotion, I'll resign at once.'

'Don't resign. But don't let Shohdi Pasha use you, either.'

'Why don't you want me to resign?'

'Why should you? I haven't.'

Yusif said firmly: 'I'm doing what my conscience tells me. The day I'm asked to do something against my conscience I will resign.'

I whispered in Yusif's ear as Showki left us, 'Why did you come, knowing he'd be here?'

'I'm used to communists. Anyone who doesn't share their ideas is a traitor and a criminal.'

Yusif's thoughts seemed to be elsewhere as he said good night to me outside my building. Tears stood in his eyes.

'I'm afraid I may forget my conscience.'

I touched his hand and blew him a kiss.

'I love you. I want you to work. So you can earn lots of money and marry. Showki loves money so that he can print pamphlets. You love money for my sake.'

He whispered, 'And what reason too?'

'Should there be another?'

'Showki's a communist. What do I want?'

I said firmly: 'You want to be true to yourself. You don't want to deceive. You want to be clean. If anything's crooked, then resign. I'll still love you if you haven't a millieme.'

'Beware of me, Samia.'

'We must try a thing before despairing of it. At worst we can always trundle a hurdy-gurdy through the streets. . . .'

But there was something bitter in the way he laughed.

18

IT WAS ONE OF THOSE RARE CAIRO NIGHTS OF WINTRY rain. People were hurrying home to escape the puddles in the rapidly emptying streets. Yusif and I were in our small flat. The carpenter had just finished the sofa and the two chairs. We had put them in our first room, and the brass bedstead and the straw mattress in the bedroom till the carpenter had finished our proper furniture. The sofa cover was green and I had chosen black for the cushions as it was respectable; bright colours would have given the appearance of a *garçonnière*.

We were silent. Yusif lay with his head on my knee. My fingers played with his hair as I listened to the rain falling outside. The rain drops made my imagination as vivid as one of the films next door. . . . I saw my marriage. . . . Perhaps if I raised the subject of marriage. . . . He would say nothing but would look tenderly and lead me by the hand to the magistrate and marry me. What could be simpler? My mother would be surprised. I thought briefly of witnesses. I might even punish Mabruka by asking Showki to be one – for how it would hurt her to hear of the details of our marriage. Why bother about her? Any two witnesses would do.

I sighed.

I was fed up with home and family. I wanted to shut myself in this tiny house and live with my love.

Once more I sighed.

'What's the matter?' Yusif spoke sleepily.

'Is it raining still?'

'Do you want to go out?'

'No, but I feel depressed . . . like watching a horror film.'

He laughed and relapsed into silence, yawning.

But I wanted our conversation to go on so that it would give me a chance to tell him why I wanted to stay here, why I was fed up with home. This would lead him to propose. I suddenly thought of a strange thing – that Yusif knew nothing of my mother. He never asked me about her. What would he say if he knew the truth?

'I'm hungry,' he said.

I was glad he was not looking at me; otherwise he might have read my thoughts.

He went on, 'I feel too lazy to go out.'

'Tomorrow we'll have a kitchen and I'll cook.'

'We have a house . . .'

'I don't ever want to leave it.'

'Let's live in it from now . . .'

I knew he understood me.

A moment long as years passed. My eyes watched his lips to see what word would come then.

'What do you think?'

'I'm ready to move in now . . .'

'And at home?'

'I'll tell them in the morning.'

He said reflectively, 'But they'll say we're mad.'

I shouted to bring my dream true: 'We are mad!'

He shook his head. 'Shouldn't I tell your mother first?'

'Mother could play the conventional role for a few moments. Then we'd leave her for ever.'

'When would you like to meet her?'

'Tomorrow.'

All the warmth of my heart was in my kiss.

When my mother heard that Yusif's salary was £120 a month, she offered no objection to the match, but did nothing to give the impression either that she was gratified or that she thought him rich. My sister sincerely rejoiced in my good fortune but my mother put on a double act, to emphasize that I was marrying beneath me and that she was only giving her consent because she had abandoned hope of a better son-in-law.

She acted beautifully. She began by talking at length about all our important relations, people I had never heard of before. Half was fantasy, half fact, all woven together in an enchanted tale. Possessions, slaves, aristocrats: a composite picture was woven from acquaintances and transformed into relations and connections. Names were dropped because they had 'Pasha' after them. This glamorous picture of the days of greatness – the days when she had played with the daughter of Rushdi Pasha, when her bosom friend had been another Pasha's niece – overawed Yusif who listened shyly as if aware of his inferior position, as if oblivious of the shabby furniture on which he was sitting. Then came his turn to be interrogated.

'Who are your people?'

'They are from Cairo.'

'But where do they originate?'

In a shy voice he admitted, 'Cairo.'

She looked down her nose.

'You have no family, then?'

'It's all in Cairo.'

'But my daughter told me you were related to Rateb Bey?'

He appealed to me for support.

'Yes, we are.'

'How?'

'Distantly. . . .'

Any outsider might have imagined that after this she would forbid the marriage. Perhaps Yusif thought this. But I smiled to myself thinking how one day I would reveal the whole joke to Yusif.

Reluctantly Mother gave her consent.

'Do as you both wish. You understand each other better than I do.'

Yusif accepted her condescension gratefully and the marriage was fixed for the following Thursday. We would have no party; it would be a family affair.

My mother dried her tears, when Yusif had gone. 'I like that young man. He seems a first-rate boy.'

Her words alarmed me and I decided never to leave her alone with him.

On Tuesday Helmi rang me up to say that he was giving a party for Rossano, the Italian director, who had just arrived. The party was on Thursday. I told him I couldn't come and that in any case I was giving up acting after my marriage. He did not press me but asked if I was going back to my old name? I was not sure what to say.

On Wednesday night I only saw Yusif fleetingly. I had so many things to do. He wanted me to go out with him but I had things to buy for myself and the house. I divided my time between the house and the shops. I thought of inviting Yolanda. I thought of having a wedding party after all, but turned it down. A thousand preoccupations. . . . My appointment for my hair. . . . My dress. . . . New pyjamas for Yusif.

I could not sleep that night and was still awake next morning when I heard my stepfather shouting outside my door:

'Yusif's gone abroad! Yusif's gone abroad!'

He handed me the morning paper.

Under Yusif's picture was the caption:

'Yusif Abdul Hamid, deputy editor of *Al-Ayyam*, has flown to Syria to cover the *coup d'état* of Husni al-Zaim.'

19

MUHAMMAD NAGI RECOGNIZED MY VOICE AND SAID curtly:

'I am busy at the moment. Please call back later.'

'You heard what's happened.'

He sounded annoyed.

'I can't talk to you now; I have a meeting.'

In my despair I cried out; this may have overcome Nagi's fixity of purpose. For he softened. 'All right, you can come to me later in my office.'

When I arrived he did not look up from his papers. I had to come close to his desk for him to notice me. He then stared at me coldly, pointing to the chair in front of his desk as if I was any petitioner come to ask a favour.

His office was large, its walls lined with books. The drawn curtains shut out the light of day. A reading lamp was focused on his desk. There were telephones all round him. His illuminated face reminded me of a doctor my mother had taken me to see as a child. All I could remember was the darkness of the consulting room, the doctor's staring eyes, his rubber gloves, my screams.

Nagi switched on a formal smile, just as I was about to scream.

'Good. . . . What service can I do for you?'

His manner made me want to leave but I could not help muttering:

'Yusif's gone abroad.'

'Yes,' he said calmly, 'he left at five this morning.'

'He didn't tell me.'

'How strange.'

'You knew we were getting married today?'

He lowered his eyes as though reluctant to speak. Then asked coldly:

'You are asking for my advice? Though it would surely be wisest to keep your private affairs to yourself.'

'I had never imagined something like this could happen. I was with him only yesterday. He left me on the clear understanding that we would get married tonight. Everything was arranged. . . . He had spoken to my mother.'

I could not stop myself from weeping.

He stood up and patted me on my shoulder as though I were a child.

'No, no, Samia . . . I thought you were more sensible than this. Tears won't help at all. You must get over this. You're no weakling.'

His words only increased my despair.

'But I love him, and I thought he loved me.'

'Look here, my girl. All you say is true. Nothing would be easier than to raise false hopes till he comes back. That, in fact, was what I had planned. I wanted you to learn about Yusif for yourself. But I can't let you torture yourself and me in this way.'

His meaning was unclear.

I wiped away my tears, eager to know what he meant.

'You may love Yusif and Yusif may love you. But you don't understand each other. If you had understood Yusif, you would have known from the very start that he would never marry you.'

I stared at his face for signs that he was deceiving me. But it showed nothing. I lowered my eyes as he picked up the telephone. He told the operator to put no calls through.

'You remember the night of my party when I told you about the Duke of Windsor who left his throne for the sake of love. I wanted to warn you then. Yusif is not a king emperor. He doesn't have a throne. If Yusif had one, I'm certain he'd abdicate for love . . . as if it was the simplest thing. Yusif's tragedy is that he had no throne. Because of that he will abdicate from his love and search for a throne. Don't blame him.' He banged on his desk. 'This is the throne he's after. If you don't realize that about him, you don't know Yusif at all. He'll forsake you, or me, for the sake of this desk.'

After a moment's silence he said emphatically:

'Recently Yusif has altered. He's not the Yusif you knew at first. He's discovered himself. He's seen the future opening in front of him – responsibility, fame, contacts with ministers and pashas, with people even more important. . . . He can play a role in politics, not love. He has persuaded himself that he can serve the country . . . fight against corruption . . . raise the standard of the labouring masses . . . encourage Egyptian industry. What role can Samia Sami play in all this? Let's talk frankly. Samia Sami is a starlet . . . pretty . . . one of the cinema crowd. Don't get angry! I respect you and I know you could have made an excellent wife for Yusif, and I think Yusif knows that too. But if he married you,' and he banged his desk again, 'he could never sit here. Because the theme of his writing would be undermined. He's going to write about politics. He'll have opponents. They'll throw you in his face . . . "Don't tell us how to put right the country . . . pay attention to what your artiste-wife is up to".'

My fear started again as he spoke of the slanders people would spread. I felt his breath on my cheek as he whispered:

'Don't cry, my dear. I too cried once, for the same reason. You have no idea how much I loved Dalal. I wept with my eagerness to marry her. I was ready to give up everything, disregard rumours and slanders. But she knew the position perfectly. She knew the society in which she was living. That she loved me more than you love Yusif was proved by her refusal to marry me. But she had something else. She had her voice. Just as you, praise God, have your acting.'

I whispered dully, 'But I've given up acting.'

He shouted, 'That's madness. Acting is your future. You must concentrate on it. It is the one thing that can give you significance. Love and marriage are nothing in comparison. You must be as tough as Yusif.'

What could I say? That he did not understand me, that I would not let Yusif go but would run after him, go down on my knees, threaten to kill myself?

The telephone rang and he picked up the receiver. I only paid attention when I heard him say: 'I'm waiting for him to telephone this afternoon from Damascus.'

Suddenly I knew that I hated Yusif. There he was in Damascus, busy, meeting people, telephoning as if I did not exist. He was a swine. I must get my revenge. I must see that it was he who ran after me . . . he'd go down on his knees. I'd make him weep at my cruelty.

'What do you think of what I've told you?'

His smile was calculated to evoke a smile from me.

I managed to say with a smile:

'It's lucky I've found out he's a swine before we married.'

'Not a swine. A swine would not have acted so stupidly. A swine would not have got himself in such a muddle. Running off like that is so childish. . . . But in the long run it's for the best. Think what would have happened if you'd gone through with it. You would have had to sacrifice your talents and become a normal, housebound woman while he got famous. You can perhaps talk of "sacrifice" today. But after a year . . . two years. . . . Love cools off after marriage. Life turns into a boring routine. He'd leave you alone so much of the time, busy with his work, with receptions, with meetings. You would have left him before he left you.'

I fought against his words. The idea of being a housewife enchanted me and dissolved my hatred for Yusif. I forgot my wish for vengeance.

'I still love him.'

'What nonsense! Is he your first love? Will he be your last? Love, my young woman, recurs. Tomorrow you'll find somebody else and will laugh when you think you once wept for love.'

This was not the comfort I had sought.

As he took me to the door, he said, 'Regard me as a friend. Telephone me when you like. I want you to be the same merry creature you used to be. . . .'

When I got home, mother told me acidly, 'You'll go to Helmi's party tonight.' Since Yusif had left me she was in command.

'When he gets back, you'll go to his office and take your shoe to him . . .

'I'll find you a far better husband . . .

'We'll get a lawyer to demand damages . . .

'That paper is run by rogues. We'll stop taking it. . . .'

I listened submissively till my submissiveness angered her. She was angrier with me than with Yusif.

20

HELMI WELCOMED ME TO HIS PARTY SHOWING A MASK of tender concern.

'I can't think how Yusif could have done such a thing . . . what a caddish trick! But forget all that and meet Rossano.' He glanced at me as though afraid I might do something that would disgrace him.

The room was full of faces I recognized from the Studios. Rossano stood near the window with Huda Murad. He was at least fifty-five, with white hair and many wrinkles in his puffy red face. He wore a blue suit and a white tie. His eyes were sly.

His first remark was to ask me in French if I would accept him as a husband.

'*Bien sûr.*'

'*Mais je suis vieux et tu es jeune?*'

He patted his pot belly: how I could consent to marry such an old man? I was in no spirit for such badinage. But he began to bait me for not answering, implying that our work together depended on my answering his riddle. Huda Murad's sarcastic laugh was the first of many; I felt desperate. Helmi handed me a glass of whisky, whispering harshly: 'Be on your mettle. He's testing you for wit. . . . Try to sparkle.'

Rossano's shrewd eyes saw through my forced smile.

'*Tu dois aimer un autre, un jeune . . .*'

I wanted to escape at any price: I thought of Yusif and his tender voice.

Rossano asked if I was an actress, then shouted to the room: 'She's nothing but a schoolgirl!'

Helmi hissed at me in Arabic: 'See the joke, cheer up! . . . What's wrong with you?'

Rossano was suspicious. What had Helmi told me?

Helmi said in his bad French: 'I told her to speak.'

Rossano made it brutally clear that he'd hoped for something better. He began to gesticulate, miming my resemblance to someone loaded down with lead. Or someone in handcuffs. I would never act until I had broken free. . . . He then changed his tack. What was my weight? Fifty-six kilos I replied. He threw up his hands! I must lose six . . . from here . . . from there . . .

Normally these jokes would not have upset me.

I no longer heard what Rossano said.

My eyes searched for Yusif with an insane hope. Surely he would ask for me? Perhaps he had telephoned from Syria.

At that moment Anwar Sami arrived with a couple of girls. Pushing them into the crowd, he shouted to me: 'Stay where you are . . . I'm coming back.'

The two girls were introduced to Rossano. It mattered nothing to me that Rossano was now advising my potential rivals to reduce.

Anwar came over to me and made me sit down in a chair next to him.

He shook his head mockingly.

'You've only drunk two whiskies? You need a bottle. . . . Clever people are always falling. . . . Why let such an idiot get the better of you? If only you'd listened to Papa's warning.'

I was in no mood to be teased.

But he insisted that he was not teasing: he insisted that I tell him everything.

'We had arranged to get married today; then he left for Syria.'

He reacted in theatrical tones:

'The base fellow! . . . I will slay him. O ministers of grace, O thunder of Heaven, wreak your wrath on this rogue!'

He laughed. 'But I'm glad he showed you the truth of my words. He'll cure your silly little head of the idea that there's anything called love. If you'd told me you'd won a million in a lottery, I might have believed you. When you told me you found eternal love . . . no, no, that's a fairy tale.' He changed his tone. 'Did Rossano see you?'

'Yes, and he didn't like me. He said I was too fat, and as wooden as a schoolgirl.'

'Don't worry. You'll get the part.'

As if he was playing a love role, he put his glass against his heart and swore: 'My beloved Samia . . . I know that tonight you want to get drunk and to forget . . . it'll be the same tomorrow . . . but at last you'll have to forget . . . and that will be the time for us to meet. I'll then give you a test to see if you've forgotten.'

'You'll help me forget?'

'I'm an expert in that art. Didn't you know?'

I drank a lot, now laughing, now crying. Anwar stayed with me the whole evening. When I laughed, he cried. When I cried, he laughed. We put on a terrific act with everyone watching. Helmi suddenly whispered that this was the best role of my life. . . . Rossano had been impressed; he was now convinced I should play the part.

After that, all I remember is leaving with Anwar and reaching a huge garage. Where were we? We had arrived. But where? Home, he said. Yet it wasn't my home in Giza. I was hardly conscious as he took me to his flat.

In the morning when I woke up I was at home. Fragments of the night whirled in my head and I smiled. And then I wept, for I remembered Yusif.

I scanned *Al-Ayyam* for news of him. I saw a headline . . .

'After I returned from Damascus . . .'

He was back. All I wanted to know was when he got back . . . yesterday . . . a week ago. How long had he been in Cairo without contacting me?

The telephone rang.

I heard his voice. He sounded triumphant.

But before he had said, 'Hallo, my dear,' I replaced the receiver and let him try to contact me for a week. I longed for his voice until I heard it, when I would refuse to listen. I told my mother that if he rang she was to say that I was out.

I had begun to feel calmer and to understand myself more. I realized that he meant more to me than my dignity and that after a time I would relent.

As I came out of the hairdresser's one day, I saw him standing on the pavement. I walked quickly away. He walked beside me and I turned on him angrily. His face was pale; he looked as though he had not slept or eaten for months.

'Samia, please . . .'

I raised my voice and he looked afraid.

I wanted to cross to the other pavement and stepped into the road. Before I knew what was happening, I was thrown to the ground; my knee and shoulder seemed on fire; a bicycle was lying on the tarmac, beside it a youth in working clothes. I was half-conscious. Yusif's face loomed at me. I felt his hands dragging me to my feet. Automatically I rubbed the dust from my dress. Blood was on my knee. Followed by the stares and voices of bystanders, Yusif led me to a chemist's where I tidied my hair and the chemist put disinfectant on my cut.

We took a taxi to our little flat. We went upstairs in silence. I tidied myself in the bathroom and then joined Yusif in the sitting-room. He took my hand and covered it with kisses; at the same time, despite all I said to calm him, he sobbed with grief.

'Stop, please stop crying.'

'I can't live without you, Samia.'

His words banished my torment, my tiredness; my pain and sorrows all dissolved.

'I want to confess everything.'

There was no need for him to confess. It was enough for me that the bad time was over. I did not want him to spoil our present moment.

But with childish entreaty he said: 'I can't rest till I tell you.' He raised his eyes shyly. 'I want your help. I'm afraid, Samia . . . I feel I am a coward. Not just a coward . . . evil.'

I cut him short.

'I've forgiven you. I don't want to hear.'

It was as though he had not heard.

'Wednesday, the day I saw you last, I heard that I had to

leave next morning for Damascus. I knew it was wrong. Muhammad Nagi said if I covered the Syrian *coup* it would establish my reputation as a writer on politics. Everyone's eyes were on Syria. I accepted with thanks – though I knew we were getting married next day. I wanted to ask for a postponement. But I couldn't.

'I could not understand what had induced me to accept so glibly.

'I think I wanted to escape. I was afraid of the responsibility of marriage. I want to show myself to you as I am, with all my weakness.

'I can't last one day without you – I will marry you. But I must cure myself. And you can help me.

'You know what put me off marriage?

'The day my mother died and left my father behind taught me there's something wrong with this world. Two people are in love. . . . They marry. . . . They must stay together for ever. The wrong is that one dies first. This is treachery – the one who dies betrays the living. The one who lives betrays the dead. There can be no real love in marriage while there is death, for death is divorce. When my mother died, my father cried, and I cried. I felt I was an orphan, condemned to live alone. From that moment I feared marriage, for I saw the loneliness behind it. Perhaps you'll not yet understand. . . . But I felt it and was afraid.

'When I was older I fell in love with Suad, Midhat's sister. I hoped she might take my mother's place.

'Then she was to marry someone else.

'I remember one morning I left the university to ask for a book I had lent her. I wanted to ask her to leave her fiancé and marry me. She stood there entreatingly.

'"What shall we do?"

'I was afraid to suggest we should get married.

'I left her, walking through the streets in tears. I was only a penniless student. The family would never agree.

'Then my father married Mabruka. I hated marriage. How could he marry my mother – and then a servant?

'I hated and rejected marriage more and more, until I fell in love with you. Then my fear vanished.

'"Don't marry," said Shohdi Pasha. "You're a journalist, you have many responsibilities, and you've still not made your mark. You must work night and day so that in the future you can be editor."

'I disregarded his advice. I was determined to marry. And I was happy, for I had overcome my fear. Being editor was not important. I was ready to give up all.

'Then came the question of going to Syria . . .

'I wanted to tell you that night but I couldn't.

'I wanted to explain myself – but was afraid you might not understand. So, like any coward, I ran away.'

He raised his eyes, filled with tears.

'Samia, let's get married now.'

'No.'

His confession had left me trembling; it had freed me from love. I did not trust the innocence in his eyes. I did not trust his frankness. I did not believe in the motives he confessed. I was sure he would betray me. He could so easily use Shohdi Pasha as an excuse. I remembered what Nagi had said about Yusif's ambition. Yusif, I now knew, was a truthful liar, an honest hypocrite.

'You don't really want to marry me,' I shouted.

'I love you, Samia.'

'I love you, too. But there's no need for us to lie or talk of marriage.'

'Don't leave me, Samia. Give me a chance to prove it.'

I said bitterly: 'You had your chance.'

'Give me a chance to respect myself.'

'What do you want? For us to be together? Enough, you love me and I love you. No need to talk of marriage. . . .'

My words wounded me as well as degraded me. But they were the only words that soothed me now. I would break myself – but not let him break me. I would refuse marriage – not let him refuse. I would lie to myself – not let him lie.

That night I gave myself to him as a street-girl to her trade.

21

OUR AFFAIR, MADE UP OF UNCERTAINTY AS MUCH AS love, had its ups and downs.

For days, even weeks, all ran smoothly. Then I was the cause of a ridiculous quarrel over Shohdi Pasha. I resented his influence over Yusif. He sulked. Why wouldn't he answer? He answered: Did I want him to be a clown? Yes, I screamed: I wanted to be amused. He said I had changed . . . I said he must take me as I was.

He tried to end the quarrel by kissing me, but I pushed him away; his look of sorrow gave me a secret pleasure.

Did he really love me as I loved him? Or was it only my body that he loved? The more I was with him the more I felt sure his love was only physical. I got bored, tired. I recoiled from his caresses. I refused to let him kiss me.

Then I would feel moments of tenderness and let him embrace me and enjoy my body. Afterwards I would despise myself for having given way.

I found myself sitting in a seductive way, smiling invitingly. He would be roused, but when he came near I would recoil and fight him off with all my strength.

Once he was so excited that he really tried to take me by force.

I slapped him on the face. He was incredulous.

'I don't want to see you any more,' I said, running into the street.

Then once again our love flowed smoothly. It was as though we were both too tired to fight. We had days of calm, days of silliness. But I quickly got bored. I revolted from his love. If he was busy at night, then I must go out, too. I revived my friendship with Yolanda. I went drinking and dancing till the small hours. I met young men and told Yusif in detail how some of these made passes at me. He flew into a rage: he would give me up for ever. Our moods alternated. I would be angry when he was calm; he would be calm when I was angry.

Was I trying to torment him – or to convince myself of his love? I don't know. I had no set plan.

I needed someone to talk to, someone to advise me.

I rang Showki.

We met on the top floor of the 'Americaine'.

He seemed so pleased to see me that he chatted away without asking why I had asked to meet him.

'I want to ask you something, on condition you reply honestly. What do you think of me?'

'You're human. What else did you expect me to say?'

'But I feel I'm hopeless . . . I feel this is everyone's opinion.'

'The fact you fear so, proves you're not . . .'

'I'm tired, Showki. He doesn't want to marry me: but he loves me and I love him. He's treated me well since he came back: but I have been horrible to him.'

He said reflectively: 'Yes, I heard he had run away from marriage.'

Yusif must have told him; and I felt a new contempt for both Yusif and myself.

'What have you decided for the future?'

'He says he still wants to marry me. But I don't believe him.'

He said sadly: 'You've lost your trust in him. . . . What a pity.'

'Something in our relationship is torn . . . it can never be the same again.'

His lips trembled.

'In my opinion, you mustn't leave Yusif as he is. You must help him to overcome his bad points. You must mould him to be the man you want. That's the solution to your problem, too.'

'You think I can do that?'

'Certainly I do.'

'And what will it lead to?'

'That depends on you both.'

I felt a new hope and telephoned Yusif to confirm our

appointment for that evening. But he had too many things to do and despite all my entreaties he would not put off his work to see me. . . . How absurd to think I could mould Yusif to my will. . . . Shohdi Pasha and the newspaper were moulding Yusif. What role could I play? It was Yusif who was moulding me.

We met next day and I blurted out:

'We must get married today . . .'

He smiled: 'But not like this.'

'You told me you wanted to marry.'

'Yes. But not just yet. Something important has cropped up. Everything is in confusion. I would have told you, except that I didn't want to bore you with my work. But to give you an idea: Muhammad Nagi is resigning. He's taking a trip to Europe. He's tired out; he needs a rest. He'll contribute articles; I'll be the editor. When everything's quietened down, then we'll get married.'

'Why not now?'

He took no notice of my question but went on: 'Be sensible, Samia.'

'You're ashamed to marry me! You must either marry me today, or I'm finished with you.'

My ultimatum did not disquiet him. Nor did I cry. I simply slammed the door and left. I would not go back to him.

But I did go back. Three months and five days later. He had become editor. I had become a different being. During our separation I had thrown myself into the world of cinema. I wiped out his memory; I hated him and I hated my heart and body which yearned for him. I repressed all thought of him as I once had of my father.

I was once again Samia Sami the actress . . . the girl men found exciting, the girl destined to be a famous star, to pass her life under a spotlight.

When I contacted Helmi, however, he had bad news about the colour film. Rossano had delusions of grandeur; he insisted on a budget of £150,000; the whole project had collapsed. But I mustn't worry. Rossano wasn't the only fish in the sea. Meanwhile I must be patient.

But I burned to get back into filming.

So I telephoned Anwar.

'So you're still alive?'

'Yes: no thanks to you.'

'You must have seven lives.'

'What news of the film?'

'Which film?'

'The Italian one. Meet me and I'll tell you. See you tonight.'

He sounded suddenly suspicious. 'You're not pulling my leg?'

'No, I must see you.'

He picked me up that evening in his car.

'Where do you want to go?'

'Your flat.'

'My flat?'

'You're afraid?'

'What on earth has happened?' He scrutinized me carefully. 'You're really serious?' His eyes were on fire.

'Yes.'

He put his arm round my waist.

'Honestly, darling, I must confess the truth – you're the most desirable creature I've ever seen.'

BOOK THREE

Muhammad Nagi

I

I AM NAGI, MUHAMMAD NAGI, THE MOST ILLUSTRIOUS journalist and writer in the Arab World. Or so I was.

Now all has changed. My place has been usurped by that specialist in hypocrisy, that pauper genius, Yusif Abdul Hamid al-Suefi. How absurd, that a boy like him should be taken more seriously than Nagi. The world's upside down.

Everything in Egypt today has become absurd. Life is not what it was. Nor is Cairo. They've turned out Farouk and swept the pashas from power. A handful of young officers, with neither experience nor education, have taken over. They know nothing of politics. They don't accept me any more than I accept them. My only hope is that their end is near.

Fortunately they've now made the biggest blunder of their lives. In nationalizing the Suez Canal, they have challenged England and France. In short, they have committed suicide.

Le Monde is talking about the French fleet's preparations at Toulon. Everyone here in Paris says the invasion will start in a few weeks.

This is my chance. Life will go back to being what it was. The faces I knew and that knew me will return. Wise, experienced hands will hold the tiller once again. I'll know how to get my revenge. I won't rest till I see Yusif with a noose round his neck.

Not so hot as yesterday. The Paris autumn has begun. Soon that north wind will blow. '*Le vent du nord emporte les feuilles mortes.*' Or so the song said when I was at the Lido three nights ago with Samia.

Samia is thrilled with Paris. She adores me for bringing her here. Every time she sees something new and fascinating, her love increases.

This morning in the hotel she was asking at the inquiry desk for two tickets for the Casino de Paris. The confident way she said, 'I am Madame Nagi,' we might have been married twenty years. Perhaps she's really happy. She doesn't mind how long we stay away from Cairo. She doesn't want me to be editor of *Al-Ayyam*. She's glad I have nothing to distract me from her. If she knew how wretched I feel.

I haven't spent a lifetime of intrigue and struggle just to become a respectable husband for Samia and a father for Sherif.

The view of the *Champs Elysées* from the window: twelve lines of cars mount to the Etoile; another twelve descend to the Concorde.

These cars alone would be enough to invade Egypt.

That would raise my spirits.

What shall I write to Cairo?

Yusif's letter enrages me. 'My dear master . . .' If he wrote, 'my dear victim', I'd respect him more.

He wants an urgent rapportage on the situation here. Suppose I let my pen write freely: Situation excellent . . . I am most optimistic . . . a matter of days and the British and French will invade Egypt and free us from the rule of trash.

He would not publish one word. He would put my article in an envelope and send it to them; they would cut off my funds. Samia needs lots of money. She never stops buying. She may act as though she has no past, as though she's forgotten the days of the cinema and her love for Yusif, but I must be on my guard. I must test her. I must make sure she isn't still thinking of Yusif.

What shall I write?

If I attack the French, how shall I fare when they win?

Best not to commit myself. I'll cable Yusif that I'm ill. He must send me money urgently for treatment.

I've still got two hours till I meet Samia and Sherif at Fouquet's. We'll lunch at the Coq Hardi. Samia will be delighted by the way the *maître d'hotel* will greet us. M. Charles will tell her about his famous patrons. She will see the porcelain cocks in the bar, the framed dollar which Eisenhower left as a tip when he was Allied Commander-in-Chief. I'll order *canard à l'orange*. She'll like that. . . . I want to display the marvels I can conjure, the surprises I can plan for every minute. Paris is at my finger-tips. I want her to be ashamed every time she compares me with Yusif.

I am Muhammad Nagi: the real man. Everything by me must be perfect, luxurious. My clothes and my neckties, my thoughts, my prose style, my food and my manners. . . . I can bear nothing cheap or mediocre.

Yet they prefer Yusif to me?

An aristocrat, a reactionary, that's what they call me in their stale clichés.

They have no idea how I built myself up, how I slaved to become what they denounce. I escaped from poverty and became rich. I escaped from being a peasant to become a *bey*. They now speak as though I had blue blood! I escaped from obscurity. . . .

Do you understand, you fools?

I escaped. Through my own efforts I escaped and pushed to the top. Then you had to come and ruin me. But the day will come when I'll trample on you.

'Reception? I want to send a cable.'

'The address?'

'*Al-Ayyam*, Cairo. . . . Suddenly taken ill send five hundred pounds medical treatment salutations Nagi.'

They'll be worried. But what matters is that they send the money. Yusif can work wonders. Lucky I left him the editorship during this crisis. He knows how to get round them. If he hadn't been there, they'd have gaoled me. Who would have thought I should be beholden to Yusif? Judgement Day would be better than what we're going through. If I was in Eden's shoes or Mollet's I wouldn't hesitate. I'd drop an atom bomb on Cairo.

I liked what Akram Bey said at the Embassy: 'These communist agents now ruling Egypt . . . they want to ruin everyone of good family . . . what do they mean by Positive Neutrality and Arab Nationalism?' Others answered. I said nothing. Some of them were probably Nasser's spies?

Akram noticed my silence. 'You are our expert, Nagi Bey. No one could explain such things to us better than you.'

Akram himself might be an agent.

I began a long-winded speech about neutralism so that if anyone received a report, it would be a good one.

Before we left the Embassy, Akram whispered:

'Between us two, do you believe all you were saying?'

I whispered back: 'Take me as you find me, please.'

'I feel for you,' he said sympathetically. 'But cheer up, good news is round the corner.'

On our way back to Claridge's, Samia noticed I was depressed.

'Don't let's see any more Egyptians. We came here to enjoy ourselves.'

But she doesn't see my critical position, my tragedy. She knows nothing of politics. I suppose that's why I trust her as I do. All she knows is I'm the great Muhammad Nagi who can entertain her every moment. This thought makes me relax. I can forget myself for a while.

I must get dressed so as to be on time. I mustn't leave the hotel too much, though. Otherwise Cairo might guess I am shamming.

How can I tell Samia all this without confessing my weakness and anxiety? As she believes everything I say, I'll persuade her that Sherif is sick.

Darling Samia. . . .

Does she return even half my love? She's so young, hardly more than twenty. I'm almost sixty. I can't keep this act up for ever. One day she'll see through me and leave me.

England and France must win the coming struggle so that I can go back in triumph.

That will bind Samia to me.

I mustn't leave the room unlocked. Samia's jewels are in the wardrobe. She refused to deposit them in the hotel safe. She laughed carelessly, 'If they're stolen, we'll buy new ones.'

Better deposit the jewels myself. I can always scold her for leaving the key in the bathroom. She behaves like a little girl who needs a nurse.

So Muhammad Nagi has turned children's nurse!

Sherif. That child can make an idiot of me. He's all I have left. But I don't have to act in front of him. I can be myself. For his sake I put up with every humiliation, for him I smile at Shohdi Pasha. In this way they'll leave me my share in the paper for Sherif to inherit.

If it hadn't been for Sherif I wouldn't have married.

'I would like to deposit these jewels in your safe.'

'Certainly, m'sieur.'

'They're not many, as you see.'

'But they're valuable, sir. Here's your receipt. Always at your service, sir.'

It's cold. Clouds have formed. It might be wiser to postpone our lunch at the Coq Hardi. Unless she insists. I must look after my health. I must have a check-up. Is there no way to bring back youth?

A young man walks with his arm round a girl. . . . How beautiful youth now seems! . . . Mine vanished without my enjoying it. An employee in the publications department of the Treasury. . . . What days! A tarbush on my head, my moustache my embellishment – what a fool I was! If Samia saw me as I was then, how she would laugh. . . .

There's a photo of me with Huriya Ibrahim.

She was the most famous dancer of her day and immensely fat. How could I have loved all that bulk and pulp? I must have still been a peasant; I loved plump women.

When people see me with Samia, what do they think, that she's my wife – or my daughter? I don't care; all that matters is what she thinks.

Is it getting cold, or am I old and tired?

Not far to Fouquet's. I'll walk faster.

In the old days, I could wander for hours in the Champs Elysées and then return to Claridge's late at night, without fatigue.

Once when I returned alone, I remember the *chasseur*'s surprise. . . .

Those were the days!

If only I could be young again for one week, to show Samia what I was then.

Here's Fouquet's. I'll sit near the door. She's not here yet. 'A dry Martini, please.'

The first Martini Samia ever drank was at my house, that night Yusif brought her to my party. She loved the Martinis, she said, but not the party; she felt that the guests were laughing at her; she was angry with me for attacking Yusif. This made me jealous.

'You really loved Yusif?'

'Of course I loved him.'

'And now?'

'Naturally not.'

'Why naturally?'

'It was like a dream. I tell myself it wasn't real. Or if it was real, it was long ago.'

'You still love him,' I said sadly.

She denied it, quietly. 'By God, no, it's finished. He's no longer the same person.'

'That's true.'

'And I'm no longer the same, either.'

'And after that,' I asked, 'who did you go with?'

She said flatly: 'No one.'

'But you must have done something.'

'No, I just sat.'

'Then why didn't you contact me?'

'Why should I?'

'Well, you've contacted me now. . . .'

'I suddenly thought of you. You're like my father.'

Angry, I laughed: 'Thank you.'

She burst out: 'But that's why I love you.'

I did not know what she meant, but when I kissed her and she yielded, she kept repeating, 'I love you, I love you,' adding in her silly way, 'because you're like my father.' This despite our affair.

Then I went to Europe several times. Every time I left she would weep, then weep again with joy, when I came back, loaded with presents. I forgot her from the moment the plane left Cairo till the moment I bought them. But when I got back to Cairo, she was the only one to hand.

Unbearable to go to the paper and find Yusif sitting at my desk. The same gossip, repeated day after day, eyes gloating at me wherever I went – hypocrites . . . liars.

I'd drink whisky till I got drunk . . . or smoke hashish . . . or spend the night with Samia. We'd meet at my flat, drink vintage wines, make love. After some months she became pregnant.

'You must get rid of it,' I told her sternly.

'No.'

'Don't be a fool.'

'It's my child.'

'Who will you claim as father?'

'Don't worry. I'll not involve you.'

'Then your family will kill you.'

She laughed. 'My family? They go their ways, I go mine.'

I threw her out.

Then rang her up a week later.

'Have you done what I told you?'

'No.'

The days without her had maddened me. Instead of whisky and hashish, I found I was addicted to Samia.

When I married her she was in her third month.

'*Maître*, another Martini.'

She's arrived. Sherif is looking around amazed. Ah, now she's seen me. She points me out to Sherif. The child smiles, then opens his arms and runs towards me.

'Was I late?'

'No, darling. You are exactly on time.'

'Sherif was playing the fool in Lafayette. He got between a woman's legs so that she almost died of laughter. "Madame, look after your child," she warned me. "I have no objection to him as a lover."'

185

How lovely she is. Will the day come when she takes a lover? Will she betray me? I'm afraid.

If she was ill . . . if she was paralysed and could not move . . . then she would die before her love grew cold.

What am I thinking? I'm wandering. . . .

'Why is the boy so flushed?'

'He walked a lot.'

'Come here, child. . . . Samia, he's feverish.'

She believes my lie, falls in with my suggestion.

'Let's go back to the hotel. We'll have lunch there.'

'Shall we fetch the doctor?'

'If he doesn't improve.'

'No, we should fetch one now.'

I agree.

I have found your weak points. Every time I see you glorying in your youth and beauty, I can get at you through your child.

Forgive me. I do this because I love you.

We go to the Casino de Paris after all. I can't bear to see her bored in our hotel bedroom.

'I thought it would be a cabaret, like the Lido.'

Are her thoughts on the cinema? She hasn't mentioned actors since we got married.

'Muhammad, someone's waving to you.'

Shukri Musa, the biggest gossip in the world. I'll intercept him. I don't want to introduce Samia.

'Hallo, Nagi Bey!'

'*Bon soir*, Shukri.'

'I swear I was just thinking of you. We were at the Café de la Paix with some of our friends. . . . What stinking times these are! They are letting Yusif write nonsense. All doubletalk.'

All I can do is shake my head and smile.

'I can't understand why they trust that boy. You know the scandal about Riri?'

'No?'

'Impossible, Nagi Bey! The rumour's all over Cairo. One of them . . . a friend of ours . . . swore that he paid her a pound. She got drunk. She began to boast that Yusif was her husband's son.'

Riri?

Is that Mabruka?

God must be avenging me in his own way. Smugly I tell him not to believe rumours.

'But I'm sure it's true, Muhammad.'

'How can you be?'

'Everyone knows it's true.'

Perhaps I can profit from this tale. There's more than one way I can use Mabruka or Riri to ruin Yusif's reputation.

2

IF I SWITCH ON THE LIGHT IT WILL WAKEN SAMIA.

She wakes in the morning fresh and merry while I feel slothful and depressed. Sleeping-pills have no effect. Shall I wake her and tell her I am ill?

'Samia?'

She doesn't hear. The sleep of youth.

And I . . a sleepless husk.

What's the time? I'm imprisoned in dark.

What are those sounds . . . firing in the street . . . a shout far off. . . . What's going on in the Champs Elysées?

I turn on the light. It's two-thirty.

Neither the lights nor the firing have woken her. I must find out what's happened. I'll go downstairs. But what if I catch cold? I'm a journalist. I can write as an eye-witness: 'The Champs Elysées: shots in the small hours.'

'Hallo . . . Hallo . . . Pierre . . . what's going on? I heard firing.'

'Something terrible, sir.'

'What's happened?'

'A moment, sir. Madeleine has fainted.'

Pierre sounds terrified. He has hung up on me. I must go downstairs. I'm not too old, my days aren't quite over. I can still get hold of news. I should like Samia to see me at work, leaving her in the middle of the night to track down crime. That will show her I'm still young. She's excited by mysteries like all young people. I've almost finished dressing and she's not stirred. I'll bang the wardrobe door.

She rubs her eyes in surprise.

'What's happened, Muhammad?'

'Nothing to worry about.'

'Why are you dressing? What time is it?'

She sits up in bed and notices it's not yet day. Her surprise is just what I wanted. I'll speak calmly, matter-of-factly.

'Nothing's happened. There was firing in the streets a little earlier.'

'Firing, and you're going down?'

She screams.

'I must find out what's happened.'

'What's it to do with you?'

I take no notice.

'Muhammad, don't go down.'

She gets out of bed and rushes to stop me.

I try to calm her, telling her she'll waken Sherif.

I must play my part firmly.

'Listen: this is work, and I'm used to it. I was there when Ahmed Maher was shot. Right beside him. I could easily have stopped a bullet; our job's like that.'

'But you're not a young reporter.'

'In our job there are no young or old. What a boy of twenty does, I must do.'

I shut the door firmly, afraid she may try and rush out after me in her flimsy nightdress. No, she won't do that. But she'll not sleep any more tonight. She won't be merry and bright this morning.

The foyer is packed with street-girls, the pretty creatures who stand all night outside the hotel.

The girls and Pierre surround Madeleine. They look up at me with surprise.

'Oh, Mr Nagi, why have you come down? So sorry you've been disturbed.'

'What happened, Pierre?'

Madeleine trembles, and Pierre looks from me to her. No one wants to answer me.

Something dangerous must have happened.

Madeleine's eyes are now open and her lips are moving.

'They killed him, they killed him in front of me. He was whistling *La vie en rose*, his hands in his pockets. They suddenly came . . . the swine . . . the police . . . *merde*. . . . Their search-lights caught him. He jumped, ran a few paces, then . . . the beasts . . .'

Madeleine stopped. Pierre said: 'They took the corpse with them. . . . They took him for an Algerian.'

A scoop!

'Was he an Algerian?'

'No, Mr Nagi, he was French.'

My scoop is punctured.

I want to see what has happened. There may be blood still on the pavement. But I've left my coat upstairs. I'll catch cold. Or the police may open fire. . . . The street girls are looking at me. They've seen me so often coming back with Samia. Their clothes are elegant. They stink of perfume and sweat. They look aggrieved: Why have you brought your wife with you, foreigner? If you'd been alone, we could have passed the night together. We could take thousands of francs off you. Can't you get rid of your wife for one evening? We'll give you a ten per cent reduction.

One of them now approaches me.

'Alone tonight, m'sieur?'

'No, my wife's upstairs waiting.'

'I've got a car. We can go wherever you like.'

'Another night.'

'Ten thousand francs.'

'Another night.'

Who knows if there'll be one? This place is dangerous. Firing in the Champs Elysées. There's no place for love!

'If you change your mind,' she says, 'I'll be standing by the door. It'll either be you or a bullet. . . .'

She is like myself. Either bombs on Cairo will destroy my enemies, or I'll wait. She waits outside Claridge's; I wait in a bedroom. Bullets . . .

'Pierre, could I trouble you for a bottle of Evian?'

'I'll fetch it at once, sir. Here or in your room?'

'I'll sit here.'

Bullets, bullets . . .

A pharaonic foyer; Parliament, Cairo. Wartime. Ahmed Maher passes through – squat physique, broad, burly face, sharp, shrewd eyes. . . . A lawyer approaches, in his eyes a strange glint. Ahmed Maher smiles. His hand in the air. A gun fires. His body slumps, his proffered hand clutches his heart; the fat, open face shrinks; the squat body crumples on the floor. A scoop. I am an eye-witness. Our circulation will soar tomorrow. Shohdi Pasha has one enemy the less. A new Prime Minister, new manœuvres. New soundings. I must get busy.

Before I write one word I consult Shohdi Pasha.

'My opinion? The country's going to the dogs. It's a mad kindergarten.'

'But how shall we treat the story? You've never been a friend of Ahmed Maher.'

His answer surprises me.

'Muhammad, now's not the time for friends, or enemies. We're all in danger. Give them a chance and these kids will ruin Egypt. Public opinion must be worked up against terrorists. Gaol for every troublemaker! Education's valueless; everyone who can write his name thinks he can be a political leader.'

Excited, afraid, Shohdi Pasha for once has lost his self-control. This is fun.

'Pasha, I want your calm opinion. After you've considered the matter from all angles.'

'I know what I'm talking about,' he retorts. 'Now's no time

for intrigues. This thing is bigger than all of us. Let anyone come to power – foe or friend – and I'll support him, provided he rids us of these criminals. The country's being ruined by trash . . . Communists . . . Muslim Brothers . . . Socialists . . . Nationalists. They're all paupers with nothing to lose. But we, we have everything to lose.'

'Your bottle of Evian, sir.'

I'll drink one glass and go up to her. Maybe she's crying. I prefer that, to having her sprightly as on a honeymoon. I'm not a young stallion to gratify her till morning. If she's ill or anxious, she'll be less eager. I can't bear to fail. It will prove that I am old. Geriatric injections are no use. Hormones, they're useless, too, like monkey glands, bull's glands. Professor Couvé is in Zurich.

'All I can do, sir, is help keep you as you are. But to bring back your youth. . . .' The eyes of the Professor twinkle. 'Perhaps we're on the verge of discovering something. In a few years' time . . .'

I failed with Souraya, but that was different. I was afraid Shohdi Pasha might catch us in the act. Souraya was drunk; I was drunk – on gin and Coca-Cola. The scene was magical. A bonfire on a Pacific beach. Tongues of flame flickering against the sand and the waves. Those were the days. . . .

Shohdi Pasha had said: 'Souraya wants to stay in Hollywood. Keep an eye on her. I'm going to Washington for two days. Then Minneapolis. I'll let you know whether to meet me in New York or St Louis.'

When we went to the airport to see him off, a technical hitch delayed the plane till 8 p.m.

When we went home Souraya said, 'I don't trust planes.'

'They'll have put it right.'

She laughed. 'Once, at Geneva, I saw the Pasha's plane take off. I went home and he walked in soon after.'

A short silence. 'Where are you taking me tonight?'

'I'm under your orders.'

She laughed again.

'Take me somewhere you've learnt about from your American girl-friends.'

No need for me to act in front of her. I took her to a bar called Minoni on the beach. Silvery surface of the sea . . . darkness inside the bar. . . . Gin and Coca-Cola . . .

'I want you to tell me about Dalal.'

They're all the same. Women hear about our affairs; they're eager for details. They feed their fantasies, they dream of being like Dalal, mad and free. I have become an expert in telling the story to such women. I know how to arouse them, make them jealous.

'How can you love her and deceive her?'

'Perish the thought!'

'Then what are you doing here now?'

I was flattered. She began to play with my hand and stroke my hair. We left the bar. The fire was gleaming on the sand. I drove. She clung to me. I put my arm round her. She kissed me on the cheek. In the hotel lift she whispered, 'You'll come to me?'

'In five minutes.'

She was waiting for me in bed. As I stepped into the room I remembered Shohdi Pasha and the plane. Could what had happened once, happen again? Was this a premonition?

As I kissed her, despite all my efforts, my mind was full of the plane. I was frightened by any sound, a car, a door. She pushed me from her crossly.

I tried to apologize.

'You're too used to whores?' she said.

I retreated to my own room. After a few minutes the telephone rang.

'Asleep?'

'No.'

'Afraid?'

'Yes.'

'Then I'll come to you.'

Souraya had been handsome in the cold, Turkish war. Today her face is wrinkled and puffy. Perhaps Yusif's flirting with her now? She must be fifty. Hardly Yusif's line.

When I had first made love to Souraya I felt triumphant.

'Souraya, the Pasha must attend my party.'

'Yes, darling.'

'Souraya, the Pasha takes no interest in the paper. Talk to him . . . criticize me . . . say you find it dull. Say it needs more rapportage from abroad.'

'Won't he get cross with you?'

'I want him to. I want him to get interested. I want him to dip into his pocket.'

How will Yusif handle Shohdi?

I was the expert at handling people. I can't understand how this weak boy outwitted me.

'M'sieur Nagi, the telephone.'

'Who is it?'

'Madame.'

'Tell her I'm coming up.'

'Are you mad, Muhammad?' Souraya had scolded. 'You really mean to marry a film extra?'

'What else can I do?'

'Muhammad Nagi . . . the hard to please . . . ends his life by marrying an actress.'

I shall walk in and find her weeping. I wish I had gone with the woman at the door. Ten thousand francs. . . . If she'd smiled nicely, I'd have made it twenty.

'Muhammad, how could you leave me alone . . . I was so afraid for you.'

'I'm back now.'

'I was crying. Fancy braving gunfire in the middle of the night . . . What happened?'

'The police shot someone.'

'Why?'

'They took him for an Algerian.'

I can't sleep. Tomorrow I'll write about the shooting.

No, first I must write to Hamdi.

My dear Hamdi . . . Do you remember the woman I got you to ask about, Mabruka, the wife of Yusif's father? I want you to contact her again. I've heard she now calls herself Riri. Pay her whatever she asks but get her to bring an action against Yusif . . . for maintenance.

Can I rely on Hamdi? Faithful in the old days. Has he changed, too? Can I risk writing?

My dear Hamdi. . . . Go to Mabruka. . . . Force her to take her revenge. This is our chance. . . . My chance. . . . Why hasn't she thought of doing this herself? She's ignorant. Perhaps afraid. She needs pushing. A court case will disgrace Yusif. Cairo and Paris are talking already. Such gossip can finish him. *My dear Hamdi.* . . . I want to sleep.

3

'I'M GOING TO SEE AKRAM BEY.'

'But you promised to stay with me!'

She really looks ill: pallid, complains of headache. She and Sherif are both ill. Their symptoms make me feel better.

'Tomorrow he's flying to Cairo and I have something urgent to discuss.'

'Didn't you tell me you wanted to avoid Egyptians?'

'But this is business.'

She looks anxious.

'What secrets are you going to discuss with Akram Bey?'

Only shock tactics can silence her.

'If you must know – politics. This is the supreme chance for us to escape from our present misery. Everything goes to show that the English and the French are planning war. The Users Association will send a ship through the Canal, then follow it up with a military landing. You think I can sit with my head in my hands till they hand us back our country? We too must get busy, Samia. You see this letter? There are people waiting for it in Cairo. Akram will deliver it. I have made my arrangements. The day the attack starts, I'll be in the fight.'

My tactics are working.

'Don't try to stop me. Either back me up, or stay silent. You didn't marry an ordinary husband. I am a politician from the top of my head to my toes. I can't enjoy myself in Paris while I see disaster falling on Egypt.'

My appointment with Akram is at the Crazy Horse, the best place for nudes. I'll make war in the Crazy Horse. I will prepare my *coup* while watching the strip-tease. You are absurd, Muhammad. . . . Your cowardly plot against Yusif. . . . Why not contact the French authorities in earnest, or go to England? You have friends in the Commons. You must do something.

'Taxi! *Au Crazy Horse, s'il vous plaît.*'

Muhammad Nagi spending his nights in the dives of Paris, how pathetic! Suppose I went back to Claridge's and found a cable from Cairo . . . RETURN IMMEDIATELY WE NEED YOU. The plane no sooner lands, than a car from the Presidency whisks me to the palace. 'We rely on your help, Mr Nagi. There's no one who can do more for our people's morale. A daily article? The country is passing through a critical phase in its history. Every word from you will help to rouse it.' 'Naturally, sir, I am yours to command.' 'I'll read your first article tomorrow?' 'I hope so. But one question, sir. What will my position at the newspaper be?' 'You can make it what you wish.' I'd have to get rid of Yusif. How could I possibly keep him while those rumours are circulating? I'll call an editorial meeting. Of course, I'll say, Yusif's a splendid chap. You all know that I, more than any of you, love him. He's been a son to me; an heir you might say. But sad circumstances compel me. . . . His absence will be temporary, until the country has traversed this crisis. Our need now is for pens the people can trust. For myself, I am confident of Yusif's integrity and patriotism. But how can I tell our readers that Yusif has been maligned? Then I'll drop the name of Riri. There'll be laughs which I'll check. 'This is not a laughing matter; it's a sad predicament for all of us.'

'Muhammad Bey, you may not notice me – but I spotted you at once.'

'Hallo, Akram. Sorry . . .'

'I've booked a table near the stage.'

Somehow, persuade him to take the letter.

The place is packed, the music rowdy, the ceiling low and the people mostly tourists, German and American bags, their eyes on the curtains.

'We can see well here. What'll you drink, Muhammad?'

The brute calls me Muhammad as if we were lifelong friends. I'd like to spit in his face.

'You're really flying tomorrow?'

'Yes, the plane leaves at noon.'

'Why not sit things out here?'

'So you think there'll be war, Muhammad? My money's run out. When are you coming back?'

'I have business here.'

If I went back to the hotel, would I find the cable? No, no one needs me.

The lights dim. The music reaches a climax. The curtains rise on pitch dark. A spotlight fingers the stage. A girl with red hair sits on a bed in her night-dress. She is attractive, more so than Samia. She writhes, yawns; it is hot and the music is fevered. She takes off her night-dress. When Samia's better, I'll bring her here. When she sees these lovely bodies she'll feel inferior. I should prefer her to despise herself – not me. Tomorrow I'll tell her she's cured.

But I am insane, totally insane! If Akram saw what was milling in my head. . . . He fancies he's sitting beside the same, elegant Muhammad Nagi he knew in Cairo.

The brute addressed me.

'Muhammad. . . .' This brunette now taking off her brassiere . . . she's by far the best . . . The music's getting louder. Now a guitar. Old women outnumber the men. Akram's lust is audible. When the show's over, I'll give him the letter.

'This one's attractive, Akram.'

'Madly.'

'Shall we invite her?'

'Whatever you decide.'

'We'll take her to your place?'

'Yes.'

'Telephone my wife . . . tell her we'll be busy till morning.'

Samia's fool enough to believe we can spend a whole night plotting.

'What about this one, Muhammad?'

'Not like the other.'

'But not bad, either.'

'We'll take her too.'

'I've only got sixty thousand francs left – but I've vowed not to take a cent back to Cairo.'

'Don't worry. I'm flush.'

The curtain falls.

'Isn't it odd, Akram, how no one claps?'

'They're embarrassed.'

'*Garçon!* Two double whiskies. With soda. Akram, I've a letter I'd like you to take.'

'An article?'

'No, a private letter for a poor wretch in need of help. To get him a job. He wrote to me. But please drop it in the post the moment you arrive. I think it's most important to be prompt with people like that. Otherwise they think you look down on them.'

He pushes the letter into his pocket. Hamdi should get it the day after tomorrow. I don't like comic turns. They're tedious, they waste time. We came for nudes. This fat comedian isn't even comic.

Hamdi's bright.

This was long ago.

'The rumour is true and not true. Yusif's father married his servant, a girl called Mabruka. She worked for them in their flat in Sharia al-Falaki. She married the old man and had a child by him. In a short time he died. She moved to Bab Zuweyla. . . . Tried to contact Yusif. . . . Even came here. He evaded her. She

197

asked the man at the desk. He came down and met her once.
Then told the man at the desk to throw her out if she came
back.'

'And then?'

'Your Happiness knows who's keeping her now? One of the
illustrators.'

'Which one?'

'Showki Mahmoud.'

I can't possibly bring Samia here. I'm basically conservative.
Better for her to remain ill.

Besides, as an invalid, she's less likely to betray me. I'll kill
her with imaginary symptoms. I'll punish her for every
moment she spent with Yusif. She loved him. Even thought
she knew the story of Mabruka:

'Do you want to hear something peculiar about one of the
men who work for you?'

'Which man?'

'The one who's not a thief.'

I was so sure of Yusif. I never imagined one day he would
rob me of all. When I heard about Mabruka I pitied him. Of
course, I was also pleased to see how weak he was. His father's
wife living in sin with one of his colleagues, and he did nothing!
I could make what I liked of such a coward. Such men make
good servants – easy to dominate once you know their weakness. Yusif could be promoted without danger. Adopt him;
mould him to my purpose: my instrument, my tool . . . I was
stupid. . . .

'Shall we arrange about the girls now?'

'You still want them?'

'It's up to you.'

'I confess I'm in two minds.'

'All right . . . don't let's bother.'

Yes, I'm in two minds. This is my shame. This indecisiveness.
Why can't I banish it?

When I decided to mould Yusif, I didn't hesitate then.

'Yusif, I want to introduce you to Shohdi Pasha. Just as I think of you as my son, I also think of you as one of the most responsible. Your relations with Shohdi Pasha must be excellent.'

He listened shyly.

Later Shohdi Pasha rebuked me.

'Who's that boy you sent me?'

'He's rather pathetic, but good-hearted.'

'You think he'll improve?'

'Just wait a little, Pasha.'

When his first article appeared, Shohdi was pleased.

And I had gained, I thought, a new ally in my struggles with my puppet-master.

'No more whisky. . . . I'm off.'

'The next turn's excellent: the snake dance.'

'You watch it. My love to Cairo. Don't forget the letter.'

I'm the one who's really ill.

All I can do is go back to Samia. To see Samia and Sherif looking ill, will make me feel better. It's cold. But I'll walk. Yet if I catch cold . . . or a car runs into me?

This torment is eternal. Death is my only rest. Dalal spoke the truth.

'And next time, Dalal? Can't you relax a little, darling?'

'I'll rest when I die. I'll leave the world without one regret!'

I'll leave it, Dalal, regretting everything. Death won't give me rest. Unless before I die, I get my revenge and destroy Yusif. Otherwise Samia will go back to him. She'll take Sherif and live with him. Because she loves him still. I don't love her, Dalal. I don't love anyone except you.

'The only thing I want you to do for me. . . . Take care of Tony. If I die, Muhammad, look after Tony.'

'And who'll look after me?'

'You're a fraud.'

It's after midnight and the fraud walks down the Champs Elysées.

199

Half drunk.

Half dead.

Half mad.

Half murderous.

Half dazed.

No. Not dazed. My eyes were open. I was on my guard. I confronted him with Mabruka to humiliate him.

'There's a nasty story, my boy, which I must discuss with you. The staff are talking. The woman with the baby who comes here. . . . She claims it's your brother.'

He interrupted me with shy frankness.

'That woman was my father's wife.'

'I know everything,' I said roughly, 'including that she now lives in sin with Showki Mahmoud.'

He did not break down, but raised his eyes to mine. 'When my father married her, I broke with him and left the house. I have never denied my relationship. I'm not ashamed. If you would like me to tell everyone on the paper, I'm quite willing. After all, many pashas have married their servants.'

'Listen to me, my boy. I'm giving you advice like a father because I love you as a son. You can't possibly become an important editor on this paper while the people you're working with all know that Showki, the illustrator, is keeping your father's wife. I'll have to sack him.'

Meekly he lowered his eyes.

'No, I'll get you to sack him. Then everyone here will appreciate your position.'

'I can't.'

He spoke as though turning a pistol on himself.

'You don't have to say it's because he's living with your father's wife. I've heard the fellow in question is a communist. You can say the secret police consider him dangerous.'

I didn't care tuppence whether Showki was dismissed or not. What I wanted was to show him how much I knew. Despite this he didn't break down, but shamelessly triumphed through weakness. Weakness was his god.

Now, weakness has overcome strength, simplicity has conquered sophistication. Was his secret that he was young and I was old? How did he defeat me?

The girls are mustered in front of Claridge's.

'Hallo . . . M'sieur's alone tonight?'

'No one's asked for me . . .'

'Incredible . . . I'll be your friend for tonight.'

'Only tonight?'

'Every night, if you wish.'

I must decide something. I'm still not dead. I'll spend the whole evening with her, Samia knows I have important business. When I get back in the morning, she'll think I've been plotting revolution.

'What about onion soup at Les Halles?'

'I should be delighted, m'sieur.'

She clutches my arm. She can't believe I've succumbed.

'One moment . . .'

'You're withdrawing your invitation?'

'No, but I'm expecting a cable. I'll just ask . . .'

I'm insane. What cable do I expect? If they do recall me, I shan't go; they might arrest me as I got off the plane. Then I'd be bombed in prison.

Shall I go up to Samia? I'm ill. How could I get entangled with this woman. She's cheap. Ten thousand francs. Muhammad Nagi doesn't pick up street girls.

'Pierre . . . any letters?'

'No, sir.'

'Or cables?'

'No, sir.'

No, no. Of course not. People don't take me seriously. Not even Samia; she still loves Yusif. This woman waiting for me at the door is more straightforward.

'M'sieur, did you find your cable?'

'No.'

'Were you expecting something important?'

'I don't know.'

'You've too much on your mind. I'll help you forget. Taxi! Taxi!'

4

'BUT YOU'VE LEFT HALF YOUR SOUP. . . . DRINK IT BEFORE it gets cold.'

The poor thing's hungry. I'll order her some more food.

'The whisky's given me indigestion. Would you like something else?'

'No, thank you.'

'But the soup's not enough.'

'Oh it's quite enough. Where did you drink whisky?'

'At the Crazy Horse.'

'Bad boy! I didn't know you were interested in nudes.'

She has a sweet smile, her voice is gentle. She's pretty. I'm only now beginning to relax. Away from Samia. Away from Cairo. Away from everything.

'Ah, m'sieur's smiling? At last I've seen you smile.'

'Because you're with me.'

'You're nice. . . . What's your name?'

'Nagi. And yours?'

'Gaby.'

'Gaby . . . you're pretty and very young.'

'Yes, but you're much younger.'

'No need for that sort of talk. . . . I'm not ashamed of being old.'

'I'm not lying. At heart you're younger than I am.'

'You don't know my heart.'

'Oh yes I do. Only very young hearts go to the Crazy Horse. Shall I confess something?'

'What?'

'I bet two of my friends that you were an important man. You are important, aren't you?'

She amuses me. I want to know what she's pictured me.

202

'A maharajah, a pasha?'

'You're getting close.'

She looks delighted.

'Better than pasha?'

'Yes, in my opinion.'

'Then you must be a prince?'

'No.'

'An ex-king?'

'No, I'm a writer. The greatest writer in the Orient.'

In this country they respect writers.

'This is a great honour for me, M'sieur.'

'The honour is mine.'

'My friends will be green with envy when I tell them. Will you write about me?'

'. . . *La reine de Paris.*'

'No one will believe it.'

'What I write, everyone believes.'

'Will you take me with you to your country? I'm ready for anything. It's not every day I meet a man like you.'

'I'll take you with me.'

She's delirious with happiness. Why not take her? I can do anything, love her, marry her, make her the best-paid mannequin in Cairo . . . the best actress. I'll raise her up. I can do it.

'I'll do anything you want.'

With tears in her eyes she leans forward to kiss me. I find it hard not to cry too.

'Pay the bill . . . let's go.'

'Where?'

'To my place, *chéri*. Or have you any other suggestion?'

'I'm under your orders.'

'Naughty boy.'

Where is the taxi winding, through these alarming lanes?

Her lovely body arouses my desire. Her beauty mesmerizes me. She's no ordinary woman. A princess, a *contessa* . . .

The street is deserted. A gloomy old house. An obscure stair, a long stair.

Is this a trap? But what can they take from me – my life?

That would be a blessing. I'm the strongest man in the world. No one can take anything from me. A quick death here would be an ideal ending.

'Wait . . . while I open the door.'

A vast bed in a narrow room, an overpowering smell of stale wood. What on earth brought me here? In the old days I never went to anyone. I never undressed in a strange house. I never slept in a strange bed. They came to me. My house was my sultanate. I never went to the kingdoms of others, the homes of others. They were the ones to go away tired out, sleep in their eyes, alcohol in their heads, swaying with exhaustion. And much I cared as I sat back in comfort, relaxing, stretching, yawning.

'I've a bottle of port. We'll drink it together.'

What will happen next?

But in my house . . . I know who's in the other rooms. The servants . . . Tony . . . I know who can come in. I know . . . I know. . . . But now I don't know anything. The port is pleasant.

There was no beauty like this at the Crazy Horse. And all this beauty is for me . . . for me alone. No one knows. I have at last got something . . . I possess it with my eyes . . . with my hands . . . with my breath.

Her white flesh blinds me. I am suffocating. Where's some air? I'm choking . . . no . . . I must do it.

She looks surprised. Be patient. Sweat's pouring from me. I'm drowning in a sea of sweat.

'What's wrong, *chéri*?'

'Nothing.'

'Ah, you poor boy, wait . . .'

Where's she jumped to?

'What's this?'

'Pyjamas.'

Silk pyjamas. How many men have worn them before me?

'You're dripping with sweat. Put them on so you don't catch cold.'

Her white flesh fills the room like a giant. She comes near me. She caresses me. She kisses me. But it's no good. I'm going to die. O Lord, don't let me down. . . . Her eyes look disappointed.

'You're tired, *chéri*.'

What can I answer?

'Sleep.'

'I don't want to sleep.'

'Sleep. . . . I'll turn out the light. I'll wake you up in the morning.'

I don't want to sleep. I don't want to open my eyes on morning.

'Sleep.'

Once I could endure tiredness. There was a place where I could rest. But now . . . I'm attacked by weariness every moment and there is nowhere I can rest. I'm pursued. Outside they're hunting for me.

'*Pourquoi tu ne dors pas?*'

Don't speak to me. . . . Give me kisses to strike fire from this corpse. She must strike fire from me. Her white flesh trembles. It torments me. My eyes are clouded. My heart beats murderously . . . Boom . . . Boom. . . . It's going to burst. This was how Raouf died. They found his naked body in his *garçonnière*. I must stop. It's no good. It's no good.

'Don't tire yourself, *mon enfant*. I'll be with you always. Try and sleep.'

In the past my strength never let me down. I was sure of myself. I stared them in the eyes, confident, calm, polite, commanding. Nerves of steel. The nerves of a gambler. I lost fortunes without an eyelid's flicker. My brain was a calculating machine. No emotions, no imaginings, no weakness. I'd advance on prepared terrain . . . I'll see you at five . . . I'll see you the day after tomorrow . . . I'll see you at 2 a.m. . . . I fixed time and place. They obeyed. Their voices sagged with desire. I had teeth, stamina, force. I cheated them with emotions. I cheated everyone with the emotions that spilled from my pocketbook, from the very folds of my clothes. I conjured them like a magician. Yet they believed. . . . 'You've a big heart, Muhammad.' 'Muhammad is sincere. . . .' Fools! I don't love anyone.

I believe no one. How easy to take them in. . . . Yusif my boy, your future's in your hands, nobody else's. Take my advice and you'll soon be famous. This girl's not the right wife for you. You'd be crazy to marry someone who goes with half the town. Don't you know about her affair with Anwar Sami?

He shouted:

'I don't believe it.'

'Don't be stupid. Anwar told me every detail.'

'I love her. Even if she went with the whole town, not only Anwar, I'd still marry her.'

'Then I'll say no more. But I must confess I knew her before you did. Nothing happened. . . . But that was thanks to me, not her. I'm afraid she's chasing you to get her own back on me.'

Tears in his eyes, he left my office.

Determined to get her, by whatever strategem, by whatever trick or lie, I changed my policy. To forge a new link between us which Yusif would not suspect, I'd convince her I was giving her advice as a friend, for Yusif's sake. 'Samia, can I trust you. . . . First please forget the past. . . . It's true I flirted with you. I wasn't to blame. . . . But now it's all over. You love Yusif and he loves you. I am now talking about his career. But promise me you'll not tell Yusif I spoke to you. Listen, Samia, Yusif's getting into deep water. . . . I think it's wiser for you to come to the flat. . . . I'll wait for you at five.'

She didn't come.

No, later Yusif came instead, in fury. As if my pet dog barked in my face, or one of my toes assaulted me! Was this slip the beginning of the end? – Yusif became Shohdi Pasha's ally against me.

Only five years ago I turned a great mill of people. I ground people to powder. I kneaded them with ink and paper. I was a baker of men. Some was good bread, some was burnt. Now I've fallen. I've become like other men. I wear the same pyjamas that they wear. I lie inert.

Yusif now turns the mill.

My mother's name was Nafisa.

This naked body lying beside me is called Gaby.

Nafisa.

Gaby.

Old Cairo.

Paris.

Ah. . . . How strange the turnings of this mill.

Sprinkling carts we'd run behind, the hem of our *gallabyas* between our teeth. Uncle Zaki hunted cats and crows to eat them. A depot of donkey-carts in a yard near us. A girl and I, bride and groom, in the yard. Mum, give me a millieme!

I never once called my mother 'Mama'. If she'd heard it, she wouldn't have understood. If she'd understood, she'd have boxed my ears. . . . Saleh, left-half . . . I was afraid of him. My chance came when he had fallen down and I hit him with a stone. His eyebrow was cut. He screamed. Blood got in his eye. I saw the blood. I threw another stone at the same place. His blood flowed on to the pavement. I pushed my fingers into his eyes, then took to my heels.

He came to see me in my office at *Al-Ayyam*. Cringing. Afraid. He wanted my help to get his son a job.

'Of course, Saleh. . . . I'll do all I can.'

He tried hard to see me again.

My mother's in her tomb. So's my father. My first girl-friend is living in a room crammed with children and grand-children. Saleh snores, waiting to go to the coffee-house in the morning and read *Al-Ayyam*. 'Muhammad Nagi, he's my friend. I've known him for ages.' No one believes him. And I'm here on this bed in this narrow room. A tomb, a new style tomb. When I die, the news will rate a line or two. The dog is dead. Muhammad Nagi's dead.

'Look after Tony, Muhammad.'

What did I do with that dog? I don't think she imagined for a moment that I would take care of him. Dalal. The only person in the world who knew my real self.

'Do you love me, Dalal?'

'Are you serious?'

'Dalal . . . you torture me.'

'You're the torturer. You want me to break my heart for someone like you? Do you really think you love me? Shame, Muhammad. Keep those sort of words for children, not for me. I'm Dalal, Muhammad, not one of your dotty admirers. I know you inside out. You're utterly conceited. You've never thought of anyone but yourself. Yet despite your faults, I love you. Real love's not like ours, though.'

'What's wrong with our love?'

'You haven't realized what our love is? It's a contraceptive, something that stops us having children. It's a whisky and soda. It's an untidy bed. Whenever I think of our love I think of my clothes scattered in the bathroom, the shower running. When you sleep, you snore like a jazz band. I lie beside you, wishing I could leave you. But I can't. I want to pray. I can't. Who understands you except me? Who understands me except me? If you were innocent at heart, if you had a heart, I'd talk to you differently. But who are you? You're the most disgusting person I know. Because I know that, you love me.'

The most disgusting person . . .

Also the strongest.

Now I can't do anything, not even disgust.

The last thing I did . . . it was Tony.

'What are you going to do about this dog, Muhammad, when we go abroad?'

'I'll kill it.'

I couldn't bear the dog's presence once Samia had moved in. Each time he looked at me, he started a record in my head: Dalal's songs, her curses, her manias, her love. This dog knew me in my days of power. He came with us to Alexandria in summer, to Aswan in winter. We'd fetch the best doctors in town if he had a tummy-ache. His news and pictures over-shadowed Ministers. Dalal had brought him to me one after-noon. He was tiny, smaller than a cat, white, his eyes were dreamy. He snuffled, yapped, chased his tail, bit at her hands.

'Muhammad, what shall we call him?'

'Tony.'

'Tony?'

'The name of a British officer, a friend of mine; he died at Alamein.'

'I thought of Tarzan. . . .'

She took him in her arms and kissed him.

'Tony . . . Tentony . . . Tonton. . . .'

'You'll make me jealous.'

'He's my real darling; he'll never forget me.'

She was right. After her death, Tony was grief-stricken. His eyes would ask me where she'd gone. I felt that he was the only person who understood me, and whom I understood. Sometimes I felt her spirit had entered his body.

'How will you kill him, Muhammad?'

'With a bullet.'

'Who will kill him?'

'I will.'

'Oh, no! Leave it to the vet.'

But Samia was pleased. She wanted me to kill the dog myself, since he had belonged to Dalal. And I wanted to kill him myself. I wanted to destroy the nightmare whirling in my head. The world had changed, and Egypt with it. People were different, I was different. Tony was a witness left over from the past.

'When will you kill him, Muhammad?'

'Tomorrow morning.'

'Will it hurt?'

'Naturally.'

'Look at him listening. . . . It's almost as though he understood!'

Before breakfast next morning I took my revolver from the drawer, a Browning six-cylinder. I knew it wasn't usual to kill dogs like this. But I did not want anyone's advice; I did not want to learn the right way to kill a dog. I charged the magazine and put the gun in my pocket.

'You'll kill him now, Muhammad?'

'Yes.'

'I'm coming to watch.'

She wanted to see blood. She wanted to watch me kill. I wanted her to watch me.

'Tony . . .'

He waddled towards me, wagging his tail.

His white body seemed gigantic as it loomed before me. If I had waited a moment more, I could not have gone on.

'Tony, come here.'

He loped after me into the garden. By the kitchen door Mansur the cook stood with his mouth open, incredulous. Suleiman almost protested, his eyes in revolt.

I whispered, 'This dog is sick. His time has come.'

Suleiman besought me, 'Please let me have him, your Worship.'

'So that you can neglect him? No, better for him to die while he's still strong.'

Tony raised his two paws and barked. He thought we were playing a game. When I pushed the revolver against his head and he tried to snaffle it, I pulled my hand back and shouted: 'Tony!'

He stood looking at me stupidly, as if apologizing for not understanding the rules.

'Let me do it,' Mansur shouted. 'Sir.'

'No.'

His white body obsessed me. I could almost see each individual hair. His wide, dreamy eyes . . . gazing into space.

Samia shouted: 'Get on with it!'

My hand trembled and I screamed, 'Tony! Tony!'

His white body quietened like a plump cow as he stood in front of me, motionless.

The shot made a loud noise. The bullet pierced his head. Blood spurted out and he gave a yelp. He leapt with the shock. He fell on his feet. He tried to move, but his head slumped. I fired again, and again he leapt, gave a little jump, and lay on the ground. His legs quivered. He tried to get up. He did not want to die, the dirty old thing. I could not shoot again. I pushed him with my foot. He yelped. He opened his eyes, his dreamy eyes, now filled with pain. Stupidly they asked: what was this game we were playing? I pushed his head with my shoe as he lay on the ground, his chest still panting. His tail stirred. His paws moved. He was going to get up again . . . if he did he might attack me, kill me, I aimed.

'Muhammad, enough!'

I almost turned the gun on her, on Mansur, on Suleiman. These bullets were harmless; the game did not kill.

I whispered, 'He won't consent to die.'

He gave a drawn-out groan; his back paws twitched, he shuddered, almost got up, then slumped back. But he was not dead. He would not die. Blood was on the ground; his white body was stained with dust. His gigantic body had shrunk. But he still stirred. If a vet had come, perhaps he could have saved him, could have extracted the bullets and made him well.

I heard voices vague as in dreams.

'Enough, sir, he's dead.'

They were lying. He was not dead. I saw a tremor in his body. His chest moved, his ears twitched.

'He's dead?'

'Yes, sir.'

Was this death? But his body still stirred, like the body of Gaby, whose breath comes and goes.

5

WHO DOES THIS BEAUTIFUL FACE BELONG TO? WHO IS this strange woman?

Where's Samia? What's happened? This bed, this room . . . ah, yesterday night.

What folly have I committed?

This is Gaby. Yes, her name's Gaby. The cheap woman who picked me last night. How dreadful. How can I extricate myself?

'*Bonjour*. What's the time?'

'Ten.'

She's laughing. She has no worries. My body's tired. If I can get through today.

'I'm late.'

'Late for what, *mon petit*?'

'I must get back to the hotel.'

'You're afraid of her?'

'Yes.'

'Oh, look at your face, *mon petit*! It's so funny – the face of a little boy who's not done his home-work. You must be brave. What will you tell her?'

'Don't laugh at me.'

'I'm not laughing at you. But you are afraid.'

'Gaby, *assez*!'

'I don't believe a wonderful man like you can be afraid.'

'A wonderful man?'

'Are you going to take me to your country?'

'I told you that?'

'You've forgotten?'

'No, not forgotten, but . . .'

'But what, *chéri*?'

'I lied to you.'

'You were laughing at me, then?'

'No, just lying.'

'So, you don't want me.'

'Gaby . . . Gaby . . . you don't understand. How can I put it . . . I am like you.'

'Like me?'

'I can't go back.'

'To your wife?'

'No, my country.'

'Why?'

'And I'm not sure if I can go back to my wife, either.'

'M'sieur Nagi, are you crying?'

'Yes, I'm crying.'

'But why?'

'It's all there is left for me. It's all I can do. I've been thrown out of my country, out of my job. I'm useless, just a worthless old man.'

Tears start from her eyes. What's happening? I'm weeping in front of her. Everything's lost. Her dreams, her imaginings, have all collapsed. I have revealed the empty truth. I'm no longer a maharajah or pasha, or prince or an ex-king. No writer, no lover, not even a man. I have failed her in everything. She kisses me, smooths my hair with her hand, caresses me, calls me '*mon petit*'. I don't deserve as much. I'm old, useless, disgusting. My head aches, my eyes seem clouded.

'*Leve toi, mon petit. Assez! Assez!*'

I obey her like a child. She washes my face with eau-de-Cologne. Combs my hair. Takes off the poor pyjamas which for the first time have covered a worn-out body. And the poor bed, it, too, had witnessed my disgrace. I can't look anything in the face. The clothes she helps me to put on – my shirt, my tie, my suit – they are a façade for an unreal man. I'm sick, feverish. How can I get out of here? My legs won't carry me. The ground sways under my feet.

'I'm worn out.'

'Wait for me here . . .'

'No.'

'. . . while I fetch a doctor.'

'No. I must leave. No doctor can help me.'

I must try and walk, try and force this inert body into action. She's so good. She doesn't laugh at me now. Her eyes brim with sympathy but not with love.

'So sorry to have bothered you . . .'

'No need to apologize, *chéri*.'

'I'm sorry I lied to you.'

'It was my fault in reminding you.'

'If we had met five years ago. . . . Only five years.'

'You're my friend now. And tomorrow. And in five years' time.'

I must give her her money.

Her fee. Ten thousand francs. It's not enough. I'll give her twenty. No. Even that doesn't compensate for all she's put up with. It won't make her forget my failure.

'My humble gift, please accept it.'

'Thirty thousand francs. . . . M'sieur, it's too much.'

'Please take it.'

'I won't take anything. For now I know everything, how you're far from your country. You'll need this money.'

'I need you to accept it.'

'I'll accept only what we agreed, ten thousand francs.'

'Gaby, please take it all.'

'I can't. You don't understand me.'

'And you don't understand me. If this was the last money I had in the world, I'd still want you to have it. Only that can give me rest.'

'You alarm me . . .'

'What do you mean?'

'I fear you may be meditating . . .'

'Suicide? No I shan't do that. Take the money.'

'All right. But I'll keep it by me. Perhaps you'll need it one day.'

'I can't find words for your goodness. May I kiss you? No, only your hand. . . .'

'You make me so sad. . . .'

'How strange. You're the only person in the whole world who's sorry for me. No, don't look at me like that. I'm not going to cry any more. You know something? That was the first time I'd ever cried in front of anyone? . . . Do you know what I'm going to do now?'

'What are you going to do?'

'Do? Did I say I was going to do something?'

'Yes, just now . . .'

'I shall do nothing, nothing at all.'

'Are you feeling better now?'

'Yes, yes. . . . I can manage.'

'*Au revoir*. I'll pray for you.'

'You pray?'

'Every Sunday.'

'That is beautiful. Remember me in your prayers always.'

'I will.'

'Now I have found the metaphor I wanted. You're a saint. The saint of Paris.'

'Please, m'sieur . . .'

'Believe me, you're my saint. *Au revoir*.'

'If you want me, I'll be outside Claridge's. I won't recognize you if I see you with her.'

How did I get up these stairs last night? I can hardly go down them. Courage, Muhammad! Don't look down. Don't think of falling. Hold your head up, pretend you're ascending. Brace up. Stop counting the stairs. A piano plays in this flat sadly, like a funeral. Its tune strums in my heart. It upsets me. The staircase is dingy or is it my eyes? Keep going, Muhammad. Breathe deeply. Keep moving. The child standing at that door has the eyes of a cat. He looks at me mischievously, dangerously, as if checking my steps. He's mocking me. He knows I'm old. So hold your head up, Muhammad. The child hurries behind me. He takes the stairs two at a time. He's reached the bottom. He looks back at me; his eyes are serious. Yes, my boy, I can't run down like you. You're cleverer than me. He's run off. Be brave, Muhammad. Only two more steps. . . . That terrible piano . . . it throttles me.

A triumph! I've managed to reach the bottom.

All that remains are the streets. Between me and the Champs Elysées there's a lifetime, centuries. When I get to Claridge's, I'll go in, very calm, very dignified, I'll speak to no one, take the lift to my room and lie on my bed and be ill. I won't give Samia any chance to annoy me. She won't find anything to scream at . . . only a broken lump, a body destroyed. A near corpse. She can talk her fill. I'll shut my eyes and ears. Her vivacity will come back. There'll be a glaring contrast between her and me, youth and age. I don't mind. The game can't go on. Only let me rest.

The road seems endless. The light is a strain. There's so much traffic, a terrible din. This is not my world. They move so fast. Their shoulders collide with mine. They frown. What are you doing in our midst, old man? Go to bed; go to a hospital; this is no place for you. . . . I can't go on walking. One more step and I'll collapse. The road turns, the people, hold on, Muhammad. Don't give in like this. Don't collapse among all these people. You won't find rest on asphalt. One more hour and you'll be in bed. One more hour. Think what you've managed to endure all these years. My Lord, don't abandon me. I'm in earnest, my Lord. I always remember you. I never forget your goodness. It's not just because I'm in difficulties I am returning to you. You're my only hope. No asylum but with you. I am your wretched slave. I repent of my sins. I will press my forehead in the dust of your threshold. You are Almighty, All-Powerful. You are also Merciful. I'll pray, I'll fast. Your light fills me. I have believed in you, God. I confess I forgot you. In the pride of my youth I forgot you. God, don't be harsh on me. Now I remember you. I ask nothing from you; I want nothing. All that I ask is rest in which to worship you. Believe me, O Lord.

A taxi. It must have been sent by God. Without this miracle I should have died.

'Claridge's in the Champs Elysées.'

I will put a Koran under my pillow. I'll pray and read God's word. I'll try and get Samia to pray. Not that I want her to believe for my sake. But for your sake. For her sake.

How busy the streets are. They ignore God's beneficence. This man hurrying so fast with his leather brief-case. You fool, where are you going? A business appointment? To gain a million francs? If only you knew. But if you knew, you'd throw away your important papers. What's the use of deals, of millions of francs? The end awaits you. If only you knew . . . all you people . . . you would flee to your homes. No hope. No hope. The end draws near. Death advances on you. Every step forward in life is a step nearer death. This driver, so vivacious and healthy, weaves his way through the traffic. . . . What an evening he had yesterday. Drunk and rowdy.

My days are gone.

I must change my way of life. Quiet. Peace. Complete rest. No anxieties, no crises. The news-vendors wave their papers. The Press holds nothing for me, only for those who are alive. For those with blood in their veins. For those who believe in the greatest lie – life.

Once I made the Press. Now, the news doesn't concern me. France invades Egypt, Egypt invades France: I am indifferent. I can take nothing with me to the grave. I want safety, that's all. The mercy of God. To meet Him in peace. God, have mercy on me.

'Claridge's, sir.'

The Champs Elysées. . . . I can hardly recognize anything. My eyes are clouded. But I know what is going on around me. Twelve lines of cars going up to the Etoile, twelve coming back to the Concorde. Beautiful girls going and coming, buying, buying, till the day comes when there's no buying. Boys making eyes at the girls, over and over. Till the day comes when there's no loving. Feet beat the pavements till they wear out. Cars run till they rust.

Good-bye, Champs Elysées.

I'll go into Claridge's, but I don't know when I'll come out again.

'Madame is waiting in the lounge. She's very distressed, m'sieur.'

'Take me up to my room.'

'And Madame, sir?'

'Don't tell her anything. Wait till I'm upstairs.'

A few moments and I shall be at rest.

This corridor seems endless. No one sees me, so I lean against the wall and feel my way to my room. There it is. At the end. Whose is this corpse face in the mirror? Mine?

Sixty years to produce this face. Living sixty years to reach this state, who can take pleasure in such a game? Forgive me, Lord. I don't intend to blaspheme your goodness. We ignore your wisdom. But I submit. I accept what you decree.

I'll open the door, then rest. I must undress. I discard the façade of a man and reveal this corpse. And rest.

She's opening the door. Her face is flushed with anger. Beautiful.

'Muhammad! Have you gone mad?'

I don't answer. I'll shut my eyes. My ears.

'Answer me – where have you been?'

She stalks me like a beast of prey. I'm poor prey, carrion most would refuse.

'Why don't you answer?'

Scream as you wish. Turn the world upside down. Shake the earth. I won't answer.

'For God's sake tell me what you've been up to. . . . Will you speak or not?'

She shakes me.

'Samia . . .'

'You think I'll put up with waiting here all night alone? I'm taking my son back to Egypt.'

'Samia, I'm ill.'

'Go to hell, you horrid old thing! Sixty . . . and out all night? You shut me up in the hotel, to go with. . . . I shall do what I want too. I'll leave you, and come back after two days. Why did I marry you? Tell me! Why should I waste my youth on you, if you leave me alone in a strange town? Get this clear. I won't live this sort of life. We'll go home at once. You'll come with me, my shoe on your neck. Or leave me and have a divorce.'

'Shame on you, Samia. I'm dying.'

'I don't care – where were you last night?'

'With Akram.'

'Liar! I telephoned him just now, before he left. He told me you left him at one o'clock.'

'We can talk about this later. Now I'm tired.'

'No . . . we'll talk now. I must know where you were.'

'For pity's sake. I can't bear any more.'

'People who stay out all night must suffer the consequences.'

'You want to kill me?'

'Stop harping on death. You can die at sixty if you like. Or do you want me to die too?'

'May God forgive you!'

'God – you should thank God you found a fool like me to look after you. Where was your Excellency last night?'

'I met some people in secret.'

'You still see yourself as a plotter? You can't lift a finger. We'll fly tomorrow.'

'All right. But let me rest now.'

'The room's all yours. I'm off.'

'Where?'

'Wherever I wish.'

6

Ladies and Gentlemen, we are now flying over Alexandria harbour. You can see it to your left. We are flying at a height of eight thousand feet. We shall reach Cairo Airport in approximately twenty minutes. The weather there is fine, with clear sky. Thank you.

'Muhammad, don't you want to look?'

'I've seen it from the air often. Wake Sherif.'

'I can see the lights of the Corniche. How long is it . . .'

'Wake Sherif.'

'You think our cable reached them?'

'Wake Sherif.'

Why are you asking about the cable? I know what's going on in your head. You're thinking of Yusif. You still love him. That's why you've come back. You've apologized a thousand times for your rude words. But I don't forgive you.

Because now I know. In one indiscreet moment you revealed your real sentiments, 'go to hell, you horrid old thing!'

We're going back to Cairo so you can betray me with Yusif. I know . . .

One day I'll catch you in his arms. I know. This is a scene I have been through myself. Shohdi Pasha found us at it. Souraya, in her night-dress, was in my arms. In her bedroom. By a stroke of good fortune I still had my clothes on. We were sure he was in Alexandria.

'Get out, you dog!'

'Excuse me, Your Excellency . . .'

'Shut up, you dog! Get out.'

Preferable if he had slapped my face, or shot me, rather than treat me in this ignominious manner, like a dog not wanted in the house.

Kicked out of his house today, tomorrow I'd be kicked out of *Al-Ayyam*. What minister or politician would help me? One of Shohdi's opponents? I would have to act quickly. I emptied a bottle of whisky and slept. In those days I was tough.

'Shohdi Pasha wants to speak to you, sir.'

Clutching my aching head I ran to the telephone. Instead of more insults, a puzzling, polite 'Good Morning'.

'Good morning, Pasha.'

'Are you unwell, Muhammad?'

'No, Pasha.'

'Then why aren't you in your office?'

I drove to *Al-Ayyam* trembling. I had never imagined I would be going there again, that the man on the door would salute me, that I would sit at my own desk again and direct affairs.

I panicked when the telephone rang and I heard Souraya's voice: 'Is that you, Muhammad?'

I whispered: 'Where are you telephoning from?'

'From home.'

My tongue was frozen. I pictured Shohdi Pasha listening in, ready to surprise us once again.

'Hallo . . . Muhammad.'

'Hallo . . .'

'Have you got someone with you?'

'No.'

'Then why don't you want to talk?'

'After what happened?'

'Weren't you worried for me?'

'I was, very.'

'No, you panicked. Imagine what he might
me. . . . You didn't care. He might have killed m
'What did he do?'
'. . . or divorced me.'
'What did happen?'
'You only ask now?'
'I wanted to be sure he had left the house.
What happened?'
'Nothing at all.'
'Didn't he say anything?'
'He laughed.'
'Impossible!'
'Really. He's a very strange man, you kno
She was silent, as if remembering someth
'And then?' I was terrified.
'And then he asked me . . . how long this
"Had what been going on?" I screamed b
mad's like my brother. I was complaining
Naturally he didn't believe me. He said:
watch this dog . . .'''
You got your revenge, Shohdi.
And now I have no hope but to return
presents.
And you got your revenge too, Yusif.
The present I am bringing you is your b

'Sherif's talking to you.'
'What do you want, darling?'
'There's light . . . down there.'
'Yes, so there is, darling.'
'Where's it from, Papa?'
'Villages with people living in them.'
'What are they doing?'
'They're in their homes.'
'Are they looking at us?'
'Who knows?'
'They are looking at our aeroplane.'

light's moved. The light's gone.'

light.'

nd you'll see it. But take care.'

e the light, my child. The light that your father

y, it's a ticklish matter. Let me explain. As you

ced you to Shohdi Pasha. I sang your praises.

t you to him for an interview he had never

took you for a mere boy. But now – and this

ing – he has great faith in you. But you don't

ts from you. Or do you?'

you as a weapon against me.'

w as a lemon.

quite normal. You're still young. You've

. The matter is simple. He thinks I've been

h his wife. Don't look startled. Trouble-

. The upshot is he wants to do me down by

supposed to be?'

ning. Perhaps he wants to win you over, to

doing. Perhaps he'll try to destroy our

u against me and me against you. Thus he

th. But Yusif, we are both free journalists,

sion. I think it's to our advantage not to

ough speaking of something sacred.

ize, Dr Nagi: I'm your pupil. You've taught

You're my dearest friend. I can't conceive of

ever. I'd rather give up journalism. I'd die

nything to hurt you.'

n't give up journalism. You didn't die.

y supplanter. Your shy smile outwitted me.

cere voice deceived me. Having learnt my

222

'Hamdi, sir.'

'Yes, Hamdi?'

'I want to tell Your Happiness about the letter . . .'

'What, in the middle of the night? Well, what happened?'

'I met her, as Your Happiness instructed.'

'And then?'

'I told her of the question. She wouldn't agree. She insulted me. I am afraid, Your Happiness.'

'Of what?'

'That she may tell him.'

You're not the only one who's afraid. I'm more afraid than you. I must get that letter back.

'Listen, Hamdi; did you mention my letter?'

'Of course not.'

'Then listen. . . . You must come to me tomorrow morning. Early. Seven-thirty at the latest.'

'Yes, sir.'

'And bring the letter with you.'

'But I don't have it, Your Happiness.'

'What have you done with it? Who took it from you?'

Disaster.

'I tore it up, sir.'

'Bring me the pieces.'

'I threw them away.'

Useless. I've put myself in his hands. He's kept the letter to use against me. He'll ingratiate himself with Yusif by showing it to him.

'Right, Hamdi.'

'I'm sorry, Your Happiness.'

'No matter. But come to me early.'

If he does or doesn't come, it makes no difference. I am now his slave.

Wherever I go.

Wherever I flee.

Whatever I try.

I am the slave of everyone I meet, of everyone I speak to, of everyone I look at, of everyone who looks at me.

7

SEVEN-THIRTY: HAMDI'S NOT COME YET. HE WON'T come. He's probably betrayed me to Yusif. Will Yusif come to lunch today?

I don't think so. He'll make some excuse for me to go to him instead.

Samia's not woken up yet. Everything's utterly quiet. This stillness enfolds the events that are to come: I must soon get in touch with Shohdi Pasha. I'll need his money. Perhaps he'll put me on the board of one of his companies. 'I have no one but you, Pasha. I am your servant. You are my only protector.'

No.

Such servility won't do. The Pasha's never had any use for weaklings. We live in a jungle. The strong prey on the weak. I must pretend to be strong. When I visit him, I'll let fall that Yusif lunched with me – at his own request. It will show that Yusif confides in me, needs my knowledge. *Al-Ayyam* reports this morning that our Foreign Minister is going abroad to confer with the French and English. I'll whisper that we're going to surrender all along the line. We must retreat: we can do nothing else. There'll be some new formula under which the French Company will take over the Canal once more. I think the Government intends this. They have no alternative.

'Mr Hamdi, sir. He says he has an appointment.'

'Show him into the drawing-room. Is my wife up?'

'Not yet, sir.'

How can I get my letter back? I had a presentiment it would be risky. Now, only Samia can rescue me.

'Good morning, Hamdi. I'm glad you came on time.'

'I can't be late for Your Happiness.'

'Shall we have breakfast together?'

'I have had mine already, sir. . . . Thank you.'

226

A silly mistake for a man like Muhammad Nagi to invite someone like Hamdi to breakfast.

'I want you to tell me exactly what you did with Mabruka.'

'I went to her, Your Happiness . . .'

'Where?'

'In her house.'

'Was she alone?'

'She took me for a client. She came out to me in a pink night-dress. She looked me up and down as if deciding what I was worth. She was chewing gum. She beckoned me into her room. Still chewing, she lay down on the bed. I did not know how to start the discussion. She laughed, seeing me still standing. "Come here". . . . I must confess I was at a loss. "I've come," I said, "to discuss something confidential. You know Yusif Abdul Hamid, the man everyone's talking about?" She narrowed her eyes at me. "What's your link with him?" "Something to your advantage. Yusif Bey is rolling in money – thousands of pounds could come your way." She spat out her gum and stood up, suddenly afraid. "Who sent you? It must be Yusif." Though I swore he knew nothing of the business, she did not believe me. She piled curses on his head which I can't repeat. With difficulty I calmed her down. But the room had now filled with women. With them was a man in a *gallabya* with his chest bare and his hair untidy. "What's up, Riri?" She told them everything. "That swine sent this creature. He wants to ruin me. I've left him alone; he won't let me alone." I felt desperate. They asked me who I was. "The bearer of a message. Somebody high up in the Government hates Yusif. He wants to cause him trouble. She'll get some money, while he'll get Yusif out of his job. We'll buy the best lawyer in Cairo." Does it make sense, I asked them, that Yusif should stir up trouble for himself? They began to believe me.'

'And Mabruka?'

'She laughed, then asked who this high up was.'

'What did you tell her.'

'Naturally I did not mention Your Happiness. I said he did not want his name known. "Tell him," she said, "Yusif's as

227

cunning as the Devil. No one can defeat him." I said, "This man can." She said, "If so, why does he need Riri?" She laughed and added something foul.'

'What?'

'I can't repeat it.'

'Tell me.'

'She said, "Your friend seems as down as me. You needn't curse your fate, Riri. Important people are in the same boat as you." Then she refused once more. I could not persuade her. She said she had forgiven him.'

'Did she see my letter?'

'Of course not, sir.'

'Where is it now?'

'I swear, I tore it up.'

'You didn't tear it up. You gave it to Yusif.'

'How can you say such things? Don't you trust me?'

'I want that letter, Hamdi.'

'I swear, I don't know where the pieces are.'

He protests his innocence. I cut him short.

'If you think you can use this letter, you are wrong. I'll ruin you if you try. Now get out.'

When disaster is inevitable, better if it come quickly.

'Samia, you're going out?'

'To the *coiffeur*.'

Of course. You must tart yourself up for Yusif. Will you see him before or after the *coiffeur*? After, I think. You'll tease him saying, Don't mess my hair. But in such a way that he won't be able to resist caressing you, and you won't mind.

'What time will you be back, darling?'

'Immediately.'

'Don't be late. We're expecting Yusif for lunch.'

'If you're going to talk business, there's no need for me to join you.'

How can I explain why she must be present?

I am in no position to feud with Yusif. I depend on you to protect me from his anger. Hamdi has given my letter to him.

228

This is a question of life or death. I'm no longer a free agent and you're my only bargaining counter. You can be his mistress, I want to live. I want you to put in a few kind words for me. While you are in his arms. Say how old I am, how pitiful. Let him give me a chance. . . . Let me be a partner in your relationship; let it benefit me too.

You're young, he's young.

You love him, he loves you.

Isn't there place for an old man like me between you? A humble place for a man with a humble request. I want to collect my salary on the first of each month. I want people still to think I'm the old Muhammad Nagi. I want people's respect. Just let me keep up this simple façade.

Will you grant me this?

'Listen, darling. All I want from you is the normal welcome to a business guest. We've forgotten the past. The Yusif who's coming today is not the same. He's the editor in chief of *Al-Ayyam*.'

'I thought of going to visit my mother after the *coiffeur*.'

'No, be sensible. Darling, think carefully. Imagine my feelings first. Go to the *coiffeur*, darling. Let him make you chic. Then Yusif will find you lovely and know you are happy with me. That's my right, isn't it?'

'Do you love me, Muhammad?'

She looks doubtful.

'Darling. Of course I love you.'

'I can't believe it. Once we were so close; now I feel you're remote.'

Yes, I have changed. You've changed, too. You speak more than you know. I have slumped in your eyes. I can no longer excite you. I can't cram your life as before. You're the one who's drifted away, now threatening me with the menace of your youth. You have dreams, I don't. You have years and years ahead of you; I only have days. Today you are afraid. Tomorrow you will escape. With Yusif.

'Aren't you happy, Samia?'

'No, I'm not.'

'Shall I put Yusif off?'

'Yes. You know what I feel? I feel you're testing me. That you want to invite Yusif so as to see us together. I can't do it, Muhammad.'

'Darling. You're quite wrong.'

But now I know the truth. She's attacking me before I attack her.

'I'm not wrong. Please put him off. I don't want him to enter my house.'

'No, I refuse to put Yusif off for such a trivial reason.'

What has made her cry?

I don't trust your tears. They, too, are lies. You're crying because I've found you out. You're crying out of regret for him. I hope you weep till the end of your life, and suffer as I suffer.

'I'm sorry, Muhammad.'

'For what?'

'For saying something silly.'

'It doesn't matter.'

'Forgive me. . . . I do love you. There's no one but you in the whole world for me. I don't want to go back to mother any more.'

'Believe me, I love you, too. And now let's be cheerful.'

'Goodness, I'm late for the *coiffeur*. *Au revoir*, Muhammad. Don't you want to kiss me?'

You kiss me warmly? Oh you liar! It is a protective screen. Do you take me for a complete fool? Go to the *coiffeur*. Go to Yusif. Then come back and tell me you still love me. There's no point in all these lying protestations. For I'll not let you go, whatever happens. If I catch you in his arms, I'll still not leave you. I need you. I need you both.

But I hate you. And I hate the day I set eyes on you. And I hate the world that threw us together.

8

THREE OF US SIT DOWN AT ONE TABLE. WE EAT QUIETLY
from one dish. If we were to open our hearts, we couldn't bear
to sit together. We would rush, each of us, to different ends of
the earth.

'I visited Shohdi Pasha this morning, Yusif.'

'What's his news?'

'Between us two, he's far from happy.'

'Frightened there'll be war?'

'To be frank, the man's a capitalist. As such, he can never be
on good terms with this régime. I can't think why they've left
him alone so long.'

'Did he tell you anything?'

'I don't like repeating things, but I have my patriotism as well
as the next man. I feel I should warn those in authority of the
danger represented by certain people. We must defend the
revolution with all our strength. For thirty years I've written
on politics. Before Samia was born. I'm optimistic that this
crisis will pass. The vital thing is to beware of defeatists. They
know they can't oppose openly. But they're quite ready to hand
over Egypt to the English, as they did in the days of Arabi.
I've met lots like that. Even in Paris. Do you remember, Samia?'

'Who do you mean, Muhammad?'

'. . . that night we met Akram Bey? Samia can tell you, Yusif.
The people we send abroad know nothing. Or at least, I hope
it's ignorance. They may well be traitors. I'm thinking of
writing a series of fearless articles. I'll demand a clean-up of our
embassies.'

He looked at me without saying anything.

I can't tell from his expression whether he likes the idea or
not. Since he set foot in my house he has spoken guardedly,
obscurely. He smiles shyly. He never glances at Samia. He
must know all about the letter. He probably met Samia before

coming here. For she too is silent. She too speaks guardedly. Her hair-style is simple. Nothing easier than to fondle it and let it spring back. You're betraying me, Yusif. But your conscience is lulled by the letter in your pocket. Also by the sense that you have won, I have lost. I no longer feel anything for you, neither love nor hate. All I want is peace and quiet. Believe me, I feel this minute as if I had been born again. I have forgotten the past. I want to wash my memories away. No sorrows, no bitterness. I will write with fire. I'll rouse the people.

'What do you think of my idea, Yusif?'

'Of course, it's a good one.'

'You don't look too keen.'

'On the contrary. I am most keen. When will you write them?'

'I'll begin tomorrow.'

'Splendid.'

He's not keen at all. His words come from his lips, not his heart. You don't believe me. You're puzzled. But I do want to start writing again. I want my articles to explode like bombs. The people in the cafés, streets and clubs will applaud me. 'Have you read Muhammad Nagi today?'

'Yusif, why so silent? Samia here has so much to tell you about Paris, the fashions above all. You can learn a lot from her.'

'I must hear everything.'

'Samia is also very quiet today. I don't know why.'

'I think I'm tired, Muhammad.'

'Young people tired while old men like me sparkle with energy? You let me do all the talking, getting worked up, planning new articles?'

A fire stabs my chest. A needle pierces my flesh. Was the fish bad? What is Yusif saying? She's telling him about the Paris fashions. The fire expands. A strange pain. Shall I tell them? No need to disturb them. I'll let them flirt. I need them. Tomorrow I'll write my articles.

Absurd.

Nobody climbs for ever. Everyone who reaches the top must fall to the bottom.

The pain increases. A ring of fire grips my heart. In my head the noise of a train resounds. I must tell them. But I can't see. A cloud covers my eyes. But I'm still sitting at the table. The food in my throat. What's she saying. I cannot hear. Everything's going. Gets remote. Stops. Is this death?

Mother.

Is this death?

Son, why did you hit him. It wasn't me, I swear. . . . Take care of Tony, Muhammad. . . . Why won't the dog die? He's dead, it's over, sir. . . . Firing in the Champs Elysées. The swine killed him. . . . He was whistling *La vie en rose* as he walked. . . . His hand outstretched, shot with a bullet. . . . His squat body crumpled. . . . Are you a maharajah, a pasha. No, the greatest writer in the Orient. Get out, you dog.

Tony.

This terrible piano . . . it strums in my head. The child looks at me. He rushes downstairs. He looks back. Don't crowd me. They frown at me. This is no place for an old man, Samia, my darling. Sherif is ill. Look, darling. The light's moving. The light's gone. Now you'll see it. But take care. Look at the paper. The presses. The headlines. Hallo. Who's speaking? Latest news. Front page. Signed by Muhammad Nagi. Written by the great writer Muhammad Nagi. Muhammad Nagi.

'Samia.'

Why is she screaming? She frightens me. Speak gently. For I'm resting.

'G-g-give me a . . . dr. . . .'

BOOK FOUR

Yusif

I

YUSIF, YUSIF ABDUL HAMID AL-SUEFI . . .

When I whisper this name to myself, I feel it belongs to a stranger, someone I neither love nor hate, but inextricably linked with me.

Who is this Yusif? The famous editor-in-chief of *Al-Ayyam*? The Yusif who sits at that editor's desk, who rings the bell, speaks into telephones, writes articles, gives receptions: in a word, the man who's got on, who has arrived?

And if not, then who?

This morning we buried Muhammad Nagi. His coffin was carried by men from the printing shop. Hundreds of mourners followed from Liberation Square to the Jerkis Mosque. I walked in the same line as President Nasser's representative, with ministers and leading business men, among them Shohdi Pasha. Sad, I walked with downcast head. Suddenly the inner voice was busy: 'Do you really think you're sad? Do you really grieve for this man who pushed you into journalism and seated you in his own chair?' To escape, I wiped my forehead as though grief wracked me. I glanced at the other mourners. Some were sad for themselves. . . . Old men saw in this coffin a foretaste of their own. Others were just showing off their best clothes: for them it was almost an official reception. Shohdi Pasha was whispering to Sayid Shahata, the director of the Economic Bank. I caught him glancing at his watch. There was no real sadness in all this sad display.

But as a funeral it was first-class. It only lacked military music to have resembled one of the funerals I remembered as a child.

And when we put his body in the tomb, I wept real tears. But even then my inner voice insisted: Are you weeping for Muhammad Nagi, or your own predicament? Though the people near me may have doubted my sincerity, they approved my making the conventional motions.

I must confront my inner questioner, I must reply.

All I am sure of is my own dissatisfaction, my ignorance of the essential 'I' within me.

Between September 6th, 1922, and today, October 9th, 1956, what was happening to me? How was it I grew up, acquired knowledge, fame and fortune, yet lost myself? We begin dying when we begin living: losing when we start to gain. Failure starts with the first moment of success.

My mother gave birth to me at one in the morning.

'What a tragedy,' the midwife shouted, thinking I was still-born . . . 'a boy, too.'

But I wasn't dead; I had simply come into this world neither crying nor smiling.

She turned me upside down and spanked me. Suddenly I wailed and she began the traditional cries of joy.

My father was away in Luxor teaching in a primary school. On the night in question, sitting up with friends over a glass of beer, more cheerful than usual, he told the maths teacher, he had a presentiment his wife was about to give birth. Next morning they brought him a telegram in class. 'Congratulations on Yusif. . . .' He could not control himself but exclaimed in front of the boys:

'I've had a baby.'

The boys exploded into laughter.

My mother's eyes would sparkle over this story: as though she was reliving the whole experience . . . the months of preg-nancy . . . boy or girl? . . . if a boy, they'd call him Yusif after her brother who'd died . . . then labour, followed by the mid-wife screaming tragedy . . . the lump of red flesh . . . her palm slapping it to life . . . my son . . . Yusif . . .

In those days I believed my father's story, his presenti-ment on the night I was born. But now I fancy he may have invented it to atone to my mother for having been absent;

to give her the feeling that somehow he had shared her pains.

It was when we were living in Haret Zaki, a lane leading off Dam Street. Opposite our house stood a small clinic which later I learnt was for venereal diseases. The women who visited it were given catcalls by our neighbours. In a shop under our flat 'Uncle' Bari sold pickles.

'Why did they beat me, mother?'

'To know if you were alive or . . .'

She would never complete her answer.

'I had to cry to prove I was alive?'

She'd laugh at my earnest question. 'Yes, that's the way things are.'

'But why are things like that?'

She could find no further explanation.

But whenever I thought of the beginnings of my life – and I thought of them often – I felt I had been given an unkind welcome. What crime had I committed to deserve beating? Was there no life without tears and violence?

I would see my mother standing at the end of the sitting-room. Overcome with longing I would rush and bury my head in her flesh and she would seize me and kiss me and I would feel life itself was embracing me, that I was alive. No twists, no turns, no complications.

If I was hungry, I screamed: 'I want to eat'. If I felt a twinge of thirst, only a twinge, I'd scream out in the middle of the night: 'I want a drink.' If my father spoke coldly to my mother, I'd scream: 'You're terrible, Father. I don't love you.' I concealed nothing, revealed everything. I was I.

What I wanted, I wanted. There was no shyness, no embarrassment, no complication. Nothing came between myself and me.

When I got older, I became the man who twists and turns, whose heart says what no one hears, whose tongue says something else which people hear.

Our innocence dissolves, our selves flow corrupt. When I fell in love with Samia, I passed torturing nights. Did I love her or not? Was it merely lust I wanted to indulge? Should I confess my love to her, or conceal it? Why couldn't I rush towards her with outstretched arms, embrace her and kiss her, tell her with a child's ingenuousness, 'I love you, I want you?' What is it that complicates life, turning innocence to folly, changing frankness into shyness or hypocrisy? What makes shame?

The first thing I loved, the first thing I remember: a strong light, shining towards me, my mother's face beside the light, a beautiful round white face, two honey-coloured eyes, and her fingers soothing something cold and sticky on to my naked back. This image of a moment I cannot forget. I cannot remember what was before or what came after. This memory binds me with such tenderness, even now I am incapable of feeling tender unless I evoke that strong light, my mother's pale face and her eyes and the cold ointment that her fingers are rubbing on my back.

When I was seven, I asked her, 'I can remember, mummy, when I was little . . . you put some cold cream on my back.'

'You remember that? You weren't yet four . . .'

'And I can remember a light.'

'That was when you had smallpox. I was so frightened for you.'

So tenderness went with a dread disease?

My mother would think back:

'Can you remember waking up half-way through the night and screaming? Sometimes I didn't get a wink of sleep for four whole nights.'

I had tormented her, made her tired. But unintentionally.

It hadn't been my fault.

But I felt it was.

Another story my father must have repeated a thousand times also filled me with guilt.

Just a month before I first went to school, my father told my

240

mother he was to meet an important official in the Ministry of Education. I heard the word 'Groppi's' repeated: I'll meet him at Groppi's. . . . Groppi's is a very big café, only rich people go there. . . . A cup of coffee costs three piastres, two for the coffee, one for the tip. . . . He turned to me. 'Would you like to come to Groppi's?'

'Yes, Father.'

To my mother he added, 'I want Mansur Bey to know I have a boy in school. This may help me to get transferred nearer home.'

By then he was working at Damanhour, near Alexandria. His holiday was almost over.

My mother dressed me carefully in shirt and shorts, combing my hair as though everything depended on my appearance. If I made a good impression my father might live with us all the time.

The next thing I remember is sitting in a garden, bored stiff, with four grown-ups. Mansur Bey was a short man in spectacles. His gold teeth smiled at me in a way I found sinister.

He suddenly directed a question at me. I did not answer him. My eyes were fixed on his gold teeth. My father shouted: 'What makes you so shy?' I wasn't in the least shy. I was trying to picture Mansur Bey eating with these teeth. My father was furious. 'You're behaving like a donkey.' Mansur Bey flashed his smile and everyone laughed. I now stared down at my new shirt, trousers and shoes. I had made up my mind not to talk to them. I turned my attention to a boy eating an ice at a near-by table.

'It's time to go,' my father said, 'you look ready for bed.'

'No, I'd like to wait a little.'

'Indeed, sir?'

'Just till that boy has finished his ice-cream.'

They all burst out laughing. I could not see what was funny. I had simply been interested by the look of happiness on the boy's face.

When we got home my father told my mother that her son had behaved like a girl and had disgraced him.

'Darling! What made you act like that? You know you must answer people when they speak to you.'

'Not only that,' my father went on. 'You feed your son, don't you? But from the way he stared at other people's food, he might have been starving.'

My mother laughed gently. 'What's surprising about that? You should have bought him an ice, too.'

Neither of them understood me. I had been neither shy nor greedy. I had merely been fascinated by the boy. That was all. I shared his feelings. I felt I understood him. I could see no use in trying to understand grown-ups.

And yet there are thousands of things one forgets. . . . They must move our depths, as the things we do remember move our minds. . . .

Somehow, I must get back what I have lost.

2

I HAD TO GO THE LENGTH OF DAM STREET TWICE DAILY on my way to and from school. The street terrified me. I was frightened each passing man might be my kidnapper; each woman swathed in black might have the evil eye; every food whose aroma tickled my nostrils be poisoned: the sweet called 'ladies' fleas', stalls selling macaroni and rice, syrupy *kunafa*, fresh cucumbers – all venomous. Both my parents had impressed this lesson on me.

Sometimes there was a fire-eating magician; or a snake-charmer. Or a monkey-trainer would set his animal to ape a country-woman kneading flour. Boys would get off their cycles, women with baskets on their heads would push into the crowd to watch. Only I was not allowed to look. My father's words thundered in my head . . . all magicians and showmen were thieves, those who watched them were good-for-nothings, boys without breeding or manners.

I would run home as if the devil was behind me, rush panting up the stairs – so many menaces lurking for me. But in the evening I would peer hungrily down at the children in the street, at Bahgat, Huda and Enfash playing football, or running barefoot after a water-cart, their *gallabyas* lifted to let the water splash their naked thighs. From my place behind the window I joined their games: kicked the ball against the goal marked on the wall beneath my window, felt the mud and water squelching between my toes. But when I heard the foul language on their lips, I'd tremble with fear: would I ever be able to answer back in the same style? Even beneath my breath I would not dare.

After sunset was the time for imagining. The houses seemed to blur, to dwindle. A veil seemed to drift over the street and its people. The lane softened; people seemed to walk softly, as in sleep. This was the moment for the demons of night to run on to the scene, clothed in yellow suits and woollen skull-caps, bearing long staffs tipped with fire. I held my breath as I saw the lights silently, quickly, catch. Now Enfash had to peer to see the game. As the gas-lamps flared, nurses leaned out of the clinic windows, chewing gum, laughing loudly. And the street-vendors pushed their little carts along the lane: cucumbers and pickled aubergines, hot flaky *burek*, cheese, and special dates were poisons I longed to taste.

My mother would call and I would leave the window to find our supper set out in the sitting-room, bread, a piece of *halawa*, Greek cheese, black olives.

'Mummy, I want some fried fish.'

'I'll cook you fish tomorrow.'

'I want it from that shop on the corner.'

'Papa's warned us not to buy fish from the market. People who buy it – God protect us – die of poison.'

'But I want fish from the shop.'

'I daren't, my son. It would give you a bad tummy and your father would kill me.'

I ate the *halawa* and cheese, my desires on the tempting evils in the street.

I wasn't only afraid of the street. I was afraid of school. Enfash used to sit just behind me in class, though he was bigger and older than me. We called him 'Enfash' because of his snub nose, the biggest I had ever seen in my life. When the teacher beat him, he used to fight back and never cry. When we filed out into the hall, he would take his revenge like an enraged demon, venting his fury on everyone in his path, particularly me.

I was thin and small. I never took part in the school fights; nor did I join the school gangs. I would sit on a bench in the hall under the school bell, feeling safer near Uncle Basyani, frowning at his watch with the bell-pull in his hand. Enfash would sometimes stop me there and come up glaring. As though what he saw did not lessen his rage, he would point his finger in my face accusingly.

'Boy, why are you sitting by yourself?'

I'd say nothing; Enfash would shout again, 'Why don't you answer? Why do you keep aloof?'

I shyly whispered, 'I'm not aloof.'

'No, you're stuck up. Who do you think you are?' Turning to the boys with him, he said bitingly, 'Just because his father's a teacher.'

Someone shouted: 'His father a teacher? I don't believe it!'

Enfash shouted back: 'What's so special about a teacher anyway? An Inspector's much better. An Inspector can sack your father, boy.'

My fear turned to anger but I felt powerless. I whispered with difficulty: 'I'll report you to the teacher.'

'You're a sneak, are you?' His heavy boot gave my thin shoe a kick; at the same time he pulled my shirt as if to tear it. 'You want a fight, do you? Go home, you mummy's boy!'

He almost made me cry but I never reported him, even when his kicks tore my shoes. I'd go home and pretend I'd been playing football. My father would scold me and blame my mother for not being stricter. This would make her sad, and then I'd be sad, too, for her sake.

The strange thing about Enfash: when I saw him close to, I feared him, but when I watched him from the window I felt a strange attraction. I liked the way he dominated the game with quick skilful kicks, his mindless shouts. I felt this strange attraction when he got into a fight, indifferent to his torn *gallabya*, to his naked back showing through the rents.

One day my dread of Enfash turned into friendship.

A new maths teacher came into class, carrying a black bag. We stood up and saluted him in our normal way.

'Remain standing,' he said that first time, quite calmly. 'You all see what I'm holding?' From the bag he took a stick. 'From now on this is Commander-in-Chief.'

Suddenly his calm voice broke into a scream.

'Hands out, everyone!'

Before we realized what he intended, he had begun to beat the whole class, one after another, without exception. The boys who shouted or groaned had a double dose which made them collapse writhing on their desks. When he had beaten everybody, he smilingly went back to his place, as if nothing had happened. But I noticed drops of sweat stand on his forehead, his breath come fast and his colour change.

One day Enfash refused bluntly to hold out his hand.

'Hold it out, you criminal!'

Aggressively Enfash refused.

The teacher gave him two blows on his shoulder, but before he could give him a third, Enfash grabbed hold of the stick and snatched it from him. Safan Effendi's manner now reminded me of a beggar who went cringing past our house every morning, wailing for 'a bit of bread and relish'.

Like the beggar, Safan Effendi now stretched his hand beseechingly to Enfash.

'Give me the stick, boy. I must beat you.'

Enfash refused.

Safan Effendi's expression became more cringing.

'Give me the stick, boy. It's for your own good.'

My smile was noticed by the teacher. It gave him a way out.

'Come up to the blackboard!'

I went up, convinced that all was over.

Safan Effendi took the stick from Enfash and turned his

attention to me. He reflected, then suddenly ordered me to sit in the waste-paper basket.

The class burst out laughing. To me it all seemed like a meaningless dream. I did not know what to do. He raised the stick in my face and I knew I must obey. I squatted on the edge of the basket, my legs inside. Safan Effendi scratched his chin with the stick while a new idea came to him. He called Enfash who swaggered towards him with bulging muscles. He called two others as well. Then told them with a wicked glint in his eyes to put 'this rubbish' in the window.

Enfash and the two others hesitated. Then with sudden delight – as if this was a new game – they picked me up and placed me on the window ledge. We were on the second floor. The other boys cheered. Safan Effendi did nothing to stop them. I sat there trembling. The least movement and I would fall out of the window. I had never been so frightened in my life. A cold breeze touched my back, wet with fear as it was. In a fever, I saw my mother screaming, I saw my father looking resignedly at my smashed body.

When the lesson was over, Enfash came up to me and patted me on the back. 'Don't worry, we'll complain to the headmaster. Tell your father. The man will be dismissed.' To the boys standing round he said: 'Safan Effendi doesn't realize that Yusif's father is a teacher. By God, you can ruin him, Yusif. No one can touch a teacher's son.'

One asked me frightenedly: 'Were you afraid?'

'No.'

'He's the bravest boy in school.'

The look in Enfash's eyes proved he wanted to be friends. I returned his smile. We strolled together in the hall. He tried to make his voice gentle and polite. At the same time with tears in his eyes he said, 'I'm going to tell my uncle too. He'll complain to the Minister of Education.'

I nodded.

'For my father's dead. Did you know, Yusif, my mother tells me we were once rich? Can you believe that? Later my father guaranteed a friend . . . the brute let him down by going bank-

246

rupt and my father died of grief. My uncle is not so rich but he sometimes helps my mother. He's an Inspector on the trams.'

I asked him respectfully.

'He inspects the conductors?'

'Not only them,' he answered proudly, 'but the passengers too. Just imagine, if you get on, even if you're the richest pasha in Egypt, and haven't paid for your ticket, my uncle complains to the conductor and the pasha has to fork out.'

We walked a few paces, then Enfash said, 'It's a very important job. More important than a teacher. Like an officer. He wears a suit in summer with brass buttons. In winter, a blue suit of English cloth, thick as thick and ivory buttons.'

I was sad my own father was not like his uncle.

But when I got home, I did not tell them a word.

'Why didn't you tell your father?' Enfash asked next morning. 'Were you afraid?'

'I just couldn't.'

He thought a moment, then said, 'Don't worry. I'll beat Safan Effendi up for you on his way back from school.'

I wanted to dissuade him.

'Isn't your uncle going to complain to the Ministry?'

He laughed irritably, as though his laughter hurt him.

'Who would take any notice of my uncle? He's a nobody.'

'Isn't he an Inspector?'

He said bitterly: 'And what's an Inspector? He's never had two shillings to spare. He wears himself out on the trams and goes home at night with rheumatism.' He shook his head mockingly. 'You're still very young,' Enfash was fourteen while I was nine, though we were both in Third C. I knew there were many things I still didn't understand. Even so, there was something inside me which guided my steps, and this something warned me it would be a bad idea for Enfash to assault Safan Effendi. It could never succeed.

Yet when, after school, Enfash took my hand, I went with him.

3

NOW I KNEW I WAS LOST. WE WERE A LONG WAY FROM Dam Street. We had walked along unknown roads which seemed to have no endings. I was not at all sure Enfash would be able to get me home. But I could not express my doubts in words. I did not want to provoke a return to our old enmity. I'd have to put up with my family's being worried; I'd endure their scoldings. To retain this new friendship I would put up with everything.

Walking the streets with Enfash gave a new taste to life. I was no longer afraid of traffic or people. With Enfash I felt strong. My friend Enfash.

Yet where were we going? How would we ever find Safan Effendi to beat him? How did Enfash know we were on the right road?

But I kept my questions to myself, since I knew he would resent them. We would perhaps not find Safan Effendi. Perhaps Enfash was lost, too. Something terrible might happen any moment. Something unexpected.

Number 5 tram was about to leave the tram-stop. Enfash rushed forward with a shout: 'We'll catch this one.' He didn't wait for me and, before I could decide what to do, he had jumped on to the bumper of the tram and was speeding away from me. With one hand he beckoned me to follow. I hesitated, then when the tram was half-way to the next stop, I started running. I heard the screech of brakes, horns, insults. I was getting in everyone's way. My heart was about to burst. I couldn't catch up with the tram. I had bitten my tongue and my mouth tasted of blood. Enfash was vanishing – and he was the only person who could get me home.

Before I realized the full horror of my position, Enfash came running back to me.

'Why didn't you jump like I told you?'

'I couldn't.'

'You're too feeble for words.'

I felt so ashamed. But the way he mocked emboldened me to ask him outright: 'Where are we going?'

'Bab al-Khalq.'

'How do you know Safan Effendi lives there?'

'I've seen him on tram number 5. Every day.'

'Do you know his house?'

'We'll ask for it.'

How could we two boys push our way into the teacher's house and manage to beat him? I pictured Safan Effendi in place of my own father, and shuddered.

'If we'd caught our tram, we should have been there by now.'

'Let's take the next.'

'But you don't know how to hang on . . . I refuse to pay.' He paused. 'Have you any money?'

'Two piastres.'

'Give them to me.'

'Then how will we get home?'

He held out his hand. 'I'll get you home. Don't worry.'

He snatched the coins, stared at them as if he had never seen money before, and said through almost hysterical laughter: 'Now you're my brother.' He spoke so warmly, I believed him.

'We'll be friends for ever. We'll play together, we'll go out together.'

He broke off and turned into a grocer's, displaying my money.

'Give me two "filters".'

He noticed my frown. 'They only cost three farthings.'

It was the cigarettes themselves I was afraid of, not the expense, but I said nothing.

He counted the change more than once, but instead of giving it back to me put it in his pocket saying, 'There's no need to do the beating up today. Let's enjoy ourselves. We'll go and watch the trains. Have you ever seen them?'

I had only seen a train once. My father had been leaving for

249

Damanhour and as his friend Abbas Effendi was seeing him off and could take me home, my father let me come with them to the station. I climbed into the train and sat in the carriage. My father interrupted his long talk with Abbas Effendi to ask me:

'Would you like to come with me to Damanhour?'

I took his invitation seriously. 'Yes, I'll come.'

He laughed and returned to his gossip.

I was thrilled at the prospect of Damanhour, of living with him in the distant city where he worked: I pictured Damanhour full of houses and trains moving in the street and myself grown up, working alongside my father. The train journey had ripped long years from my life. In Damanhour I had suddenly grown up.

The station-bell rang. My father turned to me.

'Come on, get down with Uncle. Or the train will carry you off.'

'But I'm coming with you, Father!'

I simply could not believe that I wasn't to travel.

'No, I'm coming with you.'

His quiet tones presaged anger, I knew from experience.

'Get down, Yusif, and be a sensible boy.'

I entreated my father, 'But you promised!'

He shouted in anger, 'Get down, boy! The train's going to leave.'

For some reason he had lied to me; for some reason he denied me the pleasures I had envisaged. So I sat where I was.

My father pulled me to my feet. In a moment not only my hopes but all my trust in him vanished. I burst into tears.

He slapped my face and called me a donkey. I burst out:

'But you lied, Father!'

Abbas Effendi helped me on to the platform. I stood weeping. As my father beckoned from the window, I recoiled. Abbas Effendi pushed me to the window. My father wiped my tears with his handkerchief.

'And I took you for a sensible boy.'

My feelings were now mixed. I could see he was sad, but he had lied to me; he loved me, but had slapped my face.

'Don't make me angry just as I'm leaving.'

Yet he was to blame, he who had invited me, he who had gone back on his promise.

The station-bell rang, the engine whistled, the train moved out, but I wasn't on it.

I cried all the way home, even when Abbas Effendi stopped to buy me chocolate, even when, at the tram-stop, he unwrapped the chocolate and popped a piece in my mouth, even when the conductor gave us our tickets and Abbas Effendi pointed to me as he asked for a 'half'. I realized then that I was still small. Small people could not go to Damanhour! I continued to cry till we got home. My mother then imagined I was crying because I preferred my father's company to hers, not because my father had lied to me – for if I had been able to travel to Damanhour I would have suddenly grown up.

Perhaps I would be able to take a train with Enfash. Perhaps he would board it as he had done the tram? I would follow him if he did, to Damanhour, or Minia, or any of the other provincial cities where my father had worked.

Enfash and I crossed streets and squares. Buildings got higher, noise got louder. I felt I was years away from home, my legs were tired, my breath was short, my eyes were overwhelmed with what they saw. Traversing road after road, square after square, crossing streets without hesitation, pressing ahead, leaving the old Yusif behind. . . . Finally we reached a square so high that everything seemed dwarfed, houses, cars, people. In the middle, surrounded by a large garden, was a statue of a peasant woman and the sphinx.

We threw ourselves on the grass. Enfash pulled out his cigarettes. I accepted his smoking, his need for a match. He got up, looked round him, then asked a passer-by for a light. No use. He crossed the square. I would have followed except that, for some strange reason, I was still afraid of cigarettes themselves. Was it because they belonged to grown-ups?

Enfash came back with his cigarette alight.

'Take a puff . . .'

'No, thank you.'

'Don't be afraid.'

There was a dangerous quiet in his voice.

'Have you never tried?'

'No.'

'Then you must try now.'

'No . . . I don't want to.'

He thrust the cigarette between my lips. Its bitter taste disgusted me, I spluttered.

Enfash didn't relent. 'Breathe in, not out.'

'How?'

I tried but the smoke terrified me and I pushed the cigarette away.

Contemptuously puffing smoke from his mouth, Enfash stared at me, meditating mischief. It was now sunset. Cars were lighting up. It was getting colder, night was near.

I stood up in alarm. 'It's time to get home.'

'You don't want to watch the trains?'

'No, I want to go home.'

I was almost in tears.

'How can we get home?' Enfash asked. 'We're very far.'

The brutal way he spoke increased my terror. This wasn't the right place for me; Enfash wasn't my friend; he had led me into a jam; my right place was behind my window, watching.

'If you want to go,' Enfash added, 'you go. I'm going to the station.'

'What'll you do there?'

'Take a train.'

'Where?'

'Somewhere.'

I felt a twinge of envy. But I couldn't join him. All I wanted was to get home. Desperate, I made a step or two towards home. But which way was it? The square was so big, I could not tell one of the streets which entered it from another. I would have to ask my way. But I dreaded speaking to strangers. And it was dark. I burst into tears as I stood on the pavement. A big man was striding in my direction. I rushed back to Enfash, crying.

He laughed at my tears.

'I beg you, get me home.'

'I told you, I'm taking a train.'

'For my sake, don't travel today.'

He laughed challengingly. 'So you want me to cancel my journey, just to take you home?'

'Please, Enfash.'

'All right. But you must first kiss my hand.'

He held his hand so I could stoop and kiss it. He waited, got irritated. 'I told you, kiss my hand.'

'I can't.'

He stood up and pushed his hand towards my lips, a wicked pleasure in his eyes. 'Kiss my hand, kiss my hand.'

But though he continued to press me . . . Kiss! Kiss! . . . and though part of me wanted to obey and get things over, I could not bring myself to do what he wanted. I whispered, 'I'll never kiss your hand.'

'All right, you go your way, I'll go mine.'

If I kissed his hand, no one would know. The back of his hand was dark brown, covered with scars. A quick brush with my lips, and all would be over. But his eyes still glittered with wicked joy. No, it was impossible – rather death.

My mother sometimes visited Rateb Bey and his old mother. The old lady was pious, she had made the pilgrimage and now never left her prayer-mat. My mother always asked for her prayers. She repeated every detail of her visits to my father, who listened with great attention. I would listen, too, and picture her face white as ice and frightening. On one of these visits my mother had been most impressed by the behaviour of Midhat and his sister Suad. They had come upstairs to call on their old grandmother and had kissed her hand in the most elegant, well-bred way. My mother sighed, 'When Yusif grows up, I'd like to marry him to Suad.'

My father laughed. 'What about them? Would they agree?'

I blushed, sitting as I was on the floor, pretending not to overhear. I pictured Suad as a tall bride in a white dress with

golden hair, neither speaking nor smiling, her cheeks like roses.
I stood beside her, inhibited by shyness from speaking to her.

Why shouldn't I marry her. No one would refuse what my
mother wanted; my father was jealous.

I spent the whole day dreaming of Suad, a doll bride, kissing
the old lady's hand. It was the hand-kissing that must have
given my mother the idea of marriage. It suddenly occurred to
me. I had never kissed my mother's hand. Next day I caught
my mother coming from her room and tried to do so. She
snatched her hand back, alarmed, but I seized it by force and
brushed it with my lips.

'Yusif, what are you at?'

Seeing me tongue-tied, confused, she said crossly 'You are a
man. You mustn't kiss people's hands.' She then laughed and
patted my back. But I went to a corner to ponder the puzzle of
her praise for Suad's and Midhat's manners, and her rebuke for
me.

I now said to Enfash angrily: 'I don't want to go home.
There's no need for your help.'

I walked away from him, without looking round, this time
determined not to weaken. Then I heard his steps behind me and
his voice pleading: 'Are you angry?'

'I don't need you, thank you.'

'Please don't be angry. I'll take you home.'

I had won. All the way back he vowed he was my friend, that
I was the only boy he wanted to play with.

I listened in silence which he took for assent. But in my
heart I was determined to stay clear of him and have nothing to
do with him ever again.

4

VOICES ON THE LANDING OF OUR FLAT. BESIDE MY
father, I recognized the doctor. Perhaps my father thought I'd

had an accident? If so, when he learnt the truth, he would punish me for every moment of worry. My only hope was the doctor. He was kind. He would not let my father beat me. He might stay till my father had calmed down.

They went on talking. I could hardly recognize my father's face, it had gone such a strange colour. The doctor was not laughing as he usually did. His manner was apologetic.

I was about to speak, thought better of it. One rash word might precipitate a storm.

I passed them and went in, to the sound of weeping.

My father's voice stopped me.

He did not ask me where I had been, but where I was going.

As I walked towards my room, my father's voice stopped me once again.

'Mother . . . is sick.'

He stopped, then began to cry, his whole body convulsed. I appealed to the doctor. Instead of making some move to stop my father, he seemed to accept his tears as natural.

Mother wasn't ill . . . she was dead. The lamentations, the doctor's silence, all told me the same story. The strange day I had spent with Enfash . . . that, too, proved that she was dead . . . dead . . . dead . . .

In the night, strangers, faces, doors banging, women beating their breasts, mutter of men's voices.

Our neighbour who lived on the ground floor was a sheikh, a man of religion. He came upstairs to help my father write the notice for insertion in the newspaper, and finding me half-paralysed with misery took me down to his own flat where I was given a place on the floor with his five sons. I could not sleep. I heard screams and in a corner of the room a rat was nibbling. There were voices in the street, the sound of wood being assembled. Through the shutters came a glow of artificial light. I peered out and saw men erecting the funeral tent.

But this couldn't be true. My mother would get up. The doctor would come back, he would make her well! I'd shut my eyes and count to ten. Please God: let me count to ten and then look and find her near me. The wooden structure would collapse, the strangers vanish, the screams die, and I would go upstairs to her.

In the morning I woke to find the Sheikh's sons jostling each other for the best view of the funeral tent.

The Sheikh went into the tent. My father shook hands with the pickle-seller who lived downstairs. The butcher walked into the tent, so did the gym-teacher.

The boys kept up a running commentary, only interrupted when they remembered my presence. I wasn't with them. In my mind I saw my mother lying with half a smile on her lips and her eyes closed. If only she would get up, so that this ridiculous crowd could be made to disperse.

The sound of lamentation increased. Did I imagine it or was there a faint, sad song? I wanted to cry too, but couldn't. The children were massed in the window.

'There goes the coffin!'

'The butcher's slaying the ox!'

My mother was leaving home. Where was she going? To heaven. They would lay her in the grave. Her soul would ascend to heaven. How would it ascend? Up an invisible stair? or does it fly? She will wear white raiment and stand before the portals of a huge park. The gates will open for her and she will go to live under the trees, drinking milk and thinking of me.

The children were looking at me. Bahgat, the eldest, already at secondary school, pulled my sleeve.

'This concerns you. Come. It's your mother's funeral.'

I stood up and they led me out. The tent was attracting crowds. The coffin was wobbling on the Sheikh's shoulders. My father was weeping. The coffin continued to move forward, swaying. The Sheikh's daughters were now in tears. They were joined by Bahgat, who turned to ask me, tears in his eyes:

'Why aren't you crying?'

How could I explain that all this commotion meant nothing to me?

At dusk they brought me two fried eggs and clustered round me, urging me to eat. I was very hungry and would have liked

256

to be left alone to get on with it. But instead, the Sheikh shovelled up some of the egg on a piece of bread and tried to feed me. I brushed it aside. So the Sheikh told Bahgat to eat the eggs himself. Then commanded me to go and sit in the funeral tent.

'Your father needs you. It's your duty. You're not a girl to stay at home. Nor are you all that young. You'll be taking your primary certificate next year. You're a man now. Go and get dressed.'

My father, sitting near the entrance of the tent to receive condolences, set me beside him, his eyes red, a feeble smile playing on his lips.

'She's left us, Yusif . . . we are now quite alone, you and I.'

I knew I should cry, but could not. He stroked my head.

'And next thing you'll marry and leave me.'

He had been right to refuse me to Suad. I must never leave him, never. I must simply wait for mother's return. She would come back, sooner or later.

'Mummy's left us,' he repeated, having given some alms to a beggar. 'Now you must study hard to stand on your own feet. Who knows, I may follow her soon.'

I still could not cry.

The Koran was being recited and everyone was listening. Suddenly a car hooted. My father stood up, pulling me by the hand.

'Come and greet Rateb Bey.'

This was my toy-bride's father.

For a moment I felt he had come to bring back my mother. He seemed capable of doing it. A square face inset with tiny eyes was capped by a head of hair which was thinning at the back, as I noticed as he led the way into the tent. The servant offered him coffee and cigarettes but after a moment's pause he produced his own packet and lit a cigarette with a gold tip. I thought how delighted Enfash would be with such a cigarette.

Had my mother worried at my absence with Enfash? Was that why she had left us? My fear that I might be responsible increased, as I listened to Rateb Bey talking to my father.

'I swear I can't believe it.'

'It's God's will.'

'But only yesterday I was talking to Dr Fahmi Pasha. He assured me that a heart attack is most unusual at this age. There must have been some trouble with her blood pressure which you didn't know about.'

'How could we guess? She never complained. Sometimes she had a pain in her side or in one hand, but we never imagined . . .'

I longed for him to go on. I had to know what had happened.

'When I came home she was in the kitchen. "Why are you so late?" she shouted. When she saw it was me, she laughed, "I thought you were Yusif!" "Hasn't he come back?" I asked. "Something must have kept him at school." She wasn't in the least worried. Then all of a sudden the servant screamed. She was sprawled over the table. We carried her to her room and I fetched the doctor . . . but . . .'

My father sighed . . .

'By that time all was over. We tried everything . . .'

So she had not been worried by my absence. . . . Or had she hidden her worries with a laugh, so my father would not beat me?

I listened with renewed hope as Rateb Bey spoke of this new medicine and that. Perhaps he would find something to restore her to life? He noticed me staring at him and asked my father:

'Isn't this your son?'

'Yes.'

'In which year?'

'Answer, Yusif.'

I said, fighting back a tear, 'The third.'

'The same as Midhat, but I hope you're not as lazy?'

'Thank God, Yusif works hard,' my father defended me. 'He's a good boy.'

A good boy . . . who had been smoking with Enfash! I dreaded to think what might happen if I went out with him again.

The road to my mother's grave led up a dusty hill. On the right were stables. I forget who told me that those buried in the hills of Zenhum do not rot; they hear the trumpet on the day of resurrection first, and rise the first. Perhaps I had heard this from Bahgat, the Sheikh's son.

A wooden door in a dark stone wall. On one side of a small yard a white tombstone. Near it a cactus tree.

Here, under this stone, my mother was sleeping.

The blind reciter chanted the Koran. A man sprinkled water on the earth. My father recited the prayer for the dead, then approached the grave to weep over it.

I tried to cry, but could not. Was this inability to cry another punishment? I should have cried till my eyes became red, till they became as blind as the old reciter's. But I could not.

Then one evening, a week after she died, as I was on my way home from school, tears came.

5

A HOUSE NOT LIKE OUR HOUSE, ALL ROUND IT A BIG garden, with a man at the gate. A servant receives us. We go up a white marble stairway and enter a huge hall with reception-rooms off it – gloomy and luxurious. No one who lived in this house would look twice at our house. This house is much better than ours; there is no comparison.

My father and I sat in frightening silence. From time to time he coughed, but said nothing, being as awed as I was. Why didn't someone receive us? Where was Rateb Bey? Where was Midhat?

Would I see Suad? I had never even imagined a place like this. Curtains on the windows: at home we had none. Paintings on the walls: again we had none. Here, the chairs were shiny and unmarked. Ours were all broken, with tattered covers. How Rateb Bey must despise us. The servant brought lemon juice. Something inside me said, Don't drink it. But afraid to say a word I took the glass. My father began a long chat with the servant. As if that was why we had come! My father's laughter made me feel ashamed of myself as well as him. Finally – 'Is the Bey going to be late?'

'I'm afraid, he's still asleep, Abdul Hamid Effendi.'

My father hardly protested:

'His Happiness asked me to come at five. I came exactly on time.'

The servant laughed as if he was my father's friend:

'You know how things are . . .'

My father smiled.

'Indeed, it'll probably be at least an hour before he's awake and had his bath.'

Rateb Bey . . . Abdul Hamid Effendi . . . Bey . . . Effendi. . . . What made Rateb a Bey and my father an Effendi? Why couldn't my father be called Bey? A sudden thought disturbed me. When my mother had visited this house, had she received the same humiliation. My father rubbed his hands and suggested:

'Perhaps you could tell your mistress I am here? Just give her my salutations. Then tell her that Abdul Hamid Effendi has come to give the young Bey his lesson.'

The young Bey? That meant Midhat. Would I be called the young Effendi?

The servant came back after a time and led us up some wooden stairs. The sound of my own steps scared me, as if I was burgling the house. We reached the roof and saw a small room. Inside was an old desk, a cupboard and some bamboo chairs. I liked the room. Our chairs at home were better, so was the cupboard in my father's bedroom.

'Midhat Bey will be here in a moment.'

'Ismail . . .' my father said eagerly, 'you won't forget to tell the Bey I'm here?'

The moment Midhat appeared, I remembered Enfash. If a boy like this came to school – with his fair skin and chiselled features, his soft hair and moulded lips, his silk shirt and clean shorts – Enfash would beat him up, outraged by his calm self-

260

confidence, his sense that he was better than others. He shook hands with my father without hesitation or shyness.

'How are you, Uncle?'

My father stood up to greet him. His warmth of tone, his manner of talking, were suited to a grown-up, not a boy. Midhat shook hands with me.

'What school do you go to?'

My father quickly answered for me:

'Khalil Agha . . . a mediocre place . . . not like your school Al-Nasriya.'

My father started the lesson with geography, of which Midhat proudly confessed his ignorance. His superb self-confidence even in admitting weakness deprived me of any pleasure in being better at the subject than he was.

We left without meeting Rateb Bey. When my father angrily asked the servant why he hadn't told his master we were in the house, Ismail said apologetically:

'I did . . . but he was in a hurry.'

I could see my father was upset, but he said nothing. We left without ceremony, as though dismissed.

As we sadly reached the tram-stop, my father told me I should try and be Midhat's friend.

Yet I didn't wear the kind of clothes he wore; I didn't live his kind of life; his features were not like mine; I didn't know how to exchange one sentence with him. Had my father no pride? It would be better to try and forget this new-discovered alien world.

'How are we related to Rateb Bey, Father?'

His manner changed. He threw out his chest as if expounding a lesson.

'He married the daughter of my maternal uncle's cousin.'

The relationship was too confusing to understand.

One Friday morning – our school holiday – my father was teaching Midhat and me on the roof, when we heard shouts of workmen and servants. Then the door flew open and there stood Rateb Bey.

My father took out his handkerchief and started mopping his face. His body shook, his words were hardly coherent, though effusive.

'Hallo, boys! What are you up to?'

'We're studying, Father . . .'

'And you understand your lessons?'

'Yes, Father . . .'

'Who is better, you or . . .'

He fumbled for my name.

By that time my father had pulled himself together.

'My hope was that your happiness would honour us with a visit, to see for yourself how Midhat Bey's progressing.'

'Does that mean you are satisfied, Abdul Hamid Effendi?'

'Very much so, sir.'

With a sudden laugh Rateb Bey turned to Midhat.

'Any idea what's outside?'

'What, Father?'

'Go and see for yourself.'

Midhat came back shouting:

'Ping-pong, Father, Ping-pong!'

After the lesson, Midhat asked me to play. My father, as excited as we were, stood watching, fielding the ball and shouting instructions – though he knew nothing of the game himself.

'Midhat's much better than you are . . . look how he hits the ball!'

As my racket was in mid-air, about to hit the ball, Suad ran up:

'Let me play! . . . Let me play! . . . give me a racket!'

Midhat shouted:

'Take Yusif's.'

She gave me a glance and took it.

'Now's your chance to learn how to play.'

I hardly heard my father's words, for my eyes were on my bride, the wife my mother had chosen for me. She had a long pale face, with bold, confident eyes and yet she was pretty. I would marry her if she agreed.

The ball went off the table. Automatically I stooped to pick it up, then stood motionless. She shouted:

'Why don't you bring the ball?'

'Give the ball to Miss Suad,' my father shouted. 'Don't stand like a lump of wood!'

I hated him. I carried it to her. She took it and laughed to her brother:

'Fancy bringing the ball, not throwing it.'

My father interrupted. 'He's too well-mannered.'

Next time, the ball went through the door on to the roof.

'Mabruka! Mabruka!'

A little servant, the same age as me, trotted into range.

'Stand here, Mabruka, and fetch the ball when it goes outside.'

'Yes, my lady.'

6

SOMETHING WARNS ME IT MAY BE DANGEROUS TO GO on like this, Yusif, feeding on your memories. You'll forget what you're seeking; you'll re-lose what you've lost. Keep your purpose in mind: how was the lost lost? what spoiled the spoilt? That trivial incident . . .

Not trivial.

No. Mabruka's appearance on the roof was more important than my mother's death, more important than my poverty. . . .

What happened was so ordinary. She was Mabruka. . . . I was Yusif. She was a maid working in someone else's house. I was the son of a schoolmaster. She was a peasant from the country, I was from Cairo. We had nothing in common. Nothing but the link of coincidence. She was growing up. . . . I was growing up. . . . Thoughts ran through her mind, thoughts ran through mine. Her flesh had urges, so had mine. She swept, cleaned, answered a servant's bell while I studied geography, geometry, English, French and law. Yet, like fate she forced her way into my life and I forced my way into hers. It all began with a maid coming on to the roof to pick up ping-pong balls.

And now, tonight: Mabruka lies on a bed, she tells some man that she's my relation. Her body is stark naked. The body my father embraced, married, died because of. The body that bore Ibrahim, my brother. Nothing covers it. Her voice whispers the scandal. 'Yusif al-Suefi? So you know him. He's famous, isn't he? I married his father . . . he's the brother of my boy. If you don't believe what I say – ask him.'

Is this God's will and to be accepted? With the ensuing mockery of eyes which fear my power? the false words praising my pen? the false smiles coveting my help?

Nothing covers her body. Nothing covers me.

Thinking about life drives a man mad. Life is irrational. I, who write about socialism, who urge the people to believe in planning and in a hopeful future, I who tell them that life is logical, with a reasonable purpose – what logic has my life had, to equip me to teach the logic of theirs?

Yusif, you fraud! Cut the abstractions. If you want to see what you are really made of, postulate the moment when Yusif Abdul Hamid writes his letter of resignation from *Al-Ayyam*. He suddenly stops work. No one will believe his motives. They all say that he's become suspect. That he's been sacked. I can bear that. I'll be broke. I'll give up my flat. No car, of course, no telephone. No pen. Yusif is seen daily talking to himself in the streets. He's grown a beard; his suit is in rags; his finger-nails are filthy. He recognizes nobody. His feet will lead me to Mabruka's house. My tears will wash her hands . . . no . . . her feet. . . . But what good is a lunatic to her? She'll kick me out. 'Please, Mabruka, take me as servant. I'll open the door to your clients. I'll put up with nakedness, I'll share your disgrace.'

And end in an asylum.

People's trust in what I used to tell them will collapse. Continue in your job. Write enthusiastic articles, lie to yourself. They're not interested in your real self. They want you to act for them, they want your technique, your lies.

Nonsense . . .

They want nothing. There is no right or wrong. There's no point in going on. We have no idea where we're going. A little servant, neat, wearing slippers, Mabruka . . . Mabruka at the beck of others. Standing behind Suad, standing between my father and me to fetch the ping-pong balls. Then she grows up and marries my father. If this can happen, then anything is possible. Why shouldn't the servant now pouring my coffee become a boss himself in a few years, or days?

No surety, no logic. We control nothing – except our own suicides.

I told my father not to marry her. I was furious and left home. He still married her. I didn't choose my father. I didn't choose my mother. They dragged me into this world; they gave me a name; they set my life in motion. I'm not responsible.

Was this what I was looking for – an excuse?

But, Yusif, you're not here to defend yourself, you're supposed to be trying to get at the truth.

Why were you so against your father's marriage to Mabruka? Why did you go on treating her as a servant when she was a servant no longer? Why are you so stubborn? Why are you so shy?

In your search why not actually go to Mabruka? The journey by taxi won't take ten minutes.

Or don't go.

Instead, marry Samia. Make her happy: make yourself happy.
Or don't marry.

Enjoy the feeling of being a Messiah whom nobody believes.

Mabruka's appearance on the roof doesn't really mark the beginning. Life is not as capricious as that.

A little older. The ping-pong table had long disintegrated. Now what obsessed me was my love for Suad and my hopes that we would marry. I spent long nights with an open book, hearing her voice. Long hours before the mirror, staring at my face, trying to make it more attractive, trying to improve the shape of my lips, to comb my hair and fix the waves with soap. When I looked dreamy, I had a touch of Clark Gable. My voice broke. I sang a new song:

'Twas on the Isle of Capri
That I met her . . .'

When I read novels, I'd change the names of the heroine to Suad.

I made fantastic efforts to bridge the gap between us. I forgot that I was poor, that I lived in Dam Street, that my father was a teacher awe-stricken by Rateb Bey. I forced myself to love Midhat, to love the house he lived in, to love the whole family, to feel that I was one of them, that I belonged.

I was now twelve, a student at the Khedevial Secondary School while Midhat was at the Saadiya. Father still taught us English, geography and history. At the beginning of each month Midhat would hand him an envelope containing his £3, which my father avidly pocketed. I used to loathe this scene. Yet my love for Suad helped me to forget it. For in a sense I felt I belonged to her family and was one of those paying the teacher for his labours.

When Midhat spoke of their estate, the estate became mine. When their big black car had an accident, I grieved; when they bought a new Nash, I was happier than Midhat. I included everything about them in my love for Suad.

On one of our visits, Midhat was ill in bed. While my father had the honour of sitting with Rateb Bey, I sat by Midhat. Suad's comings and goings gave me a fever wilder than his. The door suddenly opened and, leaning on Mabruka, the old grandmother walked in, her face wearing its usual serenity. The old lady had become so used to me and greeted me with such kindness that it always surprised me when she gave Midhat and Suad money and did not include me in the gift.

The old lady now stroked Midhat's hair, muttering some words under her breath. She then turned to me:

'Leave him now to sleep.'

I didn't know where to go. My father was downstairs with Rateb Bey. Should I go home, or should I wait for him outside Midhat's door?

Suad came along, as though to see her brother.

'He's sleeping,' I whispered.

She whispered back: 'I wanted to show him my photos.'

She showed me an album she was carrying.

'Would you like to look at them?'

The light was dim where we stood, so without a word she led the way to the roof. Leaning against the parapet, we looked at her feeding the swans on the Tea Island at the Zoo, wearing her school uniform, or staring seriously into the camera. She merrily described the occasion of each picture. But I could not concentrate. My whole body felt on fire. I knew I loved her. Should I tell her? The edge of my hand touched hers. She was still talking, unaware of the tumult inside me. Then she must have become aware of the pressure of my body, of the fervour of my feelings, for she stopped speaking, though her hands continued to turn the pages. I wanted to stay like this for ever. Then on an impulse I moved my lips – we were very close – and touched her cheek. She said nothing though her face was paler than usual. She no longer turned the pages. We stood there motionless until a voice called to us from below. At once she ran downstairs, leaving me with my brain inflamed.

The sun set and no one called me. I didn't want to stir. But the darkness depressed me and eventually I sneaked down the stairs, guiltily expecting doors to fly open, her mother to insult me, her father to slap my face and Midhat, perhaps, to die.

The sitting-room was in darkness. Where had my father gone?

I rushed into the garden to ask Osman. 'Where have you been? – That's the question. We were hunting for you everywhere.'

Where had I been? On the roof with Suad.

It was never easy to meet her alone. After repeated visits I knew it was hopeless, short of a miracle or Midhat's being ill again.

Months passed and I lived on the memory of our kiss. My real life seemed unreal; the only reality was us two on the roof.

My only hope was another meeting; a second kiss, the dreams I would tell her.

Years passed. My father stopped giving us lessons. We moved on from primary school and, though my father lost the £3, I felt relieved. He no longer had to display his poverty in Midhat's house and I no longer had to have him with me. There were better chances of meeting Suad alone. I would study with Midhat or pretend to. I wanted to see Suad, while he wanted to play the gramophone and learn to dance. And I strove to copy Midhat in everything, to bridge the gap of birth and breeding. I would repeat the names of film-stars with his enthusiasm and fill my speech with the French and English phrases he used. I learnt by heart his favourite songs, attended as he talked about cars.

It was better still when I went there and found Midhat away. I could wait alone for the longed-for opportunity. One day at last it came. Gazing from the roof, after a long silence I whispered: 'There's something I want to say. But don't get cross.'

She looked down and I said in a low voice:

'For years I have been thinking of you.'

'What,' she asked nervously, 'do you want?'

I was at a loss. I heard her whisper:

'Don't people . . . who feel like that . . . do things?'

'What do you mean?'

She looked annoyed and I feared she was rejecting my love. 'I love you.'

'I know. But what do you want?'

I understood: she wished me to propose.

'I want you to marry – marry.'

'Oh? You think Papa would consent?'

'Why not?'

I wasn't afraid of his refusal; I felt sure that all would come right.

'He'll just say we're too young.'

'No matter, we'll wait.'

'Tomorrow you'll grow up and fall for someone else.'

'I'd kill myself sooner.'

268

7

TO MARRY SUAD I MUST FIRST GROW UP, AND THIS TOOK
such a time. If I could be something in a flash . . . what would I
be?

I wanted to write a novel like Towfik al-Hakim's *Return of
the Soul*. It would be about Suad. I'd be famous like him, drive
my car fast as imagination. I'd live in luxury hotels, be known
to everyone, while knowing no one. I'd observe people from
afar, without their knowledge. My writings would be famous
and difficult – on Bach, Mozart, Raphael and Rembrandt. I'd
live in Montmartre . . .

Every time we stood by the parapet eating melon pips, I'd
talk to her about al-Hakim and she'd tell me about Alfred de
Musset. Now and then I'd snatch a kiss. Sometimes I'd feel
guilty, sometimes afraid, and sometimes when I saw her after a
lapse of some weeks she would seem estranged. But I was not
cast down; I knew we loved each other and it only needed time
for me to be a famous writer and for us to make a love-match
unlike any other.

Through years of frustrated love the secret in my heart grew,
while my hopes increased in scope and strength. I was now a
student in the first year of the Law College. The war had broken
out and my father enthused about Hitler and the might of
Germany. I listened credulously, but without enthusiasm. I had
an obscure feeling of waiting and watching, as if all was leading
up to some grand conclusion: the fall of France, the headlines
about bloody battles, the English soldiers filling the streets.
Students shouted, gossiped and put up posters. Sirens wailed in
practice; helmets were tried on; people equipped with gas-
masks. Volunteer air-raid wardens in leather jackets roared at
us: 'Put out your lights!' We covered windows with dark-blue
paper. Ration cards. Difficulties with kerosene and sugar. And
all the time I waited, feeling that the war would eventually,

somehow, facilitate my marriage. I became bolder. I now kissed her lips and caressed her body. The general darkness helped, just as the general anxiety somehow made me feel stronger.

While Suad's grandmother invoked God, Suad's mother discussed the difficulties of getting meat. She was alarmed at the sight of English soldiers in the streets. Rateb Bey read the papers eagerly and hunted for new tyres. He drove more often to his estate, despite his wife's complaints at being left in Cairo. All this I learned from Suad. They seemed to be getting weaker as I grew stronger. I awaited the miraculous conclusion. Would bombs fall and destroy their palace? The family would be forced into the streets. I'd stand beside them and share a hovel with Suad.

It was Thursday, the last lecture – on constitutional law. I paid as much attention as if I was a member of parliament, with Suad watching from the gallery swathed in a white yashmak like the one Queen Ferida wore in her pictures. After the lecture I went to the Engineering College to look for Midhat.

'Damn them!' he said as I walked home with him. 'I can't go out today, and there's a boat-party to the Barrage. Twelve girls. Imagine!'

'Why can't you go out?'

'Suad's future husband is expected.'

I laughed in a despairing effort to hide my sense of catastrophy. 'You mean she's engaged?'

'To a doctor with a Chevrolet.'

We reached his house and he turned to say good-bye.

At home I cried; then at sunset I heard my father going out.

As we walked together, I almost blurted out how I loved Suad. Go to her, father! Stop her marrying. Tell them we're rich, too. We'll buy a Chevrolet. I'll become Prime Minister. You're quite respectable enough for Rateb Bey to believe you.

But I said nothing and when we reached Midan Ataba, I realized my destiny was the same as my favourite author's: like Towfik al-Hakim, without a woman, sad like him, lost like him, hating marriage. I'd write a story: Men are not traitors! It's women who betray.

270

My father walked briskly, asking me probing questions about the College. I answered without spirit. He told me again how he had tried to study law himself but had been prevented from doing so by lack of money. We had owned an estate, but my grandfather had lost a law case with the Government who had taken the land for failure to pay the tax. 'You know who his lawyer was? Saad Zaghloul!' The documents written in Zaghloul's own handwriting were in a biscuit-tin – their historical value might already be £2,000. He scolded himself for absent-mindedness, for treating them so casually. The mice might get them.

Could we get our land back? Then we'd be rich.

My father went on talking about the headmaster of the law college, Mr Holmes. I paid no attention; my thoughts were elsewhere.

The café was just behind the Opera. The tables were placed in one long line and on both sides sat people playing chess.

A fat turbaned man sat brooding at his clients. The place reeked of drink and the lavatory. A midget called Mikhaili served the drinks. It was a disgusting place. My father was the familiar of these degraded people, some of them alcoholics, all of them vulgar. After watching my father start one game and lose another, after listening to constant exchanges of meaningless grunts and shouts, after thinking what Rateb Bey and Suad would think of my father's haunt, the abode of derelicts and drunkards, I took away memories which haunted me all next morning at college. I left after the first lecture and passed Midhat's college, but walked faster so he wouldn't see me.

I thought of eloping with Suad. We would take the papers written by Saad Zaghloul and sell them for £1,000. I took a bitter pride in my own fidelity.

'Mr Midhat's not back yet.'

It was Mabruka standing in the hall.

'I want to see Miss Suad. Go and tell her.'

After a long wait I saw her coming.

I asked for my copy of *Sparrow From the East*.

She asked me to sit down; I did not comply. Despite myself,

I said: 'Congratulations, Suad.' I did not mean it. This was her house – because she was rich. My father frequented a squalid café – because he was poor.

'So you're really getting married?'

'Yes.'

Confronted with her cruelty, I suddenly felt myself Towfik al-Hakim, misogynist.

'Pleased?'

'Why should I be?'

Yes, she was lying; she was pleased with the marriage. Or was I wronging her? A flash of hope. My voice came from unknown depths.

'Why are you marrying this man?'

'What else can I do?'

Marry me instead. That's what I should say. Fight! Take her hand and rush off to live as your heart demanded!

But I said nothing. My father was poor, his papers in the biscuit-tin, my mother in her grave, and no miracle had happened. The house had not been bombed; there had been no famine.

The night she got married I had a tomb in my heart. I was restless and walked in the garden to stare at the night.

8

MY FATHER'S FACE SHONE WITH DELIGHT:

'We're going to have a first-rate servant – Mabruka who used to work for Rateb Bey.'

I shared his pride. At the same time I could envisage no one from Suad's household coming as a servant to us. Seeing the great difference between our style of living and hers, would she not despise us?

'Aren't you pleased?'

'Yes, I'm pleased.'

My father went to fetch her one afternoon . . .

But I'm going too fast. I've left out the previous stage.

In those days I was too preoccupied to concern myself with the major change in my father's life. Only clashes and collisions show what is going on in the minds of others. We only see the pattern of events when they are in the past; just as we only notice a valley when we're on a mountain top. We can only understand when it is too late to use our understanding.

My father had recently retired and taken his pension. I paid no particular attention to this new phase in his life. But his behaviour got a little eccentric. He was suddenly at odds with our house off Dam Street. He quarrelled with the pickle-seller. He acted like a caged lion. His only recourse was his chess-books, which he scored with a red pencil as though he were still marking exercises. He scolded our maid Fatima, until in exasperation she left us. Next, my father began to abuse the Sheikh's children on the stairs. When he struck the cucumber-vendor it caused a major row in the lane. But I paid no heed.

Even when he announced one evening that we were going to move house, I failed to see that he was desperately lonely, that his world had collapsed, that he felt useless and old. He was, I now realize, screaming for help. And no one helped him. I can remember simply being puzzled that he wanted to leave a place associated with my mother; but my pleasure in the move was stronger than puzzlement. At last we would leave the squalor of the poor to live on the fringes of a richer life. In Sharia al-Falaki there'd be none of the dirt, the noise and the stink of our congested lane. Not far from Sharia al-Falaki was the palace of a former Prime Minister.

Our small new flat, in a new, tidy building, pleased me. We had our old furniture. Sometimes I'd feel nostalgic for our old flat, with its large high-ceilinged rooms and its memories of my mother. But more often in my imagination I'd see Suad's family bursting in – including even the ghost of her old grandmother – to deride our poverty.

When my father brought Mabruka to our new flat, her reaction as he showed her round was the reaction I had imagined.

'Where, Mabruka, do you want to sleep?'

She pointed to the dining-room. 'In there.'

She was wearing an old dress of Suad's: something of Suad had entered our house!

My father's manner towards Mabruka was quite different from his manner towards Fatima. He seemed ready to wait on her, he was so thrilled to have her. But I ignored her, refusing to accept her permanence in our home. I felt my pride demanded I should treat her, not as my father did, but as Midhat or any of her old employers had done. I kept myself to myself, and hardly felt I was leaving my own home when I left in the morning. But I had to admit our standard of comfort improved: a clean white sheet on my bed, and a neatly ironed pair of pyjamas on the pillow. My father, too, seemed much more relaxed. He'd drink tea in the morning looking utterly at ease, smiling at Mabruka as if in his own imagining he was Rateb Bey himself.

One day Midhat greeted me with particular warmth; his eyes searched mine wickedly.

'What have you been doing with our Mabruka? Now, don't play the hypocrite and hide . . .'

'Hide what?'

He laughed.

'You mean you've done nothing? Then you're a fool!'

He began to recount his own adventures with Mabruka. I was surprised, but furtively content. For the first time in my life I had the sensation of having acquired something which Midhat, for all his wealth, had lost.

I returned home with new ideas whirling in my head.

If rich boys flirted with servants, why shouldn't I? I wasn't a monk. Nor was I an artist, like Towfik al-Hakim. Why shouldn't I enjoy myself like other people? I could, after all, become a prosecutor, even a cabinet minister. The whole world suddenly seemed at my feet. Why shouldn't I drive out the English and become Prime Minister? I could eventually marry a princess.

But if Mabruka resisted . . . if she screamed? The legal penalties for rape were stern.

Yet we were the same age. If she consented, if I used no force, there'd be no crime.

If she accused me of seduction? Midhat had referred to her as a mere peasant-girl; my father would slap her face and shut her up.

I'd be corrupt – why not? All the students boasted of their exploits with girls and *hashish*. Even Prime Ministers debauched minors. The prosecutors of criminals were criminals themselves.

When my father was at the café, Mabruka busied herself in the house. Meanwhile, in vision, I was enjoying her body. Now was the time to make the vision a fact.

I went into the dining-room and switched on the radio. Tchaikovsky filled the flat. Every Wednesday afternoon at the university, Dr Grace gave music sessions in one of the classrooms. Enthusing through his pebble glasses, he'd splutter about the peaks of art, the pinnacles of beauty. Tchaikovsky was a tortured soul, afflicted with sexual deviation, one who screamed his sufferings. A genius with a flaw. Music and boiling blood went together.

I forget Mabruka's exact words, but she said something contemptuous about classical music. She wanted to change to Cairo radio.

My desire changed to detestation.

'Who do you think you are? You're just a servant.'

But in a few minutes my desire came back. She was in the shower. I could almost smell her dark body as the water splashed over her limbs.

The shower stopped, and a strange sound took over. An animal with long hair was singing. But in her voice was contempt: the house was not what she was used to, she despised me. She and I were on the same level. If I wanted her, I must come on this basis. Come! Come!

I found the bathroom door half-open. I looked down, hiding the desire in my heart and hands.

A lying voice burst from my lips, forbidding her to sing, the stupid animal.

She laughed as though unaffected by my words.

If she had only fed my dream, treated me as if I were Midhat . . .

I went back to my own room, worn out, headachy. My brain felt empty. It was my body alone that sat on the chair, papers in front of me, walls, the window. I heard the primus in the kitchen. The connection between myself and my body seemed broken. Mabruka placed tea in front of me. It was red – that's all.

9

NOW MY THOUGHTS TURN TO SAAD ABDUL GAWAD. HE is one of my secrets, shared with no one: his long pale face with the large deepset eyes. At college he was the outstanding student in my year. I knew him better than anybody.

His home was a ramshackle house in a desolate, rubbish-strewn part of Manial, set among mean huts leading through filth to the Nile. His mother, a short woman, still wore mourning for his father who had died years before. His brother Sayid was a small grocer. He had many sisters. He studied and slept in a room which was furnished only by one bed in which he and his brother slept. But when Saad studied late, Sayid would fall asleep on the rush-mat in the sitting-room. Sometimes I spent whole nights with Saad. From him I heard about Karl Marx, Lenin, Sorel, Engels and Owen. He explained the differences between Nazism, Socialism, Fascism and Communism, ideas which I had confused until then, thinking they were all words for one and the same thing.

So as not to be quite outclassed and treated as his pupil, I told him about Towfik al-Hakim, insisting I was an artist who had no interest in politics, a monk of thought, living for art and beauty and hating anything else. Once when we were talking, he abused me: 'You understand nothing. You're a spoilt boy and even when you grow up you'll need a dummy.'

'You understand everything?'

'Yes,' he shouted. 'I know the world well. When I'm not at college, do you know where I go, for two weeks at a time? I help my brother in his shop, selling olives and Greek cheese by the piastre. I wear *gallabya* and wooden slippers. Why? To feed my mother and sisters. They're all making sacrifices so that I can be educated. If I don't come first, I'll kill myself: for I must get a scholarship. I'm not rich like you.'

I almost confessed that I was not rich as he imagined, but almost as poor as himself, dependent on my father's sacrifice for my college expenses. But I took a certain secret pleasure in being thought rich. We continued friends, and I began to forget my old aspiration to be like Midhat. I set Saad the intellectual as my new model; and I posed to him as an artist he could be proud of. I read him *First Love*. It was a silly tale full of phrases lifted from Towfik al-Hakim.

'Your style's good,' he said. 'But I can't get your point of view.'

'I'm trying to show that love is a mistake; the best thing in the world is for a man to avoid women.'

He laughed. 'I'm thinking of getting married. Tomorrow you'll think the same.'

'I'd die first.'

I told him the story of my love for Suad.

'You think that's real?'

He shook his head. 'I think we're not ready for love. All that moves us now is lust. Any woman will do. Anyway, I'm like that.'

'What do you do about it?'

'I manage.' He seemed embarrassed as though he did not want to go into details. I suspected him of amorous exploits on his evenings out with a friend of his in the College of Arts called Showki, who lived in Imbaba. Sometimes this Showki visited Saad in Manial. They never told me where they went together. Until one day when we were in the final exams I visited Saad and found him with a magazine whose name was new to me: *Dawn*. He opened it and displayed with pride an

277

article entitled *Democracy in the Soviet Constitution*, written by Saad Abdul Gawad.

How had he done something so miraculous?

The words *fellahin*, workers and slogans I did not understand filled the article. But I trembled for Saad.

'And when they know you are a communist, won't they arrest you?'

'They can't. Russia's fighting on the side of England. The Censor knows about this magazine. No one's made any objections.'

It occurred to me that it might be wiser to avoid him. But I continued to study with him and listen to him expounding the Communist Manifesto. As soon as I left his house, however, I reverted to my self-flattering role of artist, someone uninterested in economics, devoted to beauty. I could escape from poverty by ignoring it, by pretending I was rich. To Saad and his brother I seemed rich, acting and talking like someone of a rich family. Midhat always treated me as an equal.

One evening I ran into Saad and Showki at the Giza bus-stop.

'Where are you two going?'

'Come and see for yourself. A party.'

Saad exchanged a glance with Showki: 'A political party.'

'I'm not interested.'

'You can't go on with this pose. Come and see. If you don't enjoy it, you can leave.'

Why was I such a coward? How long could I go on pretending the world was inferior? I would go.

On the way they spoke mockingly of Ismail Pasha Yunis, the man holding the meeting. He was a cunning politician with pro-Axis sympathies. A German victory would enable him to take power. He was a King's man, deceiving the people with reports of Farouk's intelligence and dynamism. He was one of those who believed that only the upper class were capable of governing.

The meeting was to take place in one of the large buildings of Suleiman Pasha. I wondered, before we went upstairs, if

Saad and Showki intended to break up the meeting. But on whose behalf? My worries returned.

We entered a large, luxurious apartment, brilliantly lit, crowded with workers and students sitting in armchairs. A smooth man with shiny hair and soft skin was handing round cigarettes. He spoke in exaggerated tones which I distrusted. 'I'm delighted to meet you, sir. The Pasha will be here any minute.'

The atmosphere was claustrophobic. I got up.

'Where are you off to?' Saad asked.

I pushed him aside and was half-way down the stairs when a stocky man with a neat moustache intercepted me, grabbing my arm. He smiled.

'Where are you off to, professor?'

'I'm on my way home.'

'Please come with me.'

'What for?'

'Haven't you got something on you?'

I realized I was being arrested by a member of the secret police. I laughed. My fears seemed to dissolve. I didn't know why, but I felt a new person, that I'd found a new strength.

'What do you mean? Hashish?'

He narrowed his eyes. 'No, I mean pamphlets.'

'You've got the wrong man. I peddle hashish.' To my own surprise I said this. I didn't care what he did to me.

We walked down the street, him still clutching my arm, though I increased my pace, which forced him to run to keep up with me. I felt buoyant. One day I would be in a position to humiliate this ruffian.

An officer sat at a table in the police-station.

'What were you doing there?'

'Observing.'

'Any pamphlets?'

'No.'

My pockets were searched: I had seven piastres, the flat key and a dirty handkerchief.

He took my name and address.

'Where's your student-card?'

'Not with me.'

He called one of his men and told him to go with me and get it. It all seemed trivial. I longed to tell Saad of my adventure.

Passing through our dining-room to fetch my card, I saw my father sitting with Mabruka. Best fetch my card and finish the whole matter without alarming him. But he followed me into the room. He looked terrified; Mabruka stood, pale-faced, behind him.

'What's happened?'

'Nothing, Father. They want my student-card.'

'What have you done?'

'I told you, nothing.'

My father came with me by taxi to the police-station. All the way he repeated his question and I repeated my denial. In front of the officer my father cringed, his hands trembling, his breath coming with difficulty. The officer, ignoring him, copied details from my card on a slip of paper.

'Keep away from that sort of thing in future.'

My father protested that all my life I had been a law-abiding boy. He was near to tears, and clung to me all the way home. I thought it was a lot of fuss for nothing.

10

SAAD – WHEN I TOLD HIM WHAT HAD HAPPENED – explained that the white slip of paper would be sent to a special branch of the secret police. From now on I would be watched. At the least sign of political disturbance, they would arrest me.

'But what have I to do with politics?'

'That's how they act. They drive anyone, however innocent to start with, to be their enemy.'

'Do they know your name?'

He laughed sarcastically. 'No, not yet.'

'And Showki?'

'Nor him, either.'

I was afraid. I did not like the sensation of being followed. The sacred phrases we had studied at College churned in my head: The accused is innocent until proved guilty. No guilt by association. Search warrants. The Rights of Man. The Constitution. These were the supports of human dignity. Or so we had been told.

I retreated into my books. The final examinations were near.

In the following days I went to the college in the mornings and spent the evenings at home. Although it was urgent to revise my lecture notes, I found myself unable to concentrate. Late at night I'd leave my room, and look for Mabruka. But she was never to be found. The only place she could be was in my father's bedroom. Incredible, but such was the case.

I'd smile bitterly at the thought of my father's indulging in something disgusting which I had refrained from. I'd go back and – despite the increasing heat – try to concentrate on the law. First light would come and I'd still be thinking of Mabruka. Perhaps my father was doing nothing with her; he was, after all, in his dotage. Perhaps he was afraid to be alone: perhaps he feared ghosts!

After the exams Showki told us he'd found a job – on the newspaper *Al-Ayyam*. I fervently hoped that one day I'd see my story, *First Love*, published there too.

We'd sit over coffee and a Hollywood cigarette at Mikhailo-vitch's, the café in Midan Ismailia, Showki showing us the drawings he was now publishing in the paper. We would talk for hours about Muhammad Nagi, the editor-in-chief. Saad believed that Nagi was an opportunist who'd back any party for a price. Showki agreed. I said nothing. It would be shameful for me to insult the man who would one day publish my stories. It was hardly decent, I felt, for Showki to attack the man he worked for.

My joy at passing my exams turned to disappointment when I realized that, having secured only a 'pass', I would not be eligible for the Prosecutor's Office. Nevertheless my father, delighted that I had passed at all, badgered Rateb Bey to use his influence on my behalf. Rateb Bey said that my qualifications were enough for an assistant administrator in the Ministry of Interior. Fortunately the Minister was his friend and he would do his best. I took none of this seriously; I still felt myself a student.

We were sitting in Mikhailovitch one evening when Saad spotted an item in Showki's newspaper.

'Just listen to this!' he burst out. 'It makes me feel like committing murder.' Someone from our class, it was stated, had been promoted to the Prosecutor's Office, although he had only got a pass degree.

Saad was furious. 'What a system! I get a first, and they do nothing for me, while this idiot, just because he's the son of a pasha, gets promoted above all our year.'

For the first time we realized that Saad, too, had applied for this job.

'How can you even want such a job?' Showki asked. 'What would you do if expected to prosecute a communist?'

'I'd refuse.'

'Then they'd never employ you.'

My father was as angry as Saad when I told him of the scandal. He went straight off to Rateb Bey. When he came back his anger had doubled. 'To Rateb Bey it's only natural that the pasha's son should get the job. You're just the son of an unimportant schoolmaster.'

I wanted to go out, but I hadn't any money.

'Father, please give me £1.'

'I've done all I can. It's now up to you to find a job. I can't go on keeping you all my life. If you want to sleep and eat here, you're welcome. But money, no.'

What upset me was that Mabruka had been listening. I found my steps turning towads *Al-Ayyam*.

When I told the doorman I wanted to visit Showki the illustrator, he sent me to the first floor. Showki was sitting sketching in a small room, with another young man who was talking into the telephone. As we sat there, my head swirling with the wish to work there, too, Showki and his companion rose to their feet. A man stood in the door, whom I at once recognized as Muhammad Nagi. Two other men were with him.

I decided not to stand up.

Nagi paid no attention to us. Pointing to the wall behind Showki, he told the men to take it away so as to include this room in the editorial office. He suddenly noticed Showki's drawing.

'What on earth's that?'

'An illustration to a story!'

'What do you think the reader can get from it? It has nothing to attract his attention.'

Before I knew what was happening, I had joined the discussion. My embarrassment had somehow vanished, just as when I was walking with the plainclothes-man to the police-station.

'He should have illustrated an action.'

Nagi turned to me as if we had already met.

'Isn't that so?' He turned to Showki. 'You heard what your friend said?'

'There's only space for a head.'

Nagi cut him short. 'I've told you a hundred times, the picture's more important than the story. If the reader isn't attracted by the picture, he's not going to bother with the writer. Whoever it is. Even Towfik al-Hakim. Who's the writer?'

'Mahmoud Lufti.'

'Cut the story.'

Once again I joined in. 'It would improve it.'

My opinion seemed to worry him.

'You don't like Lufti?'

'No.'

'Whom do you like?'

'Towfik al-Hakim.'

'But how many do we have like him?'

I couldn't quite say that I wrote myself. But I did say, 'Personally I don't like anyone else.'

Unfortunately he could not continue our conversation because a man came in carrying a newly printed galley proof which Nagi began to correct, ignoring me, busy with cuts and question marks. I should have liked to have told him that I was a writer, that I had my degree, that I was related to Rateb Bey.

When Nagi had finished with the proof, he told Showki to do another drawing and let him see it. He turned on his heel and left.

Showki exploded.

'Are you mad? Do you want to get me the sack?'

The last thing I had wanted to do was harm him.

'I'm terribly sorry, Showki. I didn't mean it.'

He smiled. 'You're always getting involved.'

He did another drawing. This time of a naked dancer with a cup in her hand. He said mockingly, 'This is the kind of thing he goes for.'

When he came back from showing it to Nagi, he said:

'Didn't I say, you'd get me dismissed?'

'What happened?' I longed to think Nagi had not forgotten me.

'He said you knew more than I did. He thought you were an artist too.'

'What did you tell him?'

'That you had never done a drawing in your life.'

I hated Showki. I felt that it was he who was trying to get me dismissed from my job.

'And then? What did he say next?'

'Naturally he liked the dancer.'

As I left the building I swore I would return. This would not be the end of my dealings with Muhammad Nagi.

As I approached our flat door, I heard the voices of my father and Mabruka arguing. When I went in they were standing in silence. Something was up.

Next morning Mabruka told me my father wanted me, and

284

followed me closely as I went to his room. Her eyes were fixed on me, I noticed. My father was in bed.

'Leave us, Mabruka.'

My father was staring at the door where Mabruka stood as though about to jump forward. Did he have in mind to dismiss her? He was perhaps going to tell me about the argument I had heard yesterday. He was coming to his senses and wanted my support. I sat down on the bed and smiled encouragement.

My father lowered his eyes. He pushed his hand under his pillow, held it there a moment, then drew out £5. He asked with a feeble smile: 'You need some money?'

I could not believe he would give me all this.

I whispered, 'If you can spare some.'

He withdrew his hand, wavered, then said, his head hanging on his chest: 'I have something to tell you, my son. You're grown up, you're a man of the world, you can understand.'

He wiped a tear from his eye.

'What's happened, father?'

He said through his tears, 'What can I do? It was she who left me. I wish I could rest like her. But she left me to be tormented. But praise God, no one can say I have failed you or stinted you in anything.'

What was he trying to tell me?

'I'm a sick man. Any day now I may die.'

'God protect you, Father.'

'I must get some rest.'

'Is anything tiring you, Father?'

I felt he was trying to say that he wanted to dismiss Mabruka. She must have exhausted him and worn him out. But instead he managed to put strength into his voice and declare:

'I'm going to get married, my boy.'

I could only express my dismay with a smile. I could say nothing, feel nothing.

He pointed to the door.

'I'm going to marry her.'

I looked at him with hatred. Silly old fool! I'd kill him. I'd take his neck and wring it.

'Impossible, father,' I screamed. 'You're off your head.'

I went for him, my hands gripping his neck. His fevered flesh shook, his body trembled. He slumped submissively on the bed, groaning as I raved. Then I burst from his room. I lurched at her, screamed. She was in hysterics, her screams filled the world. I ran out of the flat and into the street.

II

I FELT MYSELF AN EXILE FROM THE WORLD.

If I wanted to save myself from disgrace, I must take drastic action.

Hopeless, penniless, fatherless, motherless, I reached Midan Ismailia and the café where people sat drinking coffee and reading *Al-Ayyam*.

Could I sit down and order a bean sandwich with a cup of coffee, then run off?

No good. I wasn't up to such tricks. The *garçon* would hand me over to the police.

My mind played with a career of crime, holding up the Bank of Egypt, fleeing the city, then dying.

Should I kill myself?

I saw the tram crushing my body, the blood on the rails.

Or wait for my father's death. And my inheritance. What inheritance?

A few papers signed by Saad Zaghloul thrown into a biscuit-tin. He had wanted to take care of them. But he had forgotten. Instead he had married Mabruka.

My mother's relatives lived in the Delta. We had not kept up with them. They were poor peasants. The only relationship we had bothered to preserve was with Rateb Bey, who was rich and despised us.

Or should I go to Saad?

I'm broke, Saad, and hungry. I'm afraid. I've acted like a spoilt child. Now I'll change. I'll stop pretending to be rich, stop hiding my poverty. What shall I do? I have nowhere to sleep, no money. Shall I weep? Shall I rage? Shall I knock down that fat man walking in front of me, or slap that woman mincing down the street?

Would Saad and his grocer-brother let me help them in their shop? I must get work.

But Saad was not at home.

My last resort was Showki. I'd go to him and ask him to take me in, to find me a job, any job, sweeping and cleaning, even – at *Al-Ayyam*. I'd apologize for belittling his drawing to Muhammad Nagi. If I saw Nagi again, I'd say Showki was the best artist in the world. Will you help me, Showki?

I sat by the bank of the Nile to rest. My suit – and it was the only one I had – was getting dirty. It would wear out and I'd end up naked as the down-and-outs. I'd squat outside Sayida Zainab's mosque, farthings dropping into my shaking palm. My father would find me sick and diseased; he would implore me to go home with him, but I'd refuse and remain a beggar, torturing him with my refusal.

I hardly believed my ears when the doorman said that Showki was waiting for me in his room.

'What's brought you?'

'Catastrophe.'

'You don't look desperate.'

'I've left home.'

'What's up?'

'My father's gone mad.'

He frowned, trying to understand.

'He's going to marry our servant girl. I've left them the house.'

'But he's still your father.'

'Still?'

'Try and see his point of view.'

'An old man . . . in retirement . . . to marry a young servant?'

'What's the objection?'

For a brief moment I wondered if perhaps I was wronging

287

my father: had he not a perfect right to marry whomever he pleased? Was it any business of mine?

'But I'll not go back.'

'Tomorrow you'll think differently.'

'What can I do meanwhile?'

'Stay with me.'

He paused. 'Or we'll go and look for Saad.'

We found Saad and I shared his bed. My thoughts were fixed on the green £5 note which my father had brandished in my face. I needed it. I'd go the café next day and politely ask for it. But if he invited me to go back to his house, to eat his bread, I'd not give way.

At the chess café next morning I saw all the regular clients except him.

I did not like to stand on the pavement outside in case my father saw and realized I needed him. So I crossed to the pavement at the back of the Opera.

Suddenly I saw a huge band of boys and girls rushing into the street shouting and screaming. I heard them talk of a fire that had broken out inside the Opera. In a few moments two fire-engines drove up with their bells ringing. Among the people who had run out I recognized the famous actress Suad Resoni – she was in a transparent night-dress. Beside her stood the elderly actor Raouf Monastirli, bewildered. After watching the firemen for a few moments I returned to the café and found my father.

'How are you, my boy? Sit down.'

His welcome was as effusive as to a stranger. He could not look me in the eyes. He called the Greek waiter.

'Ask the gentleman what he'll have.'

I refused to drink anything. He then looked round and spotted a table all by itself.

'Shall we sit over there?'

When we had moved, he again tried to persuade me to drink something, but again I refused.

After a few moments' silence, he looked at the floor.

'Kismet!' he sighed. 'It's what God has decreed.'

I said nothing and he added almost inaudibly:

'We got married last night.'

I tried to smile, to show that I didn't mind.

'I was in a dilemma,' he went on. 'If you knew everything, you'd understand and pity me. I don't blame you for being angry. You had a right to be – and more than you were. But she's a minor, I'm an old man. Think of the disgrace if the police found out that I'd got her with child.'

So that – incredible thought it seemed – was his dilemma. She was pregnant. Why didn't he kill her? I lost my patience.

'I want the £5.'

He put his hand in his pocket as though the matter was beyond discussion and handed me the note.

He said slowly: 'You're coming home with me for lunch.'

'No.'

He said in despair: 'We'll leave your food in your room. Eat whenever you get back.'

'I'm not coming back.'

'Where'll you sleep?'

'With a friend.'

One of the chess-players shouted to my father.

'Why don't you come over and watch our friend here getting beaten?'

I got up and my father patted my shoulder, smiling. I felt he was being insincere. I pitied but felt disgust.

'I'm still your father. If I've done wrong, you become the father, but stay with me.'

'I just can't,' I whispered. 'Good-bye, Father.'

I walked in the streets, gazing at window displays of clothes and chocolate. I looked at the prices, I wanted to buy things; I felt the money in my pocket, I mustn't spend it. It was more precious than anything I could buy.

I remembered the fire at the Opera. Why shouldn't I go and tell Showki? If they hadn't heard about it at *Al-Ayyam*, they would be interested. Perhaps I could meet Muhammad Nagi.

I ran to *Al-Ayyam* but Showki wasn't in. So I shouted to the receptionist, 'I want to see Nagi Bey.'

'Have you an appointment?'

I said boldly: 'Tell him that Yusif Abdul Hamid, the lawyer, wants to see him in connection with the fire at the Opera.'

He frowned and picked up the telephone.

In a moment a secretary was ushering me into a large, luxurious room. I recognized the tall stature of Nagi with his quiet face, cigarette in his mouth.

He stood in the middle of the floor smiling faintly.

'What fire is this, sir?'

'The Opera's burning.'

'At this moment?'

'I've just come from there.'

He looked at me carefully as if he had not seen me before.

'I came to tell Showki. You saw me once in his office, sir. He wasn't in, so I thought I'd contact you directly.'

He gave me a smile of recognition, then rang a bell.

'What exactly did you see?'

'Actors and actresses coming out screaming from the back door. Suad Resoni stood in her night-dress in the street. Beside her Raouf Monastirli looking most upset. The girl extras were crying. Two fire-engines came to put out the fire.'

His smile got warmer and his eyes shone with a clever glint. He offered me a cigarette and lit one himself.

'Is the fire out?'

'They were putting it out when I came here.'

He said, still smiling, 'We're most obliged to you, sir. Are you interested in journalism?'

I said with pretended disdain: 'No.'

He said, ringing the bell a second time. 'Why not?'

'I don't like politics. They cause trouble.'

I realized I must establish myself in his eyes as someone important. I'd tell him how I was once arrested so he'd think me someone dangerous.

'Do you support any party?'

'None. They're all crooks. The last time I went to a political meeting the police arrested me.'

He frowned and a look of doubt came back into his eyes.

'On what grounds?'

'I didn't like the meeting and left early. But the police seemed to think I'd gone out to cause trouble. I wasn't five minutes at the police-station. My uncle Rateb Bey rang up the Minister of the Interior and got me out.'

'Hassan Bey Rateb?'

'Yes.'

An athletic young man came in. Nagi addressed him sarcastically.

'Abdul Fettah, instead of dozing here, go and cover the fire at the Opera.'

'Fire?'

'Yes, a fire. Take a photographer. Take Said.'

The young man shot from the room.

Nagi turned to me.

'You work as a lawyer?'

'Yes.'

'Why've you never thought of taking up journalism?'

I felt a show of disinterest on my part would increase his interest.

'I've never tried.'

At that moment the telephone rang. The receiver in his hand he said, 'Don't forget to give my greetings to Rateb Bey. Keep in touch. I'm most grateful. Who knows? One day we may work together.'

I left, astonished I had been able to do so much.

12

THE NEWS WAS PUBLISHED THAT SAAD ABDUL GAWAD had been appointed to the Prosecutor's Office. Jobless, penniless, I was a self-confessed failure, standing still while everyone else forged ahead.

Saad changed, and quickly. One evening I found him going

through his papers and burning lots of them, including his article on the Soviet Constitution.

He no longer liked to join us at Mikhailovitch's, on the grounds that the place was watched, being known as a haunt of young communists. He would angrily deny – particularly to Showki – that he had changed his principles, but would invoke his loyalty to his job, his sense of duty. His conscience was clear.

But Showki maintained that Saad was an *arriviste* who had arrived; who had espoused communism because of personal poverty; now the doors of power had opened, the cause was abandoned. I tried not to take sides in their quarrel; I wanted to remain the friend of both.

One evening we waited for Saad at Groppi's till closing time. Showki asked me crossly: 'What do we do now?'

'We can wait on the pavement. . . .'

'Come and sleep at my place, why not?'

Showki lived near Bab Zuweila, in a gloomy, terrifying place like a brigand's cave. A huge wooden door creaked on to a dingy hall. We talked late and Showki tried hard to convert me to communism: the only road for an intellectual.

'If you lived in a communist society, you'd be working, living. . . .'

His words impressed me, but at the same time I was afraid of his voice, afraid of the gloomy room we sat in and the ears listening. I could not bear the sense of being watched, the police at my heels. My one ambition was to work on *Al-Ayyam*. I envied Saad; I wished I could have done as well as he had. I couldn't share Showki's concern for the mass of people. The masses meant no more to me than did Mabruka. Mabruka had managed to get hold of my father; no one had given thought to me. Why should I think of them?

Next morning I found Saad in his office. He apologized for the previous night; he had been busy till midnight with a police raid on a brothel. They had arrested, not only lots of girls, but also some well-known people among their clients.

'Where did you sleep last night, Yusif?'

292

'At Showki's.'

He looked round, then whispered:

'Don't get yourself involved. You'll only regret it later. Our country's not ripe for communism – that stage will come later. What Egypt needs now is people with conscience.'

He was an opportunist posing as a man of principle, but I pretended to believe him.

He described the police raid with the enthusiasm he had once kept for Marx. The police had arrested Sayid Wahabi the iron-merchant, along with Esam Rafet son of Rafet Pasha, ex-Minister of Agriculture. Saad expatiated on the corruption and immorality of the rich.

Having promised that I'd go straight to his house – so as to avoid Showki – I went straight to meet Showki at *Al-Ayyam*. By now I was on friendly terms with several of the junior editors, whom I had often told of my role in the Opera fire; I pretended to be a person of great importance, boasting of my relationship to my 'Uncle' Rateb Bey and of his friendship with the Minister of the Interior. Sometimes I ran into Nagi on my way to Showki's office. We'd exchange a few words of greeting while all the editors gazed at me in admiration. They spoke in front of me as though their every word would be reported back to him.

I now picked up the receiver on Showki's desk and quietly asked the operator: 'Nagi Bey, please.'

Showki looked surprised. I said calmly:

'I've some news for him.'

To Nagi I related the arrest of Sayid Wahabi and Esam Rafet. I added other snippets I had heard from Saad: how the Public Prosecutor was out of favour and would soon be dismissed; his replacement would be the Dean of the Law College. I dropped these pieces of gossip as though I were on intimate terms with both the Prosecutor and the Dean. He interrupted me:

'I insist you work with us. What you've just told me is enough – I'll offer you £30 a month.'

I pretended to hesitate, then whispered:

'But I . . .'

'You what?'

'I'm an artist.'

He laughed.

'Listen to me, sir. You want to be an artist? Then you want to be an idler. You have first-class connections. You know how to get the news. Journalism offers a wonderful future. I consider you engaged.'

I gave way.

When Showki heard the news, he flung his arms round me and kissed me; he would not let me out of his sight all day. Saad's company, I thought, would be more worthwhile and less dangerous.

I found my father in his café – I had got into the way of going there to borrow small sums. When I told him I had found work on *Al-Ayyam*, he looked upset:

'With your good degree you want to work as a hack? I hope you'll find something better.'

I laughed, waiting for his reaction to my news:

'They're offering me £30 a month.'

He could hardly believe his ears, then deluged me with congratulations.

I quickly added, 'But at the moment I'm broke.'

'You've signed your contract?'

'Yes.'

'For sure?'

'For sure.'

'How much do you need to tide you over?'

He turned to the drunkard he had played chess with: 'Zaki Bey, I want a word with you.'

They went into a corner and I saw the man open his wallet. My father gave me £10, insisting I must repay it.

I took a room in Madame Rose's *pension* in a large building in Midan Ismailia. The room, which looked on to a little lane, had one wooden bedstead and an ancient wardrobe, but its blue curtains made it seem luxurious.

This was the beginning of my new life.

I felt enormously attracted to Muhammad Nagi: I could

294

imagine no one cleverer or greater than him in the whole world. Early every morning, as soon as he arrived, I'd retail the news to him as if I knew everything. Nagi never realized the sources of my news: Saad, Showki, my father and his café. From such limited sources I managed to create the illusion of contacts ramifying all over Cairo. A strange variety of people played chess: an employee from the Customs, a railway driver, an official from the Chamber of Commerce, an inspector of secondary education, a Jewish house-agent. For Muhammad Nagi I'd glean such items as the arrest of a pasha's wife with her handbag stuffed with hashish: the departure of Prince Yeken to Istanbul with his five dogs: the unsuitability of the newly-purchased railway engines: the prediction that there'd be a two months' shortage of fertilizer. Nagi would order me a coffee and offer me a cigarette while he listened, all ears.

Once I caught Saad on the point of going to investigate a murder. He let me accompany him to a tumbledown house in Bulak. We found the victim, an old man, lying on a brass bed with his throat cut. Borrowing Saad's explanation of the crime I wrote an article as soon as I got back. The criminal really to blame, I wrote, was the victim's environment. An opium addict, he stole his son's money. His new young wife had killed him with the assistance of her lover.

Muhammad Nagi read my piece, then added one sentence:

'By Yusif al-Suefi, crime reporter to *Al-Ayyam*.'

He laughed. 'We must make you known to our readers.'

'My name is Yusif Abdul Hamid al-Suefi.'

'That's not a name, it's an article. If you shorten your name, people will remember it better.'

Saad's reaction was less admiring.

'You should pay me what they give you for that piece. You quote me word for word without mentioning my name.'

One night Nagi in his office introduced me to the actor Anwar Sami.

'Yusif's someone I can trust. He comes of a good family and will cause you no trouble.'

Anwar spoke in the affected manner of an actor. 'Thank

295

heavens, Nagi Bey. What a relief to have a change from those cadging, blackmailing, sinister young men who nowadays pass for journalists. "Give me a cigarette, give me five shillings – otherwise I'll publish scandals about you!"'

He turned to me ingratiatingly.

'I'm honoured to meet you, sir.'

But to Nagi he shouted:

'Yet he doesn't look like a journalist.'

'Why not?'

'He's shy.'

To me he added, 'Cheer up, sir.'

'I fear for him,' Nagi said. 'You actors are more dangerous even than us.'

Anwar was the first artist I had ever met. He drove me that night to Cairo Studios, introducing me to Huda Murad and the producer Helmi Kamil. Afterwards he insisted I should go with him to his flat. When there he raved about Nagi. He was the first writer in the land – even the Palace feared him. So did the Ministers. All the political parties wanted his support. He lived like a king, spending money like water. But he was poor – having nothing but his salary.

'Enough that he's got Shohdi Pasha where he wants him. Shohdi's millions . . . it's all at Nagi's disposal. If I'd known how to manage Shohdi, I could have been another Cecil B. de Mille.'

He stuck out his lower lip.

'But what a price – to have to make love to Shohdi's wife! Such a bore! He must have nerves of steel. I'd vomit if I tried to kiss her.'

Anwar took it for granted that I knew what he was talking about. I kept up the pretence, but my head reeled. Suddenly he got up and fetched a red silk tie which he offered to me as a gift. When I absolutely refused to accept it, he seemed displeased.

Next day Nagi congratulated me on refusing the tie.

'He told you?'

'He was pleased, too. It proved you came of a good background.'

I was angry.

'But he's no good.'

'Anwar? Why?'

'I don't like him.'

He said in a fatherly manner: 'Look. Why do they want to know us? So we can put them in our paper. They pretend to be our friends, to offer us presents, to do anything for us: they're publicity-mad. But never imagine that you can be real friends with one of them.'

I blurted out: 'But he insulted you.'

'Really? What did he say?'

I repeated all that Anwar had said about Nagi's *affaire* with Shohdi Pasha's wife.

He smiled. 'You're still very young and very innocent. I hope you'll stay that way. Don't believe all you hear from these cannibals. Shohdi finances the paper. That's true. No paper can live only from its sales. We depend on advertisements. Shohdi's advertisements pay for our presses. This country lives on rumour. No one likes to believe that there's such a thing as honest work. We work with Shohdi – so it's a foregone conclusion that I'm having an *affaire* with his wife. The Prime Minister depends on the Minister of Finance. The Minister of Finance must be sleeping with the Premier's wife. His Majesty sacks someone. Someone's wife must have rebuffed His Majesty in his Pyramid rest-house. My advice to you, Yusif, is to disregard rumours. I need someone I can depend on. Don't let me down. You remind me of myself as I used to be. But I was bolder. If someone told me slanders, I'd give him a good box on the ears.'

I felt, as I left his office, that *Al-Ayyam* was the target of malicious plotters. Nagi was a noble warrior resisting wicked assaults. I must stand by him. Fight and defend him.

Then one afternoon the telephone rang. An unknown voice answered.

'I'm Zaki . . .'

'Zaki who, please?'

'The friend of your father, I play chess with him in the café. I'm speaking from the café now.'

My heart sank. He must be after the money my father borrowed.

'Be brave, my boy. There's been a tragedy. Your late father . . . You can hear me?'

On my way out I heard someone shout: 'Nagi Bey wants you.' I went to him. He at once asked:

'What's wrong?'

'Nothing.'

'Has something upset you?'

'No.'

As he told me he wanted me to supervise the art section, to ensure there were no attacks on Cairo's two most famous singers, I was perplexed. How could I confess that my father had died? If I did, he would want to publish the news. The other editors would insist on walking in the funeral. The truth would come out, that I was poor, that I had deceived them all. They would learn about Mabruka.

I ran to the café as if pursued. My father was dead. . . . The father I loved. Yet I had rejected him.

Guilty though I felt, I still cursed the scandalous circumstances in which he had died.

13

DISMAYED AT THE SIGHT OF MY FATHER SPREAD OUT on the café tables, my one desire was to finish everything quietly, in secret. But how? Ambulance, undertaker, police, hearse, conventional condolences, proffering of cigarettes, the horns of cars, the rattle of trams, all in the harsh light of day.

I had no money. Perhaps he had some. Could I go through his pockets? I suppose I had the right to. Could I borrow from Nagi? Impossible. Saad?

Rateb Bey . . .

His voice on the telephone pretended sorrow.

'Come here at once, my boy. You'll find I've arranged everything. No, better stay with him. . . . "No might and no strength but in God". . . . Don't worry. I'll pay the expenses.'

To him all was easy, from showing grief to arranging the funeral.

Mabruka came to the café. Now the scandal had exploded. In her arms she carried her child. Our house-walls had fallen and disclosed all that had been hidden.

I was stripped naked.

That day everyone heard Mabruka's screams. The mourners stared at her. They were probably whispering of the scandal, of how the baby she carried was my brother. I must ignore her, bury my head in the sand.

My father was carried to his tomb. Perhaps the moment they laid him underground was the best, for now Mabruka was finished, finished for ever. The world was large: she'd go her way and I'd go mine. Next morning Madame Rose would bring my tea and tell me about the film she'd seen the night before. She had no idea I had just lost my father; I smiled to keep her ignorant.

They closed the tomb with a boulder, then sprinkled dust on top, then water. It was sunset and the evening call to prayer. Everything that I would now do would be done to hide my sadness: I'd become a famous writer, make lots of money, climb to the highest peaks and scorn the people; and only those who had come to the funeral would know that my father had died and I was sorry.

I resolved I would be what my humble father had never managed to be. I would rise above poverty, tittle-tattle, scandal; to be Yusif Bey, Yusif Pasha – no £3 a month for me!

Mabruka was still wailing as Midhat led me to their large car and placed me beside Rateb Bey. They wanted me to go home with them but I asked to be dropped at the newspaper.

When Midhat insisted on coming with me, I was so happy. It was no longer necessary for me to conceal my father's death, for this elegant mourner with his large car was proof that I was the relative of Rateb Bey. Everyone could see his expensive clothes and hear his cultured voice.

I took my leave of him a moment to go to Nagi's office. Now my face could reveal the maximum of misery. He noticed it.

'What's up?'

'My father's died.'

He was taken aback. Strange feelings of sadness overwhelmed me, though I knew they were pretended.

'When?'

'This morning.'

'Why didn't you tell me? I asked you.'

'I didn't want to upset you.'

'You're mad. Is this the way to act?'

'It's over now. The funeral took place this afternoon, and my uncle, Rateb Bey, brought me here.'

'But I still can't understand how you didn't tell me. This is something unheard of.'

'I agreed with my uncle that we'd have a simple funeral.'

'But I still can't understand why you didn't tell me . . .'

'Midhat, Rateb Bey's son, is waiting in my office.'

I wanted to drop the name of Rateb Bey a thousand times.

'Good, we'll publish the list of mourners. Is it written?'

What could I say. The names were all those of nobodys. It was impossible, but I consented, when he told me to write the list there and then and send it down to the printers.

I stood with Midhat at the entrance of the building while we waited for his driver to bring the Citroën. But I wrote no list of mourners.

Two days later when Nagi asked me why it had not been published,

'I couldn't write it,' I said, 'My eyes were blinded with tears, and what was the use, anyway?'

'What a strange person you are, Yusif.'

At our editorial meeting Nagi declared that my behaviour proved I was a true journalist: my father had died in the morning, I had said nothing but, after attending the funeral, had worked normally on the evening shift. 'I prophesy here and now, Yusif has a great future with us.'

He turned and invited me to lunch and we went out, watched with envy by the other editors.

Showki blocked my way, whispering: 'Where are you going?'

'I'll tell you later.'

It seemed sad that our friendship was waning.

Nagi drove me to his house in Zamalek, a palace surrounded by a garden. A large white dog ran up to welcome us, then rolled on his back in the grass.

Nagi told me about the dog – it had belonged to his friend, the singer Dalal.

He suddenly asked me:

'Are you in love?'

'No.'

'Why are you so emphatic? Is love bad?'

'Of course not!'

'Have you no girl-friends?'

'No.'

'Where do you live?'

'In a *pension*.'

'Could you take a girl-friend there?'

'I don't think so.'

'Do you know what I call men like you, who don't know love? Ignoramuses, illiterates unable to read the meaning of life.'

I smiled shyly.

'But I'll help you, Yusif. I'll give you a key to my flat in Maspiro Street; you can consider it your own.'

After a few seconds he asked: 'Are you shy?'

'No.'

He laughed and got up from his chair.

'Remind me to give you the key before you leave.'

Anwar Sami had told the truth: Nagi lived like a king. A servant in a dinner-jacket served us our food – fish with white wine, piccata of meat with mushrooms and red wine, then fruit with Crème Chantilly. Even the coffee had cardamom in it.

From Nagi I learnt the names of the most expensive cigars, the most complicated dishes. When I spoke of the meals we had at home, however, I simply substituted those I had observed in the house of Rateb Bey.

That afternoon I left the house with the key to his flat; in my ears rang his encouragement to find the right girl to teach me how to be a man of the world.

That evening when Midhat came to the newspaper (we had previously made an appointment) a pretty girl was sitting with him in his Citroën, I had a sudden presentiment that this was the girl for whom the key had been intended.

14

POOR SAMIA. . . . AT THAT TIME SHE WAS STILL 'BAHIA', a pretty, frivolous girl, not a thought in her head, sitting beside Midhat in his car. Then I walked out . . . a stranger from *Al-Ayyam*, too shy to look her in the face. How could I make her mine? Could I persuade her to betray Midhat, or him to share her?

This was the great challenge of my life. The old, shy, timid Yusif had to die: a new young confident Yusif had to be born, an adventurer who could master women and make them his. Till then the only women I had known had been my mother, Suad and Mabruka. I needed a different kind of woman, as Nagi had said: one who could teach me the meaning of life and banish my fears: a woman I could take, outside marriage, outside any fixed aim, simply to conquer, simply to inflame till she panted for my triumph.

'Monsieur wants to go where?' she asked coldly.

We could go anywhere, I said. But eventually we would go to the flat: if this meant seducing her, or betraying Midhat. Nagi was right: I could not hope to master life if I could not first master a woman.

Yet how could I compete with Midhat? He was more attractive, richer, more experienced. He had a car.

'You write in the paper?'

I had to confess I was still unknown. I could feel their amusement at my expense.

'I want you to write about Bahia.'

The fact that she was an actress gave me hope. After all, I was the writer who specialized in news of actresses. I could make her famous, help her in her career. Midhat could not do that.

The car reached the ascent to the pyramids and I felt asphyxiated by my own thoughts; I had tasted sin, and felt a sudden nostalgia for days of innocence. Should I make an abrupt break with Nagi before it was too late?

The car stopped and I rushed off into the dark.

I was alone . . .

I had walked far; by now Midhat was probably kissing her. Where else could I find the girl to liberate me from my fears? Could she step from the dark interior of a pyramid? The gloomy path was frightening. What was it that attracted a woman to a man? His car? His wit, his repartee? His sense of humour? His money? His experience? I had none of these advantages.

Yet I must win through. Otherwise it would be better to be devoured by wild animals, or sleep in a grave.

'Where were you? Weren't you afraid of ghosts?'

I was flattered by her concern.

While my thoughts were sad – admitting that I could never be sufficiently vicious to do what I intended – her voice was sprightly as she confessed she was pregnant and expecting a child in seven months' time. A thunder clap! I was glad to notice that Midhat was as appalled as I was. She added that she did not know who the father was: Munir? Midhat? Yusif?

But impossible that anyone could be so frank. She was teasing us in an indecent way: she spoke like a man among men, I listened like a virgin. Then suddenly I realized her drift – she was talking about a new name for her role in films!

'You're brighter than Midhat!' I smiled back at her compliment.

When we reached the Studio – where she said she had an appointment with Helmi Kamil, the director – I basked in my welcome from Anwar Sami and Huda Murad. I could show her that despite my modesty I was a well-known journalist while she was still unknown. My plan succeeded. She loitered a long way off, afraid to approach, until in pity I called her over. She joined us shyly.

But she had been telling the truth: Helmi Kamil had really been hunting for a name.

Her name was given her by Anwar Sami, who boastfully named her after himself. Everyone in the Studio knew what price she would be expected to pay, and I raged inside as Helmi Kamil joked:

'But she's far too young for you, Anwar.'

Yet when you can do nothing yourself it is best to smile at the victory of others. I would publish the news that Sami had adopted a new star, Samia Sami, though it would assist him to get his way with her. That night, though almost crazy with jealous rage, I left her to their tender mercies.

But for two innocent days I published nothing about her: this would make her realize how little Anwar Sami could help her. She'd flip through the paper each morning and find nothing but disappointment. She'd complain to Midhat. I'd tell him I had deliberately written nothing to link her name to Anwar: otherwise people would jump to scandalous conclusions. I would suggest she settled on some other name, Muna Munir, as she had thought herself or Layla Fadhil. (If it weren't for Midhat, I'd have chosen 'Suad Rateb'.)

'What do you think,' I asked Muhammad Nagi, 'of "Muna Munir" as a name for an actress?'

'Why?' he asked slyly. 'Have you met someone?'

He read my embarrassment.

'Congratulations! Have you used the flat yet?'

'No.'

'Then what's all this about a name?'

'The truth is, I'm in a dilemma.'

'Splendid! Tell me.'

'It's not what you think.'

'Then what?'

'Anwar Sami's trying to build a young extra into a star. Her name's Bahia. Anwar wants to rename her Samia Sami. As an item of news it's amusing. Everyone will laugh at the idea of Anwar getting a new victim.'

'But . . .?'

'I'm not eager to publish the news. It will only help Sami to . . .'

I broke off.

'Are you still playing the puritan?' His voice was biting with sarcasm. 'How long have you known this story?'

'Since the day before yesterday.'

'What if some other paper beats us to it? We're not playing at journalism, you know. If you think along those lines you'd be better working at the Islamic University. No, this slip-up is scandalous.'

It was the first time he had found fault with me. Terror prompted me to rashness.

'It's not that I'm a puritan.'

'Then why didn't you print the news?'

'Because I'm furious.'

'Why?'

'I'm in love with the girl myself; I introduced her to him.'

Surprised, he came and sat down beside me.

'You're in love. . . . What do you mean?'

'I love her.'

'Have you any serious intentions – besides love, of course?'

'Such as?'

'Such as marriage.'

'No.'

He laughed.

'Then why so upset? You want her for yourself only? That's absurd. If I was you, I'd be delighted if she found another string or two to her bow. Each one reduces what you need spend on her. Nothing's more tiresome than a faithful woman. Every moment she rings you up: "Where have you been?" "What were you doing?" It's ghastly. Take care not to tie a millstone round your neck.'

'But . . .'

'No "buts". I asked you a plain question: do you intend to marry her? You said, No. So I tell you: publish immediately.'

He patted my shoulder.

'I'm sorry if I sound ruthless. Perhaps I would have felt the same in your place. But if you don't look out you'll be putting on a turban, dressing like a holy man. That would never do.'

Anwar was the first person to ring me up and thank me when the story appeared.

I pretended to be the zealous journalist.

'We want more news about you and Samia.'

'I'm at your command.'

'Any sensation, any scandal.'

'How odious! Do you want me to kill her?'

Then he whispered: 'Frankly, I'm going to telephone her now and arrange an amusing night with her. Thanks to you.'

I laughed as he added: 'She's charming, isn't she?'

'Indeed. But what's she like as an actress?'

'Actress, old chap? That's all a façade.'

Anwar Sami had taught me a good lesson. I had been acting like a spectator, adventuring only in imagination. Now if Muhammad Nagi was not to uncover my lies about love, I should have to get Samia or some other girl to the flat, and quickly.

Nagi asked me: 'Has she thanked you?'

'No, Anwar did.'

'A strange thing – I now share your feelings: I want to outwit him.'

'Why?'

'Enough pretence! You're more in love with her than I thought. Listen . . . take her to the flat today.'

'Anwar's invited her out tonight.'

He laughed. 'Then take her for a siesta . . . or during the evening. But take her. Our honour's at stake!'

I would never have guessed that Nagi would attach so much importance to my make-believe. Unless I plunged more deeply into lies, Nagi was likely to get more involved, perhaps even mentioning it all to Anwar or Samia herself.

Just as I was meditating what to do, the phone rang and the switchboard man announced Mabruka. She was waiting for me downstairs in the entrance hall. Disasters never come singly! I nearly told him to get rid of her, to say I was out; but a surge of pity drove me to meet her. To my astonishment I found myself smiling at her, pressing money on her and promising to go with her to the Pensions Department. I gazed at my brother Ibrahim. Mabruka was incredulous as I took in his little face – that in a way recalled my father – and all but patted him on the cheek. Why should I speak to her warmly? The world was a topsy-turvy place; she might get her pension and I might be jobless. 'Don't worry, Mabruka, I'll help you! I'll get you out of your troubles. But I make one condition only – don't come where people can see us. For I too have my troubles. My life here is based on lies. It's not easy. Every day I get more enmeshed. I must try and convince myself that they are truths. It might be nobler if I acknowledged you, Mabruka. I wish I could. But the price is too high. It would ruin everything; it would do you no good. I might even become a burden on you and your child. If I get the sack I may have to share the piastres on which you both live. I may even rob you.'

It was no use; we had to avoid each other. We were all of us at war. If we joined forces, it would really join weakness and impotence. Our only hope was to keep apart. I had to continue lying – for my lies to succeed I had to keep away from witnesses who knew too much.

Nobody noticed her coming or going. I wasn't too worried. If anyone asked me, I could say she was my servant. Nothing now came easier than lying; it only needed an increase in existing lies.

The phone was ringing as I returned to my office. It was Midhat. He and Samia were off to the pool at the National Club. Would I join them?

I rushed to Nagi.

'Would you excuse me if I went out?'

'Where to?'

'To meet her.'

'Bravo! Listen, I've an idea. What if I telephoned lots of Anwar's friends and suggested they should flock *en masse* to his flat tonight . . . when Samia's with him?'

'I'm afraid for her.'

He sighed. 'I'm afraid for you. Your love seems to be swelling to alarming proportions.'

As I left for the Club I found myself gasping at Nagi's naïvety. He was afraid that my love for Samia might grow too great. Yet my love hadn't even begun.

15

MIDHAT DIVED INTO THE POOL, LEAVING ME ALONE with Samia, whose half-naked body lay beside mine in a provocation that alarmed as much as it excited me. With the smiling simplicity of a woman who knows she has a beautiful body she suddenly asked me about love. Was she encouraging me to flirt, easing my way with the mischievous glint in her dark eyes? But I could not find the flippant, witty phrases the situation demanded. All I could do was to talk to her about Suad. I was amazed at how she believed my pretence, how she took seriously my pose of being a playboy whose speciality was married women. Suddenly her voice became dreamy and she asked me about 'tenderness'. The question struck echoes in my heart. Was she as naïve as I was? What could prompt such a body to questions about tenderness? What had the flesh of passion and wild desires to do with sympathy? More likely she was fooling me as much as I was undoubtedly fooling her. Anwar Sami was going to enjoy her flesh that very night. All I could do was to keep up my pose of being the sincere disinterested man of sensibility, the journalist who wrote about her doings with no price in view. This would make me seem as awesome to her as her body was to me. Fervently I talked of loneliness and my need for love. The tears started from her eyes as I spoke on as if to myself, till my words seemed to frighten her so that her cheerful voice sank to a perplexed whisper as if in the minutes we had been together she had grown suddenly older.

When I left her with Midhat I decided I should not see her again. I was not sure that I could make my next performance as good as this one.

To Nagi I poured out my frustration in a series of lies. I invented an exciting episode in a love-idyll: how our quick kisses had been overseen, how suspicious eyes had observed our passion, how I had tried to laugh off scandal with an innocent smile. Nagi was amused, then asked: 'You took her to the flat?'

'No.'

'But this is absurd. Platonic love is dead. You merely warm her up for Anwar.'

Instead of telling him that I was through with her, I pretended I was taking her to the flat that afternoon.

He was delighted and began to tell me all about its lay-out, where I would find beer, where whisky; there were towels in the bathroom. Two whiskies would be enough. He was as anxious as if he was going there for the first time himself.

I went to the flat and found it luxurious. There was beer in the refrigerator, whisky in the bar. I poured two glasses of both. In the bedroom I pulled the coverlet from the bed. I sat on the bed. I was alone in a flat, pretending to be there with a girl. I had the flat, the doorkey and a girl I could invite, a girl only too willing to make love. Yet I was there alone. I drank half the beer, and poured away the rest. I left what was left of the whisky, and a wet towel. I left the flat pleased with the adventure I had and had not committed.

But I was too tired to tell Nagi all the fantasies I had imagined. Instead I went back to the *pension* where Madame Rose was entertaining friends. I refused the wine she offered me – it reminded me of the beer I had thrown away – and locked myself in my room.

I tried to read a book on philosophy. Suddenly I remembered Mabruka. I had promised to meet her and had forgotten. I imagined what she would think: that I had avoided her, that I had deliberately snubbed her. But perhaps it was better so. I was in too deep trouble to be of any help to her.

Next morning the telephone operator told me Mabruka had asked for me more than once. In a panic I told him to say that I was out if she called again; if she came in person, she should be turned away.

I asked Helmi Kamil on the telephone what he had heard about Anwar and Samia. (It was my custom each morning to get hold of bits of gossips about the cinema.) But he had no news. When I told him I feared Anwar might marry her, he laughed: Anwar was too shrewd to do a thing like that.

I felt relieved; then wondered if perhaps she had been telling the truth, when she had spoken of her need for tenderness. If this was so, then an evening with Anwar might have been dangerous. I rang Anwar's number.

'What have you done to Samia?'

'I don't understand.'

'Didn't you tell me you were taking her out last night?'

'That was a joke.'

'Truly?'

'What do you mean "truly"? Do you think a cheap piece like that is worth my pursuit?'

He went on to tell me she was Nimat's daughter. I had never heard of Nimat. Anwar enlightened me: she ran a gambling house – a sleazy affair. He was embarrassed to have had his name linked with Samia's. He was glad to be off to Beirut. This made him change the subject: would I be sure to print this news, along with his picture?

She was safe from Anwar. But this still left Midhat.

My anxiety – I realized – showed my own inconsistency. One moment I resolved to see her no more; the next I worried about Midhat's intentions towards her.

When I visited him, he asked happily:

'She's sweet, isn't she?'

'Are you in love?'

'A little.'

'Marry her: if you love her.'

His eyes narrowed.

'She put you up to this?'

'Of course not.'

'I saw you deep in talk at the Club.'

'She never mentioned you.'

He did not believe me.

'Would you marry her?'

'Yes,' I said. 'If I loved her.'

He was quite angry. 'Do you know who her family are? Their reputation stinks. I picked her up on the street. They are crooks, out to make money at any price. This is probably a plan of her mother's. The old bitch will come and see my parents.' He finished seriously. 'I'll break off my relations with her.'

This was good news. Midhat must have seen my smile for he burst out angrily:

'But I suppose you'll marry her?'

He suddenly stopped, embarrassed, and I knew he was thinking of my father, who had married Mabruka.

Samia and I were joined by the sense of shame we both felt for our parents, she for her mother, I for my father. We both wanted tenderness and sympathy – but this was mad. We should ruin each other, we should stifle the fires of our ambition and remain for ever miserable and poor.

Then one morning Showki rushed angrily into my room.

'Mabruka,' he whispered in my ear, 'she's downstairs, asking for you.'

'How do you know?' He must have spoken to her himself; this was more than I could bear. 'I don't want to see her.'

'But you must, Yusif.'

I raised my voice. 'I will not see her, Showki. That's finished.'

For some time I had been avoiding Showki, though seeing much of Nagi. This was Showki's opportunity to get his own back.

'You must help her.'

'No, I told you.'

'And if she causes a scene?'

'Let her!'

A look of hatred came into his eyes. 'You are despicable.'

'God forgive you,' I said, deeply wounded.

As he left me I sat trembling, expecting to hear Mabruka's shouts echo through the building. But there was no sound and when I looked from the window, I saw Showki leading her away up the road. Wherever she ended up, I knew my place was at *Al-Ayyam*, my destiny was linked with my office.

That evening, when Showki came and apologized, I forced a smile to my lips, a smile that showed my goodness of heart.

I would have preferred him to have left things as they were; it would have given me the pretext to break with him.

'I'll help her myself,' he said. 'I know you're hard up.' He knew nothing of me. Reasons connected with my dreams for the future – not anxiety about money – made me shrink from her. His voice went on:

'There's a flat she could afford at Bab Zuweyla.'

'At your place?'

'Yes, what do you think?'

'I can offer no opinion. It's up to her.'

16

IT IS ABOUT TIME I MENTIONED SHOHDI PASHA, FOR HE marked the dividing line between my childhood of naïvety and simple wickedness and the sophisticated cruelty and wickedness which became mine when I graduated from his school: a school whose lessons I accepted without surprise.

As my self-confidence increased, in those young, energetic days, so Nagi's trust in me increased too. My responsibilities grew. Nagi told me more and more about the secrets of his work. The most important secret was the need to publish the news which Shohdi wanted published, and to ignore the things he wanted ignored. Nagi gave me the general supervision of the paper. Anything which had the least connection with Shohdi had to be shown personally to Nagi for his okay. Even the Pasha's photographs. Only those which showed him in a flattering light could be used. Only when he was with an ambassador's lady, or someone higher, could he be shown with a woman. Pictures of him at a race-meeting or watching a football match brought him nearer to the people: these were published.

Nagi frequently suggested introducing me to the Pasha. But when in my delight I asked him 'When?' he would get evasive. 'There'll be many opportunities.'

I longed to meet this millionaire whose touch affected every item in our pages. If he made a deal with America, Nagi told me to put the Washington byline on the front page. Even the football club which we encouraged made the front page – if it won. If it lost, the news was buried on page seven. Those pashas who were his friends got their news, too, published with great eclat. Shohdi Pasha was an octopus whose tentacles touched every aspect of Egyptian life. But how could I impress him? I did not feel that my relationship with Rateb Bey would much interest him. My studiously polite manner – that might make me insignificant. I was perplexed.

Then an idea came to me. I was reading Shaw's *Major Barbara* in bed. A brilliant piece of dialogue suddenly stifled my yawns. Shaw's armaments manufacturer is talking to a found-ling. The foundling admits that he is absolutely unscrupulous. Both men take off their masks and ridicule humanity, virtue and philanthropy. The foundling gets the job of running the millionaire's factories – over the head of the millionaire's son who had acquired a culture and civilization which would be quite out of place in his father's business. This suddenly showed me how I should conduct myself with Shohdi Pasha, if I was lucky enough to meet him.

When next Nagi suggested I should meet Shohdi, I asked quickly: 'What advantage would there be?'

'Are you shy, like a girl?'

'No, but he's not in my world. He's a millionaire.'

'But in himself he's very approachable; he has a great sense of humour.'

'But he's still not my sort of person.'

I felt the more I refused the more Nagi would press me to meet him.

Then the chance came. We published an item from the Ministry of Finance about protecting the small cotton merchants. Nagi was furious; the paragraph might be construed as an indirect criticism of Shohdi, the largest exporter in Egypt. Shohdi was angry too. Nagi ordered me to deduct £5 from the salary of one of the staff. I was then sent to Shohdi to concoct an interview which would make things right.

I was disgusted at Nagi's pettiness and lack of scruple. He had even told me not to tell the staff-member concerned why the fiver had been deducted, so that he would have no chance of complaining to the Minister of Finance. But I didn't feel disgusted with myself as I set out to run Nagi's errand. I felt myself a mere spectator of how the world ran. I was again the Yusif who watched other people playing football from inside the window. I gave no thought to the penalized journalist. I was engrossed with meeting my first millionaire.

I was kept waiting in Shohdi's outer office while a barber was passing in with the tools of his trade. I felt indignant, but my protest sounded feeble: 'Does the Pasha know I'm here?'

'He does, sir.' The secretary's tone was insolent.

I was admitted when the barber had left. Shohdi was reclining in a comfortable armchair with an electric heater near him. Papers were scattered round him. His face gleamed rosy pink; he smelt of eau-de-Cologne. He placed his hand on the telephone as he waved me to sit down. It was clear it did not occur to him to shake hands.

'How's Muhammad?'

'He's fine, Your Excellency.'

'What are you carrying?'

'A copy of the letter of rebuke to the editor who printed the news.'

'Show me.'

He smiled confidently as he read the letter.

As he handed it back, he asked if I worked with Nagi. When I said 'Yes', he added: 'But you look so young.'

'Not all that.'

He stared at me quizzically then pointed to his office, murmuring words I could not catch. Seeing my puzzlement, he raised his voice. 'The box is over there. . . .'

There was a box of cigars. I stumbled towards it and brought it back to him. He took one, then handed back the box for me to replace. But I must now show that I was offended that he did not offer me one. I must keep up my dignity, whatever happened.

'So you want an interview. Do you know how to write one?'

'I think so.'

My reply can't have pleased him. He fumbled with lighting his cigar, then continued scrutinizing me through the smoke. I would not lower my gaze.

'How did you come to be employed there?'

I laughed with the desperation of a suicide.

'I tricked Mr Nagi.'

His smile was deadly. All I could now do was maintain my calm in front of him, to play my role cleverly and coolly. It was war.

'How did you trick him?'

'I pretended I was rich and highly born. He believed me and gave me a job. I then showed him that my work was first-class.'

'And he still doesn't realize?'

He seemed on the point of exploding with amusement.

'What did you pretend?'

'Although my father was only a poor schoolmaster, his relative was Rateb Bey. I pretended that Rateb Bey was my uncle and my source of news. As Your Excellency may know, Rateb Bey is a good friend of the Minister of the Interior.'

'So you made a fool out of Muhammad?'

I answered firmly: 'But not in my job.'

'Where were you educated?'

'The Faculty of Law.'

I could see he wasn't sure, so I said good-humouredly:
'That's not a lie.'
He said abruptly: 'Muhammad is a fool.'
'But he taught me all I know about journalism.'
'And what do you want to do?'
'To write an interview with Your Excellency.'
'No, I mean, what are your ambitions for the future?'
'Still the interview.'
'Don't you have wider ambitions than that?'
'Not at the moment.'
His voice became cordial.
'You are a bright boy. You'll go far.'
'Thank you.'
'What do you want to write in the interview?'
'If you want my honest opinion, Your Excellency: you should support the Minister of Finance, then make light of the whole thing.'
'Why?' He sounded suspicious.
'The country merchants can otherwise make a big nuisance of themselves. They can create a fuss in the other newspapers. We don't want that.'
He did not hesitate.
'Then write the interview in that sense. Muhammad can read it to me over the phone.'
He rang the bell for the secretary. It was as though I no longer existed. But as I silently backed towards the door, he asked in his ironical voice.
'What's your name?'
'Yusif Abdul Hamid al-Suefi.'
He gave a little laugh.
'I'll tell Muhammad about your trick.' His laugh exploded. 'Let me know if he gives you the sack.'
While I was still regretting my confidence to the Pasha, sure it had done me no good, and fearing it might do me grave harm, Samia began a telephone campaign on me. I used to wait for her voice, having prepared a conversation which would lead up to an invitation to go with me to Nagi's flat. But each time she

rang, my resolve weakened. Her sweet utterances were so many bribes to get me to publish her picture in the paper – suspecting this, I changed the talk to the cinema gossip till our talk ended and the silent telephone sneered at my impotence.

At last Samia asked me to meet her. She refused to come to the paper and we agreed on the Garden Groppi's.

This was my chance to prove myself a man.

What if I failed?

But this was an examination I had to pass. I could not go through life without a woman. More important, if I failed with Samia, I would fail with Nagi and Shohdi. My very career depended on sleeping with Samia.

My first words – prompted by the thought of her relationship with Midhat – punctured my dream.

'You think I'm making up to you?' she asked angrily.

'You misunderstand me.'

'I understand you perfectly. You think I'll play around with anyone.'

Her accusation, being true, hurt me deeply. But I persistently denied that this had been my meaning, until of a sudden she broke down, to tell me Anwar had been trying to seduce her. She was telling the truth. Her story explained everything, in particular Anwar's rage. She was a pure girl; I was glad I had not broached the question of the flat. But now I should have to look for another partner; my examination was postponed.

When she left, I felt so tenderly towards her, I wondered if I was falling in love.

Nagi asked me a few days later how I was getting on with her. He smiled wickedly as he asked. I told him there was nothing doing.

'You realize, though, she went to Anwar's flat?'

'No,' I replied angrily. 'She did not.'

'But I have the details.' He said no more, waiting for me to probe, but I said nothing, stabbed by grief. So he began to recount how Anwar had taken her home and tried to bed her.

'Did Anwar tell you?'

'Not Anwar.'

'Then who?'

'Samia, herself.'

My looks must have been black, for he in turn looked troubled. 'Samia spoke to me on the phone,' he explained.

'She spoke to you?'

'To complain about Anwar. Incidentally, please keep this to yourself. There's no need for you to look so angry. Nothing happened. The poor girl was afraid and wanted my help. And I have good news for you. She confessed to me that she loves you.'

I did not believe him. I felt he was playing cat and mouse, that he had learnt how I had tricked him and was getting his revenge, and laughing at my impotence.

There was nothing for it but to seduce her, cost what it might. I made an appointment to meet her again at Groppi's.

Then the telephone operator called me in great excitement: Shohdi Pasha wanted to see me at his office at noon sharp. This meant being late for Samia. But no matter. Shohdi was more important.

He met me with a big smile. The cigar seemed to gleam in his mouth and his eyes shone wickedly.

'You asked for me, sir?'

'Yes, Your Excellency.'

'Why?'

'To know your opinion of my article.'

He could not have believed me. The article had come out weeks ago.

He said brusquely: 'I spoke to Muhammad.' He gave a little laugh and proffered the box of cigars.

'Help yourself.'

I sensed that the crisis was over. He wanted something from me.

'Are you happy in your work?'

'Very.'

'How do you get on with Muhammad?'

'Excellently.'

th me,' Nagi said with feline kindness, 'you've
enough.'
u, but I'm tired.'
he drive you home.'
ne to my boarding-house, where I found a note
e in my room.

ut when I called. I am leaving tomorrow for Sohag in
Public Prosecutor gave the order suddenly. Try and
s to discover the reason. I'll write to you at length

Your affectionate friend,
Saad Abdul Gawad.

AND RESOLUTIONS TO GIVE SAMIA UP,
ses for prolonging our friendship. To be
nan in her life – that was a role I could play
hen, as I was playing it, the desire for her
's body, would overcome me.
ve were out together she pointed to a shop-

you a new pair of shoes.'
got on are all right.'
she said with passion. 'I can't bear unsmart

some.'
whispering: 'The one's you've got on aren't all
an wait till the end of the month.'
e were like fellow-students, able to speak to
y about anything.
re should go to the flat together. She took some
finally agreed.
to the flat I felt torn: did I despise her, or love

'Muhammad is one of my oldest friends. There's no one like
him in Egypt. His pen stabs. His analysis hurts as it explains.
Or what is your opinion?'
'The same as yours.'
His voice rose: 'Speak frankly, man.'
'He's my teacher, I owe him everything, but at the same
time . . .'
'What . . .?'
His encouraging smile helped me overcome my hesitation.
'His education was not profound. There are some political
ideas which are beyond him.'
'Such as?'
'Communism, for example.'
He banged his desk. 'That's just what I wanted to hear. I
have recently read every word you wrote. When you analyse
crimes, you trace them to poverty, to the social situation. You
talk like the communist papers.'
'But I'm not a communist.'
'Of course not, or I shouldn't have received you.'
'And I would have been in prison.'
'You are too intelligent to be a communist,' he continued,
'and too ambitious. You want to get on, to become something.'
I nodded. 'I am trying hard.'
'And you can! You can even be editor-in-chief of *Al-Ayyam*.'
He saw the look of shock on my face but continued.
'We need new blood. I am a gambler, someone who loves a
risk. If I trust a young man, I put him in charge of my largest
companies. Muhammad is splendid for fighting the old
politicians, for teasing the Palace. But that's *vieux jeu*. The new
struggle is between socialists, communists and the Moslem
Brotherhood. They write in a way that attracts university
students. I need someone who can write in their idiom, someone whom they can believe.'
He paused, then added quietly: 'I want you to specialize in
politics.'
I said quickly: 'It's not necessary to deal with politics
directly. Any story can carry an antidote to communism. For

example, if I write about a poor young man who becomes rich:
that too refutes communism.'

His eyes showed his pleasure.

'Of course, you are right: the indirect approach. But try to
deal with politics directly as well.'

'And if Nagi disagrees?'

'You think he will? Then let me deal with him. Meanwhile,
do you know any communists?'

'A few.'

'Your friends?'

'Ex-friends. One has become a district attorney.'

'His name?'

'Saad Abdul Gawad.'

'Which district?'

I told him and he burst out wildly: 'In the heart of Cairo!
Left to carry on his pernicious business. The country will be
ruined.'

He wrote Saad's name on a piece of paper. 'He must be dismissed, or at least transferred.' I almost intervened to say a
word for Saad, to plead his poverty; but Shohdi might have
suspected my motives. With mixed feelings – of fear, sadness,
victory, happiness, triumph over Nagi, pity for Saad – I left for
my appointment with Samia.

She was still waiting for me. While we were having lunch in
a restaurant, and when I was telling her about Shohdi Pasha's
gift of a cigar, she suddenly asked:

'Is the Pasha still angry about the cotton merchants?'

She could have known of this through Nagi. Was she his
mistress? I suddenly felt trapped. Nagi was triumphing over me,
not I over him. I decided: in a world of foulness victory went
to the foul. I would take her that very day.

I watched her closely in the lift. I let her lead the way. Without faltering she went to the right door. There was a half smile
on her lips. She obviously enjoyed making a fool of me.

'Why are you laughing?' I asked.

'Because you lied to me. This is not your flat.'

'No, it's not my flat.'

'Who does it belong to?'

As if she didn't know!

'A friend.'

With the bluntness of a whore she asked: 'Y[...]
might come back some other time with him?'

I was so disgusted, I could only treat her c[...]
bored and we parted like strangers.

But I was still obsessed with her. She was m[...]
prove myself a man.

Then one evening, as I tried my hand at [...]
article, Nagi opened the door, his elegant, a[...]
self.

He shut the door and asked me quietly: [...]

'You've been seeing Shohdi Pasha?'

'I have.'

'Any special reason?'

'None. He offered me a cigar.'

'Good,' he said, with a laugh. 'I want [...]
relations with him.'

'That's not up to me.'

'Listen to what I say – you have a great [...]

He stepped nearer my desk and read a [...]
had been writing. He seemed embarrassed. [...]

'My boy, a silly story's going round th[...]
ployees say that a woman comes to the buil[...]
her arms who is your brother.'

I felt on fire, but managed to say: 'Yes, she [...]

He held his head high, like a rich man addre[...]

'I know everything, including the fact that [...]
Showki.'

I realized this was war to the death. He wa[...]

'You can dismiss Showki.'

'No, I can't.'

'The boy's a communist.'

I felt a twinge of panic. He would tell Shoh[...]
was my friend, and the Pasha would be indigna[...]
mentioned him with Saad.

her? Would I insist on having her, or treat her coolly? Only events would show what I really felt.

We sat in opposite chairs. The words began to tumble out of my mouth: I loved her! Yet even as I spoke I was not sure if I was telling the truth or creating a fantasy. Her face was pale as she listened. We were close together, in the same room. My words would soon run out. What then? How would I take the first step? I wondered if she would surrender or fight back, scream or let me hold her hand. Then, if she liked me, if she did not resist, what next? I had no idea how a lover behaved, if he undid her dress or took off his own clothes first. I felt so embarrassed, so confused, I went on talking.

My heart sank as Samia stood up and turned on the radio. I sensed that she was confused, too. She turned to ask me, with a boldly greedy look in her eyes: 'And now what?'

I did not understand what she meant.

'Don't you want to kiss me?'

I had been hopelessly wrong. She was not confused at all. This was no new situation to her; she knew exactly what my next move should be. And taught by the cinema and college rumours I made that next move, advancing to kiss her. I felt her breath merge with mine; this was new. I smelt a mixture of her scent and her skin; this was a physical ecstasy different from my daydreams as an adolescent or the kisses I had had from Suad.

Her hand pushed me back.

I had heard that women who wanted you did this, to increase desire.

'Does anyone know you are in love with me?'

She was afraid of Nagi, afraid he would know. She would have a dozen lovers, but try to keep each one secret from the next. But now all I wanted was her body; to get that I would make any pretence.

'No one knows.'

'Not even Nagi?'

I tried to kiss away her question, but when she persisted I said: 'He suspects.'

323

'Please don't tell him.'

'All right.'

'We shouldn't even use this flat.'

She was posing her conditions before she would undress. She was out of her mind, but her body was desirable, and to get my way I would accept any terms.

'All right.'

I began again, but once more she pushed me back to make a new condition. I must find her another flat! Again I agreed, lying. She was a fool if she thought I would furnish a flat just for her. Or was she even more crazy, did she think I would marry her? I would promise her anything, so long as I got what I wanted, now, in Nagi's flat.

But she would not let me kiss her.

'Go and sit down.'

Anger rose in my breast as I sensed she was playing with me.

'Who were you in love with before me?'

'It's an old story.'

'If you won't tell me, I won't tell you either.'

I wondered if it was Anwar she meant, or Nagi.

'If you don't tell me, I'll beat you.'

This set her off. She screamed with rage till her shouts rang through the building. Everything was ruined. I said I was sorry. She kissed me good-bye and we went our separate ways.

After a few days Nagi – who had learnt of our quarrel with ill-disguised pleasure – invited me to bring Samia to a party at his house.

Nagi was at the top of his form. Having poured me a Martini, he began to attack me, calling me a fraud. This pleased me. Clearly he was worried. Samia rushed to my defence.

Then the house filled with guests. I kept my eyes on Samia. She was ill at ease. When Anwar arrived she blanched. We kept catching each other's eye, neither certain of the other, neither enjoying the party. I would have taken her away, but I hoped to see the Pasha.

When Shohdi arrived everyone fawned on him, but after

greeting them quickly he took me to one side and asked hardly glancing at Samia:

'Is she your girl-friend?'

I whispered, laughing: 'I wish I knew. There's still nothing between us.'

'And what of Muhammad?'

'I feel sure there's something between them.'

I was afraid people would hear him as he replied:

'Then you are robbing him?'

'I wish I knew, Pasha. I wish I knew.'

Nagi interrupted us to ask Shohdi to open the buffet supper. I found myself alone with Samia and we left. As we wandered through the Zamalek streets she began to attack Nagi, saying he did not love me as I imagined, that his eyes showed his true feelings.

Was she probing for my feelings, to relay them to Nagi?

I pretended to defend him.

This roused her to further shouts: I was a tool in their hands, a toy.

Her words stung me, giving me the added power I needed to force her to the flat. When I had undressed her – aided perhaps by all the Martinis – I realized that at last I was broaching the secret of my life. In so doing I knew a pleasure intenser than I had ever known before.

When she asked, 'Do you love me?' I replied with **real** sincerity, 'I love you. Yes, I love you.'

That evening she confessed – although I told her there was no need – the whole story of her life, from her father's suicide in Tanta to Anwar's attempt to seduce her. She told me, too, how she talked to Nagi on the telephone, pretending to be a married woman.

'You don't have to tell me all this.'

'But I want you to know everything. It's lucky the room is dark. If it was light I couldn't speak.'

Then she told me that she knew whom I had loved before: Mabruka. I began to protest but she shut my lips with her fingers. 'Listen to me first. She was a maid in your father's house.

You loved her and when she married your father you continued to love her.'

'Who on earth told you that?'

'Someone.'

'I must know.'

'There's no need – but it is true.'

If I denied this, if I told her the truth, it would show that I had lied about knowing women, and she would lose her confidence in me.

'Did you see her after you left home?'

'Never.'

'Is that the truth?'

'On my word of honour.'

She had one last confession: it was she who had told Nagi about Mabruka, Ibrahim and me.

Now I felt curiously relaxed. I knew everything, and I was ashamed of my suspicions. She was much more sincere than I had pictured. The one thing I could not do was to match her truthfulness. I could not admit to her my inexperience.

She found a two-roomed flat with a balcony overlooking the Paradise Cinema. As I was signing the contract, I blushed at the landlord's question: would I be living alone? I told him I would shortly be getting married. He wished me luck.

Samia took my money and bought a bed and a mattress. From this secret world where we watched films on the balcony, eating sandwiches and losing ourselves in love, she would go to her studio while I went to *Al-Ayyam*. She was thrilled with the flat, which she wanted to furnish quickly: a sofa here, a table with a radio there, plus a pick-up to which we could dance.

At the beginning of the month I gave her my salary. She counted £36 into her bag, then asked.

'Where's the rest?'

'I paid my bill at the canteen.'

'I'm going to see the carpenter. I want him to furnish our bedroom first.'

Tapping the money, she laughed:

'When we're married, it will be the same.'

Without thinking I said:

'Of course, darling: every month.'

The idea of marrying Samia was no stranger than that of renting the flat. I had changed. I had no more fears. Samia had changed too. I would indeed marry her and proclaim in the middle of Ismailia Square, if need be: this was Samia, the woman I loved, my wife!

19

MY RELATIONS WITH NAGI WERE NOT AS BEFORE. HE made no objections to my writing on politics, he made no efforts to interfere with my work, but I felt he was not only suspicious of me but waiting for the first opportunity to harm me. I maintained my façade of innocence.

Either because I felt a subconscious desire to challenge him, or because I still valued his advice, I decided to tell him of my intention to marry Samia.

'Yusif,' he exclaimed, 'my boy, please think of your future, your career. Even if you do love her, this girl is not right for marrying. I speak from much greater experience than you can guess.'

'I must marry her.'

'There's no such thing as "must".'

'For my self-respect.'

'Has something happened? Don't worry. I have a doctor friend.'

'All that has happened is I have fallen in love.'

Now he got angry.

'Are you insane? What obliges you to marry her if there's nothing to make you? She goes with half the city. You know her affair with Anwar.'

'I don't believe it.'

'You're being stupid.'

'If she had gone with Anwar, or all Cairo, I'd still want to marry her.'

A new tone entered his voice – that of command.

'It pains me to tell you, but I must. I knew Samia before you. Although nothing happened between us, that was to my credit not hers. She's now running after you just to excite me. That's her game, my boy.'

My rage at Nagi's duplicity preceded two important interviews with Shohdi Pasha.

At the first, the Pasha told me Nagi was spreading stories against me, inspired by his jealousy of my political articles. This did not mean I should stop writing. It merely meant I should go on as I was doing and hold myself in readiness for greater things.

The next time I saw the Pasha he seemed hesitant whether or not to take me into his confidence. After beating about the bush, he blurted out:

'Frankly, I distrust Mr Nagi.'

He laughed.

'Not that it's necessary to trust those you work with. Life is like that. Nagi is famous, clever, important. He has his interests and ambitions just as I have mine.' He pointed his finger at me like a gun. 'You'll be the same, one day.' Before I could reply, he added: 'Don't argue. Though I have no doubt you'll stay by me, because I'll make it worth your while. I'll make you deputy editor, then editor-in-chief.' He paused. 'But then . . . who knows? You might change again, find your interests with someone else.' He struck his knee. 'What matters now is politics. We used to back the Saadist Party, as you know. Last week I ordered Nagi to change tack. I gave him material to use against Said Pasha, the Minister of Works.' He paused to see how I was taking his long speech. 'Tomorrow morning you'll read Nagi's assault on Said Pasha.'

'Impossible.'

'Possible. But something more. Said Pasha knows about these articles. Nagi has told him, to curry favour. Nagi has apologized to him for writing them, putting all the blame on me. He wants to back every side, including mine.'

His calm had deserted him; his sense of outrage had made him wild.

'Now I have orders for you: pick a quarrel with Nagi. On any pretext. Let everyone on *Al-Ayyam* know you have fallen out. Insult him. Abuse him.'

He was mad, I thought, but I assented.

As I was about to leave, he added 'And keep away from that communist artist. I know about the girl he's living with, your relative. If you don't let him be dismissed, you'll be responsible for him and all his views.'

I was almost beside myself when I left his office. I had been asked to behave like a mercenary who kills for a fee. I had to humiliate the man who had raised me up, abuse him in front of his own creatures, pretending that I had suddenly grown confident and strong, while in fact my confidence and strength were one man, Shohdi Pasha. I had to betray Showki too. Yet if I did as I was told I would be rich. This would please Samia. My pockets would be stuffed with money. We could honeymoon in Europe. Having conquered Nagi, I would be a hero in her eyes.

But I was still young, not yet thirty. There would be other, honourable chances. I could look for another job and start again. This would be safer. If I kicked Nagi now, who knew what other creature would not kick me, later, at the Pasha's whim? It would be better far if I resigned.

Then Samia telephoned.

Nagi had asked her to meet him in his flat by the river. At five o'clock. On the pretext that my future was threatened.

This made up my mind. I would go to Nagi's office and insult him as ordered. I did not bother to disentangle my motives: whether I was obeying the Pasha, indulging my low instincts of revenge, or chivalrously defending Samia. But I must be careful. He knew something about my future: I must get him to speak before I said my piece.

'Where were you at 5 p.m., Nagi Bey?'

'At home.'

'Can you confide in me about the threat to my career?'

His face paled.

'I don't understand.'

I trembled as I asked:

'Didn't you telephone Samia? Didn't you ask her to meet you? There's no use lying. She told me everything.'

'There is some misunderstanding, I can assure you.'

I raised my voice.

'Oh, no: I have understood precisely the creature you are.'

He said coldly: 'Please pull yourself together.'

'You are despicable.'

He raised his eyebrows.

'I despise you, utterly.'

'Are you out of your wits?'

'I simply want to tell you, in your presence, that you are a despicable coward.'

In a dead voice he ordered me to leave his room. Our voices rose as we bandied insults – criminal, dog! The office was suddenly crowded. Hands whose owners I could not recognize pulled me away from him. 'Criminal! Criminal!'

Half an hour later he crept into my office and sat cringing on a chair opposite mine. His voice was very low as he apologized to me, calling me 'his son', then added: 'On the orders of Shohdi Pasha – with which I entirely concur – I am raising your salary to £120 a month and appointing you deputy editor.'

20

I BECAME SUPREME IN A NEWSPAPER WHERE THE SMILES of the editors showed what hypocrites they were. The most hypocritical of all was Nagi who never stopped praising me, consulting me, asking me to correct his articles. I knew his smile concealed the determination to destroy me at the earliest opportunity.

Only Showki – thanks to whom I had first got on to the staff – continued to treat me as before, as if I was still the old shy Yusif.

He would still greet me gruffly in the corridors:

'How are you, Yusif?'

I'd smile back gently, and pass on. He'd shout:

'Why don't you stop and chat, brother?'

'Because I'm busy, Showki. I have a meeting.'

He asked me mockingly:

'Do you imagine you've become important?'

'Never!'

'Then stop being a snob . . .'

Although I smiled at him, I was increasingly worried at what I heard about him. He would insult the King and the Prime Minister, to say nothing of Shohdi Pasha. By repeating communist slogans he was giving Nagi an excellent opportunity to ruin me.

Things came to a head when Showki insulted me in front of Samia at a party given in my honour in an artist's house near the Citadel. He called me a tool of Shohdi Pasha and did not seem in the least abashed by Samia's presence.

I controlled myself for a few days, then summoned Showki to my office. When I pointed out to him how he was endangering not only himself but his friends, he answered back. I was in a quandary. Nothing would have been easier than to have denounced him to Shohdi Pasha: one word from him and Showki would have been arrested. But I was sorry about Saad Abdul Gawad. I did not want to destroy my friends one after another. And besides, Showki was the support of Mabruka and my brother. If he was arrested, she would come and bother me again.

Before I could make up my mind what to do, Showki came back to my office and apologized in the most abject manner, assuring me he intended to renounce communism for ever. I was glad, but felt as though I had murdered him. How ugly a victim looks to its destroyer! I would have preferred Showki to have persisted in his belief. Even though he was helping to solve my problems, his conversion gave me no satisfaction.

By this time my love for Samia had turned into a pleasant habit: I worked by day, made love by night. Then one evening of rain, my head in her lap, I found myself discussing marriage. I was aware I had crossed a dangerous line of decision, but was unafraid. I brought things to a climax by asking to arrange a meeting with her mother.

Now, her mother was a strange woman, fingers yellow with nicotine, eyes bold as brass. She made a lot of pretentious talk, despite her shabby flat, about dead pashas and old families. Secretly laughing at her I pretended to be abashed. Instead of challenging her about her pretended family, I contented myself with the role of timid son-in-law. I wanted to rescue Samia from such a dreadful place.

The moment we had fixed the date of our wedding – for the following Thursday – Samia thought about nothing but clothes, furniture and plans for the future. Love was pushed aside. I would leave her and her chatter about marriage, as though it concerned someone else. As I got on with my work, I began to wonder what Shohdi Pasha would say.

I had to tell him. I went to his office and said as casually as possible:

'So, Pasha, it seems as though I'm to be married.'

He frowned. 'To whom?'

'Samia.'

He exploded: 'Just as I foresaw. Every time I place confidence in someone he lets me down. All right, marry her. But don't imagine that it won't affect your future. Because it will.'

'How?' I asked.

'You'll ruin your reputation, you'll undermine your social standing.' His voice became calmer. 'I'm talking to you like your father, my boy. You should enjoy her, not marry her. To make her your wife, the mother of your children, would be disastrous.'

Shohdi picked up the telephone and asked for Nagi.

'What are you going to tell him, Pasha?'

332

'To stop you marrying.'

I laughed despite myself.

'Couldn't you do so behind my back?'

'That's not my way, my boy. I do everything openly.'

Having heard Shohdi express his opinion more than force-fully to Nagi, I realized now what a catastrophe my marriage would be. I would be repeating my father's mistake with Mabruka – due punishment for hurting him, perhaps.

'You know the Pasha's opinion,' Nagi said gently, 'and what he has asked me to do?'

'Yes, I was there when he spoke to you.'

'What have you decided?'

'To do what I intended.'

His hand fumbled with his cigarette. He looked pale with worry. He went out and gave strict orders we were not to be interrupted. Then sat beside me.

'The position is bizarre: it's an occasion to speak frankly. You want to become editor-in-chief: Shohdi supports you.' There was no point in my denying this. I waited in silence for Nagi to continue. 'For myself, I want to hold on to my position. That is natural. For me, therefore, the best thing would be for you to marry Samia. Shohdi would have to find someone else to use against me.'

His honesty paralysed me. All I could do was to ask bluntly:

'Why does he want to ruin you?'

'Are you acting, Yusif?'

'No, really: I've only heard rumours.'

'Then the rumours are correct. Shohdi found me in his wife's bedroom. We're all despicable. So much so that we no longer try to hide what we're doing. We sin openly. All of us, including Shohdi.'

'That's right,' I admitted, despite myself.

'But only Shohdi wins in this dirty game. For him I am a card he has played and now discards. My only satisfaction is to have smirched his honour. In a sense we are even.' He stared into my face and asked: 'But why should you get involved in our dirty game?'

'I didn't mean to get involved,' I whispered. 'I just found myself in it.'

'Think ahead now,' he warned. 'Imagine that you succeed, that you supplant me, that you become an influential man. Then, the day will come when your eyes will open. You'll see that you're just a humble slave to Shohdi Pasha. To be his cook would be more honourable: at least you'd have your skill. But it is humiliating to pretend to be someone important when in truth you're just a slave. You'll feel contempt for yourself then.'

'I feel it already.'

He said sadly: 'Listen. It is in my interest for you to marry Samia. Shohdi will throw you over. This will mean I shall keep my position, at least for a while. But the advice I am going to give you is in your interest.'

I was eager to hear. 'What do you advise?'

'That you should marry Samia. This is the chance that will only come to you once. The only true thing in my life was my love for Dalal. If she had married me, I should have lost all this. I should have been poor and unsuccessful. But I should have been the happiest man on earth.'

I could see he was telling the truth.

'Yusif, if someone really loves, he loses all interest in his dignity or other people's opinions.'

His words strangely echoed my words to Samia by the swimming-pool. I was conscious of a terrible decline in myself since then.

'I shall marry Samia.'

'You mean it?'

'I mean it.'

'Shall I tell Shohdi?'

'Yes.'

He said he envied me, and I could feel he was sincere.

I dialled Samia's number.

'I must see you, darling.'

She protested like a child.

'But I have a thousand things to do.'

'It is important.'

We agreed to meet that night.

That evening, news came from Syria: an officer called Husni al-Zaim had made a *coup d'état*. We were having an emergency editorial meeting to discuss how to cover the event, when Nagi came in and took me aside.

'I told Shohdi your decision. But he's just rung me back.'

He looked so grim, I thought I must have been dismissed.

'What did he say?'

'He wants you to leave for Syria at once.'

I felt a surge of relief.

Nagi whispered.

'Of course you won't go?'

If I went, I should escape the trap of marriage. Nagi's eyes implored me not to fall in with the Pasha's schemes. I suddenly knew that instead of marrying I would kick Nagi out of his place and make it mine. In a quiet voice I replied: 'Yes, I think I'll go.'

'Then I'll make all the necessary arrangements for your journey.'

I remembered my rendezvous with Samia. With the coolness of a hired assassin I added: 'I'll go tomorrow.'

After a meeting with the editors, at which I told them of my trip, I went to the flat to wait for Samia. I felt no anxiety, no worry. Samia arrived chattering. She was torn between a quiet wedding and making a party for her friends. I had no guilty twinges, I felt nothing, as she aired her problem. I was not the Yusif who loved her; I was the editor-in-chief of *Al-Ayyam*, the friend of Shohdi Pasha, the key journalist on his way to Syria to cover an historic event in the Arab world.

'Do you love me?'

'Yes, darling.'

'You'll give me the tenderness I need?'

'I have nothing else to offer.'

She sounded utterly happy.

'I'm sure you'll be tender, I have never forgotten what you once told me, that tenderness and love are the same thing.'

I had no sense of betrayal or deception. She was talking to another Yusif, someone who would meet her in the morning and give her the tenderness she craved. Whereas I should be going another way, by air, to Syria.

21

DAMASCUS HELPED ME PUT MY PERSONAL PROBLEMS aside. My interview with Husni al-Zaim – who reminded me of Napoleon – made me realize how easy it was to reach the top. Why shouldn't I take over the newspaper as he had taken over Syria? On my return, Nagi congratulated me on my despatches, so did Shohdi Pasha. As I stared at the newsprint with my name prominently displayed, I suddenly seemed to see Samia's face in place of my signature.

I knew, that moment, that abandoning her had been the mistake of my life. To succeed, to get to the top, that was easy. To be another Husni al-Zaim was trivial. What was difficult was to give yourself to love, to respect your love, and not to flee from it. Strange world! The things that seemed impossible were easy; things that seemed easy were impossibly difficult. It required much more effort and determination to marry Samia and suppress ambition than to supersede Nagi and stand up to Shohdi Pasha. It required the audacity of Husni al-Zaim, or the heroism of Napoleon.

I tried to get her on the telephone. As soon as she recognized my voice, she hung up on me. When I tried again, she got her mother to answer.

I forget what I did after she hung up. No, that's not true. I remember. I walked the streets for hours, hunting a miracle. I wanted my mother and father back again. I saw the coffee-shop with the men playing chess. I heard him saying: 'I married her yesterday. I had to. She was pregnant.'

'I want £5, Father.'

Tears started from my eyes. So vivid was the hallucination, I expected to see my father at the table as Mikhaili handed me my coffee . . .

That night I tried to find Showki. I would send him to Samia on my behalf. Or I would reconcile myself with Mabruka, beg her pardon and see my little brother. But Showki, I was told, had not been to the office all day.

I felt I was sitting an examination: the subject, who or what I was. Would I be able to stick to my true self, make an abrupt turn and marry Samia? Or was this a mere interlude, before I bolted the doors on my past and went on with my career of lies and glory?

The next morning marked the first question in my test.

'I love you.' I said these words on the telephone, then rang off myself before she could forestall me.

Then I saw her on the opposite pavement in Rue Kasr al-Nil. 'Samia . . .' I said, rushing across to her, 'give me one more chance.'

She rebuffed me with a strength of will I had not imagined. 'Please don't speak to me.'

Crossing the road to avoid me, she suddenly collided with a bicycle. I took her to a chemist, then home to the flat. At first my words were part of an act: 'Samia, I can't live without you.'

But suddenly I was acting no longer. I was confessing, in all my sincerity, how cowardly I had been, how despicable.

Her only answer:

'I have forgiven you.'

I blurted out everything – my trip to Damascus, my life, my father, even Suad. 'The reason I went to Syria was that I was a coward, I wanted to escape. Samia, let's get married now.'

'You don't want to marry me.'

'But I love you, Samia. Don't leave me.'

'We love each other, don't we? Then, why get married?'

I was relieved with all my heart that she was prepared to be satisfied with love. We spent much time together. I saw, I thought, a way of having my cake and eating it. Once I was editor-in-chief, no one could prevent me marrying her. But until Nagi fell, I must be prudent. There was nothing I could do to precipitate his fall; my strategy was to let him destroy himself. I proved right. In a few months a radiant Shohdi Pasha summoned me.

'Well, my boy, are you ready to be editor-in-chief?'

'Yes, sir, but what about Nagi Bey?'

'He'll send us articles from Europe. He's going on a trip in two months' time.'

'He'll never agree.'

'On the contrary, it's his idea.'

'Strange that he never told me.'

'Must he admit in words that you've defeated him?'

I resented the sarcasm in his voice.

'There's no question of defeat, since there's been no quarrel. On the contrary, we got on well these last months.'

He laughed wickedly.

'Of course, you are totally innocent. I am responsible for everything.'

I rushed to Nagi's office at *Al-Ayyam*.

'How can you leave us like this?'

He smiled. 'Luckily you're still here.'

'But I'll be lost without you.'

'You know that's nonsense. You'll manage perfectly.'

'But I depend on your experience.'

He hesitated a moment, then said: 'Look, Yusif. Have no fears that I'm going to make difficulties. I'm exhausted. All I want is to relax.' Then he added maliciously, 'And don't think I have done this for you. You may find, sooner than you think, that your dream of being editor-in-chief is in fact a nightmare. The whole thing's confidential, by the way.'

I could not bring myself to tell Samia, for she had been behaving oddly, veering from one emotion to another inside a minute.

'Where've you been?'

'At Shohdi's, darling.'

This started a pointless quarrel in which she refused to kiss me. It was obvious she disbelieved what I had said, and she

338

had reason. But when she threatened to leave me, I mastered my temper. I did not want to lose her.

Then, before the two months were up, she suddenly asked me to marry her. I agreed, as if this were a passing impulse on her part, adding, 'But not yet.'

'Why not yet?'

'At the paper everything's at sixes and sevens. Nagi is leaving, I'm to replace him.'

My news did not seem to interest her.

'It's now or never.'

'Samia, be sensible.'

'Then this is the end.'

I watched her leave with a sense of rage. This was the love for which I had been willing to wreck my life, to ruin Shohdi's schemes for my advancement. I must not put my life at her command one moment longer. I busied myself with the changes Shohdi was making at the paper. The most trying of these was Showki's dismissal.

'That communist who works with you – I've relieved you of him.'

'As you decide, Pasha.'

'I know you must feel upset, but it's better so.'

'I only fear he may be innocent.'

'Don't be absurd. You're embarking on a major venture. A leader must not surround himself with traitors.'

There was nothing I could do or say. Nagi's prophecy was already coming true.

The Pasha had presented me with a car, a Chevrolet. People thronged round me as I left the building. Just as the car drove up a small boy pushed a piece or paper into my hands. It was a plea from Ibrahim, my 'orphan brother', invoking God's name to plead for my support. It was a lie, a trick, a beggar's ruse to soil my new car and steal my money. Suddenly I heard Mabruka's voice. This was a crisis that I must handle rightly or be ruined. I must not be harsh; I must be sufficiently polite, sufficiently gentle.

'How are you, Mabruka?'

By shaking her hand I showed my lack of pride; I was not ashamed to address the poor.

'You see how he's grown?'

'It's true: he's almost a man already.'

My model was Rateb Bey, and as he might have done, I handed her £1.

'I don't want your money,' she screamed. 'You'll give me money, then forget me.'

'Then, what do you want? I'm in a hurry.'

'Where are you going?'

She had no right to ask. That was my business. I was going to meet Shohdi Pasha, to drink whisky and soda, to escape from her. My life was clean, like my office, like the Muhammad Ali Club: I would not let her pull me back into poverty and dirt. I was glad when the onlookers dragged her away, screaming. The car made off, leaving her farther and farther behind, a screaming pigmy.

But she is not far off; she is here, in my brain. So is my father, her husband. So is Samia. Samia, don't ring off. I am Yusif. Our love is over. No marriage, no mistake to ruin a life. . . . You are ready to be editor-in-chief? Of course. And Showki, I've relieved you of him. And Saad, he's in Upper Egypt, at Sohag. . . .

Enough of this comedy. I am embarked on my career. It is a big one. I have become the editor, I have ousted Nagi. I sit at his desk and drive in his car. And my little brother has brought me a petition, like a beggar, saying he is hungry and poor.

But slowly . . . slowly. . . . Don't race away from filth. Fill your mouth with it. Chew it, then slowly swallow it to the last scrap.

22

YUSIF ABDUL HAMID AL-SUEFI – THIS 'I' IS NOW THE most illustrious journalist in the Arab world: he it is who delivers the word, who invokes socialism, exalts or denounces the same.

'I' have left poverty behind. 'I' only smoke cigars, wear the most expensive clothes and douche myself in the richest perfumes. Each day I feel younger, each day my face looks more ingenuous and boyish; I am the man they trust.

The Revolution got rid of the King: Muhammad Nagi fell, and married my mistress. Each bird falls at last. Cheap people flock together. But I keep apart and so rise higher. I'm on close terms with the men of the Revolution. Shohdi Pasha grovels. Some evenings he urges me to put his ideas about economics before our new ruler. I listen, puff smoke in his face, laugh, reassure him, knowing all the time they plan to nationalize his companies. The cur would like, by making use of me, to regain his influence and continue his crimes. He thinks me another Nagi, a servile pawn. But now he is the servile pawn to whom I listen. These capitalists will have to be broken, one by one.

An officer in the secret police recently came to my office. He told me, obviously embarrassed, that a woman of doubtful virtue known as 'Riri' had been spreading rumours about me: alleging she was my father's wife.

'But,' I said calmly, 'that's not a rumour, it's true.'

I'm a martyr, risen from poverty; stripped naked, I'm a true son of this suffering people so long acquainted with oppression.

The officer gazed at me in admiration.

'You are, sir, a wonderful man.'

'I'm simply a man who's known suffering.'

'We are proud of you.'

The words flew from my mouth:

'I'm with the Revolution with my heart, not just my mind.

I've seen for myself the filth in which we lived, the filth which compelled a woman like Mabruka to become 'Riri' to survive.'

I lowered my voice:

'Will you permit me to summon Hamdi?'

He seemed puzzled as I picked up the telephone.

'Hamdi,' I explained, 'is a fine type. He's worked here for ages, on the administrative side.'

Hamdi came in.

'I want you to tell the Bey what we did, Hamdi, about Mabruka.'

Surprised, he muttered a few words, then pulling himself together began to tell the officer how, in my name, twice he had offered Mabruka £50 a month, but she had refused.

When Hamdi withdrew, the officer said: 'You tried to do what was right.'

'When I write about socialism,' I said fervently, 'I write with my blood, thinking about Mabruka.'

'That is well known to those in authority. That was the reason I came, to see what steps to take to protect you from her.'

'I want neither protection nor concealment. I'm willing to admit in the middle of the most crowded square in Cairo that Riri is my father's wife. Mabruka's no longer important. What is important is that no other Mabruka should be forced to go the way she has gone. We are all fighting for a better society.'

Tears filled my eyes; tears filled his. He left me, convinced I was a martyr, a prophet who licked the leper's sores, rising above private pains for country's sake. His report to his superiors showed results mirrored in their eyes: for me increased respect and greater glory.

Then my secretary, Kathlena, brought me a card.

'He says he's an old friend of yours and wants to see you.'

The card bore the name Saad Abdul Gawad. I rushed out of the room, disregarding her surprise, and threw my arms about him.

The years had eroded his face. His hair was greying, his eyes fading. His back was bent. A deferential smile played on his lips.

This was one of my victims. Why had I rushed to meet him?
Was this right?

'How are you, Saad?'

'I hope I'm not disturbing you?'

'On the contrary, I am delighted to see you. Where are you
these days? What are you doing?'

'The same as before!'

'Assistant Prosecutor?'

'No, a religious judge.'

'You've become someone important then, someone people
fear!'

What hypocrisy – I know that I'm a thousand times more
feared than he is.

'I'm stationed in Mansoura. I get to Cairo every week-end.
Every time I'm here I think of calling on you. Then I tell myself
you'll be busy, and will have forgotten me.'

He smiled anxiously.

I handed him a box of cigars.

'Help yourself.'

He glanced at the box. 'It would be a waste . . .'

'A waste, Saad? How can you think that?'

His embarrassment increases, his eyes drift to the door, he
thinks of leaving.

'Saad, are you married?'

'I've two boys, one girl.'

The idiot has wasted his time begetting rabbits: yet in our
year he was the most brilliant student. People like him don't
know what life is: a pathetic normal. Doubtless he'll boast to
his friends of having met me; their respect for him will soar. I
must take care. I don't know if his record's clean. Once a
communist. . . . Was that the motive behind his visit?

'Do you still have the same ideas as before?'

He's either a good actor or a good forgetter:

'What ideas?'

'Communism . . .'

He laughs despairingly.

'That was long ago.'

343

'Do you see Showki?'

'No.'

'I helped to get him out of gaol. . . . He's back working here now.'

'Here? So you see him.'

'Once in a while, not often.'

'Naturally you're very busy. But in any case he's under your protection.'

We have nothing more to say to each other; in fact his presence fills me with boredom. I gaze into space until, to my relief, I hear him make his overtures to leave.

Showki, who'd given up his communism, was, as Saad had said, under my protection. So was Nagi in his downfall. They were all under my protection.

Only Mabruka was not: the obstinate whore, the servant! If only she would die.

Yet I used her as a story, to arouse people's admiration for me, in my role of champion of the poor.

If they knew . . .

. . . knew that I was under her protection . . . knew that her fall had been my advantage.

Hamdi puts his head round the door.

'I have something to tell you, sir.'

He creeps in like a thief, pulling a letter from his pocket.

'Muhammad Nagi sent this from Paris.'

'An article?'

'Best if you read for yourself, sir.'

I read.

The fox has not unlearned its tricks. He wants Hamdi to persuade Mabruka to make a scandal that would ruin my reputation.

I smile back at Hamdi's yellow face.

'What's the matter, Hamdi? Why so troubled?'

'I don't know what to do.'

'The man's crazy. Leave me the letter.'

'What shall I tell him?'

'Tell him nothing.'

Nagi: my steps must be firm, my lips must smile, m̥
sparkle.
comes first.
ile is switched on.
voice that lets me down.
Yusif, how are you? You shouldn't have gone to s
ble. Let me kiss you.'
dead embrace?
say something. But those terrible turning lights . . .
to have a long talk with you!'
'
nd have lunch with us tomorrow?'
leasure.'
take note that Yusif's lunching with us tomorrow
you've not said "hallo" to Sherif.'
words are not as innocent as they sound. He wants
he with the child. The game of childbirth shouldn
. My brother Ibrahim's a child no longer, he's fed l
his mother's brothel, which nourishes his body – ar
Woe comes to me from children; in their eyes is t

e you Sherif? Say hallo! Gracious, are you shy?'
realize who I am.
e.
let the ogre inspect you: let him enjoy your fa
Yusif's role? He's a child like you.
d you do in Europe, Sherif?'
't reply. Samia answers for him.
the mother of this child, Samia?
Samia, if you meet Yusif, don't reject him: for
ou. He loves you as he watches the clouds (Yu
ouds). He loves you as he listens to music (Yu
music). He loves you when he closes his lids on y
sif slept). He loves you in failure and success (Yu
cceeded). Take care of Yusif because he loves yo
love you, even if there are no more clouds in
e failure and no more success.

'When he comes back?'
'Tell him you went to her and she refused.'
Nagi's letter was one more victory. I showed it to the authorities. They believed my explanation that he was plotting to ruin me, and decided in their turn to ruin him.

Nagi would go to the same prison as Showki. And Samia would come to me as Mabruka had once come. He'd be in his cell, she'd be in my bed.

Life is delicious for the strong. There is no greater pleasure than to tread on the necks of your opponents.

No, I am being cheap.

This isn't why I was trying to remember the past . . .

The night, for instance, when Shohdi called on me as I was reading the agency telegrams. It was shortly after we nationalized the Canal, when the British and French were threatening to attack us.

'It seems they mean business, Yusif.'
'You think so, Pasha?'
'I'm sure of it.'
'I'm not so sure.'
'I know the British well. The French are even worse. They won't take it sitting down. Impossible!'

A chill runs down my spine. What will happen to me if they do come? Shohdi will be the first to take his revenge. And Nagi? He'd put the noose round my neck with his own hand. A serial of my life in *Al-Ayyam* . . . Smears on my character, brand me 'the harlot's stepchild', turn the prophet into a debauchee.

It might be well to win Shohdi over.
'Pasha, I have a presentiment . . .'
'I have, too.'
'It will be disaster.'
'Of course.'

His voice welcomed disaster; his heart waited for it. I pulled myself together. The only way was for me to continue in my role: to fight to preserve my evil glory and to raise my head courageously, to continue to trample the necks of my victims.

'We'll fight, Pasha.'

'You think we can?'

'Or we'll die with honour.'

'No – with bullets that cost a farthing.'

'It's our country, it's our principles.'

He gave me his warm, soft hand and left.

Sitting at my desk I wrote a denunciation of the English and the French. Perhaps the words I was writing would one day be a noose round my neck. What a mad world – evil was turning into honour, cowardice into courage, while cheap actions were surrounded by noble dreams.

A world run mad? Or simply life?

How I wished I could understand.

23

A LARGE CROWD CAME TO THE AIRPORT TO WELCOME 'our absent chief'. The night shone with brilliant stars.

How would Nagi look? And his son Sherif? The child I lost by not begetting?

Was I once like him?

. . . There was a child called Yusif, once.

Yusif Abdul Hamid al-Suefi.

But good-bye, Yusif! For the last time: good-bye. For neither tears nor aeroplanes can bring you back.

Yet if only I could touch you once more, stroke your cheek, hear your childish voice . . . If we could laugh together, hand in hand . . . My child!

How beautiful you were!

Innocent.

Far off.

But you're still not dead. Yusif Abdul Hamid still lives, wears shorts, walks nervously through the streets, gazes at Enfash from the window, runs off with him to the station, dreams of forbidden foods.

Yusif loves Suad. Yusif is scared of from life . . .

'Yusif Bey! Yusif Bey!'

It's Hamdi shouting.

'The plane has arrived, Your Happ

'Where?'

'It's coming down now, over the

Above the runway, a star in the ni child.

'Any orders, sir?'

'No, Hamdi.'

'Everything's prepared . . . for C

'Fine.'

Everyone's staring at the sky. Th like slaves. Though now they slave smiling when I smile, frowning wh

If I hadn't come, not one of the welcome him.

The airport is enormous; peopl lights, flashing to the horizon.

'The plane, Your Happiness. Or These useless, turning lights: he But I welcome the uproar.

It drowns whispers.

'This way, Yusif Bey. We'll go Walk. Smile. The plane has lan light – a few more and we'll reach once.

It's farther to the plane than dream – that I'm here at the airp Sherif.

'They've opened the doors, sir

Night's in mourning for the d

'There's Nagi Bey . . . on the s Love is dead, Samia. The heart that marks where memories are

Can I love again?

Here i
eyes mus
Samia
My sm
It's m
'Hallo,
much tro
Can th
I must
'I want
'When
'Come
'With
'Samia,
'Yusif,
Nagi's
confront
concern u
a brothel,
my spirit.
danger.
'How a
No. Yo
The ogr
Darling
You know
'What d
He does
So you'
Dearest
still loves
watched c
listened to
in sleep (Y
failed and
will always
sky, no mo

I love you, Samia. Don't forsake me.

'This way, sir. . . . Muhammad's walked off.'

'After you, madame.'

We had almost made contact.

Al-Ayyam prints a hundred and fifty thousand copies a day, is read by half a million people. Its news is picked up by the agencies, its editorials quoted. Telephones ring, congratulating me, asking me the news. People ask for interviews. Editors besiege my doors. On my desk the cables pile up, from London, Paris, New York, Washington. The French fleet's sailing from Toulon. The 'Red Devils' mass in Cyprus. The Egyptian army prepares for action.

Events crowd in. But they stop short of the heart, bounce off my skin.

In an hour's time I go to Muhammad Nagi's and meet Samia. To me, that's the most important thing in the world.

I want to resurrect the old, chaste Yusif: to slough off more recent thoughts and enter Samia's house transformed, pure. The past is over. From now on I'll breathe the truth.

'Embattled people of Egypt! People preparing to defend our Canal!' Can you, for one second, defend me from my memories and their guilty sting?

Can you teach me what truth is, what right is?

I know.

Truth in me is a form of deceit: an innocence that achieves guilt; a childishness that ages; a body which controls me as I control it; a brain which rules me as I rule it; a heart filled with a love which fills itself on hate.

Truth; this splendid nil . . . this valueless value . . . it is Yusif's life. Reason is part of truth; so is goodness; so is love; so is greatness.

If you, the people, could bear to confront the truth as it really is . . .

Then you would know with what mixed motives you are defending Egypt: principle confused with lack of scruple, honour confused with greed. We live in a wretched splendour.

349

If I wrote an article like this . . .

But I'm no longer afraid. Awareness has cast out fear.

Honour fails to arouse me; evil to frighten me; discovery is complete.

What made me realize this?

The night at the airport?

Sherif's face?

My sins?

Inspiration?

News?

Something still is lacking.

A table, empty words, tender wounds.

Nagi asks me:

'Yusif, why so silent? Samia here has so much to tell you about Paris, the fashions above all.'

Samia has much to tell? Now I appreciate your greatness and your truth, Nagi. You are not talking about the fashions, you want us to take up our long interrupted dialogue and continue it before you. No, Nagi, you're not despairing, you're not collapsing. This shows a strange kind of consciousness, the consciousness of the great. It's as though you're taking your life in your hands. You know perfectly well that you yourself are finished. Yet you don't want to miss what lies beyond. You want to see what will happen after your death. When you leave Samia to me. Your mode of despair is fine.

'Samia is also very quiet today. I don't know why.'

Samia answers stupidly: 'I think I'm tired, Muhammad.'

Try and understand your husband's meaning: he's at the point of death. Show what will happen, how I'll come back to you, and you to me.

If you weren't coming back to me, why marry such a sick old man?

When Nagi dies, our love will revive.

Though, at the moment, he seems so terribly alive.

'You let me do all the talking, planning new articles?'

As if he's going to live.

Die, Nagi. We're waiting for your death.

Die, Nagi. I'm killing you . . . killing you with each beat of truth.

I order you to die.

His face is flushed with life, with the blood coursing in his veins.

There's not room for two great men in this one house: two truthful men.

I can't betray you. Truth prefers to kill, not betray. Samia will not accept a lover while you're alive.

You and I, we're too strong for treachery.

If Samia betrays you, it must be with someone else – someone neither great, nor truthful.

Nagi, you've reached your peak of knowledge. You cannot live: you must pass on.

Why don't you die?

He pauses, smiles – such vitality! – as if he hears the whisper of my thoughts.

I applaud you, Nagi. Your performance thrills me. You invite me to your house to draw the future, just like a god. You must die. Nagi, a god cannot sit at table eating fish. What a magnificent, unspoken dialogue: I hear you concede my triumph, your defeat. You don't hate me, you feel reborn.

Nagi, are you really reborn?

I, too, am reborn. But the world's too small.

One of us must go. If you don't die, then I must.

He's still silent. His face is pale. Are you obeying me, Nagi?

Have you agreed to die?

Muhammad Nagi screams.

'Samia!'

His face is blue; his mouth flaps without words.

She shrieks, he waves his hands, he says something in an audible voice, but no one can hear now.

His head slumps, my heart trembles, dead love revives. Your screams content me, Samia, your appetizing tender body fills my visions. As if we were back in the flat overlooking the Paradise Cinema. Death is dead.

We've buried the dead man; the woman waits at home. Shall I go to her?

Or to Mabruka?

I can do what I want. I'm very powerful. I ordered Muhammad Nagi to die, and he died.

But I can't kill Mabruka.

She who martyrized me, fermenting to knowledge of the truth. For pollution completes my truth: it is the wrong that balances my reason.

I'm thinking like a madman. My words grow less, I half close my eyes. Like a child.

To my woe, to my joy. I know that I'm a child. My words are the words of a child. Now I know! It was the child who taught me. Because he's remained with me. He didn't go, he didn't desert me. My darling child, Yusif Abdul Hamid: You were hidden, you mischievous child, inside me.